Water Baby

Chioma Okereke

QUERCUS

First published in Great Britain in 2024 by

QUERCUS

Quercus Editions Ltd
Carmelite House
50 Victoria Embankment
London EC4Y 0DZ

An Hachette UK company

A CIP catalogue record for this book is available
from the British Library

HB ISBN 978 1 52942 540 6
TPB ISBN 978 1 52942 541 3
EBOOK ISBN 978 1 52942 542 0

10 9 8 7 6 5 4 3 2 1

Typeset by Jouve (UK), Milton Keynes

Printed and bound in Great Britain by Clays Ltd, Elcograf S.p.A.

Papers used by Quercus are from well-managed forests and other responsible sources.

Water Baby

Also by Chioma Okereke

Bitter Leaf

For Boo-boo(3)

'When the food is properly done, it reaches the ant'

Igbo proverb

'All water has a perfect memory and is trying to get back to where it was'

Toni Morrison

This novel was deliberately written in '*Pidgin-lite*'.
My people: don't come for me, abeg una!

Water

1

There's an old tale where we live about throwing a newborn into the lagoon.

If the baby drowns, it is illegitimate and the mother must be banished from the community. But if it floats, the infant is embraced by all. They say fathers used to celebrate their child's birth with this test. It must have been a trick, though, as everybody knows that all babies float.

I was born in the water. That's what Papa says but it's a fiction. I wasn't born in a hospital or on land; most of us in my community weren't. We drew our first breaths on Adogbo, though according to Papa, my first moments were almost in the lagoon itself. Makoko is what the outsiders had originally called our settlement hundreds of years ago, due to its abundance of akoko leaves, and the name stuck for the community on the Lagos coast just across from the Third Mainland Bridge. To strangers, it's a slum, a metallic and wooden eyesore built over a stinking bed of ever-mounting sewage, spreading out across the smoke-filled horizon. For the government, it's the impediment between even larger coffers for them and prime waterfront real estate. But to us, who are from here, Makoko is simply *home*.

The Nigerian government likes to pretend that we don't exist, but we've been here for hundreds of years, our wooden houses resting proudly on their stilts above Lagos's charcoal-coloured lagoon. We'll remain here for some time, no matter how many attempts they make to push us out.

Mama had plenty of babies in her belly before me, but only a few of us stayed. That's not only an issue with the women in our family, as she'd explained, but with life here on the lagoon. There's a high rate of maternal and infant death among those living on the water, which is strange considering that we all originally come from the womb having been surrounded by liquid. Still, many women lose their children—although there're plenty to go around – as there are very few doctors here to speak of.

So, Mama had some false starts before Dura came and then many other miscarriages before it was my turn nineteen years ago, followed by Charlie Boy five years later. I was fearless, Papa used to say. It's why I was able to be born.

Mama had been visiting her best friend when I announced my early arrival, pounding hard on her stomach and pelvic bone. Auntie Uche had protested that it was too late for her to leave. Having had more babies than Mama, Auntie knew I was well on my way into the world, but Mama had been insistent. She'd wanted to return home to have me in her own bed, so they'd stepped gingerly into a canoe for the short ride back. Papa wasn't even there but claimed Mama's labour was so

4

painful that he'd heard her while he'd been far out fishing with the other men. Mama's voice had travelled across the water and spooked the fish, which rushed to their nets, delivering them a glorious bounty!

As I'd inched through her passageways, Mama rocked the canoe so much that they'd almost fallen overboard. Auntie Uche could only look on in fear as she prepared to rescue Mama from the filthy waters, but then something odd happened. A mighty invisible hand had reached out from within the lagoon and pushed her upper body firmly back in place. Mama let out a heavy cry and then slid to the boat's bottom so that Auntie Uche could row her home before I slipped out through her legs from underneath her wrapper. We'd stayed in the boat tethered together by our cord while my aunt screamed for help and our neighbours went to fetch the other women.

Papa was astounded when he came home later that evening, covered in sweat and scales. His eyes were large and his mouth even wider when he saw what Mama had produced. He said I looked like one of the fishes he drew out from the water daily, in shock from being extracted from their natural habitat, their eyes big with fear as their cheeks contracted from struggling to take in the air out of the water.

He retold this story many times when I was smaller. I used to ask him if I'd been slimy like the catfish that we ate in the past, which the lagoon used to be full of when it was teeming with fish. He'd reply that I was, but that Mama had cleaned me up, so by the time we met, I was dry but naked and as beautiful as a mermaid.

He said I was practically born with one foot in the water and that Mama had been helped that day by the deity Yemoja herself.

It's why they named me after the water spirit, though everyone calls me by Papa's pet name: Baby.

Papa used to say I was his mermaid because of the way I arrived. Not just because of Mama's *near accident*, but owing to the state of Auntie Uche's canoe, its plenty holes as I lay at Mama's feet, the first thing my lungs would have experienced was Makoko water. It's clearly a nonsense, but he liked to tell the story and I loved to see my small self in his pupils as he retraced our history.

Most of Makoko's fishermen believe in mermaids, although they're difficult to see here because of the colour of the lagoon. But sometimes when they're returning home from night fishing, they claim to hear the maidens playing under the bridge. It's easy to depict us as mermaids and fishermen because of our existence over the water, but I think we're closer to dragons. Creatures that are also associated with water but are highly accustomed to breathing fire, unlike visitors to Makoko. The moment outsiders step off the deck and cross the murky lagoon, the thing that stays with them isn't only the stench but the ever-present smoke hanging over the water. Our lungs are long accustomed to the black smog created from preparing fish for generations, but it's a shock to many newcomers. As if the city air is anything to write songs about!

It's never quiet here but there's peace. And like the rest of Lagos, there's always *sound*. Generators belch diesel noisily all day and night and boat motors roar by angrily, stirring up otherwise calm waters. Loud, happy music erupts out of household after household in each community. Everywhere, children are jumping between canoes, women clapping and singing at home and in church, and fishermen casting their nets out over the lagoon like Spider-Man spreading the web from his hands in the picture on Charlie Boy's faded T-shirt.

Official counts vary about how many of us are living here, but it's easily in the hundreds of thousands. The government isn't wanting to count us as it's easier to pretend as though we don't exist. But every year, more people are coming from other sites they have abolished. Houses are spreading out further and further over the water, and our home is developing like any other settlement.

There are a couple of people looking for taxis across the lagoon as I near the jetty in my canoe. At this time of the day, one can be pressed for customers, so I give thanks for the blessing. Plunging my oar deeply into the water, I draw its length through what resembles black ink mired by rubbish upon rubbish. I spot hundreds of discarded plastic bottles, carrier bags and part of a tyre among the top pile of floating refuse in my wake as I steer around them in the narrowing waterway.

I love the weight of this implement in my already leathered hands, the motion of the canoe as it skims the surface of the water like a dolphin, the burn of sulphur and shit high in my nostrils as the sun beats down on my bare shoulders. I'm the captain of my ship. Or rather, my river taxi.

'Good morning, where you wan go?' I ask as the woman waiting for a ride gesticulates wildly for my attention. Her black trousers and blue button-down shirt make me think she's a bank worker or perhaps has a government job on the mainland. She removes her hand from over her eyebrows, her makeshift protection from the glare of the blazing sun.

'Carry me to Dr Ofong's hospital,' she points off into the distance, dislodging the large handbag from her shoulder.

'Okay, enter,' I respond before she steps down into my canoe, followed by two women wearing dresses in the same pink dia-mond print. Looking around quickly, I inspect my domain through her eyes. Thankfully, despite my hectic sailing in a rush to get here, the seats are dry. The floor of the canoe is empty apart from my ever-present sweat cloth on the seat next to me with my bottle of water.

'Go quick quick, please! I'm late for an appointment,' she begs before shooting a bullet of spit into the dark water. Even if I wanted to linger in the hope of another customer, I now can't for fear of losing her.

From the way she wrinkles her nose, it's clear that she's a visitor to the community. As far as the eye can see, there's dirt from refuse spat out from the lagoon's lips a million times over or pushed in via shipping lanes and kept here by the currents. We're used to seeing the waterways filled with refuse; trash jam-packed under every house as decades of garbage bobs on the water's surface like rising secrets that want to be told. The smell of Makoko is something we are long accustomed to.

'This place go kill person,' she mutters under her breath as we glide through a particularly pungent patch of the lagoon.

My oar slides into the water like a hot comb through hair as we push off from land towards Adogbo and I listen to the chatter of my two other customers, one whose laughter reminds me of Dura, most likely hawking fish at her stall on Better Life Market, her latest newborn strapped to her back. This journey across the lagoon is what I enjoy the most. There's a bustle in the waterways and pockets of peace too, which are harder to come by among the houses.

A bead of sweat slides through my braids, and I shake my head vigorously to generate some breeze, but my executive passenger frowns at me as if I'm in danger of rocking the boat.

'You're safe, Auntie,' I say to reassure her, to soften the ice block I'm ferrying towards the community, but she looks through me before closing her eyes.

On a good day, I'll make half a dozen more trips like this before I go home to deal with my chores or to carry out one of my other side jobs. A person must have many other lives on Makoko in order to eat and sleep. But bobbing along on the water in the traffic jams created by the other boats or drifting far away with only the lights on the horizon for guidance is where I feel the most free.

Alone on the water, I can hear my own thoughts without the voices of others telling me what to do or who to be.

Many of us set our sights on the mainland, the furthest we

can stretch our imaginations before they break. Parents dream of us leaving Makoko and doing better than they did for themselves, and eventually we dream it too, all the while knowing it to be an elusive fantasy. Not many of us have done it, yet that hope pulses within us like a beacon.

I gaze longingly beyond the mainland to the skies and in those moments that are solely mine, I'm free to fantasise about the future.

One that I'm actually wanting.

2

'Don't move your head,' I scold Kemi, pulling on the end of her hair for good measure, drawing a yelp from her stupid lips.

'It's *paining* me—'

'Let me finish abeg. If you continue fidgeting, we'll be late for school.'

I complete the section of her hair I'm braiding and observe my handiwork. It's not the best, but Kemi's hair is now sectioned into eight braids to last her the week. With the two at the front stopping just in front of her eyes, she almost resembles a stag beetle. I briefly consider telling her that, but her crying will only delay us further.

We're on the deck of the house; Kemi is nestled in the V of my legs. While I plait, I bark orders to Afo, who takes even longer than Kemi to get ready for school.

'*Afolabi*,' I call out his full name for emphasis. 'If I call you again—'

'I'm coming, Baby! I'm coming,' he protests, rubbing sleep out of his eyes as he exits the bedroom.

'Your shirt is inside out,' I remark, spying the browning label on the collar of his margarine yellow and blue uniform. 'Did you bath?' I ask him, checking his face for any trace of a lie.

'Yes,' he says, reversing the shirt swiftly before tucking it into his overly short shorts in three moves.

'And did you empty the bucket?' I probe, wriggling my nose as if I can detect his waste from any others in the air around us. By the droop of his shoulders, I know he's forgotten again. 'Go and empty it,' I order him as I wipe the last bit of grease off my finger and run it down the tiny spine, created by the hairstyle, in the middle of Kemi's scalp. 'We're leaving now now.'

I go inside to put away the hair products in the turned-over plastic box that serves as a bedside table in our tiny bedroom. This is the space for the children; a collection of cousins, relatives bonded by circumstances and the closest of quarters. The floor is obscured by the two foam mattresses we share and the shelving which holds our clothing in one corner. It's stuffy when we're all inside, so sometimes I move out to the deck to escape Kemi winding her sweaty limbs around me or Tayo trying to kill us with fetid messes he never attempts to quieten, as if we're trespassers on his private premises. Sometimes I sleep in the canoe, under the grey velvet of the night sky, the slow waves rocking me gently until my eyes close.

Drawing the curtain savagely away from the window, I let daylight enter the room, making Tayo groan before turning onto his front to shield his face. I can hear Afo in the bathroom

12

scrubbing the bucket with the toilet brush through the wall separating us.

'Wake up,' I tell Tayo, even though it's of little use.

One year my junior and too stubborn to listen to anyone, including Uncle Jimi, I know he's going to ignore me. Almost on cue, Tayo kisses his teeth before raising his buttocks off his mattress to dispatch one mess that smells like rotten fish. It's enough to have me fleeing the room for the safety of the less pungent lagoon water.

I usher the small ones towards the canoe and we set off for school. Almost everyone has a boat on Makoko or access to one. On the water, Lagos is still Lagos, which means plenty of go-slow at various hours of the day. The waterways are only ever truly still in the thick of night.

In the daytime, the lagoon is as bustling as the city streets. Hawkers ply their trades as boats make their laps, piled high with food, soft drinks, clothing, even DVDs, calling out for customers that are always in high demand. Other boats are filled with fishermen or commuters making their way to work; women heaving baskets of fish to sell at Asejere and men heading to the sawmill or to dredge for sand. Little children without the means to go to school sit idle on decks or rent boats to try their hand as taxi drivers, splashing water on passers-by with their inferior piloting skills or drifting in circles, their laughter bouncing off choppy brown waves. Skilled oarsmen tut loudly as they navigate these habitual obstacles, some with their oars the length of flagpoles as they delicately ferry their assorted cargos.

Kemi and Afo giggle as we pass a large woman trying to navigate her exit out of a tiny canoe and onto someone's deck. A few more metres away, a row of children defecate directly into the water, their aim precise and expedient before they re-engage in their game of chase. Further on in our commute, two small boys play in the water, one using a large plastic bucket as his vessel while the other travels in a fuel canister with the top portion cut off to allow his body access.

Afo and Kemi have been attending Whanyinna sporadically since the floating school collapsed in 2016. Theirs is the only remaining one on the water; the others close by are on land. There was plenty of excitement when the floating school first came here; its innovative shape, a three-story pyramid like a wooden house of cards kept afloat by plenty of barrels that were also used to collect rainwater, caught the eyes of the world. But sadly, it had been no match for Mother Nature and collapsed after less than a year due to heavy rains.

Before that, many many children didn't have a chance for education. But the floating school brought us more than teaching; it had given us hope about what was possible on the water.

Now only one school remains, and even though tuition is free, many still can't attend due to lack of money. There's little help from the government, and what can you learn if there's no chalk or no pens to write? Teachers are forced to charge a small fee for the children to keep the school running, but many parents can't afford to pay the fifty naira daily fee required from each child. Many people, myself included, only go to school for a brief time to acquire some basics. One thing that life has taught us here is how to make do. Fortunately for me, as Mama used to teach, my education was more plentiful than for others.

Makoko is a fisherman's village, which was how Egun migrants referred to it when it first appeared centuries ago. Now there are many more people from plenty places that have come to make a home within the community. From Benin and Togo, even Ghana, they keep coming, and of course, many of us have been born here.

So many tribes, living and working side by side, like the Itsekiri, who sell fuel and kerosene on the high sea. Who also work in the sawmill business, like the Ijale that smoke fish along with the Yoruba and Egun people. The Igbo, my mother's people, smoke fish too, albeit mostly stockfish, as well as producing large numbers of cooked ukwa and fried groundnuts. The Hausa make very good tailors and also buy iron scraps to make and sell panels. You'll hear different languages bouncing off the water; Yoruba, French, English and Egun, eking out of every shack, day and night. Everywhere you look on Makoko, you find workers, craftspeople, artisans making something out of less than nothing. Using whatever comes from the water and the ground beneath it. Repurposing things that have been thrown away.

Although outsiders consider Makoko to be one unsightly mass, it's actually six separate villages: Oko Agbon, Adogbo (split into sections), Migbewhe and Yanshiwhe on the water and Sogunro and Apollo on the land that surrounds the lagoon. Each village is also divided into smaller communities over the water and run by a baale, a chieftain who keeps things moving smoothly and makes decisions to ensure law and order. Our outside reputation is one of lawlessness, but the truth is that life in Makoko is very safe. A long time ago, there would be people who came here to escape the police, knowing officers were too afraid to venture to these parts. We were the perfect hideaway, but such things don't happen now as they did back then. Our leaders don't stand for any type of foolishness either. As the Igbo like to say: one finger can spoil all the oil.

In Adogbo II, our small shack floats alongside thousands of others, though we're fortunate as Uncle Jimi's place is built of ironwood, which is tough enough to withstand all the trials of the lagoon. Houses crowd together in shallow water the colour of Guinness while refuse accumulates under their stilts. Many tell the story of time passing via their crumbling facades and patchy repair jobs where wood has been replaced by bedsheets, corrugated iron, tarpaulin and fishing nets. There's every kind of building imaginable on the water as households grow and struggle to utilise limited space in ingenious ways. It's an endless quest for survival. We learn to do whatever we can.

'Baby, where are you coming from?' Papa asks as I pull the canoe in, even though he already knows.

'From school, Papa,' I answer meekly before preparing to heave myself onto our deck, but he waves down at me to stay put where I am.

'Auntie Uche wants you to go help her smoke fish. Two of her girls didn't show today,' he explains as I fight to keep my face clear. I don't like doing the smoking; I much prefer my time in the waterways, but there's no point in re-litigating this matter with him. I don't see how it matters what work I do so long as I bring in good money.

'I meant to be working with Mama Ju—' I start to explain before he cuts me off.

'Then call her and explain. But go to Uche, please ... I don't have time for headache today,' he replies dramatically before disappearing indoors.

Papa thinks I'm too old to be doing my taxi work, but the truth is, I'm better at it than most. It's typically younger kids that ferry passengers between Makoko and the mainland, anything from six to sixteen, trying to captain their canoes, but I've got the skills.

I know how to keep my canoe tidy and how to avoid splashing too much water inside the boat, water that can make you sick and can cause your clothes to be stinking long after you've alighted. I'm an expert at steering away from the mountains of debris that share the lagoon with us, the sewage spreading out from underneath our houses together with the stuff pushed into our community from shipping lanes, and I don't talk too much, which can annoy passengers just wanting to travel in peace.

It's not plenty, but you can make some money from being a taxi driver. It doesn't take too much to rent boats, which is why children do it; the amount they charge one single passenger to take them across pays for the day's rental. And the price for passage doubles when it rains. Fisherwomen are charged a premium, paying for their wares which they need to take to the market. Some carry as much as four baskets of fish each day, so that's ₦800 alone, not including the customer. It all adds up as there is plenty to pay for; Kemi and Afo's schooling, rent for the house, fuel and food. Not much remains for the pocket.

Although there are many ways to make a living in Makoko, there's little in the way of prospects. I grew up watching Papa with the other fishermen, mesmerised as they departed to cross the greasy water and cast their nets before returning many hours later. I've since learned that a woman's place is smoking or selling the fish here, not to catch it. No matter how good I might be with my canoe.

If schooling's the only way out, it explains why so many of us remain where we are. Without education, there is no real way to leave. It's almost impossible to complete any kind of education, like becoming a proper teacher. Luckily there are trades, not that anyone truly becomes rich from them.

Papa thinks I should marry and have children, that plenty of my age-mates have married a long time ago, but it's not the thing I'm wanting. Still, I've known from a much younger age that life doesn't always give a person what they desire. Dura, for example, and there are plenty more.

Even before I enter the canteen, having spent all morning with my face over fire with my auntie, the smell of onions frying in palm oil assaults me and causes my eyes to prickle. Tomatoes gurgle as they hit the pot and a cook barking orders behind the curtain obscuring the kitchen area plays his spoons and pans noisily. As I glance through the premises, I spy Maureen holding court at a table surrounded by a few other girls and push my way through a couple of men drinking beer. One has feet so dry and hard it's as though his soles have converted into slippers, a feat in a settlement over water.

I arrive at the tail end of her story as fits of laughter erupt all around. Squeezing in beside Idunnu, she quickly whispers what I've missed. Idunnu is technically my age-mate despite gapping me by seven and a half months. Maureen is only one year older than us, but we've all been best friends since primary school.

Idunnu was an accomplished street hawker before she got a job inside the Platinum Star hotel in Victoria Island, while Maureen sells fish and works at the canteen to save up for some studies to apprentice with Iya Lola at her tailor's shop in Sogunro. Efe is probably the smartest despite being the youngest of our foursome. She's either working at the hair salon or teaching the children in school. Like Whitney Houston, she believes that they are the future. But her real passion lies in technology. Computers and finding a husband, whichever comes first.

In between bites of crisps, Maureen tells us about Osagie finally posing the question, despite their families arranging their pairing since they were children. While the others shriek and sigh during Maureen's story, it's only Idunnu and I that keep quiet. Maureen glances at me and I arrange my face quickly before she accuses me of being jealous. I'm not envious of her proposal at all, far from it. We're all familiar with the ever-afters of these unions, but many girls still consider marriage a fairytale. What I'm wanting is a story that nobody has yet written.

'Anyway, enough about me. Soon it will be your turn.'

I look up to find Maureen waving a cloth in my direction. Her other friends have scattered, and Idunnu is off in the corner, shouting into her cell phone.

'What nonsense are you talking?' I ask, making a face as she sits down beside me.

'About Samson,' Maureen laughs, digging her fingers into my rib. I want to be annoyed, but this always tickles me somehow.

'You're not serious—'

'I'm plenty *serious* as is he! Better prepare yourself. I don't know what you're hanging around for. Samson is a catch.'

'*Please!*' I hiss noisily. 'Then let him go and catch somebody else!' I reply to her amusement.

'Baby! I'm telling you he's *really*—' Maureen starts before I interrupt her.

'On this day you pronounce you're officially to be marrying Osagie, a future leader of the community, that you are concerning yourself with us *small fish*—'

'You . . . Keep talking your gibberish,' Maureen scolds me with a quizzical shake of her head. 'When Samson picks someone else, don't come and cry for me,' she shrugs, popping the last crisp into her mouth.

★

Some days I take the canoe really far out, so far that I no longer imagine I'm close to the city. Where there's no visible line between the lagoon and the sky. It's all one place.

It's there I sit and wait for drones to appear in the sky.

I dream of flying through the skies over Makoko like a bird, with the passage of air over my skin, so high up that the people down below resemble ants. Seeing all the houses reduced to the size of matchboxes while canals and waterways are as skinny as veins. It's what I'm wanting. To pilot the drones, the next best thing to flying. But Papa says no and there's no changing his mind once it's set. It's like amala left in a pot. Very quickly, the soft brown paste turns to stone and you need all your might to try and shift it.

Reminding him that I was a mermaid didn't get him to change his mind and many years had passed since he'd last called me that.

As a child, I'd asked why no women fished the lagoon. Papa explained that men were suspicious and believed that women were bad luck. Water sirens become jealous and don't bring fish to the boats. Those mermaids must have been the first to go from the lagoon as fishermen complain about their shrinking catches. Even their quality has deteriorated now that the water is becoming more polluted.

Had Mama been around, she'd have vanquished Papa's obstinacy by bringing him his Star beer and groundnuts. While he complained noisily over some grievance like the lid over a bubbling pot, Mama would nod her head in agreement until his voice would magically soften.

'Hear me, Baby,' Mama said one evening as she taught me how to make ikokore. 'Men are like rock, but women are water! Quiet and calming or powerful and flowing,' she told me while removing the boiled meat and fish from the bottom of the pot before dropping grated balls of water yam into the quietly bubbling broth. 'Be like water and you can break any rock.'

I hardly hear her these days but every so often she comes. Mama passed when Charlie Boy was just four years old. She became sick from a long unexplained illness that mostly manifested in chest pains. When she'd contracted a bad case of malaria it had been too much for her to carry and she'd died in her sleep. Auntie Uche thought Mama might not have been used to the work of smoking fish. She'd begun working with Auntie to help supplement her income from teaching, particularly after the school had gone on strike. I'd always expected death to come for Papa before Mama, given his occupation compared to hers, but as the saying goes: if one expects a dead tree to fall, a living one uproots itself.

In the afternoons while I wait for customers, I watch hawkers plying their trade on the water or sailboats pushing their way towards the shore by hot prevailing winds. There used to be more vessels on the horizon, but year on year that's changing. From the shrinking lagoon size and lesser quantities of fish to water levels rising alongside the rubbish enveloping us. From manmade disasters to unthinkable diseases. Life is always throwing something at us, but we hold our ground.

Makoko was born out of necessity when affordable land was in short supply two centuries ago and so people spread out over the water. Our dwelling isn't for the fainthearted, it's for survivors.

Most evenings after I've made food for everyone, I head out to the canoe again, where Charlie Boy is usually waiting. We row into the lagoon, past Migbewhe and away from civilisation. Lights from the bridge dance across the water, making it resemble ice. We talk for hours, leaving the noise of our house, of the community behind. It's only my brother and me, laughing like small children; eating Tom Toms and joking in a way we only do with each other while waves slap against the shallow sides of the canoe like high fives. Then we stretch out on the damp canoe bottom, head to head, with our legs hanging over each end of the boat and we wait. Not for shooting stars, but for planes to pass in the dark denim sky above and watch their tail lights fading away steadily like a dying match.

'One day, I will fly,' Charlie Boy repeatedly insists, his voice slowing as sleep drugs him, and I feel the weight of his cheek come to rest against my ear.

Mosquitoes sing their lullabies as they circle our skin greedily and the canoe beneath us sways gently like a hammock above the jet black waves.

'One day, you will,' I promise his closing eyes.

3

'*Baby!*'

The sound of Papa's voice bellowing my name in the morning still comes as a shock to me. He used to be out all night and asleep during the day as a fisherman. But now that he works part-time at the sawmill in Ebutte Metta like Uncle Jimi, it's difficult to gauge his routine.

'Coming, Papa,' I answer, lowering the flame on the rice I'm preparing before going to check what he's needing. After the bright sunlight on the deck outside his dark bedroom shocks my eyes. 'Can I bring you something?' I offer as my nose latches on to a foreign odour in his stale room. I look around to try and locate where the rotting scent is coming from.

'I hear Maureen dey wed,' he begins jovially before clearing his throat savagely in a way that sounds painful.

'Yes o,' I say quietly before reaching out to touch the mess of his clothes lying over the back of the chair in front of his mattress. I fold them carefully in an attempt to look busy.

'That is good news. Is that not so?' Papa says with his eye-balls latching on to me in the darkness in a way that causes my scalp to itch.

'She is very happy, Papa,' I reply.

'And what of you? When will it be your turn?' he asks, picking at a scab on his shoulder.

'My turn to what?'

'Are you stupid? You know what I am asking. Don't be wasting your life, Yemoja. Age is not your friend. You could have had plenty children by now, like Dura—'

'Papa—' I start to beg before he cuts me off.

'Don't Papa me . . . You think you can just be floating around forever, working for Mama Jumbo? You don't want to work in the market and you don't even want to use the English your mummy taught you to be teaching in school,' he continues, his voice rising with building irritation.

'Shey you know the taxi brings more money than teaching,' I argue diplomatically but he waves me away.

'Almost every last friend of yours has wedded and you're hanging around as though you're some young girl.'

'If you—'

'Don't even start your nonsense about the drones again. I've said my piece.'

'But it is good education and—'

'*Rubbish*! What can taking photographs do? Every time people are coming here and taking foto and *what*?' He holds his empty hands up at me and I watch the spittle congregating in the corners of his mouth. 'Every day the government is plotting how to remove us from here. What is it you don't understand? You want to be doing their work for them?'

'But Papa, that work isn't the government. And it's not just foto,' I try to explain without raising my own voice out of frustration. 'Mapping is *different*. It is to help us by bringing attention—'

'*Attention* brings people, which in turn is bringing the government . . . What is it you are not hearing? Makoko has enough trouble already,' Papa shouts before bringing his fist down on the floor next to him.

We lapse into an electrified silence, peppered only with his laboured, angry breathing. I tell my knees not to buckle fully despite them automatically assuming their deferential stance in front of my father.

'You know, Papa, not everybody wants to be married . . .' I stammer gently, reigniting his temporarily dormant passion.

'You be there letting Mama Jumbo fill your head with stories! *Nonsense*,' he replies, releasing a sound from his lips like a peanut shell being cracked open. 'Baby, a woman needs a husband just like fish needs other fish!'

'Then why is Auntie still single?' My lips challenge before my brain even registers what they're doing. I stare at Papa, horrified that my insolence will not go unpunished.

'That is not my business,' he says, dismissing my petulance. '*You* are my business. Making sure you make something of this life! *Marry* . . . Have your children . . . That's how we do things! Now, bring me water, please. All this talking has thirstied my brain.'

'Yes, Papa,' I say, relieved now that our awkward conversation has ended.

I fetch a bottle of water, open it and place it on the floor beside him. With almost three gulps he consumes most of the bottle before belching satisfactorily.

'Some women are too much for a man,' I hear Papa say while I'm exiting his room as though his brain has finally sourced the answer for my previous query. 'That Mama Jumbo na plenty.'

I wake Tayo, whose job it is to fetch water from the borehole. You can't drink the water from the lagoon though some people think that boiling it is enough. Uncle Jimi says it's fifty per cent shit and piss. Still, sometimes in an emergency, it can't be helped.

Tayo has always been close to useless. That's what everybody says because it's true. His other family isn't like that, so who knows how water entered into the stalk of the pumpkin? His only future prospect is surely an area boy; him and his layabout friends becoming roughnecks that roam the streets in gangs, causing trouble and extorting money from passersby.

The son of Auntie Bisi's sister, he was sent to us when his mother could no longer handle him. The idea was that Uncle Jimi would straighten him out and steer him from a path leading towards destruction, but his head is like a brick. He just doesn't hear word. It's almost as if he's suffering from sleeping sickness. Refusing to fish, fired from the mill where Papa worked and only occasionally follows Uncle Jimi to the boat builders where Uncle earns his main income. It's a wonder

Tayo is still here at all, even if he's only occupying space while contributing less than nothing.

Once I finish with Tayo, I hurry into my trousers and head to my job with Mama Jumbo. As her name suggests, Mama Jumbo's a large woman. Not that she cares, her weight is a veritable sign of her success. She's a delight to see on the waterways, manning her canoe in her eye-catching boubous and her ever-present multicoloured head-tie to match the necklaces around her neck. Everything with her is *extra*. The make-up on her face, her large teeth flashing like sugar cubes, the gigantic gold hoop earrings hanging from her earlobes. Papa always jokes that it's any wonder her canoe doesn't sink from its load. He says that due to her weight, she'd be better served riding in two canoes; with one foot inside each one like water skis.

With her goods stacked up around her, Mama Jumbo laughs her big laugh as she passes by, encouraging people to come out and buy something. She's also the elder sister of Mama's best friend, Auntie Uche.

Mama Jumbo's name is Auntie Agatha, but we've always referred to her by her business name. I don't even think she remembers her former one. We used to visit Auntie Uche regularly after Mama passed away, but it was Mama Jumbo I was most interested in. Auntie Uche sells stockfish along with some other women, but Mama Jumbo sets about building herself an empire on the water. As they tell it, she used to be dating a boat builder, which is why she has so many canoes. But she started off with just one and built up a large supply of steady customers as a result of her bullishness and charm until she was unmatched in the nearby waterways. From one canoe, she now has at least four on the water at all times, selling biscuits, crisps, peanuts and soda, while another sells cooked food. Her other canoes are piled high with tomatoes, onions, mango, yam, Maggi cubes and pepper. All the things people might need for their cooking. This year she's branching out into clothing, offering slippers, jeans, T-shirts and dresses.

As I watch Mama Jumbo chuckling so that her necklaces jingle and release their highlife, it's hard to believe what Papa says about every woman needing a husband. Maybe at one time that was true, but it's not something which should be compulsory. Mama Jumbo has never married and doesn't seem like she's missing anything. Even with the money she must have, she doesn't *need* to ride a canoe all day; she can happily employ another person to take her place. But she enjoys her life on the water on her own terms. She doesn't appear to require a husband for that.

'*Baby*? Is something bothering your head?' Mama Jumbo asks sharply, yanking me out of my thoughts.

I turn around to find that surprisingly, she's crept up behind me as I'm surrounded by boxes. Her deep octave has spoiled my counting, and the total has scattered in my brain, so I begin removing the packets of instant noodles from the carton to start over again.

'What is it?' Mama Jumbo probes before using her big teeth to destroy one oily-looking puff-puff. My stomach rumbles enviously as I watch her chewing the delicious, pungent pastry slowly. I bite the inside of my cheek to distract myself from my hunger.

'Papa is saying I should marry,' I reveal, stocking the noodle carton before moving to her collection of biscuits lined neatly on her shelves to replenish the load for one of her canoes.

'Who is it he is expecting you to marry?' She snorts and her laughter rumbling inside behind her breasts causes them to shake like rattles.

'He says na time . . . That a woman needs a husband and that fish need each other,' I explain with a sigh so heavy it hangs in the air between us like a full stop. As I fill up the boxes on the floor around me, I mentally picture the canoe outside that I can see out of the corner of my eye, to try and assess if there's anything else I can add to the floating merchandise before I begin to replenish her stocks of clothing.

'You wan marry?' Mama Jumbo asks me while wiping crumbs off her front so vigorously she becomes a one-woman orchestra.

'One day . . . But now what I'm wanting is to join the drone exercise,' I repeat out loud. Mama Jumbo already knows about the project since it was to her that I made my first confession about wanting to be a Makoko Dream Girl. I would have told Mama if she were here and she would have helped me bring Papa to some level of understanding. Still, it had felt good to confide in Mama Jumbo.

'Don't let anyone tell you what you want from this life, Baby,' Mama Jumbo instructs before digging the nail of her little finger between her teeth. 'Me? I left school in primary three. You think all this came to me for free?' she adds, waving her arms around the dark room piled high with her assorted inventory. 'Na *me* fight for every scrap I get and it was sweeter for doing so,' she says, planting her hands on her hips like a lesser-known superhero.

'I know if Olachi was here, she would tell you the same,' Mama Jumbo adds as she beckons me towards her and then grips my shoulders tightly, leaving the grease from her pastry on my skin as if it's body lotion. 'If that is what you want to do, then you must go for it. You hear me?' she asks, shaking me gently.

'Yes, Auntie,' I nod, feeling emotional all at once on hearing my mother's name coming from her lips.

'And tell your papa I said a woman needs a husband as much as a fish needs slippers.'

Everybody heard about the mapping project when it arrived in Makoko. News of it spread like the floodwaters that routinely rush our houses and schools, causing plenty of commotion. People started to talk about being drafted to learn to pilot the drones, young women especially, who would be taking pictures of all of Makoko as a way of mapping the surroundings. All the images will be stitched together to form one big picture of the place.

As I listened to all the gossip about the project, I imagined how much fun it would be to fly the drones and where the project could lead. I'm not particularly interested in technology the way Efe is, it's the flying I like. With my knowledge of the canals and waterways, I know I'd be good at it, more than I would be selling fish in the market. The reasoning behind the project is that the better we know our community, the more we can help develop the place and make life easier to live on the water. There are so many issues with sanitation, the lack of clean or running water, and getting electricity safely to us, so we don't have to rely solely on generators. We're already suffering from no hospitals and a lack of proper public schools. Plus, every year there's more flooding and fewer fish. They're all dying in the dirty water, choking on all the rubbish inside the lagoon. I can see the importance of this work that will show the world who we are, but it isn't something Papa's wanting. It's mostly the older members of the community that are suspicious of the project. There's no such thing as free kola nut, they protest. They don't trust people from abroad who say this work will help us. Most likely, it'll assist the government, who are already trying to take our land. To take us from the water.

From time to time, people come to Makoko to see how we live. Reporters within Nigeria or from overseas calling us the Venice of Africa, as if we have a clue what that is. Sometimes it's tourists from all over the globe. From America, from Thailand, or from England. They've watched something about us on the news or on the computer.

There are people coming here to try our food or to buy our art stuff as it's cheap. They explore the fish market and see so many things they've never witnessed before in their lives, like watching the women assembling the fish in the smokehouses, joining the heads to the tails with palm fronds, so they look like circles, like bracelets before placing the panla over the hot flames. Proper mainlanders even come here to use our make-shift clinics or to visit our traditional healers. They venture here, wrinkling their noses like they're smelling shit as they're ferried across the lagoon, then choke on the diesel fumes and the smell of fish in the air that's like an invisible cloth on the body, though we who live here are long accustomed to it. They come to observe us as if we're animals in a zoo or in the wild, and are almost taken aback when they realise we're just people. Hardworking people; living and loving like the rest of the planet.

They come in ignorance and they leave with wonder, with their eyes and lips wide, and their bodies stinking of fish.

Everybody knows that living waterside is coveted even when the water is greasy and filled with dirt. They want to shift us from this place and then clean it up so they can sell it for millions. Create another Banana Island-style place like in luxurious Ikoyi, where the houses are the opposite of our wood and tin; they are *first class*. Proper electricity and running water. Streetlights, sewage systems and telephone lines with satellite. *Everything.*

They have tower blocks, the kind that are covered in glass so that they glint at all times of the day when the sun strikes the building. Auntie Bisi, who works for a family in Ikoyi, even says they have tennis courts, running tracks and a swimming pool almost the size of the lagoon itself, if you can believe her. The houses are colourful too, like in Makoko, except they are more cream, white, blue and pink than brown and black. Instead of wood, they're made of brick, concrete and glass. Instead of one small shack with twelve people living inside, one big mansion houses maybe the owner and his wife. Can you imagine, more bedrooms than people living in the property? That's how all the millionaires and billionaires are living. The bankers and the people with oil. The people in government, in politics, even the recording artists. They're all living in paradise.

As soon as they shift us from Makoko, the government will do all the things they are currently saying aren't possible, like real electricity, unlike now where we're forced to run power lines from the mainland over the water. They'll bring schools and proper hospitals and police stations. The air will be real air instead of smoke and the water will run clear instead of grey and brown. Fish will return, swelling the nets like they used to do when Papa was fishing the lagoon. They'll tear down our stilted homes to erect skyscrapers and luxury villas so that people crossing the bridge no longer have to cover their eyes and pretend not to see us like they did when we were next to them.

That's what Papa is fearing.

That they will take Makoko, leaving us without a home.

All around Victoria Island, luxury properties are sprouting. It's only a matter of time before they snatch our community. Papa says the government and developers are no more than armed robbers waiting for the moment to strike, so we must always be watching. We should always keep our eyes open and our mouths closed.

If we give them more opportunities to step into Makoko, that's how they'll come inside and take everything from us.

It was Maureen who first told me that Samson was having feelings for me. I never had a clue. I'm not sociable like Maureen, yappy like Idunnu, or beautiful like Efe with her high cheekbones and her naturally tinted lips, the colour of ube, so that she doesn't even need lipstick.

I'm the tomboy in the group, not that I mind because it's easier to pilot the canoe in trousers without anything flapping and distracting me. I'm not in danger of showing my pant to anyone, like if I'm wearing a skirt or wrapper.

I know Samson better than the others from riding the waterways. He's an expert at repairing boats already at his age and makes a healthy living from it. Maureen had pulled me aside at a naming ceremony and told me that Samson was toasting me but I didn't want to believe it as she assumes that everybody's goal is to find a partner and make children. Now she'd managed to achieve that before twenty-one like she'd always wished.

I hadn't particularly noticed him before that, but after she told me about his feelings, some juju had made him appear in my daily life, at the jetty while waiting for passengers, on the water or on the occasions that hunger drove me to buy some-thing at Grace's Canteen. When we went to church, I'd find him sitting inside my eyeline and sometimes on my way to watch the fishermen gathering their nets or to meet Charlie Boy, Samson would stop me and make idle conversation. Part of me wondered whether Maureen was pulling my leg and trying to get me to embarrass myself for her entertainment. Or perhaps he's just painfully shy. Either way, his current undeclared status doesn't bother me too much and has some advantages. He fixed the small hole in my canoe several times without payment and also buys me plantain chips and soda every now and then.

I'm waiting for Idunnu on her deck while she finishes bathing when Samson appears on the waterway with his friend. I dislike Koku, who thinks he's funny when he's not and talks too much; meanwhile, his breath smells worse than the lagoon. I don't understand how it doesn't offend Samson. How can he spend so much time up close without giving his friend chewing stick?

Of course, it's Koku who is bare-chested onboard, his scrawny body and wiry arms looking like Afo's even though he's twenty like Samson. I wave as they pass by before dropping my gaze to my lap quickly, but I can hear the sound of the propeller increasing and know that they're coming this way. I steal a glance at Samson's face as he steers the boat, the three ever-present parallel lines on his forehead, his tight shoulders and lean muscles evident underneath his skin, ebonied from working under the sun. He's had this latest hairstyle for close to one year, a low Afro with the tips of his hair twisted, perhaps when his fingers have nothing better to do. He's also been experimenting with facial hair, but scanty hairs under his chin don't quite amount to a full beard. Nevertheless, he has a pleasant face. It's soft, not hard like Tayo, who carries so much anger at the world that it's twisted his features. Samson's skin is smooth, unlike Koku, who is riddled with so many pimples they look like tribal markings.

'How far?' Samson asks sheepishly when they pull up in front of the house. My mind plays tricks on me and I imagine I can smell Koku's breath as he opens his mouth despite the long distance. It's just the lagoon as the breeze hits the waves.

'Notin spoil,' I reply instinctively, turning towards where Idunnu is invisible behind the wall. I watch Samson's eyes flit over to her doorway, checking to see if she's on her way out. If he hasn't had the courage to ask me out directly when we're alone, then I'll most certainly be spared now that we have an audience.

'They say rain is coming,' Samson says before Koku knocks his friend playfully no doubt because of his poor chat.

'The lagoon is thirsty,' I reply as I study the cloudless sky above us.

'No be only lagoon—' Koku says as he pulls a face before cackling devilishly, and Samson throws him a sharp look.

'If you want, I can come later for your side, help to put cloth down for your—'

'Our house no dey flood like that!' I shake my head quickly, shooting down his offer before Idunnu appears, her hair frosted with beads of water and her skin gleaming from freshly applied lotion.

'*Cassanova!*' Idunnu sasses as she emerges from her doorway and strides over to where I'm sitting. 'Shey you came here for me?' Idunnu jokes as Samson kisses his teeth at her. 'You know say you get competition?' she calls after him cheekily as he powers up the boat and pulls away, waving to me as he departs.

'Leave him,' I tell her playfully, even though I enjoy her making fun of him on my behalf. But the truth is, while Samson is a kind man and a viable husband candidate, my heart isn't catching fire. I'm hoping to feel something more. If not for him, then for some other person.

Before I can digest another empty conversation with Samson, Idunnu sits beside me on the deck and delivers her surprise.

'I'm pregnant,' she says heavily and her revelation chooks me so much that my mouth becomes immediately dry as though I've drunk cashew juice.

'It's a lie!' I yell like a mad person. My exclamation loosens my tongue, but I can tell by the way her eyes are running that it's true. She's looking over at me as if I'm a bowl of red onions she's been chopping.

'By Moses?' I whisper, and she nods her head before falling into pained silence, heavier than her shoulder against my own as we press our backs against the heat of the wood. Moses is her part-time boyfriend and part-time dredger off the coast to supplement his diminishing income from fishing.

'When you find out?' I inexplicably ask. I don't even know why, but my brain doesn't know what to ask since it's afraid and excited at the same time. I'm fearful for her and the life change this news has brought Idunnu. I feel my nerves racing as if I'm the one about to run a race, not her.

'A week or so. But I was praying it was not so,' she reveals, wiping the beads of sweat peppering her forehead.

As I study her, I think I can already see the difference in her face. A browning of her usually yellower skin, the fuller shape of her cheeks. I tell myself it's a nonsense, that my eyes are dreaming, and we fall quiet as a series of boats pass by, some women selling snacks and a canoe full of children being piloted by one not much older than them, screaming and giggling in the way we ourselves might ordinarily be if not for Idunnu's announcement.

A part of me is joyful, I recognise, as I imagine Idunnu staying in Makoko now that she's to be a mother. She's endlessly plotting about how she can save up to go leave. Without education, it's a hard thing to master, but some people work hard and secure work elsewhere. Some others are just lucky.

'So, you will be wedding like Maureen—' I begin, but Idunnu cuts my sentence quickly like scissors.

'*No!*' she looks at me crossly before clapping her hands together. 'Moses? For where!'

'But why are—?'

'What he doesn't know cannot hurt him, Baby. I am not having pikin or becoming Mrs Adenuga and working to the bone smoking the fish he catches or waiting to hear that something bad happen for his work.'

I picture Moses alongside the other men that dredge for sand, descending wooden ladders into the depths of the lagoon. Submerging themselves totally before returning with a bucket full of sand that is emptied out onto the floor of a boat until it's slowly filled. Weighed down by its cargo or wet sand, they move slowly to shore, where the sand is then loaded onto trucks before delivering it to building sites around Lagos. Dredging is truly dangerous work. Plenty accidents – and worse – regularly happen.

As we sit side by side, my legs gap Idunnu's by the length of my whole foot. The wood of her deck floor is so jagga-jagga and the space between each beam is wide in a way that brings to mind our pastor's teeth.

'What are you saying?' I ask the question at last, even though I don't need to. The answer has already appeared in front of us on the deck like a surprise visitor.

'Don't tell Maureen. Don't tell anyone, Baby,' Idunnu pleads while squeezing my forearm forcefully. 'I'm not having it,' she whispers with a shake of her head. 'One way or another, I am leaving Makoko, I tell you. This is not stopping me.'

In the afternoon, I watch out for the people with their drones, but they don't appear. Wunmi had told me which area she was meant to be capturing, but perhaps she'd shifted the time and I'm too late to spot anyone. I float lazily on the lagoon instead and look at the birds drifting so slowly across the burnt orange sky, as if they are suffering from heat stroke.

I repeat what Mama Jumbo said earlier in the day, but when her voice reaches my ears, now it's only the level of the mosquito instead of the drumbeat it was when she first spoke. Every passing second quiets her words. I try to imagine Papa's face as I tell him that he and I aren't desiring the same things.

I think about Idunnu and the confusion in her head and the trouble in her stomach. For a few moments, I pretend that I'm as free as the birds, that I can pick up my canoe and ride on the lagoon away from Makoko, Papa's instruction and people's expectations. If I'm hungry, I will fish. If I'm thirsty, I'll build a system to remove the dirty from the water. No one will tell me what to do. No Tayo polluting the air with his night-time emissions, no Kemi running to me crying about her brother's nonsense or trying to steal my clothes. I allow myself to feel the temporary delight of my childish dreaming, but I know that real life isn't as simple and my thoughts stray to Charlie Boy, who I know I can never leave behind. Even now, bobbing freely on the water, the grey haze hanging over me isn't the smog but the weight of familial obligation. Women must be one way, men another, and any deviation is tantamount to disobedience. Sometimes I wonder, would I have had an easier pathway if I'd been born a boy like my brother?

My gaze falls over the handmade lettering on the canoe's side. The *Charlie-Boy* in capital letters that has been faded by the sun and diluted by rain and water. I pick up my paddle firmly, tasting the frustration that burns at the back of my throat.

I'm late in returning home, but lucky for me, Papa's sleeping from the traditional medicine he drinks for his pains. Uncle Jimi has returned. I can hear his voice two houses away with some other men, joking and laughing. He must have instructed Kemi to start on dinner as the smell of palm oil and crayfish greets me as I alight the canoe. Kemi's happy to be pushed aside as I take over from her, making the ewedu soup she's started preparing.

Charlie Boy's annoyed with my tardiness. I can tell from his tight mouth and his hands he has rolled into balls at his side as he glares over the water. I pull out the carrier bag at my feet, revealing the chin-chin and Sprite I've brought for our surprise picnic and his eyes start to shine like one of the lights on the bridge.

As we eat, I tell him about Mama Jumbo and what she said to me about not having to marry. He isn't really interested, but he listens anyway while his eyes comb the skies in search of his planes. I'm jealous of him still, I realise, as my insides stress from the pressure I feel on account of my sex. I wanted to be a fisherman, but Papa said it wasn't done and then Charlie Boy was finally born and could live my dream. He wasn't worrying about who he should marry even though in Makoko women typically have more money than the men, although that income is small. Even now, Charlie Boy is free. He's always free in a way I'm not, which makes me feel uneasy inside.

I tell him about the drones, but he doesn't understand what they are, so it's easier to stick to watching for planes and we wait for them to intersect the thick darkness hanging over our canoe like a fever.

'I will fly one day, Baby. Mark my words,' Charlie Boy whispers before his nostrils begin to blow a tiny flute.

'Me too, Charlie Boy,' I reply, staring up into nothing.

4

I dream that somebody has mistaken me for a fish and is reaching for me in the smokehouse. As I'm about to protest, they chook my mouth with a stick, pierce both my lips so I can no longer talk and before I know it, I'm in a circle like a smoked titus fish and heading for the fire. I feel the hot black metal against my skin and wake up, my body pouring with sweat.

Rain comes down on the roof overhead as if someone is playing steel drums. It washes away my dream before I rush to check on the water level to see how much it's rising and if we need to start removing our things from outside.

Business never stops on account of the bad weather. Fish still need selling in the market, clothes require stitching and wood must be chopped. The rain only really affects school as the water pours in and disrupts the children too much. Everywhere else, things go on.

Tayo refuses to wake up, so Afo and Kemi go and collect water for the household instead. I'm about to complain to Papa but catch myself before I enter his bedroom just in time. Papa would only use it as another opportunity to bring up marriage again or to tell me to follow Dura to the market. But that's not where my better life is coming from.

The morning is quiet. I only pick up two customers who want passage to Makoko. I feel bad since it means that my cousins will miss out on school. After we've paid the rent for the house, there'll be very little remaining since Tayo and Papa don't bring in much income to speak of. We're fortunate that Auntie Bisi's work as a housekeeper is regular money. It comes with a sacrifice as she only returns home once every two months for the weekend and then over Christmas, or sometimes when the family that employs her travels overseas.

As I'm finishing with Mama Jumbo, Efe texts me to tell me to come to the hairdressing salon where she works. Before I enter my canoe, Mama Jumbo comes rushing out to hand me a plastic bag. Inside is a portion of maize flour, along with a bag of tomatoes. That's the benefit of working here as I'm truly her favourite employee. She's always giving me small small things: onions and tomatoes before they spoil, the remnants from larger bags of rice and beans, some pepper, Maggi or stockfish if we're in need. It's good to know people in high places.

Only Efe is there when I arrive at LABELLE, the small salon sandwiched in an already crowded waterway. Her boss normally finishes late afternoon for the bar, leaving her to sweep up the hair and tidy the stations in preparation for the next day. I push open the door and find Efe leafing through a tattered magazine.

'You've changed your hair,' I comment, admiring her shiny new braids crisscrossing her scalp in an intricate grid pattern with extensions so that their ends are just above the small of her back.

'It's nice, sha?' she cackles before swinging her head expertly so that the hair behind her billows out in the breeze she's created. 'Come and sit down,' she says, beckoning me towards a wooden stool which I happily accept as I crouch in position in front of her.

Efe begins unpicking my cornrows that have been in too long and whose formerly crisp lines have now become furry. As I listen to her cracking her chewing gum while she fills me in on the gossip she has ingested from her day's work, I feel bad because I know something juicy about Idunnu. Instead, I press my lips together to stop the story from escaping.

The smell of cooking oil floods the salon even with the door closed and my mouth begins to water as my nostrils pick up the aroma of stick meat drizzling their fat onto hot flames as they cook along with roasted plantain.

'Are you coming on Saturday with us?' Efe stops her activity briefly to confront me.

'Coming where?'

'I knew you weren't listening,' Efe replies, mischievously snagging my hair with the tail comb. 'To the protest,' she says.

'Oh yes . . . I don't know,' I say, my brain imagining hordes of angry people congregating. 'I have to ask Papa,' I explain, listening to her blowing the air out of her mouth in exasperation.

'Baby, we are all going. It is during the day, so you don't have to ask anything, especially as you know what he will be saying.'

President Buhari condemned this latest attack that had made international headlines as yet another assault on innocent civilians targeted by terrorist groups. Loggers, farmers and fishermen were accused of spying for the army and pro-government militia; this is why they were attacked. Alternatively, they'd failed to pay the tax imposed on them by the group leaders.

'Since when are you political?' I change direction, wondering why the youngest out of us all, let alone the one always painting her nails and wearing blouse and skirt is so adamant to take to the streets.

'After last year, of course!' she replies swiftly, reminding me that she'd gone to the EndSARS protest with her older brothers. 'It is our duty, Baby,' Efe answers passionately. 'It is our country,' she adds and I find myself humbled by her words.

'Besides, my friend, the streets are full of people. *Fine* people,' she stresses with her generous lips so that her pout makes me laugh. Efe drops her hands from my hair to pick up the magazine from the counter. 'There are even celebrities there, Baby! I can meet Wizkid! They even say Davido might be attending in Lagos, like he did in Abuja for SARS. Can you imagine?' she squeals, raising both hands towards the ceiling that looks like a wooden checkers board with no pieces.

'You dey pray for real?' I ask incredulously, watching her eyes close and her hands clasp together between her breasts. 'Efe, you're too foolish!'

'I tell you, Baby, I will find a husband on Saturday. If you like, stay there waiting for one to hop inside your boat!' she replies seriously.

Kemi's noticeably quiet as she watches me make palm oil rice. Her eyes blink protectively as the pepper meets the oil, but I'm long used to the assault of ingredients as I cook over the stove. Aromas fill the air as the pot heats up and I see her looking around for what to eat.

We're cooking in anticipation of her mother coming home to visit, even though Auntie Bisi always wants to do everything during the times she returns. But this welcome meal I can easily do, to show her how much growing Kemi has done in her absence.

After preparing the meal, I take the canoe to the traditional clinic to pick up Papa's medicine. There are so many things reeking inside the clinic, so many individual ingredients that the combination blocks my nose so soon I no longer smell anything while I wait. Plenty people are waiting in the room too, using all the air so much so that I start to feel lightheaded, like sleep is coming even though it's only the afternoon. The walls of the clinic are painted entirely in green. Green for the walls and green for their ceiling. I'm considering going outside for one minute to wake myself up a little, but I'm certain to lose my place in the queue as people are always impatient for their treatment.

Papa's been using this medication for a long time, not that it's helping, but he believes in it. He suffers from low energy and aches and pains from chopping and loading lumber at the mill. The thick black liquid that can clear the hairs from your nose is meant to fortify him, but it's so disgusting that Papa takes it with soft drink before letting whoever's at home finish the rest so that Afo and Kemi usually end up fighting over the warm Fanta or Mirinda like chickens over a kernel of corn.

I focus my attention on the small boy clutching his stomach in the clinic to keep myself awake. He reminds me a little of Charlie Boy when he was small, right down to the gap in his front teeth. I wonder what his ailment is as he touches his abdomen and his behind in equal measure. His mother doesn't even stop him or remove his hand. Nothing moves on her face, as though she's deaf and can't hear him. *Maybe there's nothing wrong with the child*, I think to myself. *Maybe she's the one suffering.* Next to them, a woman with a bright yellow head-tie tries to stop her identical twin girls from fighting over a dirty doll baby with a missing leg.

As I'm observing these children, my mind wanders to Idunnu and her predicament. Her parents don't complain as much as Papa because she brings in good money from the hotel, along with her two sisters who work as house-helps in Apapa and Lekki. Whatever my current problems, I'm grateful that my situation only involves me and not a baby inside my stomach. I wish I hadn't agreed to keep her secret as Maureen, who'll be wedding soon, probably has the most life experience out of all of us. Even Efe knows more than me when it comes to men.

It's quicker to come here for medicine than to the Aiyetoro Medical Centre where by seven in the morning, there's already a long queue because of the good work they're doing there. When it opened, there were plenty people coming for emergency services and more. They were helping many women and children suffering on Makoko as childbirth is no small business. They even had a maternity ward for women who are having babies and are planning to build a floating clinic as well. I wonder whether Idunnu will go to the proper clinic to remove her baby or if she'll use traditional medicine that some women use to stop a baby coming or make it leave once it's here.

I'm formulating my future advice for her when a man exits the healer's room with two other men under his armpits as they support his left leg. He's wearing tattered trousers revealing grey ankle bandages from where his blood has dried. Every step they take draws a sound from his trembling lips and the sweat from their exertion leaves all three of them damp and shiny as though they've come right out of the lagoon itself. Quick quick, I jump from my seat as the mother with her crying baby tries to go in front of me to meet the healer, but I'm faster. I hurry and collect Papa's medicine while she tends to her child.

On the way home, I take my time rowing past the Church of Deeper Meaning. The sound emanating from the church's evening service bounces off the waves as the harmony of women repeatedly thanking Jesus fills my ears.

Every time I pass there, I remember Mama singing with her friends at the devotional service. Our community has many churches like the rest of the country.

It's really a true that God is everywhere in Makoko, from The Believing Faith Church of God, Word of Life Ministry, Church of Christ the Redeemer and the Ministry of Celestial Worship, where the congregation dress in white for their regular services. I believe in God but too often, He's quiet inside my head. Sometimes I'm jealous of the people who know Him better than I do, like Auntie Bisi and Auntie Uche. When I talk to God, he doesn't hear my voice, like the mother at the traditional clinic.

I don't hear Mama's voice as she hijacks my thoughts, but I know what she would tell me in this moment. *Be like water,* she would say.

Find a way to do what I'm wanting.

All around me, I realise as I drift on the waterway, I'm surrounded by people following their desires. From Maureen to Idunnu and Efe. Even Tayo, who sleeps through the better part of the day unchallenged.

As if by magic, Mama Jumbo passes by in her canoe, banging the side of her aluminium caldron with a large wooden spoon as she hollers to announce her presence on the water.

Her deep voice reaches my ears and tickles them from the inside, and our eyes connect as we move in opposite directions. My heart jumps behind my ribcage like a grasshopper and I know the excitement I feel is from the seed of my thoughts, a decision taking root and the water I'll need for my flower to flourish.

5

The morning's heat causes my limbs to swell. When I open my eyes, a headache presses down on my temples, so I move from the deck, where I must have fallen asleep last night, and enter the darkened bedroom.

A musty stench rises from the sleeping bodies like breath. Pushing the pile of shed clothing on the floor to one side, I lie down on the dusty wooden surface and watch pearls of sunlight bleeding through the slats of our ironwood home, cresting Kemi's sleeping features in beautiful bronze. I hear someone close by dragging fishing nets off their hanging posts outside and a nearby mother shouting at her children. Endless movements over the water graze the pain above my eyebrows like a nail burrowing deeper into a wound and I try to distract myself with the words Mama would sing to me as a child to settle me: *Onye mere nwa nebe akwa.* Who made my baby cry?

Before I even get to my favourite part that comes after the pepper soup, I've thankfully drifted off to sleep.

The sound of Auntie Bisi's voice stirs me awake after what feels like hours and I notice I've sweated through my cloth as my hands run themselves slowly over my temples to check whether I'm still intact.

Kemi has long since abandoned the battered foam mattress she shares with Afo; only Tayo remains dreaming in the room with me, his body hostile even in sleep. His naked back is contorted in harsh angles and the knuckles on both his hands are clenched as if he's on the verge of throwing a punch.

I'd been so happy when Tayo first came to stay, someone closer to my age that I could get along with. But where his parents had failed, so too had Uncle and Auntie. It's almost as if Tayo didn't want to be reached. He always reminds me of that passage in the Bible, the one likening the devil to a roaring lion looking for people to devour.

I get up slowly, relieved to find that the beating in my head has subsided, and escape to the unoccupied bathroom. As I'm cleaning myself, I listen out for the children. Since Tayo has abandoned his duty of collecting water, I hear Auntie Bisi order Afo to go and get drinking water with our neighbour's children. Crisscrossing the lagoon bed are pipes leading to boreholes in neighbouring Sogunro, where we procure the clean water.

I've barely been in the bathroom for five minutes when Auntie Bisi pounds on the door, threatening to reawaken my headache.

'Auntie, I dey come,' I protest through the door while wiping soap away with my cloth.

'Baby! Better hurry o . . . We're going to be late for Iya Gloria's naming ceremony,' Auntie Bisi yells.

*

Every minute, someone's being born on Makoko. There are plenty plenty children, not all of which survive. But there are so many naming ceremonies here that they take place once a week, almost as though it's church.

We're deadly serious about naming ceremonies in Makoko. Everybody knows that a name can take you far. Take our former President Jonathan, for example. Surely, it must have been his first name—*Goodluck*—that propelled his career to the highest station.

In Igbo land, while there's no official naming ceremony for a birth, a family announces a new baby by rubbing powder on their necks and then a child's dedication follows three months after they are born. It's much more of an event for Yorubas, who perform a ceremony beginning with a small prayer and an introduction to the baby. Prayers and songs of praise follow, to welcome the latest addition to the family.

By the time we reach our destination, Auntie Glo's house is already heaving with plenty people. It's a wonder there's room for another baby with all the bodies already crammed in their household. I'm momentarily grateful that in our house, there are so few people in permanent residence there. At least at times, when the talking becomes too much, I have the canoe on which I can find some small respite.

We locate Auntie Uche, who has saved us some space, if you can call it that. My gaze falls on the lightning bolt running through Auntie Uche's hairline, widening more each time I see her. I'm certain it's the smoking work that ages her, whereas

Mama Jumbo comparatively still looks in her prime. Wedging our bodies inside the crush, Auntie Bisi and I join in the singing before the presiding elder at Iya Glo's event begins to officiate the ceremony, talking through the presentation of the seven symbolic items that are traditionally used to express the path or hope of a successful life.

The new baby – a small boy – is quiet in his mother's arms as she jostles him gently to keep his eyes closed. From the small gap in my viewpoint, I notice the child has taken after his father, his wide-set eyes and deep forehead magnified further by his barely visible eyebrows. His tiny face reminds me of the end of a yam. I'm no longer listening as the elder speaks while rubbing the salt on the boy's lips, but as people start to react to the baby's pained expression, I'm pulled from my thoughts by their laughter. The boy remains surprisingly calm even after the palm oil, but with the application of kola nut, he begins to wriggle and cry as his eyes open in alarm.

The small breeze that Auntie Bisi creates with her make-shift fan that's actually a handkerchief pulled from her neckline is a relief as yet more people arrive even after the newly named Adewale has been announced to the world. For everyone, it's one more owambe, another opportunity to congregate, to rejoice and most importantly, to eat.

I'm not overly surprised that Idunnu hasn't turned up, even though I was expecting her to come. She's avoiding welcoming a pikin, and knowing her full situation, I don't blame her. After I've filled my belly with moi-moi and rice, I push my way over towards Wunmi, deep in conversation with a tall skinny boy with a nose so pronounced he looks like a camel. Her eyes light up opposite him and I wonder what's so sweet in their conversation that her brain is willing to overlook the superficial. Moving past the people gathering around to get closer contact with the child and family we're here to celebrate, I grab hold of Wunmi's arm as her man friend disappears in the throng of people before she can start talking to someone else.

'Wum-wum, how far? Did you not see my text?' I ask her, using the same nickname we called her in school. I notice her eyes comb over the fresh cornrows Efe did for me in the salon.

'I no get credit,' she explains, looking through me as she tries to find her friend's frame in the crowd spread over the large deck shrouded by blue, green and once white but now grey fishing nets that are more decoration than utility since more fish is imported here than pulled out of the lagoon at greater and greater distances from Makoko.

'*Ah*, but I've been messaging you *now* . . . How is your work going?' I ask her, trying not to sound too needy.

'I'm enjoying it o!' Wunmi says while drinking her Fanta.

'Can I see your phone again?' I ask, referencing the smartphone she was given for the project.

'I no bring am today, Baby,' she replies gently as her soft brown eyes scan the crowd until defeated; she refocuses her attention on me. 'We are learning so many things! And there are so many new discoveries in Makoko. On Friday, Ayo found a butcher specialising only in dog meat. She say for sure that's where Rover, her dog, don perish.'

55

Inside my top, my heart pounds with borrowed excitement from Wunmi's stories. I swallow my envy as I listen to her, one of the six young women selected in the first wave by the Code for Africa project, although the project has plans to expand.

'Can I come with you? Will you take me, please? Make I help you—'

Abandoning my earlier reserve, I start to beg, but her gaze shifts. I turn around to see the man she is talking to before heading towards us with a red plastic plate. I can smell the fried tilapia even before he arrives next to us.

'Yes,' Wunmi agrees distractedly before using her hand to surreptitiously push my waist. Her way of telling me to vamoose. 'Your auntie is calling you,' she announces loudly as the camel holds out the plate towards her, smiling at me briefly.

I move away to let them flirt in peace while I wiggle my body inside the cluster of people waiting to collect food from the table. I pile a fresh plate high, my appetite reinvigorated by my success. Whether she likes it or not, Wunmi has agreed to take me and deep down, a part of me is jubilating. I'm one step closer to my dream job on the water.

Asejere Makoko fish market is right next to our settlement and is a place that's always noisy. Kemi and I shadow Auntie Bisi under the guava-like glow of sunlight on the verge of ebbing before evening properly comes. She winds her way through the sprawling market, seamlessly avoiding bodies as vendors coax customers to buy and sellers balance products overhead or between their fingers in spectacular fashion. The call of merchants is like music as they try and entice everybody, from businessmen to students, to buy their evening meal.

It's croaker fish that Auntie Bisi's after to cook for a friend of hers who's fallen sick. We push through until she's found the seller she's seeking out, an athletic-looking woman sporting a green lace boubou with a turquoise and yellow leaf print wrapper across her waist while her cropped Afro is hidden underneath a brown basketball hat. On the wooden table in front of her are plastic buckets filled with mackerel, tilapia and the croaker Auntie was searching for to prepare her fresh fish stew that's legendary among her friends.

Behind us, a boy curses while trying to push his wheelbarrow crowded with assorted livestock through the throng of people. Kemi and I exchange funny looks as we observe the woman's impressive offerings, the beautiful silver frames of her barracuda with their sharp-toothed grins. Auntie Bisi stocks up on fish and some other ingredients we need for cooking before making our way back to the canoe.

When we pull up at home, Papa and Uncle Jimi are making plenty commotion on the deck. They're not alone but are surrounded by fishermen friends I recognise by sight but only know a few of them by name. Bottles of drink are scattered at their feet between them, bottles that will soon be dispatched into the water, adding to the floating junkyard.

Despite much of her time on land, Auntie Bisi's always graceful alighting the boat even with her bulbous behind that has carried many a baby like any purpose-made highchair. At her request, Kemi and I put away things as she sets to work on the fish, setting loose a spray of scales before dismantling the heads and extracting their guts in one fluid, deft move. I latch onto the men's conversation metres away as their voices rise with indignation and as a result of their drinking.

'There is no fish!' I hear the one they call Yarwood proclaiming before the other fishermen around him murmur in agreement. 'Three, *four* hours we are going before we can even set our nets,' he continues exasperatedly.

'How much are you bringing back?' I hear Papa's question before he releases a string of chest-clearing coughs.

'If we're lucky, forty kilograms,' Uncle Y replies, his voice laden with disgust.

'That's not even a third of what we used to get!' Papa exclaims before someone scatters the bottles outside and the sound of glass rolling over wood overtakes the chatter.

By the time the palm oil has risen over the simmering tomato and onions, the level of their conversation has mounted and the word *China* can be heard ringing out repeatedly.

'It's not just them! They're all at it . . . Spain, even Netherlands,' Uncle Y hollers, uttering the latter's name in a way that makes it sound like three separate countries. 'Fishing our waters, bypassing the restrictions—'

'But the Chinese are the ones selling *our* fish back to us,' Uncle Jimi weighs in before Papa interrupts him.

'*Eh- heh*, and what is the government doing about it? See us, fishermen living on the water, yet we are chopping frozen fish from Republic of China!'

★

Charlie Boy hugs his belly as I replay the discussion he missed out on earlier at home. I embellish Papa's drunkenness, from his round belly protruding through his open shirt to the scattering of the bottles before Uncle Jimi persuaded Auntie to relinquish the fish stew so that only a little remained for her friend. While making fun for my brother, I reflect on the words of the fishermen as I repeat them to him. It's true that the fish are disappearing, and with that, so too are the jobs of the men in a dying industry.

'Is this not a reason to embrace the new, like the mapping project that'll make people see us?' I ask out loud as my brother slips one finger quickly into his nostril. 'If the government doesn't want to acknowledge we exist – and our people want us to be invisible to the outside – who'll come to help us?' I continue, reaching out for his elbow to shift his hand.

Charlie Boy shoots me a defiant look before shifting in his seat and setting the canoe in motion. The waves that appear are as plentiful as the questions in my head about the future. How will we improve the water and return the fish and maintain our livelihoods in this place? If women are adapting by selling more and more frozen fish, aren't the technological jobs – the ones shining a light on Makoko like Code for Africa – not adapting as well?

Departing fishermen are highlighted by the moonlight, their frames casting inky shadows on the waves as their voices vanish in the darkness surrounding Charlie Boy and me. I wonder silently if my brother wishes he were heading off with them instead of being here by my side, laughing about the day and worrying over what will become of us. Ironically, he's always shown little interest in fishing, the boy who's allowed to. His passion has always been in the sky.

'Electric birds?' Charlie Boy repeats pensively, scanning the cloudless night as though he hopes to see one. I'd finally found a way to explain to him about drones. After all the weighty questions I've thrown out, this is where his brain is.

'You're going to fly one?' he asks, reaching his hand out over the rim of the boat, as if to touch the water until I stop him.

'Yes o,' I answer emphatically. 'I am.'

As a sleepy look overtakes him, I sit up and prepare to row us back to Adogbo.

'We're going back?' Charlie Boy's voice startles me as his eyelashes flutter open. 'Why?'

'Auntie Bisi will be looking for us,' I reply, feeling the oar in my hands being teased playfully by the water.

'But we haven't seen the planes yet,' he protests. 'Ten more minutes, please.' He pleads softly and I know I can't refuse him.

'Five,' I counter, watching him release a yawn as he stretches dramatically before standing up and observing the inky horizon.

'*Seven*,' he negotiates cheekily with a knowing nod.

It's always nice to have Auntie Bisi back for a visit as it means I'm not the one endlessly cooking or clearing up after the men of the household. So, it's annoying this time that she's home, she insists we *all* clean instead of her ordering us outside so she can do it properly for a change.

We do the same thing within the community; a monthly clean-up where we attempt to eradicate a small portion of the mountains of rubbish swept in through the canals, particularly after rainfalls. All of the city's water drains into here, from Akoka, Bariga, Shomolu, Oworonsoki and Macgregor Canal. It's not solely our problem, yet we're the ones blamed for the mess. We're the ones falling sick from the water, whether it's cholera or diarrhoea attacking our people. But cleaning here is an impossible task. Even if you do a little, more pours in. It's not a battle we can win by ourselves.

I watch Auntie Bisi, bent from the waist so that her backside is high in the air like the sun in the sky overhead. The dirt she sweeps floats around from one place only to end up in another corner of the communal room we use for eating.

It's easier for me to clear away my cousins' things rather than have them underfoot, complaining about the task in sweltering heat or breaking out into arguments after they unearth long forgotten treasures, like Afo's kite, that originally belonged to Charlie Boy but was abandoned with a broken spine after Afo's pilot journey. My cousins are messier than my brother and I ever were, but there's no real authoritarian policing their behaviour besides me. Deputised as a result of my age and gender, I tidy their belongings, packing away the clothes on the floor into their Ghana Must Go's before collecting the foam mattress and dragging it outside.

It's Mama that taught us how to do this. Taking the mattress outside to beat it with a broom before allowing the
sunshine to clean it as best it can. The mattress isn't heavy and
I can easily manipulate it myself, but I make sure to bang into
some things purposely to disturb Tayo, currently imitating the
dead in a star shape on his own mattress. He still hasn't shifted
when I re-enter the room, so I begin my own sweeping, knowing that the sound will harass him in his sleep. As I near his
bed with my pronounced strokes, he stirs grudgingly, his eyes
when they appear are angry torches.

'Baby, stop your *nonsense*! You no see I dey sleep!' he shouts,
trying to lie back down, but I'm feeling surprisingly defiant.

'*Auntie*?' I call out innocently over the sounds of my
sweeping.

'Baby!' she yells back in recognition.

'Shey we need water?' I ask, waiting for the inevitable. In
the pause before she responds, Tayo's breathing changes gear
on his mattress and he flinches even before his name is called.

'*TAAAAAAAYYYOOOOOOOOOO,*' Auntie Bisi's
foghorn rings out loudly. Her ability to drag his short nickname out of her lips so deliberately that it hangs in the air for
at least five seconds is outstanding.

Tayo eyes me viciously before getting out of bed, bumping
against my shoulder with his sour body as he passes on his way
to the bathroom.

It's a small one, but a victory nonetheless as I drop my broom
to collect his meagre possessions and dump them in an untidy
pile on the chair. There's no way I'm cleaning for an ingrate.

I reach for his mattress, flattened beyond redemption and reeking from his sweat and accumulated messes, and pull it away from the wall. But as I lift it, I spy the small brown bottles on the floor. I don't even need to read the label to recognise them, scattered all over the streets and waterways, accumulating under plenty houses. My eyes start to count them automatically, but I hear footsteps behind me and drop the mattress at the very moment Auntie Bisi's face appears across the threshold.

'Did he hear me?' she asks, looking over at the wall as if she has X-ray vision into the toilet.

'Yes, Auntie, he is going,' I reply quickly as I reach down for the broom to avoid any eye contact.

6

The moment you cross Makoko and hit the mainland, you're bombarded by large billboards competing for your eyesight all over Lagos. Advertisements for churches, toothpaste, for chicken . . . For anything you're wanting.

Banks upon banks, oil and gas suppliers, and numerous pharmaceutical companies, try endlessly to get your attention. We learn all the brand names from the rubbish that swims into our community. We're not safe on the water from the vices and the addictions that are taking hold of people in Lagos proper.

Codeine cough syrup can be deadly, but it hasn't stopped people from guzzling it like it's Gulder beer for the cheap high that it gives. Plenty of young people are drawn in by the sweet strawberry flavour which masks the chemical taste of the drug and, before long, are so hooked on the euphoria it produces that they are unable to stop. It's a growing problem in Makoko, where many people, children mostly, remain idle. For some, it's the only chance of escape they can get: drinking cough medicine or inhaling diesel. Many adults are addicted to the syrup too, even grown women, hiding their cough syrup inside their handbags as I ferry them in the *Charlie-Boy*, pretending not to notice.

Maureen lost two of her brothers to addiction. They'd left Makoko by then to sell medicine on the streets of Lagos. A year later, there were reports that one had been killed by an okada and the other was never heard from again.

It used to be easy to tell who was abusing the medicine because it was rotting their teeth, making them resemble ojuju. That and their zombie-like eyes, or their shivering and shaking when they are going through withdrawal. But people have since learned and adapted so you now see boys on the street tipping their heads back expertly to pour the medicine directly into their throats and preserve their tooth enamel.

It's not something I expected of Tayo.

For someone as stupid as him to utilise that clever method to hide his affliction.

The situation I discovered about Tayo is the worry bead consuming most of my thoughts. If I report him, Uncle Jimi and Auntie Bisi will surely throw him out of the house. He was sent to them as the last resort, and even though I've been waiting patiently to see life deal him a hand, I'm still fearful of being the one to set things in motion.

I wrestle my guilt about burying my head in the sand. Not everyone that is using the cough medicine has a problem, I try to convince myself. If Tayo was addicted, surely we'd all have noticed? It's not as if he's really aggressive or getting into trouble. His only real crimes seem to be oversleeping and general laziness.

I'd been holding my breath throughout Auntie Bisi's stay, waiting for the inevitable *what are you doing with your life?* conversation. I kept quiet about Tayo before she left, not wanting to be accused of ruining her trip with bad news about her nephew. It'd have been easy to unleash as well, to distract from her focus on me before she returned to Ikoyi with her quiet but deadly parting shot: *You should be cleaning your own house.* Code for the marriage agenda everybody is always pushing. No other order of business for me as far as the olds are concerned.

These days, marriage and weddings are the only things anyone can think about. Especially Maureen, who's finishing all our credit discussing her upcoming nuptials. She's one of the lucky ones, in that she's marrying a son of a baale, one of the village chiefs of Makoko. Meanwhile, Efe's still dreaming about celebrities. I'm not envious of Maureen's situation or her bride price for that matter. On top of who knows how many bags of salt, rice, sugar and alligator pepper, she's getting shoes, lace and a wristwatch which is absurd as if there's one person that can't tell time, it's Maureen.

Idunnu kicks my foot under the table, bringing my attention back to the magazine Maureen has positioned under our nostrils after summoning us to the canteen to discuss the gele, iro and buba she's contemplating for the big occasion.

'See this one's mind! Blank like a fish!' Maureen teases me as she moves over to the grease-filled rotary fan in a corner of the canteen to reposition it so that the paltry breeze blows in our general direction.

'I don't know why you're asking me,' I respond in my defence. I'm hardly the queen of fashion as they're always proclaiming. 'It's Efe you need for this nonsense—'

'*Nonsense?*' Maureen hisses, her nostrils flaring wildly and her eyes accusatory as though I have just called her mother a prostitute. She stands up with such force that the table shifts noisily.

'That's not what I'm saying—'

'*Idunnu*, I'm boring Baby with my wedding. Tell me, am I boring you *too?*' Maureen exclaims, looking between me and Idunnu, whose face is asking how she's suddenly been caught in the middle of our squabble.

I know for Idunnu, Maureen's wedding isn't the centre of her interests. After all, there's something more serious inside her centre. For a moment, I wonder whether Idunnu is about to tell her, from the long pause she's taking to gather her words and feel a wind cool my back where before beads of sweat were racing to my pants.

'Me, I like this one,' Idunnu replies quietly, pointing to an ornate purple wax fabric in the battered magazine.

Maureen raises both eyebrows at me before resuming her chair, suitably appeased. A customer clucks to get her attention and she ignores him before the cook shouts in the back. As soon as she's gone, I turn my attention to Idunnu.

'You want to tell her about . . . you know,' I ask quickly, eyeing her non-existent belly obscured by the table.

'If I wanted Moses to know, I would tell him myself,' Idunnu hisses, nodding in Maureen's direction. 'Telling that one is the next best thing.'

A group of children in varying degrees of nakedness are playing on the silt and mud of nearby Apollo as I approach with my boat. Some attempt a haphazard game of football with a deflated ball, while others are engaged in an intense kite-flying mission that reminds me of Charlie Boy when he was little. He was so eager to do it by himself that he'd barely relinquished the line when others tried to teach him. As the kite lands close to a pile of rubbish, its bright blue colour reminds me of the first kite we'd tried to make ourselves, from shredded plastic bags and sticks of wood. My brother and I had been so proud of our work until we tested it. Our failure had brought tears of laughter to Mama's eyes as she'd observed our effort.

I wait patiently, my attention flitting between the children, the mid-morning heat and my phone, in case Wunmi's a no-show in her standard fashion. Not long after, I see her coming in a grey and white dress whose pattern mirrors the kind you see on good armchairs on TV, the type they cover in plastic to stop them from getting dirty. In today's temperature, I envy her close-cropped Afro that draws more attention to her birdlike features; her long, lean nose and her small round eyes. I hadn't considered her attractiveness before this point, or perhaps I'm only just now witnessing her blooming.

Wunmi's English is slightly better than mine since she's constantly using it, another reason I'm sure she was selected to be a Makoko Dream Girl in the first place. It's what the young women chosen to participate in the project were christened and each time I hear the name, the butterflies in my belly turn to sour stones. I should have been one of them if only Papa had allowed me to attend the workshops and learn how to use drones to collect geographical data.

Once Wunmi enters, we set off in two canoes; a gentleman along with three other women in a canoe piloted by a former classmate whose name escapes me and Wunmi and myself in the *Charlie-Boy* so that we can talk in private.

'Are we collecting the drone?' I ask after a while, making sure to follow the other canoe without being disrupted by the noisy go-slow on the waterways.

'Today is just the mapping exercise,' Wunmi explains before plucking at a loose thread on the seam of her dress. 'But if you come this afternoon, when I'm meeting Ayo, I can show you,' she adds and I breathe a sigh of relief.

Wunmi shifts her weight in the seat ahead of me, causing more water than I'd like to leap in over the boat's rim. 'Careful,' I warn, assuming authority for our passage until the mapping officially commences, but she ignores my tone.

'*Baby*, in exchange for what I'm teaching you, you're going to pick me and take me to see Ebenezer,' Wunmi says as more of a statement than a question.

I blink back at her as my brain tries to acknowledge what she's said, and who she's talking about.

69

'*Ebe* . . . The boy from the naming ceremony?' I enquire after finally conjuring up the young man with camel features.

Wunmi nods shyly and her pupils grow in size instantly as she giggles as if I've just cracked a joke.

'Na so?' I answer, but my mouth's already smiling. All things considered, it's actually a pretty good deal for getting what I'm wanting.

We start off in a part of Makoko I'm less familiar with: Yanshiwe. Our sprawling communities have personalities of their own inside their labyrinth of waterways. While bobbing on the water, our canoes knocking against each other sound like coconut shells dropping from a tree, and I listen to their discussions before we proceed in earnest.

Wunmi extracts her coveted location-tracking smartphone from the handbag she's strung across her body and I watch her scroll through its navigation until she turns to show me where she's landed. A point of interest list appears from which she can make selections after identifying a site. Mosques, churches, markets, boat terminals, clean water sources and storage facilities – the list is quite extensive. We *are* literally putting Makoko on the map, one premises at a time. A map that the whole world will be able to see. No more pretending we don't exist.

Wunmi selects 'head of community residence' from the list of suggestions and I realise that our first point of interest is a baale's house within the district. It bears little distinction to many of the other homes on the water as I recognise the iron-wood we also have instead of the cheaper variants of wood some homes are fashioned from that quickly degrade over time. The size of the baale's house is, however, much larger than other buildings nearby. For a moment, I contemplate Maureen's new life after she's married officially to Osagie and leaves her current home for Sogunro, but Wunmi makes a sound with her teeth – commanding me as if I'm her goat – and we press on to the next location.

My brain is spinning with so much new information as we crisscross Yanshiwe and Migbewe, the neighbourhoods of some of the girls in our mapping party. I take in parts of the wider community that my eyes have never seen before. We unearth various waste dump sites, a cassava processing plant and a small health facility run by twin sisters. I know sections of Makoko better than some as a skilled navigator of the waterways, yet I'd been ignorant of many of the businesses hidden between the houses in various neighbourhoods.

We make a note of everything, roads, water sources, even sewers, and I barely notice the time going by as we explore and mark out formerly invisible sites, areas without names or addresses. After discovering a street with two barber shops, a tailor and an artist selling paintings and sculptures made from salvaged rubbish, we stop for a rapid-fire exchange of ideas on how to tag the area.

'What do you think?' Wunmi asks. The question directed at me feels like somebody's suddenly chooking my temples with knives as I feel the weight of everyone's scrutiny on me and think quickly. Astonishingly, the first thing that comes to my mind is my brother's T-shirt – a faded multicoloured top bearing Spider-Man in his official costume, crouched mid-leap while shooting webs out with both hands.

'Parker Parade,' I answer, my voice coming out jagga-jagga with my nerves before bracing myself for ridicule, but none comes. My suggestion is written down, and just like that, I've put something on the map that was never there before. I can't believe it. To those that don't recognise our work in the community, we're a simple motley crew of young women.

Little do they know that we're a new generation of pioneers.

Sometimes, I find myself wishing that the *Charlie-Boy* had a motor. It's hard not to want one when my arms feel like lead; strangers not belonging to my own body after a long day of rowing. But a motor costs about half a million naira, almost four times my monthly income, so it's simply out of my league. I've been saving for a smartphone and a computer if I can afford it. A sophisticated phone means more than business, it's a means of education too.

On the occasions I spot Samson on the lagoon and watch him fixing the boats or racing across the black water easily on his speedy boat, I fantasise about him giving me a motor instead of only crisps and Coke. Maybe if I was pretty like Efe, or outspoken like Maureen, things like that would happen for me, I think while wishing every day wasn't so much of an effort. Then I remember Mama Jumbo's hard work and the sweetness of her rewards, and it's enough to power my muscles again.

As I'm dropping Wunmi back off on Apollo, almost like I've summoned them with my thoughts, I spot Koku by the shipyard before I see Samson a few feet away, focused on a boat. Koku, on the other hand, is making a spectacle of himself as a couple of young women pass by. Whatever he's saying is clearly amusing them as they giggle like fools and push their breasts out against their filthy dresses in a way that makes saliva rise in my mouth. Then, as one of them shields her smile with her hand as she laughs, I wonder if she's covering her mouth from Koku's breath now that he's moved closer to them while making a game of trying to tickle them under their armpits.

It's as if Samson senses me because he looks over in my direction. I'm not sure I have energy for another stilted conversation, but I nod at him anyways. There's a part of me, I recognise, that's flattered by his attention. I might not be overly consumed by girlish things, but I'm still a woman. I know I have something.

When I was much younger, I looked like I was hollowed out of the same wood as my father. Our dark walnut complexion, deep-set eyes and our proud, prominent nose. But as I reached puberty, my mother started to appear in my features, softening what used to look angular and unyielding. Here, there are plenty of boys looking for girls in an absence for what else to do, but that's never been my thing. Even though I'm predominantly surrounded by trouser-chasers like Maureen and Efe, who welcome this ogling and heckling from supposed suitors, I'm glad to have Idunnu who's more like me, despite her having an unofficial boyfriend. One good grimace from Idunnu can turn any man to stone. I've seen it with my own eyes. It can shrivel the *dodo* between his legs so fast that the man will just be standing there touching his cheek, wondering how she slapped him without ever moving her hands.

One of the boats used by sand diggers is in front of Samson. Up close, it looks as if the only thing holding it together is prayers. I take in its impressive sail, made up of a variety of rice sacks. When the sails are puffed out by the wind on the water, they often resemble beautiful tapestries or colourful batik fabric. I take in the damage to the boat's hull that was the object of his attention before I appeared while he puts down his tools and reaches for a cloth to wipe his face that's sweating so much it looks as if he's poured a bucket of water over his head. His chest rises and falls dramatically as though he's been running.

'Afternoon,' Samson says sheepishly, pulling his damp grey button-down shirt away from his skin.

'You dey work hard, sha,' I say before walking around the boat slowly to observe his handiwork while I wrack my brain for meaningful conversation.

'Na Wunmi dey with you?' Samson stares into the distance behind me and I nod as I run my hand over the mint-coloured wood of the boat's hull.

'*Yes*. I was a Dream Girl for the day,' I admit, instantly regretting my outburst the moment it slips out. The less people know the better, before Papa catches wind of my rebellion.

'For the day only? How can?' he replies jokingly. 'You na Dream Girl, *finish*.'

We share a moment of shock because he's finally said the quiet part out loud and I opted for laughter instead of any

verbal comeback. Our serenity is shattered by a hawker trying to offload his bundles of peanuts that we refuse, much to
his dissatisfaction.

'Are you thirsty?' Samson continues after the small interruption, his fingers mimicking a bottle of soda. 'Happy Success
Grill is just there,' he adds, gesticulating over his shoulder.

A part of me is resistant to giving him hope where I truly
feel there's none, but another part is still feverish from the
day's events, and before I know it, I embrace my recklessness
by agreeing. At least I'll have something to tell my friends
later.

'Baby? What brings you this side, or should I say *who*?' Koku
starts, before baring his teeth and gums like a simpleton.

'Wunmi,' I answer emphatically.

'*Wunmi*? That one fine o . . . Make you call her for me so I
can talk small—'

'*Small*? Wunmi no get interest for small man,' I yap him
quickly before turning away, and while he's searching for a
suitable comeback, Samson and I fall into step without him.

While walking, my mind replays his audacity in calling me a
Dream Girl. There's more to Samson than his quiet exterior, I
sense, as we amble side by side, but if there's buried treasure
within him, it's so deep one might suffocate before reaching
it. Less awkward without Koku, Samson seems intrigued by the
mapping project when I tell him about my excursion discovering pieces of the community. But each time I try to imagine his
hand coming towards mine, I feel the urge to karate chop the air
around me as though I'm trying to vanquish a mosquito.

75

Distracting him with stories, I get to relive the euphoria once again at finally being up close with the drone as Wunmi demonstrated how to use it carefully while I fidgeted behind her like an impatient schoolchild. As we'd watched it make a quick journey overhead, I'd wondered who else was waving to it from inside as they spotted it in the sky above them, who else we were delighting that we couldn't see.

'Na so,' Samson mops his brow with his hand after I finish. 'That one pass for real work?' he asks with a small laugh that I echo halfheartedly, adding his slight dismissal of the activity to my instinctive objections about him.

'What of you? What of business?' I manage to question. If I ask him what he's wanting, there's a risk he might answer that it's me.

'We thank God … It's flourishing. I'm happy,' he replies softly.

It's an honest God-fearing answer that still bores my spirit somehow, but thankfully we arrive at Happy Success, which stands out before us with its colourful paint combination of bright blue, orange and green. Someone had attempted to paint trees, the sky and the sun – I'm guessing – but must have been overpowered by the task as none of that is properly recognisable, but it's still nice to look at. As Iyanya's latest song pours out from openings in the walls and on the street in front, a line of children concentrate on executing a complicated dance routine.

It's not a place I've been before but there are plenty people milling around with drinks and food even before we enter.

From our arrival and his recognition of people as we go inside the hot box that it is, it's evident Samson's no stranger to this bar. The smell of long-cooked food is sealed into the interior's dark wood and even the air inside is so greasy it causes my stomach to flip flop.

'You want chop?' he asks without waiting for me to answer as he presses his way through bodies towards the bar. I linger close to the entryway, where there's more air circulating and observe the children. One prima donna in the middle tries to impose his will on the others on either side of him, an effort requiring much negotiation. Even after the song changes, he's still the one calling the shots.

Hearing my name over the music, I glance over to see Samson brandishing a plate of fried fish and two bottles of malt in both hands while trying to beckon me over. I spy the table that has become free that he's rushing towards and push my way through the bar. As I'm passing by the window, I do a double take outside as my brain registers what my eye has taken in a moment later: a group of young men sitting in a poorly drawn circle. I can hear their laughter as one of them throws stones at a stray dog that has approached them looking for scraps. The dog's ribs protrude from underneath his sandy fur as though he's swallowed a xylophone.

At the young men's feet lie empty bottles of cough syrup. Tayo looks up at the window and I can't be sure if he sees me, feels my presence mere metres away from him. Something in his face closes and he stops laughing alongside his friends. I watch as he extracts a bottle from inside the pocket of his shell

77

suit jacket and tips his head back slowly. As he pours the ruby liquid into his mouth, his Adam's apple moves skilfully like a snake devouring its prey.

Samson slides my drink and the plate of fish towards me as I sit down heavily opposite him, but the thrill is gone and I push the plate away.

After what I've just seen, I no longer have an appetite.

7

My body aches from my night's sleep in the canoe. I'd escaped the house after cooking to avoid the tension of any troublesome interaction between Tayo and me. Afo detests porridge beans, like my brother, but it had been all that we had. After quelling the mini protest with some fried plantain, eventually Charlie Boy and I had drifted to sleep outside with the motion of the waves lapping against the canoe.

Creeping into the bedroom in the morning – stretching the cramp out of my neck as I go – I see I needn't have bothered as Tayo still hadn't returned. Afo's small frame is on Tayo's bed while Kemi is a perfect right angle on the other mattress. For a moment, I watch them, sleeping peacefully as a result of total occupancy of a bed. Kemi's lips move in her sleep as if she's reciting a speech, while a steady line of drool exits Afo's mouth to make its home in the already sullied bedding.

I bathe quickly and prepare some ogi for breakfast for the household. In my hip pocket, my phone sounds repeatedly but I only check after sweeping the house from top to tail. I'm confronted by a barrage of messages from Efe making plans for the demonstration taking place later in the day and asking me not to disgrace her with my attire. It must be the fashionista looking for a husband in her speaking and not the budding politician, but even so, I take time considering my clothing before selecting my good denim, the one that's dark blue and bears the least sign of use. It's *jump-up*, but even so, the way it hugs my ankles; I think I can get away with it. It almost looks like style.

I reach for my black and white top before hesitating. From what I recall of the #EndSARS protests in the newspaper, there were plenty people and plenty commotion at the demonstration. I understand the importance of adding our voice to the choir but I'm reluctant to lose my best shirt for the cause. I choose my red singlet instead, which has a lacy upper part, before searching the bedroom for the only handbag I own.

The excitement brewing in my body isn't solely about attending the protest, I realise, as I gather my things together. Part of me is still buzzing from the clandestine outing as a Dream Girl.

Charlie Boy's eyes had been larger than flying saucers when I'd told him about it as we'd floated in the canoe; his mouth pausing the suck on his sweet so that his left cheek was bulging as if he'd been beaten.

'And *you* were piloting it?' he'd asked, his eyes combing the sky as though the object of our conversation would miraculously appear over us.

'Not yet, but I know exactly how to use the controls,' I'd explained proudly, my fingers mimicking the familiar movements I'd watched Ayo and Wunmi making with their hands on the console of the drone.

I replayed Wunmi's laughter at my evident awe as I finally saw the drone up close, smaller than I anticipated, a metallic praying mantis or stick insect rather than the bird I'd initially described to Charlie Boy. I'd taken in its long body and four-winged appendages; its two eyes on its front with the circular camera head underneath it that reminded me of a frog's expanding vocal sac underneath its chin.

'I'm dead,' I'd exclaimed with excitement as Wunmi slotted her smartphone into the carriage of the console and after a few manipulations, the contraption came alive.

My brother had been in hysterics when I told him about Samson and his failed attempt at a date. Not that it was entirely Samson's fault that the mood had been soured by our cousin, but he'd been with me at the time so my brain had put all the emotions involved with Tayo and Samson in the same place and I had no general interest in sorting the jumble. Even though my ears are hearing whenever people proclaim he's a good prospect due to his job and family, as far as I'm concerned, Samson is stale biscuit. For someone starving, he'd be a great miracle, but I hadn't reached that kind of hunger yet.

Papa's anxiety about my status was his and his alone.

After he'd finished laughing, Charlie Boy had fallen silent and I saw what looked like fear creep into his chocolate-drop eyes.

'You like him?' he'd asked quietly and I'd made a comical sound by way of response. Everything I'd relayed about

Samson spoke to the contrary, but a small part of my baby brother was afraid of separation, should I depart to become someone's wife.

'*Ah*? You're the only boy for me, Charlie Boy,' I teased him gently while running my hand over his natty, sand-filled hair. Surprisingly, he hadn't ducked to avoid contact as usual but surrendered under my touch.

'I won't leave you,' I'd assured him quickly and without scolding him as he'd swept his fingers through the blackish night waves.

I make my way to Efe's watching the young boys, aspiring fishermen, casting their nets off the rickety walkways just visible over the lagoon water. Most of the boys in the community begin early, shadowing their fathers on the boats and learning the ropes until their time comes with age. It looks like these boys are idle and killing time with their nets that were bound to come up empty at this impractical location, not that it mattered to them. One of them has made their attempt into a sport and takes off speedily over the slimy pathway.

'*Careful!*' I yell out at the top of my lungs as terror creeps up my spine at the thought of him slipping. I'm royally ignored but at least I've tried to warn them.

As I approach the other side of Adogbo, a separate community in its own right, as the vastness of our location has created natural neighbourhoods among the shack clusters, I notice a shift in today's temperature, the breeze blowing through my clothes and am grateful for my outfit. Efe's neighbour is blasting

'Billionaire' by Teni as I near their house. Instantly my spirit is uplifted as I burst into the bedroom where Efe and Maureen are settled, having kicked out the rest of Efe's siblings.

'*Well*? Am I fine?' I ask cheekily, pirouetting like a top model before striking a pose in the doorway, cocking my right leg at an angle.

Efe turns to inspect my attire. Her expression isn't communicating excitement but nor is she horrified, so I consider that approval.

'Borrow my earrings,' she commands, pointing towards the corner table with her chin. I go in search of her jewellery and she plots my path behind her without moving her head. 'The gold ones,' she elucidates and I reach for the small earrings that resemble horseshoes before coming to sit down on the floor next to Maureen.

Efe has the best products as a result of her work in the salon and is always bringing back samples. The end of products or snatches of hair from mismatched bundles. Old nail polish where the end's almost over even after diluting it small small with nail polish remover.

I watch Maureen scooping a generous dollop of Blue Magic hair pomade onto the back of her hand. She then distributes it between her curly braids as she oils her scalp. I'm marvelling at her ability to complete this task while simultaneously eating a piece of fried meat; being careful to avoid gripping the morsel with her elected oiling finger.

I'm surprised that Maureen and I are the ones ready while Efe is still taking her time. I watch her wearing a denim pinafore dress which stops at the knees, showing off her smooth skin. Underneath is an orange and gold Gucci top that I'm sure Gucci doesn't know they've made, despite the initials broadcasting from across the entire fabric.

'Maureen, is this really *you*?' I joke, bumping my shoulder against her own. 'Did Efe tell you the wrong time?' I ask out of genuine curiosity.

'*Me*? I'm not going with you guys!' Maureen scoffs. Meat finished and fingers licked, she proceeds to massage her scalp with all her fingers.

'Why no—'

'I am to be *wedded*! I can't be running around Lagos and putting myself in jeopardy,' she replies, shaking her head.

'Don't mind her,' Efe chimes in after she has completed her make-up. Her lips are glinting from the petroleum jelly she's used and around her eyes is a strong line of black kohl pencil. She looks incredible. 'See if I no get husband, today *today*! Keep your son of a chief . . . When I come back with Kiddwaya, you'll see pepper,' she replies, flicking her hair over her shoulder.

We're still laughing about her delusional fantasy of bagging the *Big Brother* contestant when Idunnu appears.

'Sorry o,' Idunnu offers before resting her body against the wall. I can see that she doesn't look like herself. 'I was running late. Efe, you get water?'

Efe nods and exits the room to yell at one of her younger siblings to bring some water for Idunnu to drink.

'Are you okay?' Maureen asks, her eagle eye for gossip armed.

'I'm fine but my stomach dey turn all night,' Idunnu explains with a deadpan expression. I notice she refuses to make eye contact with me as she replies.

She downs the water in one go when it is brought before coming to hover by my side. While Maureen's distracted by Efe, I whisper to her as discreetly as I can.

'Are you sure you're fine? You don't have to come.'

'I'm okay,' she replies quietly, smiling at me fleetingly with gratitude in her eyes. 'I was vomiting all night. I'm surprised anything dey for my belly! But I swear I'm going with you today. God Himself knows na distraction I need.'

There's a go-slow on the water as we head towards Lagos Island. Crowds of canoes push their way forward amidst idlers and vendors shouting over one another, children playing and canoes transporting carefully piled stacks of wood.

Many people appear bound for the same destination as us; shocked into action by the news earlier in the year of yet another bombing by a jihadist group that once again attacked rice farmers and fishermen in the North that saw almost a hundred people killed. In the newspapers littering the lagoon, it was unclear which group was responsible for the attack. Some locals had claimed it was Boko Haram, others thought the Islamic State West Africa Province the likely culprits. Either way, for decades terror and violence have escalated, even spreading into neighbouring Niger, Chad and Cameroon, which led to a regional military coalition being created to fight the militants.

After three weeks of demonstrations all over the country in 2020, voices crying out against police brutality, change came to Nigeria. For once, the people not only had the ear of our government but the ear of the world.

SARS, the Special Anti-Robbery Squad, was notorious throughout the country for a long string of historic abuses. It was originally set up as a masked police unit to carry out undercover operations against violent crimes like kidnapping, armed robbery and car snatching. But like everything else in Nigeria that wears uniforms, there's plenty of corruption and the SARS unit was no better than the criminal groups that brought about their creation in the first place.

In early October a video was released of a SARS police officer shooting a young man in Ughelli before driving off in his vehicle. The four of us had huddled around a computer screen in the entertainment centre to witness it with our own eyes. Despite the shaky, pixelated footage and the shouting in the brief clip, the truth had been there to see.

Papa and Uncle Jimi's complaining kept the story alive in our household and then only days later a new report surfaced that *another* SARS officer had killed the musician Sleek, just twenty years of age. So, the latest demonstrations against this unit began and caught fire. They weren't listening to us; they weren't seeing us before, but magically the rest of the globe knew Nigeria. Naomi Campbell, Nicki Minaj, even Queen Bey shouting for our people! As a result of the mass demonstrations, the government was forced to pay attention and agreed to disband the unit.

As Nigerians rose up against uniformed officials, fuelled by Fela's music that was blasted in the streets, small small we lost the fear he bemoaned we possessed. That made us resistant to stand up for ourselves. Little by little we are learning the power of demonstration.

I hadn't attended the protests for SARS. As Papa had warned me many times, it wasn't my business. Even though I understood his reasoning, I don't think he was correct. As the demonstrations continued over days, the Army had been brought in, not to mention police officers who opened fire on crowds of peaceful and unarmed protesters. Even from the water, the mainland had looked raging, fuller than usual as more bodies and vehicles swelled the already crowded streets. Traffic which is always heavy in our megacity was brought to a standstill by the demonstrations in Yaba, at Lekki Toll Gate and near the airport. Eyes aflame, Efe had recounted how Nigerians in their thousands came to voice their frustration until they were sent fleeing by water cannons, tear gas and live rounds of ammunition, no matter what the government said. Though luckily, they'd missed most of the danger personally on the day they went.

The reports over the radio and in the papers had all been too much for Papa. It unearthed too many wounds from eight years ago when the government had come to forcibly push us out of Makoko.

★

Say what you want about our waterways and canals, but the streets of Lagos are just as bad. There are so many potholes that their streets resemble a never-ending game of oware. Most of us learn how to play the pit and pebble game from childhood. Moving the hard, pale green Bonduc seeds round and round the board in the hope of winning the most at the end. But nobody's winning in this country with a government that refuses to look after its people.

After we navigate our way through a tangle of boats vying for entitled access, we're confronted by the cries of children on a nearby veranda as well as in the water.

'*Yevo, yevo!*' they yell, pointing at two approaching canoes before they scatter in different directions.

Idunnu, Efe and I look around for the white people they're referencing and sure enough, we see the canoes, with their mixed complexioned cargo and cameras. We discuss what they might be coming to witness. From their expressions, they're novel visitors to Makoko. They appear transfixed like some of the people in church when listening to the gospel. Their eyes are agape as they take in our wonder as though they are on safari.

We're accustomed to tourists in Makoko. People have been coming over time, usually with cameras in hand. From the missionaries or journalists to people looking for fish that hear about us from the mainland; they all jump into canoes to voyage to our side. But just because we're used to strangers visiting doesn't mean that everyone's receptive. Many children shy away from this contact with foreigners. Some see it as an opportunity to make a bit of money if they can get away with it without their parents finding out. On the whole, the community is wary of visitors taking photographs because government officials don't like attention being drawn to the very place they're wanting to ignore.

The older generation have trusted before, only to see our community pride repackaged as pity once it passes through the photographic lens of an outsider. Some of them have long since stopped believing in people coming here for our stories or promising to raise funds. Promises that hit our ears but never seem to reach our bellies.

'I don't want trouble o,' I remind Efe fearfully as we wind our way through the streets as more people join the flow of movement behind us. Heaven forbid that something happens and I'm forced to tell my father where we've been.

'We'll be okay,' Efe sighs as she eyes the growing crowd on the lookout for Mr Right. 'Nobody is dying today,' she adds determinedly, hurrying me on.

Beside me, Idunnu's hair is frizzing steadily with the climate. I observe its length changing each time I look in her direction as her hair recedes from just above her shoulders to graze the bottom of her ears.

If the SARS protest wasn't our business, then this protest certainly is as we march in solidarity for our fallen fishermen in the North. We three are armed with only our voices, but others in the gathering, even some from Makoko are carrying placards and Nigerian flags and scarves as we press on foot in a three-hour journey towards the governor of Lagos State's residence in Ikeja. Some people have even tied green or white materials around their necks to make capes.

I'm surprised by our numbers. There's volume everywhere in Lagos – Makoko included – but this crowd is impactful on the streets as businesses in Yaba and Ilupeju grind to a halt and traffic becomes gridlocked on Ikorodu Road. Only roadside vendors aren't interrupted as their business continues, peddling roasted meats, pyramids of tomatoes and onions, and piping hot akara and moi-moi underneath colourful parasols to escape the blazing sun overhead.

Somewhere between my thirst evaporating and Idunnu losing a slipper so that she's forced to buy a new pair from a young hawker, my fear dissipates. I no longer think of Papa somehow sensing my betrayal from his bedroom in Adogbo, I am no longer terrified of uniformed soldiers bursting through the streets to take our lives. I'm just another part of this moving unified stream.

Songs bubble onto people's lips that we adopt, singing in unison until our throats burn. One Nigeria, one anthem. I understand why Efe was invigorated at her first protest. Even if the government is a big fish in the ocean, confronting a large school of small fish can also be intimidating.

As we walk on, Efe reaches down for a sign someone has lost on the journey. It's a piece from a cardboard box with the text 'in solidarity' scrawled on it. She holds it above her head as we march, joined by people on motorbikes too. Even cars caught up in the traffic jams honk their horns along with us, or so it seems, even though Lagos is a place where people are always talking with their horns.

I surrender to the moment like a canoe on the lagoon being carried away by a storm. Little more than a piece of drift-wood. As our chanting builds, I can feel my soul being swept up like a sail filling with air. But that air is our voices, our breath and our sighs. *Our frustration.* Our despair over more mindless killings, over the lack of protection from our government, the state of our country.

I look around, imagining we're all screaming over different things as we are gathered together as one. I feel my rage bub-bling through me about other injustices, the futility of youth in a country that considers its people little more than cock-roaches. The condition of our community and the lack of fish in the lagoon. Even my anger at Papa emerges, bursting through my throat at the thought of always being constrained. Having to keep how I feel and who I am hidden. The realisa-tion leaves me feeling momentarily faint.

I feel Idunnu slow beside me and shoot her a conciliatory look. She's grimacing through some discomfort so that her lips have now become a thin line, but she shakes her head at me sternly, answering my question even before my mouth has asked it.

We're just beyond the city mall and almost at our destin-ation without having encountered any military force. The only impediments we have come across are the burning tyres and tree branches that people have assembled to impede the inevitable government response should it begin while demonstrators are passionate but peaceful. But there's a bottleneck up ahead and we come to a stop, the whole throng throbbing with anticipation and frustration as we wait to be on the move again. Efe points to a man in the crowd with twists in his hair and a goatee. His eyes are obscured by expensive-looking sunglasses as he bears a sign recycled from the SARS demonstration. Nevertheless, its message is still applicable: OUR LIVES MATTER.

'Is that, *is that Burna Bo*—' Efe begins before Idunnu kisses her teeth loudly. As if stumbling upon the major recording artist would be that easy.

'This one is hallucinating!' Idunnu replies before we burst into peals of laughter.

We're still cackling as the smoke starts to appear. We follow the willowy trail to its black epicentre from a bus shelter up ahead, an angry cloud getting larger. Other people start to notice it too and quickly, the mood changes. What feels like a natural reaction to witnessing danger – some jostling in the gathering as we try to move away – shifts and bodies become more forceful. Our mantras become individualised as the crowd starts to disband. Suddenly the sound of a lorry's backfire peppers the air, or maybe it's actually real live gunfire. Either way, chaos breaks out.

It's the full-blown fear in Efe's features that sounds the alarm for me. I'm not even thinking of my personal safety as I look over at Idunnu, being pushed and pulled like a doll-baby. As my gaze falls to her stomach, her hand is protectively in front of her midriff, even for something she's not wanting.

I react quickly, grabbing them both by the hand as we turn back on ourselves and away from Alausa. There are so many moving limbs inside my vision as I run that I don't know which are our own and which belong to other people, some of whom have the same survival instinct as us and are rushing in the same direction. Efe's braids are whipping me as she runs ahead of us, but I don't care. I try to shield Idunnu as best I can from other people as we escape.

We only stop for breath when we reach Oregun, pausing to clutch our stomachs outside the 7Up bottling company and again by the Unilever building. Idunnu's hair is completely beyond salvation. She looks like a scarecrow that birds are no longer fearing and have set upon with relish.

We thread our way through unfamiliar roads before winding up on Olanrewaju Street. There's a lack of footfall that relaxes us as we fall into step with the few pedestrians on the street compared to the throng of moments earlier. We head naturally towards the busier end of the street that becomes gradually more populated as hair and phone shops appear, along with the yellow and black taxi cabs that commandeer any Lagos street. Idunnu looks the worst for wear after our sprinting. Fortunately, I see a mini market up ahead and coax her on just a little further.

Our nerves are shredded but when Efe begins to laugh from the adrenaline, Idunnu and I join her. Hollering in the street like mad women until a large black SUV appears in our eyeline. Instantly I recoil, even without processing the vehicle in full, without taking in the absence of either the green and yellow stripe across its body or the white lettering signalling the police force. We begin running again, our feet lifting from the dusty street as we seek sanctuary at the threshold of the mini market as the vehicle passes and joins the traffic jam up ahead without any altercation.

At the door, I pull the handle just as someone inside is about to push. Through the glass, I see the astonishment on the young man's face as his body – still fully in motion – emerges from the store with a jolt and we collide. My mouth rushes to apologise but I realise it's no longer functioning. I'm also unable to drag my eyes away from his own, from his face, even as from my periphery, I can see the oranges he must have purchased rolling past our feet on the ground and into traffic like rats escaping a broom. *What's wrong with me?* I'm asking myself, but as the question forms about why my body's also not moving, I become aware that he's also frozen and staring back at me.

Some fish want to be caught. That's what Papa used to say years ago, when he would return home with nets heaving with their catch of the day in the period when the lagoon used to be giving. He'd declare that the fish were practically forming a line in the water to enter their nets; their capture had nothing to do with his skill.

Suddenly Idunnu's hand appears between us then, brandishing three sandy oranges. At last, my eyes blink and the spell is broken.

'I'm sorry,' I say finally, when my tongue has unglued itself from the roof of my mouth.

'*I'm* not,' he says with a deeper voice than I'd expected to exit his tall, wiry body. I follow his hand as he reaches over Idunnu's, still proffering his fallen produce, and opens his palm towards me as if we're two people assembled for a business meeting. 'My name is Prince,' he adds as we shake.

'*Trust you*,' Efe scowls while twisting her lips as I ferry them back to Makoko as the light begins to dwindle.

I can't help it. A giggle escapes me at her frosty reaction to my good fortune. Prince's image is placed proudly on a mantle in my mind. He's shining bright as I recall his gentle face, the two dimples on his cheeks and the perfect symmetry of his bald head like a toasted eggshell.

'It had to be *you*,' Efe continues over the sound of lapping water. 'Of all the people dey meet man,' she adds, as though me finding a handsome man is such an impossibility.

The audacity.

'You think you're the only one that is Cinderella?' Idunnu yaps before breaking out into laughter that rocks the canoe gently underneath us.

'Don't forget it's my earrings you're wearing,' Efe replies with a sour twist of her lips. Determined as ever to have the last word.

8

'Would you like to run one of my canoes on the water?'

Mama Jumbo's question stuns me as she watches me coming in and out of her house with produce bound for sale.

Her query is another indication of her success, so much so that she needs additional employees while many others in Makoko are forced to eat pap night and day for lack of anything better to fill their stomachs. I'm aware it's an honour to be asked; that the other canoes are piloted by her children or relatives, so I try to arrange my face quickly before she takes my hesitation for something bad.

'I'm thinking of branching into the markets,' she explains while fanning herself with a wooden fan that creaks with its energetic workout at her hand. 'Selling big fish and crabs, prawns, crayfish and lobster for people with money,' she adds, casting her gaze far away in the overall direction of the mainland. 'Hotels and caterers are where the big money is! Maybe even transport, though what do I know about managing a bus fleet? Anyway, it's certainly not here, though we make a living. Thank God,' she sighs as I lean against the wall in front of the chair she's occupying like a throne. 'Ugo will handle the market,' she continues, referencing one of her daughters. 'But I need reliable people on the water. I'm too old to be training people or rooting out *thieves*!'

'Auntie, I am grateful—' I begin before she interjects sharply.

'*But*?' she challenges gently. 'I can hear the but coming . . .' she replies, eyeing me in a way that makes me uncomfortable. Like she's seen under my skin and bones and knows what's hiding there.

'No but, Auntie. I just want to think about it,' I answer sheepishly, my lips parting to display the grinning teeth of the imbecile I feel like.

'What is there to think about?' she asks rhetorically. 'Or do you have a better offer?' she adds, eyeing me suspiciously. I shrug my shoulders dramatically and resume my activity. Busying myself with packets of spaghetti, I can feel her gaze boring into my back before the sound of her fanning recommences.

As I head home after my shift, I mull over what Mama Jumbo said about the future. Those that are still fishermen on Makoko give the fish they get to their wives, which is where the business begins as they smoke the fish prior to selling or offload the fresh fish in the markets with all the skills of financial traders. Unmarried women like Mama Jumbo need to go further in search of their fish. To Aja, Epe, Lekki or Ikorodu, spending anything from two million naira on their stocks of fish to last a couple of weeks. Ice blocks are fast becoming big business in Nigeria too. It's costly but necessary in the fish trade.

I can see the opportunity I'm being given, to learn from her experience. For a steady job, which might also allow me the possibility to save real money, but something inside is holding me back. It's not the feeling I had when I was in the boat with Wunmi and Ayo. When our faces were turned up to the clouds, watching the drone passing through the sky and confusing birds. It's not the highlife that moved through my body even before my skin touched Prince's warm palm, giving me an electric shock.

With my arms functioning on autopilot, I allow my brain to fill with him again, even though it's a madness. After our introduction outside the shop where I was forgetting myself, Efe had dragged me inside almost as though I was her child. We entered to buy water, plantain chips and groundnuts and were giggling like boisterous schoolchildren while the scowling woman at the counter was eyeing us as we moved around the shop as though we'd been plotting to steal something.

'*Why* was he introducing himself?' Efe had questioned, irritated as if he'd just pulled down his trousers to expose his dodo instead of simply telling me his name.

'I thought it was nice,' I had admitted, my cheeks flushing with the memory of our eyes locking.

'*Madam!*' Idunnu called out to the woman at the register. 'You get ginger? For your sour stomach, Efe . . . Before jealousy kill you!'

No one had been more surprised than me to find him still outside when we exited the store. He was sitting on the low wall behind the parked cars, fiddling on his phone and swinging his legs gently. As soon as he saw us, he stood up and headed up to us.

'You're still here?' Efe had yapped, making an expression that made her look temporarily possessed. Prince had taken off his glasses then and eyeballed her directly, his dimples deepening as he smiled in her direction.

'How often you dey bump into three beautiful women? Are you sisters?' he asked politely, and like a menacing guard dog pacified by some chop, Efe dropped her head and giggled.

'*Friends o,*' she replied as I felt Idunnu nudging the small of my back to push me closer to where Prince was standing before I was eclipsed by Efe, who'd by then registered his attractiveness.

'Where are you coming from?' he asked.

'The protest—'

'Oh *yes* . . . I wanted to go but I get shift,' he said, holding his carrier bags up by way of explanation.

'What do you do?' Efe leapt on the question before I could think of what to say. It was as if we were playing with a skipping rope and I was too afraid to jump in under the swinging cord.

'I'm training to be a chef. I work at the Viceroy hotel . . . Just ten minutes from here,' he explained.

With his answer Efe rapidly appeared to have lost interest and shifted her attention to our carrier bag in search of the plantain chips.

'Were there many people?' he asked as he put his sunglasses back on, so I'd been disappointed to have lost sight of his whole face.

'*Plenty*,' I replied. 'We came from Makoko to demonst—' I started to tell him, but he cut in excitedly.

'From the water?' he asked as if we were mermaids that had appeared on land before him.

'*Eeehn*,' Idunnu nodded as she reached for the carrier bag Efe was holding. 'Wait o . . . Did we not buy water? Come and help me,' she said, pulling Efe by the arm.

'Are you blind? There's—' Efe started to protest before Idunnu womanhandled her.

'*Abeg, shush!*'

'Should I come too?' I'd turned to ask stupidly, but Idunnu had shot me a dirty look.

'And what do *you* do in Makoko, Baby?' Prince asked as Idunnu dragged Efe back inside the shop. I realised then that she was trying to give us one minute alone without an audience.

I told him about my work with Mama Jumbo as well as my taxi work on the *Charlie-Boy*.

'So, if I want go around Makoko, na you I dey call?' He latched onto my words quickly.

'To do what?' I asked, fighting my giggles.

'Isn't that where all the fish comes from?'

'What do you know about our fish?' I teased and saw his eyes light up.

'Abeg . . . obokun, owere, shawa . . .' He reeled off more varieties expertly in a way that made me impressed by his knowledge and I felt pride in the community. 'I rarely even get time to get to the market, let alone to cross the water.'

'Where are you from?' I'd asked, studying his features.

'Ekiti. I dey here two years,' he replied, reaching for his phone. 'What's your number? I'm *serious* . . . I see a need for a taxi in my future,' he'd continued with a straight face before a smile tugged at the edges of his lips.

'And what of *my* future?' I teased after I'd given him my number and he'd flashed my phone so I could save his own.

'Hmm . . .' Prince had remained pensive for a moment as he'd held his chin with one hand. 'I'd say that your future is looking bright.'

Maureen has already heard my news before I enter the canteen in the morning as she's wiping down tables. She flings down her cloth as soon as she sees me.

'If it isn't the conquering bride!' she booms, making me blush even though I'm currently the only patron of the establishment.

'You're so foolish,' I cry as she chuckles.

'Who told you? Was it Efe?'

'Of course! She and Idunnu came in yesterday. Her face was looking like this . . .' Maureen says, using two fingers to pull down her lower eyelids before curling her lips. 'I don't know what is doing her. I told her she's the youngest! She has plenty of time,' she continues, shaking her cloth at a fly making noise between us.

'Na curse of beauty,' I sigh dismissively before perching on a table as she cleans up around me.

'*Oya*, come on . . . What happened?' Maureen asks, flinging the cloth in my direction playfully.

'But you already know!' I respond, bemused.

'Then tell me again,' she demands greedily and I willingly feed her gossip monster.

Not even an hour passes before the canteen starts to fill up. From fishermen returning from the night's work and seeking food or drink before slipping off to sleep to the idlers with enough in their pockets for some bottles and some conversation. Grudgingly, Maureen goes off to fulfil her waitress duties, so I head out onto the veranda to wait for Wunmi to arrive.

I listen to the conversation carrying itself in the wind. Another camera crew is touring Makoko for another reportage about the community. There's some disagreement about whether they're from the US or the UK.

Many of the camera crews that visit our parts need permission from community chiefs first. Even with that, it's often difficult to get people to engage with them for their shooting as very few locals have a good grip on the English language. We were certain to see them up close on the lagoon today as they'd be near our location once Wunmi arrived from her other job and we set off for the day's tutorial.

My brain slinks back to well-thumbed thoughts of Prince when my mobile suddenly pings beside me on the floor. I hold my breath before looking down at the screen. Fire shoots through my veins as I take in his name, followed by the message underneath.

Fine Baby! On much reflection—na three oranges you're owing me. How we go rectify this injustice? When can I see you again?

Pain in my cheeks alerts me to the fact that I'm grinning like a fool. Part of me contemplates running inside the canteen to ask Maureen for advice. Thankfully, I stop that impulse in its tracks even though I can hear my heart pumping through my ears. I close my eyes and conjure up Idunnu, the calmest and sassiest of us all. Imagining her response, I let my fingers type it out.

Why exactly is your recklessness my fault?

I set the phone down and cast my gaze over the lagoon, staring as a woman passes on the water with a boat so laden with provisions that its tip is out of the water like a shark about to strike. What if he doesn't reply? The fearful thought creeps into my mind when my phone pings again, making me jump.

Was it not you that bumped ME? So it is your fault that I am a wreck!

I type out my response: *Maybe you should see a doctor.* Before my nerves get the better of me, I press *send* and settle the phone in my lap. Not even ten seconds passed before he was writing again.

Let me see you first. If my pulse dey race still, then I'm fine.

I'm laughing to myself about our exchange as Wunmi pulls up in a canoe filled with people. Still reeking with the aroma of freshly smoked fish, I size up her mini skirt and skimpy top combination together with her lipstick in the shade of Bazooka gum.

'See how you don dress up for droning,' I say before she waves her hand around herself dismissively.

'*Please,* Baby . . . Carry me for Ebenezer,' she pleads breathlessly and I feel my spirits plunge despite my euphoria moments earlier.

'But I thought . . . You said I could fly today—'

'Ayo will take you! *I swear.* See the message wey I already send her. But all of his family are away now. This is our only moment to be alone,' she begs anxiously.

I observe her frame as she stands over me. I measure her feelings against mine as my initial excitement diminishes. As much as I'd been excited about flying the drone, how can I stand in the way of what she's wanting? Especially now that I'm having pins and needles just from my small encounter with Prince. I resign myself to agreeing when Maureen appears with her cleaning cloth draped over her shoulder like a scarf.

'*Na waoo, Wunmi!*' Maureen exclaims, dragging out her name before letting out a short whistle, having appraised her outfit.

'We better get moving,' I tell Wunmi as I stand and put my phone away, although my mind is still working on my response to Prince's last message.

'Where you dey go?' Maureen's eyes flash eagerly. 'Where are you off to?' she presses on at the top of her voice as I'm ushering Wunmi onto my canoe. I pull away from the edge of the canteen, giving Maureen a majestic wave, but she eyes us before strutting back inside. The town crier denied another morsel of intrigue.

'Thank you, Baby,' Wunmi sighs a few minutes later, reaching out to touch my arm briefly as I glide my paddle through the water.

'Ayo will let me have a turn?' I enquire again about our agreement with the drone, to satisfy my restless soul.

'She will,' Wunmi assures me.

As we near Migbewhe, I slow down to avoid the disturbance on the lagoon as two children disappear underneath the dirty water before coming up routinely to swallow air. Wunmi and I take turns yelling at them to exit the grimy water as streams of refuse and excrement float by their chattering mouths. They refuse to comply until, at last, one of the boys emerges triumphant, clutching his reward above his head. The kite that must have been piloted into the water.

We wait for them to come out of the lagoon, watching the naked one without the prize racing after his older compatriots. Beads of water fly from his skin like black diamonds. Try as you might, there's no keeping people completely out of this filthy water filled with plastic and metal scraps. Where human shit and hazardous chemicals combat for dominance. You can't stop them from entering the lagoon that has mercilessly taken children one way or another.

After dropping Wunmi off, I try to control my trepidation as I chart a course to Ayo's location and am pleasantly surprised when she's sitting in her canoe writing in a notebook. She smiles shyly as I near her and her lips split to reveal the gap tooth that has beset every member of her incredibly fertile family tree. Ayo is a mother already at seventeen and has been married since fifteen. Her grandmother looks after her two daughters while she works.

'Wunmi go see doctor?' she says by way of greeting and I nod in agreement, corroborating my friend's lie. *Dr Feelgood is more like it*, I think to myself and catch my words before they tumble from my lips.

I tie the *Charlie-Boy* on the jetty beside her and climb inside her nameless canoe. It leans to the left as she rows out into the lagoon past the steady traffic on the water. Sitting behind her, I eye the drone kept carefully inside its container as we avoid splashes from nearby collisions. It's a rare opportunity for me to relax in a canoe. For once, my arms aren't the ones rowing. The breeze caresses my cheeks as it passes, reminding me of Kemi's breath in the mornings. While Ayo makes idle chatter, I pull out my phone to reply to Prince.

We have traditional clinics on Makoko just in case, I type in reference to my earlier crack about him needing a doctor and save it to send later.

The sound of children in school drifts towards us and I latch onto their chanting of arithmetic. I'm transported instantly to a childhood version of myself, sitting on the floor alongside other children facing the blackboard adorned with hieroglyphics. Going through the same motions that brought us no closer to proper tutelage.

Ten minutes later, we're clear of traffic and the only canoe in our location. Ayo moves for the drone and quick quick, I stop my daydreaming.

'Before you even *start*,' she begins loudly, giving me a know-ing look, 'I know you want pilot am, but first, you must watch me. There's only two of us today and I'm not having anything going wrong.'

'I *know* now—'

'Shey you know, but just be patient. After this, we're going to Oko and you can take your turn.'

I comply like a little child, sitting down meekly as I observe her carrying out the same routines as the last time, paying attention to her record-keeping in her notebook before hand-ling the drone. I drink in every action while my lips retrace each step at a whisper, so I don't forget anything when my turn comes around. Ayo's eyes are trained on the contraption in the sky. Her breath is even as her hands make slow, repeated patterns as though she's performing a traditional dance. I'm salivating as I wait for my turn at the controls and thankfully, time passes quickly. Ayo doesn't spend long in the sky; enough to trace a few wide circles while I look on over her shoulder.

As we push on to our next location, I offer to row and she accepts, taking the opportunity to remove the baseball cap on her head and lift her face towards the sun obscured by the haze of perma-smog hanging over us. I listen to her drink water greedily as she sits up ahead of me, the curve of her spine echo-ing the gentle arc of the canoes that crisscross the water every day, like symmetrical slithers of hollowed-out gourds.

There's more activity here, more boats passing, as we pre-pare ourselves to power up the drone once more. I remove the shirt tied around my waist, clearing away any distractions as if

I'm an athlete getting ready for a race. We're about to start when there's more commotion. I look around, irritated to see the visiting camera crew looming into view just behind a cluster of lagoon commuters. We watch them for a few minutes, observing their disturbance of daily life as locals shift around them to get out of shot or to move closer in the hope of perhaps liberating some money from a guilt-laden pocket. Then Ayo taps my arm, a signal to get a move on.

I feel the nerves in my fingertips. Suddenly they're so tingly, they no longer feel like a part of my body. I close and open them a couple of times to get the blood moving properly before she places the controls in my hand.

'It's okay,' Ayo says gently, watching my shaking appendages with what looks like familiarity and empathy. 'Just do what I did and what I tell you,' she instructs slowly. I nod my head, but the simple act leaves me feeling dizzy.

I can't help it; my eyes dart over towards the boats in our periphery and she senses the hesitation within me.

'Allow ... make them no vex you. Just *focus*,' Ayo says authoritatively.

I take a deep breath as I stare at the drone in front of me on the floor of the boat. Then I exhale.

It's only when Ayo's voice pushes past the blood pounding in my ears that I hear myself screaming. I wasn't aware I was making the sound, but out of me it pours as I stare between the screen on the console and the drone in the air at my command.

'Shut up!' Ayo barks, laughing at my hysteria before a fleeting look of panic overrides her features. '*Relax, Baby!*'

I can't think of words. Only expressions and sounds exit my mouth – not real words or sentences to convey thoughts – in the way Charlie Boy used to while first learning to fly his kite. I'm no longer in the boat with Ayo but high up inside the sky, pushing smoke and clouds out of the way to view the thousands and thousands of houses emerging out of the charcoal waters of the lagoon, so plentiful they resemble an army on a liquid battlefield. Plumes of smoke erupt from smokehouses that float up and join the sky, while light shimmers on the surface of the lagoon and renders it inviting from such a distance.

Houses of all shapes lie next to one another, exhibiting different colour roofs, including one that's been patched up with some billboard advertising so that *Smile Bright* appears like an order that I follow as the drone plots its path. It's make-believe, my eyes are telling me. It doesn't look real, more like a painting that has been brought to life. Canoes that should be *still* on canvas but are pulled across the artwork by magic. People appear, going about their business or looking up at the drone in wonder, just as I'm doing, mastering the machine. Roads and sewers emerge through the collection of houses; it truly *is* a map I'm seeing of our world. We're real. Now we're existing in a way nobody can deny.

'Bring it around slowly,' I'm hearing Ayo say from what feels like a great distance as the wind whips my cornrows against my neck as I'm flapping my invisible wings high up in the air and feasting on spectacular views of the community.

It looks so different from the water level with the garbage

drifting by and the noise and the people. It looks like the place people are dreading. But from the sky, the wooden house posts jutting out of the water, the proud columns and squares of aluminium and wood, the boats gliding by like endless smiles, Makoko is a thing of beauty.

Behind Ayo I hear other voices, but all my attention is on the console and the sky. My neck should be hurting from its work supporting my head for so long and I notice that my skin is pulsing from head to toe.

It's only as my body turns naturally to follow the movement of the drone that I notice the camera crew looking in our direction. The lens is pointing directly at our canoe, the video camera that could swallow us whole with one bite.

'Okay, let me take over,' Ayo suggests as she takes over the console, accustomed to guiding the drone easily with an audience.

I grip the edge of the canoe as I sit down, but adrenaline's still shooting through my core, my back slick with sweat. I imagine how I must look, my skin polished on account of perspiration, but I don't care. I flew!

After Ayo lands the drone safely and makes her notes, we begin to head back to our starting point. The camera crew is still hovering in the water, taking footage of the community as a white man with hair that looks ginger once the light strikes it talks to the camera while sweeping his hand around in every direction. Slotting into the line of canoes that forms, we try to make it past the visitors unnoticed, but as soon as we approach, the camera swings over our way.

'Hello! Do you speak English? Could we talk for a second? What are you doing with the drones?'

Ayo and I both flinch at the rapid bombardment of questions as we keep rowing, trying to avoid direct contact with the video camera one man is hoisting.

'What are you doing?' an eager voice asks again.

'We're mapping Makoko,' Ayo reveals quickly as our boats cross in the water.

'What's your name?' the ginger-haired man calls out and Ayo and I look at each other, trying to hold back our laughter and slight irritation by the unexpected encounter. They are stationary in their boat, and mere moments later, there's distance between us as we drift out of their reach.

The cameraman's eyes are blocked by his equipment. It's almost as if he has a disfigurement, like the machine is growing out of his face. But I feel its magnetic pull, and no matter how much my brain tells me to drop my head, I'm locked onto the lens.

I read his lips as the gap between us widens. The people on his boat all take turns shouting the same questions at us to draw us back into a conversation.

'*We're Dream Girls,*' I scream spontaneously in their direction, raising my hands to the heavens as Ayo titters behind me. I join in with her laughter, giddy after my outburst and my virgin piloting of the drone after soaring high above our home place. My brain's racing in an effort to remember everything exactly as it happened so I can share it with Charlie Boy when I see him.

★

111

I abandon the dish I'm preparing over the fire to tend to the commotion in the bedroom. Afo has Kemi in a semi-headlock when
I reach them and he's trying to prise a piece of paper from her
hands. Of course, Tayo is ignoring the situation while sprawled
on his mattress. I notice his headphones and the flickering screen
of his mobile as he wastes another day watching nonsense.

'Let me *see*,' Kemi squeals at half tempo due to her squeezed
neck. I'm surprised at the fight in her for someone so small.

'What's going on in here?' I yell, attempting my best Auntie
Bisi impression. It is long-suffering, managing these children,
but alas, it is my portion. Afo hesitates and it's enough time
for me to snatch the paper out of Kemi's hand, which triggers
her brother's instant release of his hold.

'It's mine,' Afo protests, rushing me to retrieve his work,
but I hold him at bay with an outstretched hand.

'Can't she *look*?' I say before peeking at it myself. It's a pencil
sketch of the view from the veranda, the row of houses opposite with their ombre stilts rising from the water. A young girl's
reaching out to touch the edge of a fishing net that has been
laid out by a fisherman.

I study Afo's meticulous line work and shading. No one has
taught him this skill, and in recent times, he has spent more
days at home than in school.

'Afo, this picture na really *good*,' I tell him, watching his
bottom lip jutting out in confusion at the sudden praise of
his handiwork.

I'm sure to him, it's just a drawing. Something to kill the
boredom of his days before all delusions of education are

exhausted and he starts following Uncle Jimi to work or begins to fish like Papa once did. But what I notice is genuine talent, something that can carry him through life if he develops a passion for it. Makoko is in need of more artists, of people with skills that fall outside of fishing in a place where the lagoon has stopped giving.

My compliment has softened his annoyance, and as soon as I return his painting, he hands it over to Kemi. I creep out of the room to rescue my cooking, serenaded by the sound of them playing calmly with one another. The peppery tomato sauce is boiling furiously in the pot by the time I add the cassava flakes to the mix and stir and stir. I watch the stew turn into a gloop, binding the onion and stockfish. The chilli fumes rush up my nostrils and tug on my hairs, causing my eyes to water. I take care preparing the galidodo, Charlie Boy's favourite, turning it slowly until it thickens, making sure the bottom of the pot doesn't burn.

I keep a close watch on my phone while I cook, and sure enough, it pings to signal a message has been received. I know it's Prince. A glance at my screen confirms my suspicion. My gut is as hot as the food on the fire with the exchange of each message. It's what I was missing with Samson despite Maureen trying to push me in his direction. From our mounting communications, Prince is taking shape in my mind, despite not having seen him again since that first time. I've only been sharing things with Idunnu since Efe has jealous tendencies and Maureen only has time for herself. It's a madness, spending so much time talking to someone that's not here, but

113

he already feels familiar. Moreover, it's not something I'm sure I want to control.

Papa and Uncle Jimi make a lot of noise on their arrival from the sawmill. Papa's medicine is not giving him much vitality in that he has deep black rings underneath both eyes, almost as though someone has punched him well well. They disappear to wash the dust off them before returning as we run around them, bringing drinks and something for them to chop. As Papa and his brother discuss the protests, I bury my gaze on my top, working out an old stain with my spit and two fingers.

The experience at the demonstration in Ikeja replays underneath my lowered eyelashes as they debate what they've read in the news and heard from other locals that attended. He's none the wiser about me making it to the march. The uselessness of the government is a well-worn subject in most households in Makoko.

I absorb their rising voices as they repeat familiar accusations across from each other at the table. As bitterness about the past rises on their tongues, they spit repeatedly to exorcise it. It's never far from Papa's thoughts – the cruelty of those in charge – and only inevitable that it's on his lips today even after so much time has passed.

We shuffle around them; Kemi and Afo as they dance around, trying to vanquish a halo of mosquitoes while I replenish the drinks Papa and Uncle Jimi are consuming. We're rarely included in these types of discussion, no matter that we're no longer little. But we're children, privy to every grown-up conversation yet somehow invisible.

As I wipe the spilt beer off the table in front of Papa, he stops talking to look directly at me as though he's only just become aware of my presence in the room.

In that moment, he's not the same Papa of today, the one that's worn with age, but a younger version of himself. No protruding stomach or hairs peeking out over the rim of his nostrils. Black coils on his head instead of a matted grey field.

I bite down on the resentment that bubbles up within me suddenly – about the government, even about Makoko itself, as I wonder what we truly have left that it can possibly take from us.

'Tell me again about the drone,' Charlie Boy says when he has finished his celebratory feast of galidodo followed by his preferred Tom Toms sweets.

'*Ah ah* . . . You no dey bored finish?' I ask him, amused by his latest obsession and delighted at the opportunity to relive the experience once again now that I'm with him. For a brief moment at home, I'd contemplated telling Tayo about my achievement before remembering him as a fully accredited thief of joy.

'*Baby* now,' Charlie Boy implores and I give in, sharing my anecdote until the weight of his body sinks into mine.

'Happy birthday,' I sing again as my brother reaches over to intertwine his fingers with my own as we stare into the darkness in our makeshift celebration.

'Thank you!' Charlie Boy replies excitedly. 'How old would I be?' His question catches me off guard, disrupts the semi-silence we've fallen into.

'Fourteen,' I reply and the realisation only dawns on me after I perform the calculation. Three years older than I was when I'd lost him.

In July of 2012, Makoko became cluttered with flyers. Paper decorations that grew and fluttered against houses and in the water like strange insects. Colourful as they'd been, they weren't broadcasting some imminent festivity within our settlement but rather the government's plans to tear down Makoko. As Charlie Boy and I collected the flyers to draw on their blank sides later at home, we barely paid attention to its message of complaint about our unwholesome structures occupying the water without authority. But the news spread through the community quickly about the government's effort at baring its teeth, only nobody had anticipated how speedily they would strike.

Seventy-two hours later, the authorities had sent men armed with machetes.

We were still rubbing sleep from our eyes when Papa shook us awake. The alarm of voices screaming and shouting signalled trouble and fear gripped me as though I'd been waiting for Papa to brandish his whipping stick. Peeking out from behind him, as he watched through the window, we saw part of the commotion as these strangers infiltrated Makoko. They began chopping down houses, hacking off the legs so that they plummeted into the water while the police looked on from nearby boats. As the sound of homes crumbling, the scream of chainsaws destroying properties crept closer and closer towards where we huddled. Glued together by our sweating bodies, Papa ordered us to pack as quickly as we could. There'd been no time to cry, even as the steel in his voice propelled us to action, before it was too late.

I'd grabbed a shell-shocked Charlie Boy and pushed him towards the veranda as Papa and I assembled as much as we could before we all hurried into the now-cramped canoe. Around us, other families were doing the same thing. Trying to gather all their belongings, yelling at unswayable men who wielded electrical tools like true power, heartless to our pleas in their desire to destroy our homes. Papas and Mamas everywhere had ushered children and old people into boats quick quick before their homes were attacked and their belongings plunged into the lagoon. I heard the animal cry of a mother as her baby fell into the water amidst the chaos before being fished out by some neighbours.

As we'd rowed away from the home we had shared with Mama before she passed away, Papa had told us not to look. By then his face was granite, his eyes ice as we sailed away from the monsters delighting in their handiwork, sending bamboo and driftwood back into the lagoon from whence it came with the fury of their weapons.

I'd covered my brother's eyes with my hands as he shivered between my legs. His breath warmed my fingers that trembled violently but hadn't parted to give him a view of the home we'd known sinking from existence. The place we'd learned to walk and talk. The lopsided living-room floor that I'd scratched my initials into with a bottle-top, where Charlie Boy had sat and stared, mystified as his nephew – Dura's firstborn – was thrust into his five-year-old arms. The deck where Mama and Dura used to fling Charlie Boy high into the air inside a wrapper they held at either end to make him sleep; where Mama had shown me how to use the grinding stone when teaching me how to cook; where Papa had split his trousers open while laughing at our efforts to remember the rhyme he and his brothers would sing about the scorpion trying to steal the conga eel's teeth.

We'd arrived at Uncle Jimi's house visibly shaken. The destroyers hadn't targeted that side of Adogbo yet, but they would be coming. Papa immediately departed with his brother to go back, along with other willing men, to stand guard over what was taking place until they had time to figure out a plan of action. Auntie Bisi had ordered Damola, Ade and Ewa, her older children, to help us bring our things from the canoe. Then she'd dragged us into her bosom forcefully before pushing us away so she could grab at her headscarf and her clothing. Wiping the dried tear stains that had streaked our hollow faces, she'd cleaned Charlie Boy's nose with the edge of her wrapper while he watched our haphazard pile of possessions mount on their deck as nearby onlookers sighed pitifully.

We at least had a place to lay our heads, but sleep didn't come. Afo, who was two (Kemi was not yet born), had squeezed in with his parents to allow us more space. I'd held onto Charlie Boy, feeling his body quiver in our new setting on the floor between the two foam mattresses with their older occupants. It felt as if someone had scraped out all my insides, like scooping out melon seeds, only not stopping until all that remained was the rind. I'd tried to picture Mama, to conjure her up in our old home before the buzz of the saw cut through my thoughts and made her disappear.

In the days that followed, nothing was the same.

The dismantling of our allegedly illegal constructions continued the next morning; homes macheted and burned, people displaced with nowhere to go. At least we had our relatives. For some others, their boat would now take the place of their fallen house.

On the third day, our tempers were exhausted. Uncle Jimi came home and reported the story that as residents tried to reason with the devastators, a policeman shot and killed a local leader. The news horrified people as our predicament gained more attention globally, and two days later, the demolishing stopped abruptly.

Papa had recalled the time before that, two decades earlier, when they'd destroyed Makoko before to build their McMansions. Eko Atlantic, the luxury district created from space stolen from the community that had resided on the fringes of Bar Beach long before the millionaires moved in and commandeered the waterfront.

The community reeled from this latest devastation that uprooted so many families. Haphazard wrecks that were once standing properties and jagged beams had at last been transformed into the genuine eyesores on the lagoon the

governments classed them as. Hundreds tried to salvage anything they could from the water and people tried to find what
and whom they'd lost in the disarray. As parents held endless
discussions among themselves, we children were ushered outside so as not to cause distraction.

After the first three nights at Uncle Jimi's, Charlie Boy
regained his boisterous energy, largely because it hadn't been
his responsibility, as it was mine, to help Auntie Bisi incorpor-
ate our belongings into their thankfully larger home. But I
and those older than me were still zombies. Now that we were
permanent fixtures, Ade, who had been standoffish at first, was
forced by Auntie to acquaint Charlie Boy with the neighbours'
children, some who were his age, while I spent time unpack-
ing the jumble we'd managed to slip into our boat before the
authorities butchered our home.

I'd been occupied with the household, Papa with the government and Charlie Boy, as usual, with boats. I hadn't taken
the canoe out since we arrived and it was still acting as storage
for some of our possessions. As Charlie Boy began insisting on
going out to watch the planes, I brushed him aside, waiting
for him to drop the subject.

'We can't go now,' I'd told him warily. 'Too much dey
happen.'

That Tuesday morning when I'd woken up, my brother wasn't
in my arms and by the time I rose, he hadn't emerged from the
toilet. When Auntie Bisi called us all to eat, he was nowhere to
be found.

I knew instantly what he'd tried to do and hurried towards our canoe. It had been tied where we'd left it and I breathed a sigh of relief that I was mistaken, that he hadn't tried to pilot it himself.

It was only when Uncle Jimi's children had taken their own boat out later that day that we discovered him, his beautiful broken form in his Spider-Man T-shirt, his tattered blue short knicker blending into the rotting pile of rubbish accumulating between the stilts underneath the house.

When they pulled his flaccid body from the water, from the scum accumulating around the house's wooden posts, we saw the gash on the side of his coconut head from where he'd slipped, trying to enter one of the boats in the middle of the night and conked himself out before drifting off to his death.

The one eye that had remained partially open – the one looking in my direction accusingly before Papa closed it and laid his head against my brother's sodden chest – had been the colour of the lagoon.

Earth

9

'Baby!' Papa calls my name with a volume I'm certain the neighbours across from us can hear. I answer, dropping the clothes I'm in the process of washing back into the bucket, and hurry towards his room, wiping my hands on the back of my skirt before he can abuse my name again.

'*Where* are you?' he begins even though I'm standing before him, looking into his milky eyes. 'Nobody is seeing your taxi—'

'I'm working, Papa, I promise!' I rush to answer.

'I hope so,' he continues, scratching his stomach so loudly that my own skin begins to sting at the imagined contact from his nails. It's as if a tiny cricket buried in his chest hairs is rubbing its legs together. 'I was saying no be like you to forget your responsibilities,' he adds, bringing his hand down on the mattress and releasing a layer of golden dust into the air.

'No, sah. I have been helping Mama Jumbo,' I lie rapidly, pushing the images of me mapping Makoko with Wunmi and Ayo and my moments with Prince to the back corners of my mind.

'You know the young ones have not been to school and they are raising the price of fuel . . .' he presses on and I listen quietly, nodding when I'm required.

Once he's finished his rant about the daily extortion that is life in this country, I slip out to my bedroom. Kemi is its only occupant, sleeping ferociously in a position that resembles someone doing a front crawl in the lagoon. I close the door gingerly and inch back my dressing table as quietly as I can. Removing the small piece of material I've hidden there that masquerades my savings, I pull out the notes to count them again. I'm not as close to my smartphone or my future as I would like, but I peel off some notes anyway to give to Papa, contemplating how quickly the extorted becomes the extorter.

My heart had been thumping like a generator by the time I arrived at Makoko fish market to meet Prince. As I scanned the gathering crowds, I fought to decipher the features I'd committed to my memory within the bodies jostling for attention.

Hovering near the entrance, I pretended to ogle buckets filled with abo, squid, crabs, shawa and shrimps of all sizes. I watched a vendor shelling the bowlful of prawns purchased by a customer with the skill and speed of orange peelers on the streets and allowed myself to become transfixed by her rhythmic hand movements. I pulled out my phone to reread the encouraging text from Idunnu, the only person I'd told about the date. I was on the verge of relaxation when a text from Prince appeared and I geared myself up for disappointment. Instead, what I'd read was a message telling me to 'look up.'

126

Tearing my eyes away from the market woman, I saw him standing a few feet away in a bright white T-shirt with the words NO LIMITS wrapping across his chest and some dark jeans with zippers over the kneecaps. His eyes were clear as his sunglasses were riding at the top of his bald head like a child climbing on their parent's shoulders. He smiled at me and my bones started turning to jelly inside my skin.

After Prince touched my shoulder playfully, he became quiet. I felt the same way, overwhelmed after multiple texts and now being confronted with the person in the flesh. All of a sudden, I acknowledged how much he knew about me, and me about him, and felt as vulnerable as the fish eyeballing us from inside the braided baskets scattered around the market.

He'd never visited before and I was proud of myself for suggesting the location. From the expression on his face, I'd brought him to a carnival. His mouth had opened like the massive eja-osan lying in vats of water – fish longer than my whole arm – waiting to be purchased. His attention was piqued by the woman selling yellowtail, a large fish with a distinctive arrowhead marking near its tailfin. Next to her was a group of energetic women selling barracuda. I'd stood behind him as he successfully bartered the price down from fifteen to eight thousand naira, after which he carefully pointed out his two preferred fish.

I enjoyed his childlike wonder as we walked through the market slowly, marvelling at snails bigger than adult fists and prawns with exteriors so intricate they resembled tortoiseshell jewellery. He'd stopped to try and take a photo of the teenage boy balancing a white snapper in a shallow bucket atop his head. The fish was almost the same size as the boy's young companion that followed beside him, eating a cup of gari mixed with water.

Conversation came easier then as Prince ran around the market, pointing out things like a child in front of a sweet vendor. I'd let him impress me with knowledge as we admired shine nose, croaker and catfish. All around us the market was teeming with people eager to pick up their own purchases before the heat of the day struck. I directed his attention to the cleaning quarters, where girls and women stood waiting for customers to request their services: scaling, cleaning and chopping the fish for speedy use at home. We stood at a safe distance and watched them setting free showers of fish scales that covered the wooden stumps they used for chopping. Young girls, unfazed by blood and the overpowering scent of spilt guts, wielded cleavers skillfully, showcasing their incredible agility. Next to the cleaning section were the smoking quarters, where platters of fish wait for their turn over the hot coals. Again, some customers hovered noisily for their purchases to be cooked on the premises, pushing and shoving to be heard above the din. The aroma from the roasting section made us hungry, so he'd purchased a portion of small fish that we'd eaten while we walked. Alongside the fish sellers, other vendors shouted to draw attention to their products: water yam, tomatoes, cooking and cleaning utensils and endless supplies of plastic goods.

No one paid any attention to us inside the market, our bodies clashing on many occasions by accident and sometimes on purpose. It was funny to listen to a man who knew so much about cooking. For all Papa's life as a fisherman, I'm certain he could only point out the fish's head and the tail, but Prince had been talking about every ingredient inside the market like a professor.

'Have you always wanted to be a chef?' I'd asked him as he'd been sorting through chillies in front of a woman with a child strapped to her back, much to her bemusement. When he held one up to his nose, she'd eyed him savagely, clearly on the precipice of running her mouth before he'd stopped sniffing them and purchased a bagful.

Prince had shrugged, evidently unnerved by my enquiry as he removed the backpack from his side to add the peppers to the other items he'd squirrelled away. The fish he'd carried in the plastic bag brushed my bare legs as we walked.

'I wasn't good at many things,' he explained softly. 'But cooking . . . I don't know. For me, it was like a language I could speak. So, I just followed it, even though it—' He fell silent and his gaze dropped to the ground.

'Even though what?' I pushed, turning to face him.

'Never mind,' he replied before shaking his head. 'Just watch me . . . I go put Nigeria on the map well well,' he boasted, pointing to the message on his chest. With these words, my skin prickled as I recalled the drone being piloted by my hands, the mapping work being carried out on the lagoon and the similarity of our intentions.

'How so?' I asked, arching my eyebrows as I pored over his wonderful face.

129

'One mouth at a time,' he laughed, dropping his gaze to my lips.

We'd exited the market, pushing past a woman yelling to attract attention to her handbags. She'd threaded ten through each arm while she wore others across her body and balanced at least four perfectly on her head as she wound her way through the bustling crowd. I observed her, musing over who'd come to shop for mackerel, only to instead leave with a colourful satchel.

Stopping by the first bar we found, we'd taken the chance to rest our legs as Prince ordered us two malts and we talked some more about life on the water and at the hotel where he stayed. Then fearing for the health of his fish purchases, he'd carried his load and we'd set off again after a quick pause where he'd rushed into a shop to buy some ice that he'd thrown into his bag with the fish. Before I knew it, we'd arrived at the jetty. I laughed as he'd taken care of his footing on the walkways which looked precarious to those unfamiliar to them. It was only after he'd begged me to hold his hand and our fingers had connected that I realised it had all been a a ploy to touch me.

I approached the *Charlie-Boy* and hovered awkwardly as he looked between me and the settlement spreading out over the water. He hadn't even batted an eyelid at the smell.

'Are you afraid?' I asked as fear worked its way through my body that this might be too much for him to take in.

'Me *keh*? *Never*,' he'd laughed, rocking back and forth on his heels. 'If I no get my shift, you would see pepper,' he teased, holding up his carrier bag. 'Next time, you will be my taxi driver!' he added, his head dropping in the direction of the boat.

I smiled as my heart throbbed with excitement at the prospect of there being a next time as I climbed into the boat, minding my entrance in the mini skirt I'd worn to impress him.

Picking up my paddle, I'd hesitated as he'd remained still on the walkway, watching.

'You dey wait for me to ride into the sunset?' I joked.

'I hope you're a better rower than that, Baby. We haven't even reached eleven,' he said, studying the imaginary watch on his wrist.

He hadn't been joking. He'd indeed come for his trip to Makoko, arriving earlier than we'd planned so that I'd been collecting a canoe full of passengers when I saw his long limbs waving at me through the people gathering at the water's edge. Evidently, he had a wardrobe filled with empowering messages as this time he'd worn a grey T-shirt bearing the message: BE THE BOSS.

We managed to squeeze him into my canoe as the last passenger as I ferried two women and their empty baskets, along with a couple laden with bags from the market. I watched the women pass a baby equally between themselves for the duration of the ride – taking turns to rock its noisy mouth to peace – so that it was impossible to discern its rightful mother. While steering the boat in the early afternoon traffic, I'd stolen quick glances at Prince, who smiled back over the heads of the other travellers. He'd been furthest away from me as the last onto the canoe. I could tell he was becoming overpowered by the stench of our waters now that we were in it and the shocking sights assailing his virgin eyes, but he tried valiantly to disguise his discomfort. We'd only begun speaking directly after I'd dropped off my final passenger.

'Well . . . what do you want to see?' I asked him as he shifted gingerly inside the rocking canoe, inching closer to me until he was sitting on the pew opposite mine with his legs spread out on either side of me.

'Show me everything,' he replied, holding onto my hands briefly before they resumed their work, carrying us across the water.

I took him on a long voyage across Makoko, pointing out the various communities while he drank in all the different scenes taking place in people's private homes and verandas. The barbershops and the tailors, loud and busy as always, the churches with their roster of services in the week, for bereavements or expectant mothers, or for enticing wayward sheep back into the fold. He watched children running around and playing endlessly in the water and outside of it. Babies being washed inside the lagoon, dunked into the water the way one does unceremoniously with a chicken into scalding water before removing its feathers. Some children in a nearby canoe tried to engage us in a race and we'd obliged, letting them think they won, until we sailed out of their reach to their deafening amusement. My thoughts strayed to Charlie Boy, and for a moment, I tried to imagine what he would be like if he was still with us. Would he have inherited the wiry but power-ful arms of Papa or been off fishing with the other young men? Would I even have had ready access to the canoe, or would I have been smoking fish for years without any complaint? My path could have been entirely different as a result of one adjust-ment. I might not even have arrived at this exact point on the water with Prince, showing him my neighbourhood.

He'd requested to visit a smokehouse, so we'd gone to visit Wunmi, who'd been surprised by my sudden appearance with an unfamiliar man. Still, we'd crouched behind the group of women, watching their gruelling work through the thick smoke as they grilled endless amounts of fish while hacking due to the environment and chatting simultaneously. We sam-pled some of the fish they had and its spicy sweetness, its warmth under our fingers as we broke through its blackened exterior to expose the moist whiteness within seemed sud-denly worth all the runny eyes and fuzzy chest it took to prepare it.

We stopped for a snack at Maureen's canteen. I hadn't had to worry as she didn't work on Wednesdays and Iya Fowoke, who did the cleaning and sweeping that day, had no interest in our small lives. We passed a boat full of girls I recognised were on a mapping excursion, but I couldn't see anyone I knew well enough to approach them, not that I'd wanted to in that moment. As the afternoon wore on, Prince seemed more and more undaunted about his watery surroundings. He didn't even mind that I hadn't brought him close to my house.

He'd wanted a turn taking charge of the boat and so I'd let him control the paddles. I sat beside him, quietly amused as he attempted to sail through our tricky waters, navigating countless floating obstacles and trying not to crash into other commuters on the lagoon. I'd been telling him about the mapping programme and was directing him towards the place where I'd made my debut drone flight when I heard Mama Jumbo's voice cutting through our conversation.

It had been too late to hide. She caught up with us in the water and there'd been no time to whisper anything to Prince, let alone wrestle the oars from him.

'Baby? Na you? I thought so, but it's not often I find *you* taking taxi,' she offered dryly as I greeted her quietly. The name of my canoe was visible to anyone, Mama Jumbo included, so it was clear that she knew we were messing about in *my* boat, even if Prince seemed to enjoy being temporarily mistaken for a local boatman.

'Will I be seeing you later this afternoon?' she asked with an arch of her eyebrow and I blushed as though she was catching me out in a lie or bad behaviour when we were doing nothing wrong.

'Yes now, Auntie. I was just showing my friend around the place,' I explained before my words faded into nothingness.

'Do you have a name, *friend*?' Mama Jumbo ogled Prince, her face suddenly serious despite the musicality of her attire.

'I be Prince, Ma,' he'd replied politely. 'Is that efo riro I am smelling?' he continued smoothly.

'It is indeed,' Mama preened, looking over the pots of cooked offerings sharing her canoe with her. 'You want?'

'*Yes o*—'

'A man that likes his food!' Mama Jumbo made a sound between a laugh and a rumble as she prepared a takeaway container for Prince. Her bosom undulated with the movement of the waves, and as I waited for the encounter to end, I wondered if my own scrawny chest would ever know such weight or if I would always look like an ironing board.

It was only when I heard the word *chef* being repeated at Mama's earsplitting volume that I realised I must have floated away into my thoughts and their conversation had progressed more than I'd anticipated.

'Where is that?' Mama Jumbo asked with evident interest. I noticed the shift in her eyes that had dropped their initial guard towards him after only a fleeting conversation. Mama Jumbo wasn't rock like Papa, but perhaps Prince had more water in him than I realised.

'In Ikeja,' Prince answered. 'The Viceroy—'

'I don chop at the Viceroy! You mean to tell me *you* cooked my food?' Mama asked, dropping her bottom lip with such comedic emphasis that there'd been no other option for us but to laugh.

'I be sous-chef, Ma, but . . .' Prince was explaining sheepishly, the look of pride evident on his face.

The thought had crossed my mind about whether Mama Jumbo was making polite conversation or telling the truth, but almost as soon as it occurred, she spotted it and gave me a knowing look.

'What is it?' she asked, swivelling her head to direct the full force of her face towards me.

'When did you go to the hotel?' My lips mumbled in an attempt not to overstep more than they already had.

Mama Jumbo kissed her teeth dismissively and rolled her eyes at me before pointing at her canoe. 'You dis girl . . . You think I don't have legs?' she asked comically, looking down at the appendages hidden by her wrapper and her canoe full of cooking utensils. 'There is more to life than this water,' she added, waving her finger at me as if casting an inaudible spell.

In this early morning light, the lagoon almost resembles polished glass. Charlie Boy and I sit silently, hypnotised by the mist rising from the water, snake-like coils that disappear as they rise and meet the air.

'One day I will fly,' my brother says as a fish pokes its head out of the water briefly to inspect our canoe before swimming away.

'I believe you,' I murmur, my head still thick with sleep.

I hadn't intended on staying out all night, but between taxi shifts and helping Mama Jumbo during the day and walking the streets of Lagos with Prince, my body was exhausted. He'd taken me on an endless trek, it seemed at one point, to find the stall with the best corn, as he'd proclaimed while we marched down busy roads. As far as I knew, maize was maize, but I'd eaten my words when I sank my teeth into the vendor's fire-kissed, sweet, moist kernels served with perfectly roasted and smoke-scented ube.

'I have to go,' I say out loud, watching my brother nod as I reach for the paddles, drinking in the final moments where the lagoon is mostly ours alone before the rest of the world awakens.

'You can leave me here,' Charlie Boy says, staring across the waves in the direction of where the night fishermen usually position themselves.

'I'll see you later,' I reply.

'I know,' he says with a smile.

Slipping the oar into the water beneath us, the canoe lilts to the right and I move my weight to centre the boat properly. It only takes a few seconds, this simple shift in my seat, but by the time I look up again, my brother has gone.

When I arrive at Maureen's traditional wedding ceremony, she looks like a flower. Her braids have been arranged in an intricate up-do that almost resembles petals the way they're coiled in a bun. The beads strung around her head like a crown match the plenty beads around her neck, the ivie-uru that are traditionally worn by her people for their ceremony.

Underneath her sheer coral veil, her eyes are covered in a shimmery pink powder and blackened with kohl pencil and on her lips is another kind of pink with a glossy overlay. She looks so different from the last time I saw her, three days ago, when the four of us crowded her deck and talked until the early hours of the morning. Efe was going to get into trouble, not that she cared, as we'd whiled away hours gossiping about things that might be harder to communicate once Maureen officially became a married woman in another household.

Idunnu and I had huddled together as Maureen went through last-minute details about her engagement and the preceding introduction that would take place in the morning between only the family members, where they went through the formalities of ensuring that they were not related and matters relating to the bride price. We'd listened to our friend amidst the ever-present noise of Makoko and I'd had to remove Idunnu's hands from her abdomen on more than one occasion when sleep started to catch up with her. From a nearby house, we heard and ignored the cries of a woman being beaten by her husband before the wail of distressed children overshadowed their intermittent shouting. Maureen had shrugged over the commotion, accustomed to the routine outbursts of her neighbours. We'd ignored the incident as best as we could to enjoy these last moments of our friend's life before marriage.

After four of her cousins have been rejected by the groom, in the ritual pantomime that takes place before Osagie's family recognises Maureen as the rightful flower they have come to claim, Maureen is welcomed through the jovial crowd by singing and clapping. The short walk in front of her isn't made easy by intention. Barriers must be cleared out of her path on her journey to be wedded. The bodies gathered in close quarters make this part amusing, as people shuffle aside to gradually grant her access but not before showering her with banknotes as she passes by to stand next to her father before Osagie unveils her.

I study the sweetheart neckline of the shimmery red material she'd finally settled on, bordering on crimson in the sunlight. The other cloth she'd selected for the marriage – pale turquoise with a leaf motif – looks so different on all of us wearing it in varying styles; the women in her family, along with us, her closest friends, while the groom's side is decked out in reds and gold.

Efe and I had opted for tunic dresses, but Idunnu is wearing a skirt with a long-sleeve, peplum-style top. I can't help but think how we are all at different stages of womanhood and crammed into Maureen's house as the ceremony gets underway. I watch words exiting Maureen and Osagie's mouths, but after a few moments, I begin to picture Prince and me staring out at everyone instead of the bride and groom. I pinch my elbow to get a hold of myself. This is what Papa hopes for me, this moment with someone dry like Samson. To be like Maureen or Dura, who moved to Apollo to become the volatile Tokunbo's third wife and baby-making machine at sixteen for the sake of the family. To me, it is an existence. Somehow I just know it's not *my* life.

The crowd's laughter helps to pull me out of my fantasy as Maureen's family spokesman puts Osagie through tests, as is standard practice in a wedding, to demonstrate that he's worthy of their daughter. He holds his own, putting on a show in his bright white outfit with his orange beads, his black fedora and a matching cane with a gold lion's head. Maureen plays her part too, answering in the affirmative when asked for the last time if Osagie is the man she intends to marry, to the delight of the gathered audience.

I fall into the rhythm of the ceremony, chanting, nodding and clapping in the right places. It's hard to see from where we are as relatives from both sides shift to get better vantage points of the wedding ceremony. Then Maureen is ushered over towards Osagie's father, where she lands her bottom on his lap gingerly seven times to the whopping sounds of all of us. Osagie's father rises with Maureen before placing her on Osagie's lap and their union is sealed. Osagie grips Maureen around the waist proprietorially before he releases her temporarily as they exchange the cup of gin that passes between them.

Idunnu and I squeeze each other's hands as we watch Maureen and Osagie feeding each other a sugar cube and a drop of honey before biting into a kola nut. The symbolism of this is obvious: that marriage is both sweet and bitter. They must be prepared for what comes. Be *patient*.

As Maureen and Osagie kiss, I picture Prince and I, drifting aimlessly back to his day on the lagoon, following the trajectory of a pair of abandoned water drums filled with all kinds of rubbish.

'Can I tell you something?' he'd asked and I nodded, feeling the canoe lurch underneath us as he moved closer to me. He held out his hand and cupped it as if he wanted to whisper in my ear, but suddenly his fingers had moved to cradle my face and he'd brought his mouth down onto mine.

Everything else faded away; the backdrop of tower buildings in the far distance, the noise from nearby boats. Only the gentle undulation of the water beneath us remained that had mimicked the pressure of his lips before he slowly pulled away.

'You think you're sharp?' I'd said once my eyelashes unknotted themselves in time to spy the cheeky smile creeping over his face. Then before I could stop myself, my hands reached out for his shoulders and I leant over to kiss him again quickly and grabbed the oar at our feet. 'I guess I had something to tell you too,' I'd added before taking over the rowing, his mouth wide with surprise like a grunter fish.

With heads bowed, Idunnu and I whisper to each other as both sides of Maureen and Osagie's families offer what seems like endless prayers for the success of their union, but I can intuitively feel Maureen's gaze on me and look up just in time to catch her eye.

There's so much food, we don't even know where to begin amidst the mountains of party rice and the endless platters of fish at the banquet table. Palm wine, beer and soft drinks are flowing and we inch our way through wedding guests as children tear around, hyped up on choco-sweets and puff-puff. They buzz around like flies and are shooed away endlessly by grown-ups piling their plates high with the spectacular feast. Efe, Idunnu and I find some space on the veranda to eat our food and gossip before we move back inside to watch Maureen dancing with her husband, surrounded by onlookers. She appears happy but tired as her dance moves become more robotic with each rotation they make.

I wasn't wanting this before. *Before* I'd met Prince. Maybe that's what's causing my slight suffer-head. That or seeing my friend's wedding day up close, I'm afraid about the inevitability of my turn. Or perhaps even after all my detachment as Maureen bored us endlessly about her nuptials, I'm surprised that I'm actually swept up in the moment, now that it's finally come, the way sometimes in church what the priest is saying strikes a chord and for one minute you feel something.

As if she knows what I'm thinking, Maureen throws me a penetrating look as they sway in our direction. I stick my tongue out at her childishly and she hides her face inside Osagie's neck.

'You feeling okay?' I manage to ask Idunnu after Efe's joined in on the dance floor. Efe jiggles her waist like someone taking a lot of effort to pound yam while her arms make a motion like a flapping chicken.

'This thing is not easy o,' Idunnu whispers with eyes that suddenly seem much older than her twenty years on this planet. I feel sorry for her. At the same time, I wrestle with my guilt at feeling lucky I am not in her situation.

'What have you decided?' I ask, ignoring Efe as she signals over to Idunnu and me, trying to beckon us onto the floor. She looks dejected but only for a moment before one of Osagie's groomsmen, a stocky man with a deliberately lopsided high-top, starts to gyrate his hips in her vicinity. Behind Efe, Maureen's mother is carrying out a move that makes it look as though she's riding an invisible donkey.

'I went to the traditional clinic. They don give me some-thing to take,' Idunnu replied quietly. 'But I may need you to help me, when it's time,' she adds softly.

It's as close to a plea as I'll get from Idunnu, the strongest of us, and I reach out and stroke her hand fleetingly, admiring the henna we all did in solidarity with Maureen.

'How much do you think she has made?' I ask, drawing our attention back to the bride who, fresh off the dance floor, is being accosted by guests waiting to convey their congratula-tions or to spray them with more banknotes to bless their new lives together.

'*Ah*, this one and her celebrity wedding?' Idunnu states emphatically with a lift of her eyebrows, 'More than the three of us *combined*!'

We giggle quietly, observing Maureen on what's undoubt-edly the best day of her life and the moment she's been dreaming of. Efe, whose eyes are shining close to where Maureen and Osagie are holding court, is the same. For them, there's nothing bigger than this. Me, I'm not so sure.

'It will be your turn next,' I say to Idunnu, who clucks her tongue and shakes her shoulders. A swift rejection of my pre-monition if I ever saw one. 'Not even one day?' I probe as her gaze flickers.

'You know at the hotel, the things I've seen,' Idunnu begins with her eyes glazing over and I recall some of the tales she's shared about cheating husbands, high rollers and prosti-tutes in the seedy venue. 'The kind of money some of these girls are earning ... No be small o.' She swallows visibly before sighing.

'One day *keh*? *It*'s more than I can make in a week, and then how much is left for my pocket once Mama don carry am!'

I sigh in commiseration, thinking of my own measly savings and the burden of helping to prop up a household.

'These women can do what they like, can buy whatever they want without having to justify,' Idunnu whispers, eyeing Maureen and Efe, who is now dancing with another boy, one that isn't wearing the groom's colours.

'Can you imagine?' I say, thinking momentarily of their freedom and not the price they have to pay for it.

'No restriction ... No permission,' Idunnu continues passionately before clucking her tongue. 'No obligation or tradition, just going with the flow! I don't know many things, Baby, but I am positive that life of certainty is not for me,' she concludes cryptically, staring at the newlyweds.

Hours later, the feasting, drinking and singing start to subside and the numbers have thinned as the groom's party has made their way home in anticipation of Maureen's arrival. We wait for Maureen's tearful goodbye with her family; her wedding momentarily transformed from a celebratory affair into a sad farewell as her mother breaks into sobbing, no doubt resulting from copious amounts of hot drinks.

The three of us climb into the larger boats destined for Osagie's along with Maureen, her older sister and cousins that are her wedding party and some other married women from her household. As we sail through Makoko, we rehash the wedding, the gifts bestowed on the family and listen to her relatives regaling Osagie's panache. But the merriment becomes subdued the closer we get to his place and reverence takes hold of the group, who begin to pray over Maureen. I close my eyes and allow the voices of her relatives to wash over me, to bless all of us too at this transition that Maureen is making. We alight from the boat and complete the short journey on land to his place. Voices from Osagie's house ring out in anticipation of our arrival. 'Bride! Be proud!' they call out until we finally come to a stop next to his property. Osagie's graceful auntie emerges with her spectacular head-tie shaped like a bronze bird of prey in flight; it had caught my attention so many times during Maureen's ceremony. She brandishes a bowl of water that she holds out for Maureen. We are silent as Maureen slips her hands into the bowl, inside which is floating money and some cowry shells. Osagie's auntie washes Maureen's hands before drying them on a new head-tie clutched underneath her armpit.

I swallow the unexpected sadness that bubbles up within me as Maureen stands beside her wedding party on the threshold of her new community. She seems younger there as she holds onto the head-tie and the money from the bowl in front of her. Her lips quiver briefly as though she's only just realised the distance between us or is facing the reality that this is her home from now on, that it's not just a fleeting visit as part of the wedding show. She'd be expected to dine alone in her husband's house, but these days the rules are relaxed slightly and her sister and her cousins will stay behind with her a while longer.

We greet some of Osagie's family, who are now lined outside to see us, proffering yet more presents bound for Maureen's family. We say our goodbyes before heading back to the boats, where echoes of their revelry in his house can still be heard and bounce off the waves around us, serenading us as we make our return voyage to Maureen's former home.

The three of us linger at the back of the boat, craning our necks over homes in Sogunru even though our friend is long gone from our view and well into the start of her new life.

10

As I'm watching Prince sleeping, I'm wishing that I had Afo's skill with drawing so I can capture the moment. His mouth is partially open, but nothing's coming out, unlike with Afo or his sister, from which a thin line of drool would exit, glueing them firmly to their mattress.

Sleep renders his face younger. Not that at twenty-four he has old features, but with his eyes closed and his eyelashes trembling as he dreams, the armour he usually wears while awake is gone.

Ghostly sounds leak through the walls of the staff quarters into Prince's bedroom, where we are, behind the plush Viceroy hotel. The place is dark owing to its grey cement walls, but air circulates through the large paneless window in the corridor.

It feels strange, this period of inactivity in the afternoon when I'm normally working on the water. But when Prince suggested sharing his day off after all the extra time he'd accumulated, I grabbed the chance and sent Mama Jumbo a message, telling her that I wasn't feeling well. Things had moved quickly between us, although it felt painfully slow due to the stretches of absence between our meetings where we stole kisses on the water or held hands freely when we were away from Adogbo. At least an inter-community romance meant a chance for random sightings. But with Prince dwelling on the mainland, every encounter had to be carefully planned in advance.

He'd met me in Makoko and organised an okada to take us back to the hotel. I'd been squished between their two bodies, holding onto the motorcycle while Prince gripped onto me from behind as we wound our way through Lagos traffic, leaning and swerving dangerously as our driver hurled abuse at each car we passed and narrowly tried to avoid the limbs reaching out to curtail our progress through the city gridlock.

As we approached Ikeja, I recalled the protest, when the streets had been crammed with bodies shouting and marching. So different to a standard street scene, where buses and vehicles stopped and started in the street, and hawkers tried to navigate the busy road, running between cars to sell chewing gum, oranges, Nollywood DVDs, water and even jeans. On the sides of the roads were the ever-present food sellers and a smattering of people on foot going about their daily lives. I stopped recognising the streets as we'd passed the point at which Efe, Idunnu and I had turned back that day in our escape before colliding with Prince. As if he'd been reading my thoughts, his fingers had clasped me tighter and our bike had made such a sharp turn to the right that I'd closed my eyes for fear the three of us would surely go crashing to the ground.

When I'd opened them, I caught sight of the impressive white building framed with a long row of palm trees and bright lights in the shape of rainbows that adorned the arches that appeared to be the hotel's signature. The Nigerian flag fluttered in the air proudly at the end of a long flagpole alongside other countries that looked familiar, but I couldn't place them due to my scanty schooling. The only one I was certain of – other than Cameroon, Benin and Ghana – was the one belonging to the United States.

Prince had paid for the okada as we'd climbed down, and we walked slowly towards the hotel, my legs feeling rubbery after our journey. He had pointed out some landmarks along the way, but I hadn't been listening as I processed the fact that I was parading on the streets of Lagos with a boy when I should've been filling boxes with merchandise for sale on the lagoon. My guilt was easier to focus on than my fear and excitement about being alone with Prince. My insides felt so jittery. My body was tingling so much that I was convinced a strong breeze could carry me away.

After passing the security gate, we'd explored the hotel via a different entrance, taking in its grounds slowly, from the impressively clear swimming pool to the garden filled with the kinds of plants and flowers I'd never seen and decorated with grey and white striped lounging chairs. There was an outside eating area for guests and what looked like an outside kitchen too for chefs to prepare meat over fire for barbecues. Prince waved his hands in the general direction of the hotel's supposed spa area and tennis court, but by that time, my mind was full. The hotel was bigger than I expected from what he'd said about it in our conversations, but we hadn't seen many people as we walked around. Some of the staff recognised Prince and gave quizzical or approving nods, most likely as he wasn't wearing his uniform and clearly had a visitor.

After Prince settled me in his room, he'd slipped out for close to half an hour while I observed the bare surroundings he lived in. Inside his closet, his clothes were folded more neatly than I could have imagined a boy doing without a woman's help. Aside from his bed and chair, he had little in the way of possessions. I studied closely the one picture he'd stuck to the wall above his bed next to his diplomas from the Culinary Academy. It wasn't a recent one as he appeared a lot smaller in it, but I'd taken in his fuller face and his close-cropped Afro as he stood alongside what I read to be family members from the whisper of resemblance across their faces. While he and his siblings were smiling for the photograph, his parents, shorter than all of them and sandwiched in the centre of the shot, wore all the seriousness of those who still believed cameras captured people's souls in addition to images.

At the sound of my mobile, I went to retrieve my bag from the floor. As I bent, I noticed the things underneath his bed and dropped to my knees for a closer inspection. I flipped through the old, well-thumbed magazines about cooking, pausing at the pages he'd turned the corners down on to see what had caught his attention before retrieving the books under his mattress. One was about French cuisine, another was a whole book about bread. I studied the third one: *Tale in a Pie*. The pictures on its cover caused my stomach to roar so loudly I put all the books away quickly in case the noise alerted people to my presence in his room. I'd just returned everything to the place I found them when Prince opened the door with his back facing me. When he turned, he was holding a tray carefully with some silver domes. He laughed as he took in my expression while gingerly setting the tray down on his table and removing the covers with an expert flourish. I moved over to him to stare down into the food he had revealed.

'Na you make this?' I asked, looking at the crab eyeing me from a white bowl filled with what I'm ashamed to say resembled water from the lagoon.

'Of course. Since I can't carry you go kitchen,' he explained, pushing cutlery in my direction. 'This way, I'm bringing it to you. I didn't know wetin you like, so one is chicken and the other is fish.'

'*Okay*—'

'But try the two,' he ordered softly as he saw my gaze leap towards the chicken, which was presented in a manner that was closer to its original form.

I copied his movements as he spooned the broth with the crab into his mouth. The shell had only been for decoration. Extra to the *max*. He'd removed it to show that he'd already scooped out all the meat, which floated inside the soup along with unfamiliar vegetables and herbs. I watched his face over my spoon as he

151

awaited my reaction. Swallowing had never seemed more important, and even before I had, he'd laughed at me.

'It's as if I'm bringing you poison,' he teased, and I playfully hit him on his arm in response.

'It's *sweet o*,' I responded genuinely, as I took another spoonful of the broth. It reminded me of the perfume Auntie Bisi's employer gave her last Christmas. It was almost flowery on my tongue, so light and fragrant as an aroma of coconut and other foreign spices tickled my nose before soft sweet cushions of crab disappeared between my teeth.

Prince put the tray down on the floor so we could both sit facing each other. As I'd gone to sample the chicken, I noticed that he'd stopped eating and was just watching me as if I was on television.

'What happen?' I asked, mortified that I had accidentally left food on my face, or I shouldn't have picked up a piece of the chicken covered with little black seeds. 'You're not eating?' I probed before licking the tasty sauce from my fingers.

'I'm saving it for you!' he replied cheekily. 'Who knew someone so scrawny could actually eat?'

The smell of fried egg and palm oil infiltrates the open window in Prince's room and pulls him slowly from his dreams. I follow the movement of his hands across his bedsheet slowly as though he's expecting to find my body alongside his own, where I was before he fell asleep. I watch as he opens one eye to look for me, and when he finds me missing, the other one does too before he lifts his head up.

'Why you dey there? Did I snore?' he asks softly. Not fully awake yet, I can see the confusion on his face as he finds me on the floor facing him. I shake my head and then avert my eyes from his gaze, which feels different now, even though I'm back in my jeans and my black and white top. When I look up a moment later, his pupils are still on me. When I catch my reflection in them, I'm naked.

'Do you want to go?' he offers gently then, reaching for his T-shirt that is on the floor between us.

'No,' I say, surprising myself when the words exit my lips.

He smiles but I've already changed the mood, I realise, as Prince continues to dress. For a moment, I see myself from his perspective. Me with even my shoes on and my bag by my side. I don't even remember dressing after leaving his soft bed to look at him.

'It's *okay*,' I mumble, but the rest of my sentence disappears as he comes towards me and lifts up my chin with his hand.

'I understand, Water Baby . . . Mermaids can't stay out on land for too long, abi,' he replies with a knowing wink.

The sound of a boat's motor peeling off into the distance wakes me up and I open my eyes to the sunlight reluctantly. My body aches in a way that makes Prince feel nearby, as though he's just left my insides, even though I'm on the veranda in Makoko watching Iya Clara's four-year-old daughter spreading her backside over the water to shit into the lagoon.

I look away, searching for the origin of the sound of wind chimes drifting across slow-moving waves. At last, I find it at the house in the far-left corner of my eye. What I'd mistaken for chimes are two shirts jingle-jangling on warped wire hangers in the distance.

I return the wave of the passing children in a canoe bound for the school. The boy at the back of the boat resembles Charlie Boy so much that at once, my scalp goes cold and my head shivers as I recall my brother in his school uniform. I nurse a small sense of remorse that I'm spending more time away from him, sneaking away some of my availability to get to know Prince. Charlie Boy doesn't appear to be offended or aware of my omissions, but nevertheless, I chase away the guilt wrapping itself around my throat as I think about the secret I'm keeping from him. It might even be shame; perhaps they are the same thing. We talk about the sky, about planes and drones and the family, but my mouth cannot bring itself to confess about Prince fully, no matter how much I'm wanting.

He'd like Prince too. That much I know. My brother, who was so passionate throughout his short stay. He'd like that Prince has a goal he is striving towards. A big dream, like us. He'd fall about laughing at Prince's dry sense of humour.

The backs of my eyes begin to sting, but I allow Charlie Boy to remain in my mind until the canoe carrying the children disappears from my eyeline. I hear Afo and Kemi in the bathroom together when I enter the bedroom. The room stinks from the stench exiting Tayo's body, so I draw the curtain vigorously to allow the air from outside to penetrate.

'*Baby*!' Tayo yells as usual, but when he turns towards me, I notice the discolouration on his face. My expression makes him remember and he reaches out towards his cheek, where the blackened bruise is, before stopping his hand mid-air and eyeing me defiantly.

'What happened to you? Who did that?' I ask as he lies back down and covers his face with his hand.

'Na your business?'

'Did you fall?' I press on, coming to stand over him before I become aware that my shadow's giving him the darkness he requires for sleep and so I step away to allow the sunlight full access to his face once again.

'Stop disturbing me, *abeg*—'

'Don't bring trouble for this house o, I beg you, Tayo,' I begin as my frustration bubbles out of me. 'There are children here to fall under your influence—' I continue before his wild laughter interrupts my train of thought.

In what could only be a matter of seconds, Tayo jumps up from his mattress to tower over me. The anger coming off his body is like a force field that keeps us only inches apart and I feel my body immediately slick with nervous sweat. I brace myself for a blow, but it's only his spittle I feel on my face as he kisses his teeth before he backs away from me a little, satisfied I'm aware of the damage he can do if he feels so inclined.

'You are *mad*,' he rages on, touching a finger to his temple theatrically. 'You have lost your *mind*—'

'I'm not afraid of you,' I announce evenly and cross my arms over my chest. It's a lie, and we both know it.

'What is your problem today?' Tayo asks, his sour breath like an added assault as the movement of his upper torso releases waves of his stale sweat that make me want to retch.

'What you are doing is not good, Tayo! I know about your cough medicine and your bottles all over the place,' I say, pointing towards his mattress. 'Just don't bring it back here is all I am asking.'

'What about *you*? Wetin you dey do?' Tayo spits at me, his eyes aflame as if he's possessed.

'What am I doing?' I ask him, keeping one eye on the door in case the children want to enter the bedroom.

'Who is that man on your boat?' he replies swiftly, looking triumphant.

I hesitate at his question as a scroll of scenes replays in my mind. I know immediately that he's seen Prince and me. What I'm uncertain of is where and what he's seen us doing. '*Well*?'

'Tayo,' I begin, but he dismisses me with one savage look.

'You think you are the only one who get eyes? Why don't we ask your papa which one he's more interested in?' His breath tickles the perspiration on my face. '*Abeg*, mind your own business, and I'll mind my own,' he remarks cuttingly as he moves past me to close the curtain, an act symbolic of the end of our conversation.

11

Efe has spent twenty minutes boring us senseless about some boy she's been exchanging messages with. As she reads out his last text and asks us all to translate the hidden meaning behind his four or five words, I catch Idunnu stifling a yawn as she peeks at the door waiting for Maureen's arrival. Thankfully, that comes a quarter of an hour later, despite the fact that the three of us have already been gisting for thirty-five minutes.

'Sorry, *sorry*,' she mouths breathlessly but for once gets a pass for her tardiness instead of a row of scowling eyes. This is the first time we've been together as a foursome since her wedding ceremony and we're too excited to be angry.

We barrage her with questions about her new situation, watching her preen as she fills us in about married life. I bite my tongue while listening to her discovered wisdom. It's not as if she's been married for years, but it's clear a transformation has taken place, if only in her mind. Efe tries valiantly to steer the conversation towards Dapo, but none of us are having it and Idunnu distracts her by rehashing the latest gossip on Adogbo.

'Did you hear about Egebe?' Idunnu asks Maureen, whose face lights up as she braces herself for some intrigue. She raises a hand to pause Idunnu temporarily as some people enter the canteen to greet her and ask about her wedding. She doesn't have a shift today, so she takes her time, enjoying the attention this life event has brought her, while we wait impatiently to resume our conversation before the working day beckons us separate ways.

'Where were we?' Maureen says as she reclaims her seat at our table with a half-smile.

'They came to take Michael Egebe away . . . For beating his wife—'

'He didn't just *beat* her,' Efe jumps in to overtake the story-telling. 'They say that when they came to help her, her lip was hanging *here*,' she continues, motioning with her hands in a way that makes all of us wince.

'Is that his fourth?' Maureen asks. 'Shey the one before died?'

'What difference does it make?' Idunnu counters swiftly as I nod fervently, given that she's plucked my very comment out of my mouth.

'I'm just saying. She must be young *now* . . . You would think she can fight,' Maureen sighs before chewing on something invisible.

'Like *you* would be able to fight if Osagie put his hands on you?' I challenge Maureen, who throws me a dirty look.

'My husband would *never* lay his hands on me! That is why, ladies, you must pick *well*—'

'So, it's her fault her husband is a brute? Is that what you dey say?' Idunnu's voice is low as she questions Maureen. We all know this is a bad sign and an indicator of an imminent explosion.

'That's not what I'm saying,' Maureen replies sheepishly as I try to make eye contact with Idunnu to stop her before her transformation into a raging beast. 'But this thing dey happen plenty for Makoko,' she continues with an air of resignation. 'You have to be prepared.'

Idunnu is still vexing when we enter my canoe. Instead of taking her directly home, we do a slow crawl through the neighbourhood so she can calm down.

'It's not her fault,' I say by way of de-escalation, watching Idunnu's lips turn into one hard line.

'Everyone is so small-minded here,' she replies sharply before releasing a spittle bullet into the black water. 'The way it is, is the way it is,' she mumbles, looking wistfully across the water.

'But things are changing,' I offer weakly, knowing my statement will do little to salve the wound paining her.

'Not fast enough,' Idunnu whispers.

Two canoes almost come to blows on the water as one refuses to let the other pass. The two male drivers give as good as they get, but it's the one with the boatload of passengers that wins the day as the power of the crowd succeeds. We

159

wait patiently, observing the exchange of abuse between them. A woman, easily Auntie Bisi's age, reaches into the water to flick the other driver as their boat drifts by. It releases some of the pent-up energy of the lagoon as those witnessing her childishness break out into giggles, including Idunnu and me. But I can't help thinking there's something hanging in the air. Some foreboding that all these random acts of violence are alluding to.

Now that we're alone, I tell Idunnu everything about Prince and me, which is easy to do as there's no judgement from Idunnu, which is why I like her. Plenty of lip but never any real scolding.

'So, the man is good with his hands,' Idunnu teases gently.

'*Stop*—'

'But it's nice he's impressing you. It's a good sign. Some don't even try,' she adds seriously.

She seems amused by my update, and for a brief moment, we're free without any stress hanging over us. But soon, I notice the discomfort overriding her expression, the grey sheen that hijacks her features the longer we cruise on the water.

'Is it the boat?' I ask, concerned for her well-being as she dry heaves over the side of the boat but stops short of vomiting.

She shakes her head and looks down at her belly in exasperation.

'Baby, I think I am ready,' she says in a voice that sounds as though it's coming from somewhere very far away.

'Are you sure?' I ask even though I know the answer. After all, it's Idunnu I'm talking to.

'What will happen?' I ask her quietly.

'When I take the medicine?' she shrugs noncommittally. 'I have to swallow the drugs first before drinking some liquid. It will help my body to remove it,' she explains.

'Will it hurt?'

'I think yes, but the tonic should help. That's what the healer said.'

'What do you want me to do?' I ask as I slow the canoe's movement now that we're coming off the main waterway and within earshot of the houses we pass.

'I no know how long it will take to start. After I take the medicine . . . But if I do it tomorrow, then it can be over soon, and I will be well before Mama returns from helping Nene's itoju omo,' Idunnu explains with a look of sadness. It dawns on me how doubly painful this is for her. Contemplating the end of the life she's carrying while her mother is aiding Idunnu's sister-in-law Nene with her newborn.

'I will take it before my shift. My supervisor is my friend, so if I'm sick, she will let me go . . . Then I will call you.' She explains the plan she's concocting out of thin air. 'Is that okay?' she asks, almost as an afterthought.

'Of course,' I assure her before I set the canoe into motion. 'Just call me, and I will come.'

I wipe off my face about twenty yards from Wunmi's boat before going closer. I try to remember all the things Ayo showed me before, as well as the basic keyboard tutorial Efe had treated me to at the centre in case today's mapping lesson involved more intense data entry. It's only when I hear some male voices that I inspect Wunmi's canoe more fully and take in the nicely dressed passengers she's transporting across the water. I read her body language before her eyes catch mine and use my oar to stay the progress of my vessel. She offers a small shake of her head and I let my shoulders sag in defeat for a moment before paddling away from Yanshiwe to get an early start on my work shift.

When I don't hear from Idunnu, I send her a message in the afternoon. But it's almost when I'm finishing with Mama Jumbo that her reply comes in, telling me she isn't going to drink the medicine after all and that she'll explain later. Confusion wraps itself around my brain, yet something eases in my chest at the thought of her not drinking the traditional medicine. Many girls have perished believing in such rubbish. There was no way to guarantee what you were taking. Not that I'd said anything to Idunnu about my doubts. But for all the vitality drinks Papa had been consuming, I wouldn't be at all surprised if the traditional healer was selling him Guinness mixed with goat shit.

Mama Jumbo's engaged in a phone call so loud that I wonder why the phone is even necessary at all. I'm pretty sure the person she's shouting at can hear her across the lagoon. I make a face as though my ears are paining me before rearranging my features when she scowls in my direction. As I listen to her discussing the situation with Egebe's wife with her friend, I begin to see Mama Jumbo in a new light as I gather little pieces of the conversation while sweeping up the stockroom.

'If the elders don't reprimand him, then I will,' Mama Jumbo booms before holding her phone away from her ear while her friend responds. 'You know me, Marion, I no dey play! Let them try that church nonsense—' Mama Jumbo begins before casting me a glance. She then switches to rapid-fire Igbo so that I'm only able to catch about one out of every fourteen words.

'And that's where you and me dey differ,' I hear the annoyance in her voice after the lengthy response from the other end of the line. 'You say it's not our problem, but I think it's *everybody's* problem,' Mama Jumbo replies before their call comes to an end.

'Baby!' Mama Jumbo jingles a little while later and I answer. When I come back into the room, having swept all the dirt off the edge of the veranda, she's furiously rooting around in her cleavage in search of something. The rattling of her bracelets comes to a halt and she extracts her fingers grasping a tissue and wipes her face with a sense of relief. With so little wind today, the hot air hangs like Koku's breath.

'Remind me, are you planning to be sick this coming Friday?' she asks.

The shock of her question hijacks my body, but I manage to keep my face frozen.

'No, Auntie! *Why*—'

'I no dey too old to remember young love,' Mama Jumbo answers while picking up another handful of nuts.

163

'I, I'm . . .' I stammer, but she cuts me off before I can present a legitimate defence.

'Shey he's treating you well?'

'Yes, Auntie,' I respond shyly, keeping my gaze fixed on her shed sandals between her bare legs on the floor.

'You know you can come to me if you have any problems? Me or my sister, *eh*? We are here for you. That is what we promised your mother . . . God rest her soul,' she continues, looking heavenward.

'Yes, Auntie,' I answer again on autopilot.

'There are plenty *bastards* in this world. And in this very community,' Mama Jumbo announces with pure venom in her voice. 'But your friend seems like a reasonable person. Maybe you were wise to look further afield.'

I don't know how to respond to her, so I try to make the same face I do for church and when I was in school, to convey that I'm listening when my mind is really on holiday.

'No matter what anyone tells you, it's not okay for your husband to raise his hand towards you. Do you understand what I'm saying?'

'Yes, Auntie,' I say again for good measure.

'If that ever happens, you come and tell me. I'll show you how to put that hand of his down, once and for all.'

I must have fallen asleep after making beans for the household as the sound of my phone ringing chooks me out of my dream, where Prince is teaching me to cook a dish and calling out the names of various ingredients that all sound made up. Placing the phone to my ear, it's not Idunnu's usual voice that I hear but a pinched and whispery tone. Sleep vanishes from my brain instantly, as though someone has poured cold water all over my body. For some reason, I'd assumed after her message yesterday that she'd decided not to go through with it again, but from the tone of her voice I know she's gone ahead and taken the medicine, without the explanation I'd been expecting this call to be.

'Baby! You've not been answering—'

'I fell asleep,' I begin before remembering what really matters. 'Have you done it?' I ask.

'*Eeehn*. Late last night when I saw chance. It started paining a few hours ago,' Idunnu says before letting out a long breath that I understand from my own bleeding is her trying to manage her pain.

'Where are you?' I ask, picturing her expression through the phone.

'I dey Sandra side . . . Please come *now*,' Idunnu implores.

I jump up from the mattress and Kemi stirs by my side but doesn't wake up. One of Afo's eyes opens to observe me, but from the evenness of his breath and his open mouth, I know he's still sleeping.

By moonlight, I creep around the room, looking for things and throwing them into a carrier bag. My towel, a wrapper, and the dress I wore the day before in case Idunnu needs a change of outfit. Papa snores loudly when I crouch and listen outside his door. Inching the door open slowly, I remove his vitality drink and pour some of it into the empty soda bottle

165

one of the children has left behind. I push some paper into its head and snatch a bottle of water and some biscuits and jump into the canoe.

I sail as fast as I can to meet Idunnu, enjoying the burning of my arms that stops my brain from spinning as I pull my way through inky waves on an almost-empty lagoon. When I reach where she is, it's hard to discern her in this thick night, but then her eyes appear like miniature moons and I wave my hand. I help her enter the canoe and at the sound of her laboured breathing, feel my nerves shoot up another notch. She gives me a knowing look and tries to smile through her agony, but it only makes her look like a mad person.

'My supervisor was sick yesterday,' she explains, panting between every word. 'So, I couldn't do it until after my extra shift. And then Moses came when I—'

'It's *okay*. Save your breath,' I tell her as I guide the boat around a large mass of pungent, floating debris.

'Where we dey go?' she asks while rubbing her belly in repeated circles.

'Don't worry,' I answer as I row into the darkness.

I follow the pinpoints of light until it dawns on me to fight my instinct to paddle far into the lagoon, where she can cry all she wants. If something happens to her, there'll be no way to save her, and I can't – and won't – carry her demise on my shoulders. A fish announces itself in the water before jumping back into the waves and I take that as a sign and navigate us towards the fish market.

In my mind's eye, I recall the Pentecostal church not far from the market's location and the construction of the apartment block not far from that. At this time of the night, we would be hard-pressed to come across other people.

We're born in the same year, but as I cradle Idunnu in my arms as blood runs out from between her legs, it's like I'm her mother. I rock her calmly and sing nonsense as it appears in my mind while trying to stop her from twitching as the pain exits her body along with her unborn. I'm glad I had the good sense to bring my towel, not that it provides much comfort for her on the hard ground. But we're shielded from sight by the eucalyptus tree and the cement wall of the unfinished build-ing takes Idunnu's weight. She's sodden and delirious by the time the real pain has passed. She's still bleeding, but it's man-ageable and some colour returns to her lips she's chewed through. I use my wrapper to wipe the film of sweat from her face and force her to drink water, which she does greedily. When she refuses the biscuits, I make her sip Papa's vitality drink. She barely has two mouthfuls before it comes back up, drizzling down her chin and soiling her shirt.

'*You want to kill me?*' she accuses gently before another silent wave of pain assaults her.

My knees ache from crouching on the ground but I don't complain. I'm alert to her every movement and to every sound around as the night becomes diluted and slithers of light begin to appear. With my help, she manages to remove her pants and skirt, which we place in the carrier bag to throw away. She'd brought black trousers but opts for my dress, owing to the ease of putting it over her spent frame. After padding her fresh pants heavily, she takes my arm willingly as we amble back towards the canoe to make it back to Adogbo while darkness remains.

I only become aware of how exhausted I am when Charlie Boy appears. His fingers unsettle the water as he plunges them into the lagoon, resuscitating my drooping eyelids just in time to save me from losing the oar slipping out of my lazy grip. He knows Idunnu's face but doesn't seem concerned about her state when he asks me what's happening and I tell him as quietly as I can. I'm grateful when he offers to help me sail so I can relax a little. I share the burden with him while Idunnu floats in and out of consciousness on the bottom of the boat.

'Who are you talking to?' Idunnu's question startles me as we pull into the waterway. The lagoon is quiet without its traffic. The sound of the water never rises above the level of the sucking and gulps created by a thirsty person drinking water as we move steadily towards her house.

'My brother,' I reveal quietly. I'm too drained of energy to lie, and in her state, I don't believe she'll even remember my admission.

'Charlie Boy,' Idunnu says calmly, looking directly at the end of the canoe where he's sitting with his arms stretched wide as his fingers surf the gentle wind as we travel. I study Idunnu's face intently as my body prickles with electricity. In this very moment, I'm convinced she's seeing him too. 'Am I dying?' Idunnu asks softly, with no hint of fear.

Her voice breaks then and she makes low sobbing sounds that quickly stop as sleep catches her.

'*Is* she?' I look towards him for the answer as panic squeezes my chest.

Charlie Boy leaves his position to straddle her frail body. His little legs make an upside down V as he bends to peer over her face directly beneath his.

'Not even close,' he whispers and I let out a sigh of relief.

12

I hope my face is unreadable but I'm surprised when I see Samson waving while he heads towards me as I'm finishing washing clothes on the veranda. I put my hands over my eyes to get a better look, but there's no sight of his sidekick anywhere. *At least that's one good thing,* I think to myself while wrestling a sudden frisson of guilt over his unwanted attention. Kemi and Afo are playing in the canoe, but I ignore them as I pour water out of the bucket into the lagoon before disappearing inside while Samson completes the journey to the house.

He delivers a friendly greeting, which I return, wondering why he always seems out of breath when he's riding in a boat with a motor. My brain's still pondering this conundrum, so I'm caught completely unawares as he scrambles around underneath the grey sheet at the back of his boat before whipping it back with a dramatic flourish. I stare down blankly at the motor he's revealed. From the edge of our deck, I can smell his fragrance that competes with the diesel he also smells of. The combination of both is offensive, like when Auntie Bisi started her job in Ikoyi and began to spray air freshener after Tayo shitting. The effect that's invariably worse than the original odour.

'I have been working on it for a while. From some old parts,' he explains nervously as I process the present he's meaning for me to have.

'*Na so*? But we can't buy it,' I begin frantically as the children stop their playing to climb up so they can see the machinery up close as Samson masterfully picks it up with both hands and heaves its mass onto the deck behind us. I know where he's going; the motor might as well be two cows and a bag of money sealing my fate.

'I'm not selling it,' Samson chuckles then, tipping his head to one side as he laughs awkwardly. 'It's a gift. For *yo*—' he adds before Papa's shouting inside the house makes him visibly flinch.

'*Baby!* Who goes there?' Papa belts out aggressively.

Both Samson and I freeze as we hear shuffling sounds emanating from the house. I recognise them as Papa trying to lift himself up from his mattress and picture him scrambling for a vest to put over his round torso.

'Who is it?' he asks before clearing his throat and I motion to Samson before heading to the door as Papa's head emerges.

'Papa, na Samson,' I say, all at once feeling like a child as Samson fidgets behind me, bending his head politely towards Papa.

'*Samson*! It's some time since I see you. How far?'

'Good, sah. Notin spoil . . . We thank God.'

'And your business?'

'It's good—' Samson begins, but Papa doesn't even wait for Samson to finish before he continues with questioning.

'Is your father well now? After his operation?'

'Yes, sah . . . They carry him for Aiyetoro, but he's fine.'

'After your brother's wedding?'

'Yes, sah . . . they waited until Elijah married.'

'Tell him I said hello,' Papa says before he catches Afo and Kemi nudging each other over the motor. 'What is that?'

'Samson brought it for Uncle Jimi,' I shout quickly, ignoring the strange expression Samson's making while noticing his mouth doesn't contradict me.

'I don do some repairs on an old boat. They were going to destroy it, but I thought some parts could be saved,' Samson stammers feverishly as Papa shoots the children a look that immediately freezes them.

'It's for Uncle Jimi?' Papa sniffs suspiciously as a nervous tick appears on Samson's face and I feel my armpits begin to sweat profusely.

'*Yes, sah.* Baby and I dey talk a while ago. She mention something about a motor. I thought you could use it.'

'*Ah ah!* Thank you, Samson. That's *very* kind o,' Papa says, holding his hands out. Samson moves closer to my father, standing in the doorway. Papa's eyes are small, black pinpricks as he acclimatises to the full sunlight that he usually avoids in the daytime by hiding out in bed.

'So, you two have been talking . . . How old are you again, Samson?' Papa asks in a voice one octave higher than before.

172

'Twenty-two,' Samson croaks while tugging at his shirt collar.

'See how scrawny you are still! I hope there is someone cooking for you? A hard worker like yourself needs someone to be feeding him when he comes home . . . Baby cooks quite *well*, you know,' Papa says, winking at me while I pretend to rub at something lodged in the corner of my eye.

'You get somebody special?' Papa asks with raised eyebrows as Samson starts to visibly melt in front of him. I transform myself into a stone statue, mortified.

'No, sah. Not yet o—' Samson manages, keeping his gaze fixed on the wooden panels of the house.

'Well, you're still young,' Papa scoffs before he retreats back into the gloomy interior. 'Don't take time,' he shouts from inside as his feet slap the ground noisily.

I can no longer look at Samson and am grateful when I hear him make his hasty goodbye before rushing for his vessel. Afo and Kemi are reanimated as his motor roars to life at the back of his boat. They wave at Samson as he disappears behind a spray of fetid water, pushing past me as they run towards Papa to ask questions about our new motor.

My brain is a whirlpool as I try to digest what just happened on our veranda. Papa's only made it to the living room but is now looking at me as if I'm some money he's found in his pocket.

'Shey you and Samson be good friends?' Papa asks slowly.

Words have abandoned my throat, so I nod my head slowly as tears glaze my suddenly peppery vision.

'A *fine* boy . . .' Papa professes, parting his lips to reveal meaty gums. 'A person could do worse.'

He begins stroking his stomach underneath his shirt like it's a small animal and I feel a knot in my own belly tighten.

When I wake up, I feel the familiar grinding in my womb and back that tells me my period has come early this month. I check the mattress that Kemi and I are sharing before lying back down to stare at the darkened ceiling. A part of me wonders if my cycle has shifted in solidarity with Idunnu, my friend. Since the ending of her pregnancy, she'd slid into one type of low-level mood as if something has quenched her batteries. I was relieved that she was safe after taking the medicine, but my worry for her had transformed from her baby to her overall well-being.

At her house, I'd watched her over-salting the stew she'd been cooking and participating in our conversation halfheartedly when I came to visit. Outwardly, Idunnu looked the same. In fact, where I'd expected to see fragility, I encountered more hardness to her already steely edge. Her relatives floated around us, carrying on their business and chattering in a way that hadn't allowed us to talk properly, but we'd tried as best as we could to whisper a hurried private conversation.

'Do you think anybody suspects?' I'd asked, looking around her large family shiftily. Three children were engaged in a game of tormenting an ailing cockroach and one older woman with a boubou as voluminous as a parachute exited the house with only half of her braids unloosened so that her natural hair stood up in defiant contrast to the eight remaining cornrows to be tackled. After throwing a bucket of rubbish into the lagoon, she disappeared back inside.

Idunnu observed her familial portrait along with me. Then she'd raised her eyebrows knowingly before shrugging.

'You don't seem happy,' I whispered as the children ran in circles around us. My suffering was more of restlessness, but Idunnu's felt deeper, in a way that made me worry despite her habitual attempts to mask it behind a steely exterior. I'd reached out to stop her from adding yet more seasoning to the bubbling pot on the fire she'd been staring over.

'My dear . . .' Idunnu sighed heavily as she tapped the tomatoey spoon against the flesh of her palm to test the food she was preparing. 'Just because I've escaped the hook, doesn't mean I'm free of the net.'

'Morning 'til night . . . Work and suffering! Is it too much to wish for something good to come? I mean, am I mad? Am I waiting in vain for a miracle or is this all there is?' she'd asked in a pained voice before I'd departed, stirring her stew as if it were an oracle from which an answer would appear.

I'd reached out and squeezed her hand tightly so that she'd turned to face me. I wished she could see how wonderful she was, how much joy she brought to all of us around her. There'd been no point in telling her how fearful I was that she'd taken the medicine that night; how terrified I'd been of losing her, like I'd lost my brother.

'Idunnu . . . I'm looking at one,' I'd said with all the sincerity I could muster as I stared into her tragic eyes, praying that her soul would hear me.

Kemi's knees, on the verge of digging into my spine, pull me sharply out of my memory and I escape to the bathroom to wash. Pouring cold water on my body and face, I enjoy the small shock that temporarily removes me from the cramps brewing in my body. As I clean myself, I imagine that along with the dirt, the sense of defeat Idunnu and I were discussing is also washing away. I understand her frustration too well.

Maureen and Efe are different. Not that they're easily satisfied, but for them, how it's always been is enough. Idunnu, however, is another case entirely. She's simply not a fish made for Makoko water, I'm coming to realise, yet has seemingly no means for survival on land.

I follow Wunmi and some other girls out on another mapping mission around Oko Agbon. None of them appear to mind my attendance and I'm grateful for their inclusivity as we move around the community through the day like seasoned treasure hunters. When we finish the work, I take Wunmi to visit Ebenezer. I busy myself exchanging silly messages with Prince as I close my ear to whatever's taking place quietly inside Ebenezer's house.

I'm hoping Mama Jumbo won't notice when I arrive late for my shift, but her foghorn calls me abrasively as I'm creeping out of the canoe to tiptoe on her deck. She hollers my name again and I hurry towards her, concocting my tale about go-slows on the waterways, but when I reach her living room, I find her on the telephone.

'Bring that for me.' She motions dramatically from the long bench she's reclining on by twitching her nose to point towards her beer, cold-sweating, on the table a short distance away. I bring the drink and take the opportunity to disappear into the stockroom, where I speed through my tasks. It's only a short while later before I hear my name for a third time. Mama Jumbo's finished her phone call and is now working through the bole wrapped in newspaper on her lap as I return. My stomach flips unexpectedly as the smell of roasted plantain reaches me. I wasn't hungry before but something about the way Mama Jumbo eats with such relish always awakens my appetite.

'You know you have not answered me about my boat? Are you going to pilot one full-time?' Mama Jumbo eyes me as she prises some sticky plantain off the end of her thumb with her teeth.

'I'm still thinking, Auntie,' I reply sheepishly.

'When you see opportunities, you go take am. Do you understand what I'm saying?' Mama Jumbo lectures between bites of dodo. 'That's the problem with you youts of today . . . You no get *fire*! See me, see trouble,' Mama Jumbo sighs as she points an oily finger in my direction.

I fix my eye on her lap, watching the disappearing plantain she's guzzling that has turned the white pages of the news-paper orange.

'Let me know next week, or I'll assume you don't want again. You hear me?'

'Yes, Auntie.'

'Please . . . Help me to count the rice so I know what to reorder,' Mama Jumbo says, her fingers hovering over the last piece of plantain.

Spying my face, she scrunches the newspaper over the dodo and hands it to me instead of eating it. I blush with embarrassment but take the gift willingly, my mouth already watering at the thought of the soft sweetness to come.

Disappearing to the stockroom, I perch in front of the sacks of rice and open the newspaper. While I polish off the dodo, my eyes scan the soiled text of the *This Day* paper lazily. As I turn the page over, my eyes are drawn to the photo occupying almost the full page on the other side. A small piece of plantain lodges in the back of my throat, cutting off my oxygen. I re-read the headline a dozen times, but the words on the page don't change: *The Pearl of Makoko*. It's not a hallucination, I'm seeing what I'm seeing.

I pore over the image, the close-up of a face gripped by joy, staring up towards the sky. I blink again, but it's still my face on display in the paper, my teeth glinting as if I'm advertising toothpaste.

My legs buckle underneath me before my brain short circuits like NEPA taking light on the mainland. I try to hold on to the only surprising thought in my head. Not why my image is in the paper at all, as I feel my body floating towards Mama Jumbo's floor, but the astonishing fact that I've never looked more beautiful.

13

When I come to, I'm lying on Mama Jumbo's bench in her main room. She's fanning me with some paper that I snatch out of her hands greedily to search for my picture again.

'Baby, have you gone mad?' she snaps as she moves away from me to a safe distance.

It takes a few seconds to process that this paper is a newsletter from the church, so I begin fidgeting frantically on the bench, searching for the newspaper I must have dropped.

'What is it?' Mama Jumbo asks with one hand raised as though she's on the verge of covering herself with the sign of the cross.

'I was reading the paper,' I start foolishly and she gawps at me as though I've lost my mind. 'The newspaper from the plantain,' I add, but her face is only a picture of confusion.

The only thing to do is to locate it, so I scramble up from the bench and run back to the stockroom. It's lying on the ground where I must have collapsed. I don't even have the memory of making contact with the floor or Mama Jumbo carrying me back to the other room. I race back in, waving the paper in front of me as though it's a winning Lotto ticket.

'*See!*' I declare, brandishing it in front of her until she takes it out of my hands.

Mama Jumbo squints while reviewing the page slowly. My heart pounds in my ears as I follow her lips, mouthing the headline before her eyes trace the page and recognition strikes.

'*YE-PA!*' Mama Jumbo bellows, clutching at the shifting head-tie on her head. 'Baby, *is this you?*'

I nod my head as she turns the page over, as though expecting the article to continue as if someone's done a real interview with me, like I'm a superstar or a politician. She begins to laugh quietly, but then the sound increases and becomes more maniacal, no doubt with the absurdity of the situation. I can't help it. I join in with her until tears are running from both our eyes and she's pinching her waist as though laughing is causing her pain.

'*Pearl of Makoko.* Olachi! *Heeeeey!* It's as if they know that is your mother's name?' she says, brimming with emotion.

Again, I blink at her by way of response. I have nothing to do with my face in the newspaper. It's as much a mystery to me as to anyone else. I shrug as I reach out for the paper. She hands it back to me.

'*Up you!*' she says, her voice steeped in pride as she wipes the tears from her face. 'You resemble her so much here. It's strange. Not so much your father . . .' she adds quietly, her face registering her words as the dig they were intended to be.

At the mention of Papa, I feel my head grow light again.

180

I imagine the sheer number of newspapers that have been circulating the city, all bearing my smiling face and my Dream Girl title. I wonder how long it will be until the news reaches him.

'Maybe he will not see it?' Efe offers diplomatically but light's shining in her eyes way too much as she says it.

I glare at her as she moves the broom around the hair salon, sweeping up hair from between Idunnu and my feet.

'Or maybe he will not recognise you? *Abi*? It almost *doesn't* resemble you—' she continues, squinting at the newspaper on the counter before Idunnu butts in.

'*You* . . . your jealousy no get limit? Of course, it's her! But maybe he won't see it,' Idunnu destroys Efe before bringing the conversation back to me as she notices my fears mounting again at the thought of Papa discovering my disobedience.

Maureen's a no-show to my emergency meeting, but she's already chimed in via a phone call, finishing up by asking what's the worst that can happen? It's true. It's not as if my picture can be undone. Still, my fear is genuine, even if it's been some time since I've experienced a beating.

As we kick around various options, including hoping he doesn't see it and doing a wide sweep of all the newspapers coming close to the house, Mama Jumbo's words replay themselves in my mind: 'No matter how large the fingers are, they will not be bigger than the nostril.' In other words, there's a natural order of things. And sometimes, when we don't make a decision in life, the universe decides for us.

I'd intially taken her use of proverbs as something to do with the manning of one of her canoes, but now I understood that it applied to Papa too.

'Why are you even in the paper, sef?' Efe asks after a moment of silence falls between us. Both Idunnu and I turn to stare at her, but there's no visible malice in Efe's features. All I find is curiosity.

'What do you mean?' I ask.

'Why is the paper featuring you? No be jealousy I dey talk . . . *Wait*—' she commands as her attention's captured by someone passing by the salon.

Idunnu and I are puzzled when Efe dashes out of the salon and returns, dragging a young man by his elbow.

'This is Sunday,' she explains breathlessly as she steers him to the counter. 'Sunday, *please,* show us your phone,' Efe begs with a generous bat of her eyelids. 'Na only you get special phone! Big man that you are,' she adds, touching his arm playfully.

It's almost possible to see the steam exiting his puffy ears as he pulls his Galaxy phone out of the pocket of a too-small polo shirt.

'Fetch the internet for me,' Efe demands and instantly, underneath his fingers, his phone springs to life.

Efe snatches his handset while Idunnu and I approach her and we watch her type in the newspaper's headline before the search engine throws up results. Plenty of them.

'What is happening—' I snap, engulfed by a large wave of fear, but Idunnu's arms are already reaching across my body to press the phone's screen, opening up one of the links where Rihanna's regal face blinks at us from the page loading in slow motion.

Through the screaming blocking my ears – shrieking all three of us are making – I stare at myself underneath whatever Rihanna's talking about. It's not just a photo this time, but a video of me standing in Ayo's canoe with my hands on the drone console. So much sun is reflecting on the lagoon water that it looks bright orange instead of its usual dirty black. The footage is slowed down and in the absence of silence, there's some sleepy instrumental music playing, the kind that makes your insides feel sad unexpectedly.

'*Baby!*' Efe's squeal eventually unblocks my ears, bringing me back to the present situation. 'You are famous! You are *Rihanna* famous. Rihanna knows who you are,' she yelps, jumping up and down. It occurs to me a moment later that Idunnu – so subdued recently – is exhibiting the same behaviour.

'You're *everywhere,*' Idunnu stresses with her eyes as bright as the sun.

'Check Twitter,' Sunday's deep baritone chimes in helpfully as he greedily accepts the hug that Efe unexpectedly bestows upon him.

Idunnu follows his suggestion, all the while trying to shush us so that her fingers can type. Efe and Idunnu battle for the phone as only strange sounds are exiting both their mouths before they begin chanting 'Pearl of Makoko' in unison as if I'm a footballer that's brought us home the World Cup.

'You don dey trend . . . She's a virus,' Sunday proclaims before his faux pas brings Idunnu swiftly back from the land of euphoria.

'No be virus! She dey go viral,' she corrects him quickly while flicking her fingers towards me in another sign of her happiness.

It's too much to take in, so I remove myself from the huddle and go and sit on a nearby stool. I let their words wash over me as they open link after link, trying to piece what led to what before Sunday reclaims his phone. *This Day* might be where I first saw myself, but it turns out they are one of the last to cover the story. The small piece about Makoko that occurs routinely as some do-gooder visits the community and makes an inconsequential report about how we live in a foreign newspaper. Only this time, it was a picture and some video that mattered. *My* picture and *my* video. Who even knows what Rihanna was watching online before she saw it? That's what led to others discovering it and exploding the internet.

When I look up, what feels like only moments later, Sunday has disappeared and Efe is running tongs through Idunnu's hair.

'Welcome back, Daydreamer,' Idunnu quips before flinching when Efe accidentally grazes her ear.

'Papa go kill me,' I say as the blood drains from my face.

'*Ah!* He can't kill you now, Baby. You're a *celebrity*,' Efe responds wisely.

★

I take my time dropping the two of them off after Efe has closed the salon. I'm dragging out the inevitable reckoning at home, but I don't care as I allow other boats to pass in the crowded waterways, much to the bemusement of chancers on the lagoon. My mind starts to play tricks as I observe some people staring in my direction. Are they recognising me already from my newfound fame? Averting my gaze, I steer home, grateful as the sky darkens around me, cloaking me from extra attention.

The deck is still when I pull up the canoe. Perhaps luck will be on my side. Papa and Uncle Jimi have gone out to see some friends. Maybe they will drink beers until their bladders are the size of calabashes and return home too late for any kind of encounter.

I slip onto the deck with the grace of a ballet dancer. My gait is so light that the wood underneath me doesn't even announce my presence. As the adrenaline pumps inside me, I start to foolishly believe that I can make it unnoticed until his voice emerges from the quiet house.

'Who is that?' Papa shouts.

The whites of his eyes and his teeth are what illuminate his face in the darkness, highlighting the sharp contours of his features as he waits for me to appear with his arms folded across his chest.

'Oh, you're back?' he starts off quietly. 'Sit down there. Why don't you tell me what it is you've been up to, *Pearl*?'

14

All of a sudden, we're superstars.

Visitors to our house are endless as news of my appearance in the paper grows. Others who are more social media savvy in the community also learn of my fleeting VIP moment and are grabbing the chance to view me in the flesh. Papa and Uncle Jimi's days are temporarily disrupted as some people drop by with booze, kola nut, even chicken to give thanks for the universe's unexpected benevolence on our family. Of course, others pop in, hoping to benefit or out of an uncontrollable sense of curiosity. I'm forced to ring Mama Jumbo and explain to her that I can't come to work, and – even more surprisingly – she's understanding.

I watch Papa in his good vest and his grey shirt combination during the late visit from a group of women from church. After flocking around me and bestowing their noisy prayers, they've encircled Papa, beseeching him for bits of gossip as though he has any information to offer them. But he's accustomed to this now, after several guests have come round and is now waxing lyrical, as though the papers asked his permission before shadowing me on the water.

I bite my lip as I observe them chatting and laughing about this current affair. A part of me is annoyed at him for claiming what isn't his, yet I'm relieved at his public reaction after shouting so hard at me that it called Mama from the heavens to visit me in my dreams. As I'd poured my defence into my pillow, hot tears running into my ears – and into Kemi's mouth, who could sleep through anything – Mama had whispered to me soothingly in Igbo, singing as though I was still her small child. Her voice had been like soft waves slowly rocking the canoe and I'd drifted off to sleep before the headache that had been stalking my temples could strike.

'A whole you can disobey me just like that?' Papa had hollered like a wounded animal. I couldn't look at him directly, so I'd fixed my gaze on my cousins, intermittently cowering by the bedroom doorway and fleeing whenever my father turned his head.

'Ayo was just showing me,' I'd begun feebly in my defence but with a raise of his hand, I closed my mouth.

'It's not even only your disobedience, it's your *ignorance*! All these years, I've been telling you there are people seeking to uproot us! They want to take this place away . . . Are you forgetting what happened to your brother?' he shot at me.

It was a small spark, but I'd already suffered the third-degree burns of Charlie Boy's death years ago. My skin had thickened as a consequence.

I chose silence over answering back. Over telling him I could never forget my brother, that I communed with him every day, that he was as present as he ever was.

'Now the elders will be looking at me like I don't know how to raise my children! With your face all over the papers as if you're a criminal! *Abeg*, get out of my sight if you don't want me to beat you! I don tire,' he'd yelled, his eyes hard and wild. I hurried out before my legs lost power and pulled me to the ground at his feet with the force of a riptide.

It was Uncle Jimi that had calmed Papa down the following day. The disobedience aspect aside, he'd thought about the elevation this temporary notoriety could bring at the boat builders where he was angling for a promotion and at the saw-mill. Even more than that, there could be more possibilities for the community as well.

'It is a good thing they're doing. We have more sense of who we are on the water,' I hear a woman's voice drop into the conversation as some people around her murmur and shift on our rickety furniture in the living room.

'We know who we are,' Papa's tone is gruff as he responds. 'And we know what *they* can take from us if we give them an opportunity,' he adds. Another woman clucks her teeth in support of his statement.

'We have done what we can for Makoko! Isn't it time to let others also find a way forward? What is it they say? The future is for the young,' the first lady proclaims, squaring her shoulders.

I admire her indigo boubou with its detailed gold, green and purple embroidery down its front and on her sleeves. As

188

she senses me gazing her way, she smiles at me quickly before returning to the conversation and I take the time to commit her face to memory. Whoever she is, I decide I like her.

Now that you are famous, will you be charging to make your appearance?

As I'm rereading Prince's latest text message again, the edges of my lips stretch into an uncontrollable smile. At least his warmth is compensating for Papa's cold shoulder behind closed doors. I'm momentarily distracted from my plate, which is when Tayo strikes, using his dirty hand to swipe my meat. I eye him viciously, thinking of abuse to hurl his way, but his eyes flash knowingly before he curls his arms around his body and purses his now-greasy lips to make kissing sounds. Nudging past him in disgust, I leave him to his nonsense and fling my remnants away now that he has sullied them.

From using my pillow to pocketing the small change Papa left for me on the table, Tayo's evil is outdoing itself, but he knows I'm fearing he'll reveal my secret or embellish upon it. If Papa doesn't stone me for impropriety – despite repeated insistences that I marry – then after demanding to meet Prince's people, he would have me wedded faster than the hit producer Don Jazzy can create another banger track.

My notoriety within the community is enough wahala for now, so for the moment, I'm choosing to hold my tongue.

It's only Prince's humour getting me through this situation as I watch for the light or the ping on my phone announcing his messages like an antelope grazing in front of a lion. Prince, whose head is buried so deeply inside kitchen pots that it was me who told him about my predicament rather than him finding out on the internet. Afterwards, he'd combed through the hotel trash until he'd found an old copy of the newspaper and told me my picture was now hanging on his bedroom wall beside his diploma.

I send a reply worthy of his foolishness and wait for the women to clear the veranda as they take their time entering the two canoes that had brought them to our house. My new friends wave at me as their boats move away into the distance and I wave back vigorously until they are no longer visible from where I'm standing.

It's Wunmi who first tells me that the drone people are after me. The paper mistook me for a Dream Girl, albeit with my help as my mouth had run away with myself after my pilot flight. So now, according to the world, I was part of the project, which had been news to the organisers.

When Murtala Sada arrives at our house, I'm filled with apprehension as I stand between Papa and Uncle Jimi on our veranda. I feel like a prisoner sandwiched between them even though I've no intention of escaping, no matter how speedily I can row on the water. Mr Sada isn't alone but has come with two other men and a girl I recognise from my first mapping expedition though her name has flown from my brain.

We enter the living room and I'm dismissed to go and bring refreshments for the group. The girl looks at me conspiratorially but doesn't move from the stool where she crouches, at a slight distance from the men as though her age precludes her from being a legitimate part of the discussion.

I return as Mr Sada is asking Papa why I wasn't at the introductory meeting for the drone project that took place and I squeeze my eyes shut and pray that Mama can come and pluck me from the room before Papa says anything too embarrassing.

'We are very busy people, my daughter included,' Papa replies condescendingly as his shirt strains against his stomach. 'Every day we are working hard ... There is no time for fairytale—'

'Between her taxi and working for Mama Jumbo, there was little capacity to attend,' Uncle Jimi butts in more diplomatically. 'But clearly, where there is passion—'

'There is *potential*,' Mr Sada finishes swiftly before taking a satisfactory slug of his cold water. The deadpan of his expression is broken when he throws a wink in my direction before returning to appeal to my father. 'It is this potential we'd like to discuss with you.'

The whirlwind of the past few days is still making me dizzy. My world has been spinning ever since the discovery of the article and my belly has been churning in a way that makes me imagine whether this is what Idunnu was feeling like when she was carrying her pikin.

It was still hard to process that the drone project had offered to make me an official member of the team. A part of me had been terrified they'd paid us a visit to reprimand me for masquerading as a Dream Girl or would charge me with theft of their equipment. If I hadn't stolen it outright, then perhaps kidnapping might have been an accusation they could have made. But even after they'd explained their endeavour in more detail, Papa's expression had been one of stone. If Mama had been with us, she'd have known the way to appease him with her water so that their words would penetrate his ears, but he wasn't having it. Still, at least he hadn't said no immediately. I had only Uncle Jimi and not myself to thank for that.

Soon after Mr Sada and his team had departed, we got word from our neighbours that some news crews had made contact with the community leaders about interviewing me. Not just local channels but even foreign crews wanted permission to gain access to Makoko to film and ask me some questions. Papa and Uncle Jimi had left in his boat, but not before giving me a hundred menial tasks to complete while they sailed off to discuss my fate.

Kemi and Afo had fidgeted around me, imploring over again that I tell them about the mapping trips and what it had been like flying the drone. Even the usually errant Tayo had made several appearances at home to torment me and take advantage of the excess of food we had as a result of all of the impromptu visitors wanting to be touched by our amazing stroke of good fortune.

By the time I'd rowed out to see Charlie Boy that evening, Papa and Uncle Jimi still hadn't returned. I relayed everything to my brother, who'd sat facing me with a mouth perfect for

192

attracting flies until I'd finished my last sentence. That was when his brain remembered to close his jaws. His eyes had shone like stars in the sky as he held up the newspaper pages in the dark and traced my face with his fingers. The drone wasn't visible in the shot in *This Day*, but I knew he was picturing it in his mind's eye as he drank in the image while we sat in the boat pondering the result of Papa's discussion with the community elders.

Papa had broken the good news to me the following morning, except coming from Papa's mouth, it had only sounded like news, not anything to be happy for.

'The elders think it is a smart thing for you to do the interview,' Papa had decreed as though someone was forcing him to eat shit from a bucket.

'What do *you* think?' I'd asked foolishly, hoping for a fleeting moment of paternal affection to override his authoritarian disapproval.

'I think that I am a small fish,' he replied with a pronounced sigh. 'But I beg you, just don't bring any disgrace to this family, Baby. After all, *you* are a small fish *too* and—'

'I know, Papa,' I said, finishing the adage for him. 'Na the small fish dem go chop first,' I recited knowingly.

I'd done three interviews in my black and white top over two days. The first with BBC Africa, followed by a local AIT reporter, and the next day a white man flanked by a fast-talking Nigerian along with a lanky East African had come to do a report for Euronews.

Papa refused to have reporters inside the house, even if it belonged to Uncle Jimi, and ultimately it had been his decision. In the end we settled on interviews on the veranda for BBC Africa, but the other two had wanted me in the canoe, where Afo and Kemi had been allowed to sit at the other end on the condition that they were quiet and mostly out of shot. I'd answered their questions in as few words as possible, doing my best to avoid the scrutiny of their lenses pointed in my direction and their nodding heads, trying to encourage me to relax. Only *how* was I meant to relax when the whole of Adogbo was glaring at me from their houses or nearby boats on the water, observing my brush with fame?

'What does the mapping project mean to you?' I'd heard this question from every journalist that had interviewed me and had hopefully perfected my answer by my final interview.

'For us, it is a better way of navigating the community,' I explained in my best English. Mama would have been so proud. 'But also, it is a way of showing the world we are here. We are not invisible, and we should not be treated like it.'

Their cameras tightened on my face as they barked instructions while producers fussed about capturing several shots of me on the water like a movie actor. Staring into the distance, rowing the boat, pointing out various sites in Makoko, even talking and pretending to laugh with my cousins. It wasn't exactly work, but it had been gruelling, and by the end of each day, I'd fallen asleep as though my soft drink had been laced with palm wine.

Another invitation had come in then, not for an interview in Makoko but for an appearance at a British Council event on

Lagos mainland. The TV interviews had also been recompensed, but the money being offered for the evening's reception had made Papa choke on the yam potage in his throat before tears started springing from his eyes.

'Wetin she go do?' Uncle Jimi had asked Papa after the visit from the woman from the council who came to dangle the invitation.

'Present something to some person . . . That is *it!* An award. As far as I know, it's a special event in conjunction with their arts programme, followed by a banquet,' Papa had bellowed, exposing his gums wide.

'So, them dey pay your daughter to chop?' Uncle Jimi had replied before he and Papa had cackled while scratching their temples with incredulity before drawing straws about who should attend alongside me. Both men were staunch longtime resistors to stepping outside of Makoko if they could help it, so in the end, they'd decided on Auntie Bisi, who was already on the ground in Ikoyi and Mama Jumbo, the most successful businessman they knew.

Papa had given me some of the interview money to buy new clothes for the event in Maryland and it was Maureen who offered to help me, now that she was a seasoned wife, not to mention her fashion acumen she was training for if she didn't end up with a baby first.

I met her in front of the jetty and we performed the fastest of shopping trips at the tailors she was getting to know in her new location. In Latia's Boutique, we found what she'd been looking for, ready-made dresses in modern styles at eye-watering prices, though there were a few on a rack in the corner in what the seamstress declared was last year's fabric. I reached for a long dress with sheer sleeves, but Maureen stopped me in my tracks and picked up a bright red dress in a stretchy material that had come to just below the knees. Heading behind the curtain shielding a narrow dressing room, I tried it on before exiting nervously to check myself in front of the mirror Latia had removed from next to her makeshift counter and held out towards me. It looked very costumey to me, my thin frame barely pushing against the fabric, which had the partial peplum design at the side that accentuated my nonexistent hips. The more I stared at myself, the more I wished for Mama Jumbo's curves to help the fabric hang right. My muscly arms jutted out proudly in a way that made me feel ultra-exposed.

'You look like—'

'*Michelle Obama!*' Latia offered confidently.

'Yvonne Nelson,' Maureen had countered with the name of a striking Ghanaian actress-slash-everything.

The red dress was almost double the amount of the other one, but Maureen pounced on my indecision with the speed of a jungle cat.

'Baby, you are in the *public eye* . . . You can't be wearing one yeye dress! Who knows who you will be sitting next to? What if you meet your husband?'

'Shey you know I have a boyfriend, Maureen?' I reminded her swiftly.

196

'*Who*, the cook?' Maureen's head swivelled sharply to face me as I nodded defiantly. 'Your star is rising, Baby. So should your aspirations,' she had smirked, handing Latia my new red dress.

Mama Jumbo in her black, yellow and orange regalia is a sight to behold. With her magnificent red and orange head-tie atop her head, she resembles a mighty cockerel. I admire the confidence emanating from her body in steady waves as I hover at her side like her lowly maid. One would be hard-pressed to ascertain the true epicentres of attention at this gathering, but truth be told, I'm happy that she's pulling some of the focus off me.

When we arrive at the Oakum Events Centre, Auntie Bisi is already waiting for us. She takes in my new outfit and fresh box braids approvingly as I shuffle behind Mama Jumbo's voluminous skirt, wishing I could crawl underneath her hem and hide inside it.

Auntie Bisi waves to us from the bustling reception table, that was three tables in a row, decorated with name tags and manned by six people in matching ill-fitting suits, talking over one another and arguing over the two clipboards they're using to usher everybody in. The reception area seems like an unofficial place where everyone is congregating and preening in front of the cameras, greeting friends and acquaintances while sizing up strangers.

I wipe my sweaty palms on the bottom of my handbag hanging off my shoulder while Auntie Bisi and Mama Jumbo catch up as though they're staring at each other on the stinking lagoon instead of in a hall filled with noisy people whose clothes and perfumes are doing combat.

A few people approach us, telling us how they'd caught my picture in the paper. They flash exaggerated smiles that are as off-putting as the camera flashes from eager photographers shouting '*hello hello psst*' in our direction. Ten minutes later, some organisers start to coax us towards the auditorium.

The room resembles a huge cake. White material is draped across the ceiling and everywhere, there are bright lamps that look like earrings hanging down over the round tables covered with pink tablecloths and flowers. I thought I'd be sitting between Auntie Bisi and Mama Jumbo, but it's Auntie Bisi whose name is the centre, whereas I am to sit beside a woman whose name I'm reading on the name card and watching to see who she might be in the crowd.

As people finally take their seats, I notice the white people are sprinkled on each of the tables like garnish. That is when my table mate arrives; a woman with hair the colour of straw and pupils I can't help double-taking at since I've never seen green and yellow combined. She smiles as she feels my attention on her. No doubt she's used to people being thrown off like I was due to her Ghanaian last name.

'I'm Helen,' she says, even though the name card has already introduced her.

'Yemoja,' I croak.

'Mother of the sea,' Helen replies. 'I know . . .' she continues with a warm smile I fail to return.

An organiser stops by our table before crouching beside me and motioning for my attention.

'Someone will come tap you when it's time for you to present,' the man says hurriedly. 'Just follow them to the side of the stage.'

'You'll be fine, Baby. It will finish quick quick,' Auntie Bisi says softly as if sensing my mushrooming anxiety. Like it's medicine I'm about to take.

My head starts to throb as the pressure about speaking in front of all these people bears down on me. I remind myself I'm not the one getting an award. All I have to do is say the person's name, and then we can eat, and then we get to go to the hotel. It was the only thing I'd insisted upon when suggestions were made about where they could put us up for the night free of charge.

Everything else had been mostly out of my control, even the red dress I'm wearing that's making me look like a half-eaten lollipop. Once I made it through the event, we'd be staying at the Viceroy for the night. Almost under the same roof as Prince.

The master of ceremonies is wearing an impressive agbada in a snakeskin print, but his vibrant orange handkerchief peeking out of his pocket mimics the colour of the hat on his head. A hush falls upon the crowd in a way that hadn't existed before when some of the organisers in bulky awkward suits had been mumbling into the microphone, conveying one type of bureaucracy. I'd turned my ears off too, while scanning the gathering, trying to get a better sense of the company we were in.

'Thank you so much for coming here today. We thank our sponsors, the British Council, the *Star Journal* and VQ Mobile, for putting together this vital event that showcases the impressive artwork from our local communities—'

As the tables explode into warm applause, I join in with them.

'The arts, and indeed *artists*, play an important role in our society. Much more than just creators and provocateurs, they are custodians of our ancient cultures, as well as historians . . .'

'I hoped I'd get the chance to meet you, Yemoja,' Helen's voice so close to my ear pulls me away from the man speaking on stage. Discombobulated, I turn to face her, but the loud clapping from something the man has just said is too overpowering. We can't speak even if we wanted to, so I sink back against the white cloth covering of my chair.

Auntie Bisi and I are glued shoulder to shoulder so that eventually my body adapts to her rate of breathing, which relaxes me before I feel the tap on my shoulder that I've been dreading. I follow the woman who leads me to the side of the stage, where a man with a complicated-looking headset is motioning instructions to nearby people. He waves me over kindly before pulling me behind a small, erected screen that obscures me from the nearby tables as I wait for the young abstract artist on stage to finish his speech.

'Okay, someone will introduce you before you walk on stage. Just read what is written on the envelope in front of you on the podium before you hand it to the winner,' Mr Headset whispers, pulling me aside abruptly to let someone pass. 'Do you understand?'

'What is *podium*?' I say shakily, not recognising my own voice.

'That stand thing there,' he points and I nod in comprehension.

My name appearing over the loudspeaker unsettles my nerves once more, but then a separation happens unexpectedly from hearing my given name when I'm so used to being called Baby.

I try to quell my mounting fear by telling myself it isn't me. That I'm a ghost drifting across the stage as the spotlights on the ceiling blast my forehead, shining it instantly as the master of ceremonies is reminding everybody I am the Pearl of Makoko. I force myself to look at the crowd to find Auntie and Mama Jumbo but stop myself as the sea of faces glancing towards me makes my head dizzy and my stomach begins to lurch.

Suddenly, Mama's voice sounds in my ear, telling me to be like water and my feet, turning to lead inside my tight shoes, comply by lifting off the ground. I reach the podium and grip its sides tightly to steady myself as the MC stands behind me.

I glance down nervously. As explained, a pile of envelopes are there and I scan the text on the back of the one on top and brace myself to speak.

'*Go, Pearl!*' I hear an invisible voice say in the audience and there's a ripple of chuckling which dies down quickly.

201

'Thank you,' I say inexplicably, internally chastising myself as the words swim on the page in a different order as though they're trying to trick me. I feel the weight of the videographer's lens metres away from me and contemplate my awkwardness being captured for all time in his recording. 'In the category of digital photography, the winner is Abimbola Olawale,' I announce, relieved when the applause drowns out my voice that was no louder than a whisper.

The winner's hand trembles as she takes the envelope from me, the one containing the details of her grant or perhaps even the prize money itself. We could be classmates; she's no older than me as we exchange a knowing look about our shared fear of this public scrutiny.

As she races through her thank-you speech, I sneak a glance at our table, where Auntie Bisi and Mama Jumbo are beaming proudly in my direction. My stomach roars powerfully, my hunger announcing itself now that my time in the spotlight is mercifully over. I look around sharply and apologetically at the MC standing beside me, but if he'd noticed my growling belly a moment ago, he doesn't react. His gaze is fixed on the worn notes in his hand that are his guide throughout the ceremony.

After a series of uncomfortable photographs are taken of all of us, presenters and winners, we're finally free to return to our tables. There's a murmur of approval as I return to my seat from the others at our table and I bask in their adoration while waiting for the food to appear on the buffet tables arranged on one side of the hall. Servers posted behind each silver platter are ready for us at the long table but are still no match for national greed as they field shouts from men and women haggling over portion sizes and particular pieces of meat from the laid-out spread.

Not long after we've eaten and drunk, the mood around the table begins to stiffen. After repeated attempts to engage me in conversation, Helen extends her reach to Auntie Bisi and Mama Jumbo, who give her the experience she's been after, providing her with more information about life where we live. Helen explains that she works for some clean water initiatives with projects all over the world and is interested in learning more about the difficulties we face on the lagoon. I lean back in my chair as I pick through a jollof rice drier than the Sahara desert and let the women talk across me as if I'm not there. It's when one woman across from Mama Jumbo makes a face while Auntie Bisi's talking that Mama Jumbo sparks.

'I beg your pardon!' Mama Jumbo snaps at the woman who hasn't spoken. Her face – already light from bleaching creams – is rendered paler from being addressed directly. Her mouth opens either with fear or indignation before she glances at her husband by her side, who shrugs dismissively before devouring the large piece of beef on his plate.

'*Ozugo, Agatha*—' Auntie Bisi engages her Igbo to stop Mama Jumbo from exploding, but Helen disarms the situation by asking the woman sitting between Mama Jumbo and the scowler a question about the fabric she's wearing.

I watch as Mama Jumbo's upper body shakes like a bird whose feathers have been ruffled. She delivers another long eye to the woman who annoyed her – who at least has had the good sense to quickly rearrange the disgust on her face while lowering her gaze – and when the woman and her husband return to the buffet table to restock their plates, Mama Jumbo speaks the words that have been bubbling within her.

'*See* her . . . Acting as though her shit doesn't stink. Meanwhile, we're the ones that watch it floating by in our water,' she says irritatedly to Aunty Bisi.

Before we leave the event, Helen pulls Auntie Bisi aside for a brief conversation while Mama Jumbo and I contemplate collecting some of the flower displays before deciding against it.

'What did that one want?' Mama Jumbo asks when Auntie Bisi returns, looking overwhelmed.

'To exchange contacts. She says she wants to try and help spread awareness about the community now that Baby is getting attention. I'll believe it when I see it,' Auntie Bisi answers with a twist of her lips that Mama Jumbo mirrors before she and I escape to the toilets. The toilets are almost more impressive than the auditorium itself as I drink in the cool white tiles of the fresh-smelling room with its long bank of sinks and mirrors and the wooden doors of the individual cubicles that we disappear behind to do our business. Sitting down, I wrestle a laugh about the fact that the cubicle is more exciting to me than the whole dinner, but at the sound of Mama Jumbo's flush, I pull myself together and exit.

'Remember, Baby, no nonsense when we get to the hotel. You hear me?' she asks my reflection in the mirror beside me.

'*No o,* Auntie,' I reply faithfully.

'It's our secret,' she continues, referencing the situation with Prince that only she knows about. 'So, you are trusting me . . . But I'm trusting you too.'

Mama Jumbo falls asleep as soon as the car arranged to take us to the Viceroy sets into motion. Her head rolls back and her face lifts towards the car roof before deep snores leave her mouth, no doubt a preview of our night together in the hotel.

The bright lights of Lagos are like a masquerade, a riot of colours and sound. Even at night, everything's still going on; the people on the streets, cars rushing on the road, the smell of petrol and suya penetrating the lowered window on the driver's side as he sticks his arm out to conduct traffic. My eyes power back up when the car stops moving. I must have been dozing next to Mama Jumbo, but suddenly I realise we're at the gates of the hotel before we're ushered through by two men in uniform. I send Prince a text as Mama Jumbo stirs to life and begins to try and reposition her head-tie that has drifted to the left before we exit the vehicle.

The driver removes our bags from the car's boot, and even before he can drop them on the pavement, a man runs out from inside the hotel to collect them. Although the driver looks at us as we hover by the car's side, he doesn't ask us for any money before climbing back inside the nice motor and departing.

The young woman on reception in the maroon uniform is very polite as Mama Jumbo declares us in front of an impressive-looking counter.

'Yes, I have your booking. Everything has been arranged,' the desk clerk explains while staring at me approvingly as if I'm Genevieve Nnaji instead of a canoe taxi driver from the ghetto. 'Emmanuel will take your things up. If you just follow him?' she adds, pointing to the man whose bottom is so sharp inside the tight confines of his trousers that it threatens to burst through the sheerest of linings.

I hold my breath inside the lift as the doors close and magically carry us to the fourth floor, where our room is located. Mama Jumbo closes the door behind Emmanuel calmly as though we're not in Ikeja but in her house, stinking of diesel and smoking fish, but my eyes inside my head are screaming. The beige room is easily the size of all our bedrooms combined. In it, there's a black dresser that looks like polished glass, over which is a television. There are two large beds in the room, not the one I'd been anticipating occupying with Mama Jumbo where her snores would roll directly into my ear. But there's easily space for my mattress in Makoko to lie between the two beds so white and soft they look as though they're moulded out of pounded yam.

From the corner of my eyes, I glimpse Mama Jumbo as she pushes open the door to the bathroom before closing it behind her. It's a spectacle of glass, marble tiles and mirrors. The shower floor is so long, I could happily sleep there, should Mama's snores prove too much in the middle of the night.

My phone pings, alerting me to a new message, as I'm running my hands over the white bed cover but I'm far too busy adoring the hotel room.

'*Baby!*' Mama Jumbo booms as she exits the bathroom. The head-tie is now in her hands and her ear-length twists are on full display. 'Answer your phone! That must be Prince. What are you waiting for?' she says, pointing towards my mobile on the dresser and eyeing me as though I'm one mumu. 'If you're not back in one hour, heaven help you!'

I grab my phone and handbag and race for the door. While waiting for the lift to arrive, I read the message from Prince, telling me to meet him by the telephone bank near the reception desk downstairs.

When I reach the exit door at the end of the corridor, it flies open and there is Prince, so handsome in his black uniform.

'*Psst!*' he hisses, beckoning me towards him with his fingers. '*Yepa!* Na you, Baby? I mean, *really*! See your fine hair! You are a top model,' he drools after flicking his fingers dramatically before laughing as he twirls me around briefly to admire my red dress from all angles.

'Stop it,' I laugh, feeling my skin tingle everywhere his eyes land.

'Where's your auntie?' he asks, peeking behind me at the still-empty corridor.

'It's okay, she's upstairs, but time no dey plenty,' I reply.

Taking me by the hand, he leads me outside into the velvet air that covers me like a blanket after all the artificial air conditioning of the hotel's luxury interior. The chirp of crickets welcomes me from inside the cropped hedges as we follow the row of spotlights around the courtyard to settle in the far corner of the seating area. A couple that appear to be guests are huddled together on a single lounge chair, but the only occupants of the wide paving stoned terrace seem to be staff, engaged in a late-evening barbecue. The scent of onions over open flames causes my mouth to slick with saliva as we approach and I feel their attention turn towards us as Prince puffs out his chest before pulling me a fraction in front of him by way of introducing me to his friends and colleagues.

'Aha, the Pearl don come!' a man brandishing the barbecue tongs pronounces, pointing them towards me and the small gathering bursts into laughter as we join them before they pull both Prince and myself into a warm conversation.

They make jokes about my celebrity status, but it's less about me and more to tease Prince affectionately. He wears the mockery proudly as he boldly threads one arm around my waist. The music coming out of one member of the staff's phone is tinny but just enough to soften the mood as they unwind at the close of the night. Once we finish our snack, Prince pulls me away towards the small, illuminated garden to steal some alone time before Mama Jumbo sends security guards after me.

As we dwell in the darkness, I remove my shoes to feel the grass beneath my feet. Prince watches in silence as I press my toes into the soft, yielding ground and, for a moment, think of my life over water back home.

'*Why?*' I ask out loud as his shadow moves towards me and he traces both my shoulders gently with his hands.

'Why wetin?'

'Why is this happening to me?' I ask of the sudden weirdness of my life.

Strangers know my face and my name. People are inviting me to things and celebrating me as if I'm a national holiday. I'd always wanted something unique, but maybe this was *too* different. As exciting as this sudden notoriety is, it's even more terrifying and I allow my guard to slip.

I watch Prince reading the fear on my face with his finger-tips before he leans forward to kiss me. His lips taste of the onion and orange of the barbecue marinade.

'Does it matter?' he asks as I lower my head against his chest and inhale his scent.

His heart pounds away underneath me at a rapid pace. 'Maybe because of SARS, the eyes of the world are upon us, or because your beauty is captivating,' he adds before I pinch him playfully. 'In Makoko, do fishermen ask why the fish enter their nets or are they simply grateful for the catch?' he continues wisely and I digest his question in silence before he pushes me away a little to get a good look at my face.

'It's okay to be afraid, but don't ask *why* is what I'm saying. Just enjoy your moment, Baby. It doesn't come for everyone,' Prince says quietly before pulling me into his arms.

15

Once again, the house is full of people. Every time I think that the news has subsided about my picture in the paper and the interviews, more visitors appear. Today, thankfully, it's mostly family. Auntie Uche arrives along with Dura, her husband and their three children that Afo and Kemi run around with before crowding the baby, prodding it carefully as if she's a toy they're waiting to trigger into action. The whole house is fragrant with the smell of Auntie Bisi's cooking – newly returned home for *urgent* family business – as the aroma of her fish stew boiling fills the air.

As I'm cleaning up the bedroom a little so that the baby can lie down in peace for a few moments, I see the writing pad from the Viceroy peeking out from the edge of Tayo's mattress. I'd given it to Afo as a gift, along with the pen that came in the plush hotel room where we'd stayed. I figured they would come in handy for his drawing. I gave Kemi the packet of biscuits that had been next to one small electric kettle, along with two teabags and a sachet of coffee. She'd polished them off even before her brother had started admiring his present.

I'd kept the small-sized shower gel and soap from the bathroom that smelled like fruity flowers.

I'd updated the girls about the event in Ikeja, along with the stay at Prince's hotel, much to their entertainment. Even Efe managed to put aside her envy to ask questions about every inch of the hotel room and even guests, in case I'd unwittingly come across a star in our short time there. I'd assumed that the reception was the peak of my moment of fame, but then Uncle Jimi had told us about his call with Auntie Bisi over dinner and the letter that'd arrived for me through her job in Ikoyi from Helen, the woman who had sat at our table at the art awards. Auntie Bisi had been beaming ever since as if she'd received a letter from the Queen of England!

'Wetin be Davos?' Auntie Uche asks for the benefit of anyone who might have been missing over the last two days of rehashing the invitation that had been bestowed upon me.

'It's a place. In *Swizza Land*,' Auntie Bisi replies with a confidence clearly coming from her phone calls with Helen since Auntie Bisi never went beyond primary two in school. 'A big meeting is taking place there every year—'

'The World Economic Forum,' Dura reads slowly off the letter Auntie Bisi has passed around the living room as if it's a diploma.

'*Eeehn*,' Auntie Bisi nods before rising once again to check on her cooking.

'And you will be presenting there or what?' Dura eyeballs me as I come back into the living room to scoop the snoozing baby up from her lap.

'*No!*' I shout, louder than I should for one holding a baby, but thankfully, Cindy doesn't fret.

My niece's eyelashes flutter open for a millisecond before she falls back asleep as I cradle her gently against my shoulder. I can't help the thought that appears as I fleetingly imagine my sister and her husband lying together. Tokunbo with nostrils so large that one toilet roll can easily enter. Father, forgive me; I don't know how she does it.

'They want a convoy from Makoko to attend, including Baby because of her *profile*,' Uncle Jimi explains, pride deepening his voice across the room. 'Top academics, politicians and businessmen from all over the world will be there discussing! We have a chance to bring global attention to Makoko,' he adds, looking over at Papa, who has remained silent but has been taking out his frustration on his peanuts this whole time.

'Up you, Baby!' Auntie Uche says approvingly and Uncle Jimi grunts in confirmation.

'Who dey go from Makoko?' Dura asks before I disappear to settle my niece on my mattress.

'That is what we need to decide,' Auntie Bisi explains. 'There will be four in all.'

'What about passports?' Dura says, going through the same range of questions that sprang to our minds when Auntie Bisi first told us of the offer.

'Na, the H2All people go handle all of that . . . So long as they have birth certificates, they will arrange all their papers before the trip in mid-January.'

Dura shakes her head as if something has come loose inside her skull. Then she begins to laugh until tears pour from her eyes. Everyone joins in except Papa who's biting on a peanut forcefully as if it's my head he's picturing between his teeth.

'Baby! In *Swizza Land*? In the abroad? *Hyah*! Luck has always fallen on you,' my sister says, springing from her chair suddenly to put me in a gentle headlock. It's a little too tight for praise, so I wonder if her subconscious is inflicting small pain out of jealousy.

'Nothing is decided yet,' Papa's voice cuts through the air of jubilation like a dagger. The mood changes so swiftly that Cindy feels it in the other room and begins to cry. Dura releases me and moves on instinct, but I'm quicker on my feet.

'Let me go,' I tell her as I hurry to the bedroom to gather her child in my arms. As I stare down at Cindy, I thank her wordlessly for allowing me to escape the tension of the living room and hope she fusses for a while so that I have an excuse to linger.

The lagoon is choppy when I leave to meet Charlie Boy. I imagine it echoes my insides, the ebb and flow of my worries as I contemplate a journey overseas.

When I see him, the world falls away and it's just me and my brother. No commotion related to my viral explosion, no drama from trying to cultivate a relationship in secret. I feel bad for neglecting him a little recently, but he doesn't appear to mind. I'm unchanged in his eyes, despite my brush with fame. I like that I'm the only version of Baby he knows.

Charlie Boy is stunned into silence when I tell him about the invitation to attend the World Economic Forum conference alongside big people in society. He's less focused on the event itself but the fact that in order to get there, I'll need to get on a plane.

'Are you *joking* me?' he says, at last, blinking as he returns from his blank state. 'We're *really* going on a plane?'

'Yes, we are,' I laugh in spite of my sincerity. But the situation *is* comical.

All the years we've spent looking up at planes and fantasising about something that's out of our grasp, and now it has fallen in my lap by pretending to be a Dream Girl.

'Are *you* afraid of going up there?' Charlie Boy points up towards the cloudless sky above us and I shake my head somewhat unconvincingly.

'Maybe it no dey happen,' I reveal heavily before his excitement topples our canoe over. 'I know what Papa will say,' I add, waving a mosquito away from my ear.

'No, Baby! We have to go!' Charlie Boy scoffs before going quiet, his deepest desire all at once extinguished. Even he has no words of encouragement to cover me from the killjoy that is Papa.

'You know what Mama would say,' he replies at last as the dim light of a trawler in the distance illuminates the dark edges of our vision.

I *do* know, as I cast my glance across the never-ending water that surrounds us. If any part of me wanted to chicken out, I'm more determined to go now I've seen my brother's enthusiasm. Still, I have absolutely no idea how to use feminine wiles to break Papa's rock.

Although we don't know the family too well, Idunnu, Efe and I attend their naming ceremony for the free chop. It's a plan that backfires since Oluwa's house stands close to a generous mound of refuse, the smell of which drifts over on the breeze, spoiling the taste of the rice they've put out in enormous plastic coolers.

'Baby, it really isn't up to your father,' Idunnu says over the noise coming from the drummer *konkoronko-ing* not too far away from us. 'Efe was right a while ago . . . This is bigger than you now. This is about the community. Even if he wants to say no, the elders will insist—'

'Won't they have the same mind as him?' I ask as the beat from the drum gets louder.

'If so, they would not have allowed the mapping to take place,' Idunnu replies as Efe makes her way back to us, clutching three bottles of soft drink. 'He's just gesturing the way Papa dey do . . .' she explains while squeezing my arm. '*Look,* our people are stuck in the past, but not all the leaders. After all, it's not corrupt Naija government, but *international,*' she continues, stressing the word. 'It's a chance to—'

Her sentence is swallowed up by Efe's return at a lightning pace.

'Your future husband don reach,' Efe announces cheekily, glancing back over her shoulder before distributing our drinks. I spot Samson making his way through the gathering.

215

I slide my body instantly towards the floor to hide. It's not enough that he'd shown up to the meal at our home at Papa's invitation, much to my aunties' and my sister's delight, but now he was here where I was safe from my family's reach. Strategically sandwiched between Kemi and Afo while he sat close to Uncle Jimi and Papa, I'd tried to conjure up an imaginary future with me as his wife – admittedly a much better situation than Dura's portion – but my brain had filled with black lagoon water that had been impossible to see through. Thankfully, Tayo had been absent and Papa couldn't draw any attention over my cooking as Auntie Bisi had prepared the entire spread. Samson had been sweating so much even before ingesting Auntie's peppery fish stew that I'd half expected water to flow between my toes under the table as he quietly flooded our house.

'Baby has no time for Samson,' Idunnu says, marching to my defence and bringing me back to the present. Something chooks my leg on the floor, but I don't dare move in case he spots me.

'Her papa get time . . . But maybe you can ask Samson to talk to your daddy? He might listen to his future son-in-law!' Efe yaps viciously.

In the darkness of the decrepit bar Prince and I are sitting in, Makoko feels like a universe away. The lettering on Prince's T-shirt has started to fade so that the *POWER* reads more like *POW*. Either way, he's handsome enough to pull it off. As he tips his head to one side to ogle me, I chase away the guilt

I feel over the thought of using Samson small small to help me with Papa. Any attention I pay him will be viewed as encouragement – as will Samson, making my case for me – but the more we'd discussed the idea of using a man to try and shift Papa's position among ourselves at the naming party, the more it made sense in my mind.

'How long would you go for?' Prince asks, using his finger to clean his sunglass lens before reaching for my wrist.

'The conference is four days but there are events before and after that. And there is also the trip to Italy—'

'I thought it was just Switzerland you were travelling to?'

'They are neighbours now.' I explain my recently acquired geography quickly as disappointment hijacks Prince's features momentarily. 'And how can we not see the *real* Venice while we are so close?' I say, repeating Helen's words per the invite. When I bite down, it's on trepidation rather than excitement.

'*Water Baby*,' Prince sighs as his knee taps against my own underneath our table. We watch a fly tracing a clear square outline dizzily on the tabletop.

'I know,' I reply, echoing his sigh.

At Auntie Bisi's insistence, we've used some of my interview money on a new stove and dining table. The old one was leaning too much to one side so that things would slide off. After many years of trying to even out its legs, Auntie has declared that's enough.

We all received some new clothes too; a pair of jeans for me that are light blue and cover my ankle while Kemi got a new shirt and both Tayo and Afo got trousers. Even Papa hasn't remained angry all the time, since this good fortune is infectious. He treated himself to a new mattress and dashed the old one to Afo, who's been ecstatic with his bounty. No more having to suffer with Tayo or begging for the edges of our own. Of course, now there's barely any visible floor around the three foam linings. Still, it's a small price to pay for his comfort.

Tayo is publicly exhibiting good behaviour the way he does when Auntie Bisi is around. He's even been less of an irritant to me now that people are knowing me, but you can never tell with him. His association to me has brought him more notoriety among his mates and no doubt more cough medicine, only he's no longer storing the empty bottles inside our bedroom.

When Uncle Jimi returns from work, he brings out his new radio from the bedroom and floods the living room with music. It's a rare sight, one typically viewed at Christmas or at weddings, but witnessing Auntie Bisi drunk is a spectacle to behold.

Afo and Kemi are sufficiently embarrassed by their parents swaying in front of us to Ebo Taylor before the rhythm overtakes them too and they join in with the dancing. Papa's too stiff in body and in mind to participate, but his toes tap in time to the music as bottle after bottle of beer falls at his happy feet.

I start to remember when we were smaller in our house before they chopped it down. Papa would play his radio loudly in his bedroom and Mama would sing while she finished cleaning. Her syrupy voice was like a balm that would calm the household and send Charlie Boy, me and Dura to sleep before they started to make jiggy-jiggy in their room.

Before sleep would catch me, I would listen to the lyrics of the songs she sang back to Papa as he waited for her, wondering what this big love felt like and wishing to be old and happy like them. I never once thought that I would lose Mama so early. More shocking still was that after she passed, the gruff but playful Papa we knew as children would cease to exist.

As the booze and soft drinks flow during the celebration of our windfall, shaking the stresses out by the movement of our bodies, I glance at Papa, whose face almost looks relaxed. Our gazes meet and for one split second, I think I see him, the younger him from those days, whose pupils would sparkle like glitter before breaking out into reluctant laughter on the odd occasion Mama would put him in his place with a sarcastic word. Papa sees me too and for a moment, my heart swells at this brief episode of familial closeness that even Tayo has joined in with, despite his effort centring mostly on finishing off what's left of the yam porridge.

I want to tell Papa that I'm still here, that I'm still me – his Baby – but I can't find the words. I hadn't even noticed his disappearance at first; we'd all been too devastated by Charlie Boy's death to discern the transformation and gradual detachment in my father. And could anyone blame him? He'd already lost so much. Is it any wonder he didn't feel like holding onto anything else too tightly after that?

Then, just as quickly as it was cast, the spell is broken. For a moment, my brother's image is reflected briefly in Papa's eyeballs before they turn back to granite while my aunt and uncle chuckle beside him.

I wake to the sound of boats passing on the canal. Prising one eye open, I watch a parade of canoes pass by, carrying the same cargo: sticks of bamboo destined for a house-build somewhere nearby. The five occupants of those boats make enough noise to chase away the dream I was holding onto and I stretch myself fully awake before I notice the itch from the mosquito that has bitten its way down the length of my arm as I slept on the deck. The heat of the day hasn't yet descended, but the sunlight hitting the water gives it a tangerine glow as a hawker beckons over to me as she passes in the water with a boatload of goods.

Auntie Bisi makes an appearance and asks me to help wake up the children now that we have some money to send them to school. In the bedroom, Afo's sleeping like a king on his new mattress, a star shape with his arms behind his head in a way that makes me smile as I rock his body steadily until his eyes open.

'Time for bath,' I tell him before I move over to Kemi and do the same. Tayo must have slipped out at some time during the night, hopefully without opening his mouth to Papa about Prince.

When they are both ready and have eaten, I ferry my cousins to school. Still buoyed by the household's party mood, I listen to them playing 'I spy' as we cross the lagoon before tiring of the game and trying to invent a song in my honour, the chorus of which is repeated chants of Pearl of Makoko.

After dropping them off, I take my time returning home. From my position on the waterway, as I approach, I can hear the shouting emanating from our house and slow down the canoe. There's time for me to row away from whatever argument is taking place inside. Sure enough, it concerns me and this trip to Europe. But despite my fear, I dock the canoe and board the deck gingerly.

Papa rushes noisily out of the house but stops when he sees it's me. Turning back on his heels, I follow him into the house, which has lost the morning peace I left it in. I notice immediately that the sparse items in the living room have been scattered and a pile of Papa's belongings have formed a messy mound in the narrow corridor.

Uncle Jimi finishes yelling into his mobile phone before he joins Papa to shout with him in his bedroom while Auntie Bisi moans and mutters like some of the church women speaking in tongues. I manage to bring her out of her trance by pulling on her hand, which was oscillating between beating her breast and bashing her headscarf.

'*What's* vexing everybody? *What has happened?*' I ask frantically.

'*Tayo, Tayo, Tayoooooo,*' Auntie Bisi repeats, winding herself up again so that her bosom shakes.

'What happened to him? Is he okay?' I implore, shaking her arm to get her to focus as fear chills my centre. It's not his addiction I immediately think of, but Charlie Boy's limp body resting on the trash before being raised from the water.

'Is he *okay*?' Papa's voice behind me, repeating my words, makes me jump. His breath is sour from beer and sleep, his mouth is open wide like a bear's. '*No*, that boy is *not* okay,' Papa yells, spit pooling in the corners of his lips, twisted with rage.

'*Dotun*,' Auntie Bisi calls Papa soothingly, in an attempt to calm him as I wait to find out what Tayo has done that has enraged him.

'He better not step foot here again, if he knows what's good for him!' Uncle Jimi adds with anger that matches my father's. 'Or there is truly *madness* in your family!'

'Wetin he do?' I ask quietly and the three of them turn towards me theatrically.

'*He don thief all your papa money*!' Uncle Jimi reveals before the pieces of the puzzle in front of me make sense. The disarray of the house and Papa ransacking his bedroom in search of Mama's satchel, where he keeps important papers and his savings.

My ankles turn to concrete on the living-room floor as the news about what Tayo has done sinks in. The money from my interviews and my appearance at the art show, and whatever else Papa had, is gone. Riding in Tayo's trouser pocket next to his stupid *dodo*, no doubt to be blown on cough medicine with his degenerate friends.

At the baale's house, I kept quiet in the corner as the group of assembled leaders, along with Papa, Uncle Jimi, Auntie Bisi and even Mr Sada from the droning project, discussed the invitation from H2All. Although I'd seen one or two of the community leaders at certain points in life, at church, a thanksgiving ceremony, or perhaps just passing in a boat, it was the first time that I'd viewed these big men up close, dressed in their colourful agbadas with matching hats and their necklaces befitting their status as heads of the various communities around us. Waterside, Egun, Adogbo were all represented. We'd gathered on a well-assembled deck with two fans at different ends blowing air at one another, where we sat underneath the covered awning to protect us from the sun.

My eyes had kept straying to the gold watch on the wrist of our community leader, so elaborate and large that it could no longer be classified as a watch and was closer to the size of a clock on the wall in my old school.

It was Uncle Jimi who'd bought the drinks we came with to show our respect as we informed them of the NGO's proposal about Davos and to hear their wisdom on the affair.

Things were still tense at home after Tayo's abscondment. Papa had ordered me to track him down, but none of his layabout friends had seen him and of course he wasn't picking up anyone's calls. I can't lie that I was less bothered by his running away after the shock of his theft had worn off. Tayo was trouble and with him gone, he couldn't give me any more. At least he had vanished without revealing what he knew about me and Prince.

I'd gone to the canteens he frequented close to the shipping yard and the entertainment centre with the pool table and loud computer games that jobless wonders spent all day at, all to no avail. Then I'd tried some of his friends' places, but the ones that I could find had no information worth sharing. It was only when I'd returned home after the fruitless day of searching that my brain had started chooking me about my own hiding place in the bedroom and I went to check it feverishly. Even before my hands reached for the limp, wrapped pouch, I knew that my money was gone.

Papa wanted to find Tayo not just to recover the money, which would have been good, but to teach him a lesson. Thieves were paraded around the community to alert people to their actions and to shame them. It had proved a surprisingly effective deterrent within Makoko. A part of me had wondered, as I searched fruitlessly for Tayo, whether he'd disappeared before he could be publicly labelled and potentially shunned. I suspected it was the side of me that still hoped for Uncle Jimi's nephew to be redeemable. If he was worried about his perception, then perhaps a grain of good remained.

Although Tayo's misbehaviour had plunged the house into a sullen silence, it had ironically helped to advance my situation, now that Papa's savings had been wiped out.

'You're even lucky you have people advocating on your behalf. If it was up to me, you wouldn't go,' he'd declared stubbornly while accepting his bowl of gari, before finally giving in.

His reluctance about the trip was overridden by the money the organisation was prepared to pay to compensate for our attendance, not to mention the daily stipends and whatever the exposure would bring. Samson hadn't needed to work his magic by the time he came to the house to speak to Papa about Switzerland. Tayo's theft had dynamited a bit of Papa's rock, leaving him surprisingly vulnerable.

'This is a great great thing,' the Egun community leader expressed after Uncle Jimi had spoken on Papa's behalf. Papa couldn't muster the enthusiasm in his voice to speak for the family, but Uncle Jimi was a worthy orator in his own right.

An approving murmur followed from all the leaders as they took turns reading the letter whose contents had already been made clear.

'We would be on the world stage. Have the world's ear—'

'But what is important is to remember what we *want*. And that is education for our children and a hospital,' our leader said before another flurry of rapid-fire exchange took place.

That they were up for the invite was so apparent, Papa had made no attempt to challenge them. He sat back in his chair between Auntie and Uncle as though he was their child. In his mind, I'm sure he was thinking of all the ways to beat Tayo if he ever got hold of him again.

'Iyawa is *far*! And the health centre they are supposedly building is too far as well,' I heard the man in the lavender and grey print complaining so vigorously that the sound of his gold bead necklace reminded me fleetingly of Mama Jumbo. In the universe's comedic timing, a woman had crossed the lagoon in front of us in a canoe filled with produce. Her voice boomed out of the black megaphone she pressed to her lips, securing her competitive edge over nearby hawkers in the water.

'Are we not fishermen? Don't we contribute to the economy of the state? We must have a say in these things that affect us—' another leader chimed in, echoing the sentiment.

'*Agreed*! We must think about our priorities and find the right people to allow us to achieve our ends,' Egun's stately head declared before our community leader raised his hand and silenced the conversation.

'*Yemoja,*' he'd said, addressing me directly for the first time, and I pulled my gaze away from his watch to face him. 'You have brought this unexpected attention to us and we are grateful. Your father has raised you and named you well,' he added, bestowing a warm smile at me before facing Papa.

'Allow us to discuss the matter more seriously. We will determine the two people who will represent the community on a higher level in Switzerland. That will leave Yemoja – who they've invited as well – and one other for you to choose to go with her on the trip. Come back tomorrow for our decision.'

16

I'm pulled from my sleep by the unmistakable sound of my name. Rubbing my eyes, I glance at both Kemi and Afo bathed in moonlight from outside. They're sleeping serenely and the room feels lighter with Tayo's absence despite the circumstances. I sit up and pitch my ears towards my doorway, but the rest of the household is silent. Lying back on the mattress, I'm on the verge of dreaming when I hear my name again: *Yemoja*. Even though everyone knows not to do it, I answer. It's a superstition we believe in, that to answer a call without seeing the person is to respond to a ghost. Don't I do that anyway, with my brother? I peer into the darkness, waiting to see if any response appears. It's Mama's frame I'm hoping to emerge before the weight of my eyelids pulls me under.

With Auntie Bisi in the house over the last few days, I realise how much I'm missing Mama during this time. She'd know what to do, how best to soothe Papa, still seething from the injustice carried out by Tayo but brought about by me and my picture inside the newspaper. When you draw a line to

Papa's misfortune, one end of it always arrives at my person, or so it seems.

As I clean my face in the bathroom, I'm shocked when I see the reflection in the mirror is less my own and more Mama's before a trickle of soapy water clouds my vision. I hadn't realised how much I'd changed over the past few months, how I'm resembling her more and more as proven by my magnified face in the newspaper. I stare at myself in the broken pane, wondering whether this resemblance is contributing to Papa's inability to look at me these days. Is my behaviour just a disappointment, or am I a walking reminder of the things he's lost?

I almost choke on my ogi when Papa declares that Samson is to be my companion to Switzerland. As the breath leaves my body and dots appear before my vision, I will myself not to pass out on the edge of the deck. Too much time will be lost if I escape this moment by fainting and I need to be alert to lodge my protest.

'Isn't it supposed to be people who are speaking English?' I blurt out while frantically thinking up a million logical objections to the prospect of going abroad with Samson. I would rather stay here and join Dura in the market until the day I die!

'Must he talk to everyone? He will be there for *you*!' Papa huffs satisfactorily as if his decree must be carried out, before requesting I fetch him a soft drink so that he can dilute his tonic.

We have no more soft drink at home, so I take one of the rickety paths between the houses to go and buy some bottles from Sojemi, who sells drinks from her house. If I opt to take the canoe out, I might drift out on the lagoon and never return.

It's not possible. There's no way Papa really wants me to go away with Samson. I'm convinced it might even be his way to get me not to go on the trip at all, or else he's trying to push me into wedding. It's a good strategy because if I refuse to travel – or tell him about Prince – then I'll remain here within striking distance for him to push his marriage agenda, and if I'm not going, then what is Samson doing in the abroad?

The community leaders had decided overnight who to pick for the trip, informing Papa and Uncle Jimi when they returned the next day that our community leader's son would be going, along with Dr Hariri from the general clinic. They thought it would be wise to have a doctor there as part of the group to speak in a professional capacity about the health challenges for the people of Makoko. Since that decision had been made, all that remained was who would escort me on the trip. Even prior to any discussion taking place at home, I knew that neither Papa nor Uncle Jimi nor Auntie Bisi had any intention of setting one foot on an aeroplane, not to mention foreign soil.

I'd broached the subject with Mama Jumbo when I'd gone to work, noticing her slightly relaxed attitude towards me since we attended the art show together, so that we talked more than we worked during my shift as she caught up with how things were changing in my life. It had been so subtle, this slide from employer to confidante, that I'd never seen it coming, grateful though I was for its appearance. Mama Jumbo wasn't the surrogate mother figure I'd been expecting in life, but maybe Mama had had a plan when she'd asked her and Auntie Uche to watch over us.

Of course, Mama Jumbo had rejected my invitation to accompany me to Switzerland, waving the offer away as though it was a cockroach flying in her direction.

'A whole me, *keh*, on a trip over there?' She shook her head, setting off her entire orchestra. 'Who will look after my empire?' She'd laughed, spreading her bejewelled fingers out in front of her to sweep the room. It only occurred to me afterwards, as I made my way home, that perhaps she didn't have a birth certificate that would allow the organisers to procure the paperwork necessary for the trip.

I listen to the idle conversation around me as I'm queueing to buy drinks at Sojemi's makeshift kiosk. Children are running around everywhere, circumventing rubbish while causing destruction. A naked boy with a swollen stomach chases after his older siblings in vain before the stern hand of his father pulls him off his feet. Another woman is bathing a newborn girl in a shallow red bowl outside. Her daughter's repeated little whimpers remind me of a kid goat.

I buy the soft drinks and make my way back home slowly, contemplating whether there's a tonic I can give Papa to make him forget this nonsense with Samson. Or if I'm lucky, Samson will have an accident that takes him out of the running. As I'm fantasising about the demise of one or the other, my

not-quite-dream from last night comes back to me suddenly –
me calling out to Mama during my sleep – and I lose my footing in a puddle.

My right leg is soaked in my new denim, but I don't care; a
light has gone on inside my brain as an idea comes to me. I
know it's from Mama, so I thank her quietly as I run the rest of
the way home with the drinks clinking inside the carrier bag
in my hand. My heart races as I enjoy the lightness of my step.

My water alone might not be enough, but I see now a way
to break Papa's rock.

In the late afternoon, I take Auntie Bisi to the market to do
some proper shopping. We're alone in the canoe and I use the
opportunity to speak to her unguarded.

'Auntie Bisi,' I begin cautiously, 'what do you want for
Kemi when she is grown?'

'To be learned, of course. For her to have an education and
a job . . .' she answers pensively, squinting at a massive pile of
dirt in the water. 'But I want my children to be happy,' she
adds before letting out a deep sigh.

'You think Papa feels the same way about me?' I question,
rowing us away from the children drifting in small buckets on
the lagoon. Auntie Bisi affects a kind of half-nod but doesn't
say anything with words. 'Well, Samson no go make me
happy,' I confess loudly, my mouth trembling with the weight
of my revelation.

'*Ah*, then you must tell your papa that—'

'How can he even ask Samson to go to Switzerland with me?'

'*Baby,* your father is your father . . . Not to say he will always get sense. It is hard for him to see you as a woman,' Auntie Bisi reveals before shooting a well-aimed spittle bullet into the water.

'It is hard for men to see women at all,' I reply gravely. 'But everywhere you look in Makoko, *women dey.* Is it not so? So why should I be the only woman going?' I ask.

Something in my tone reaches Auntie Bisi, whose expression changes as her head nods conspiratorially with me. 'What does that say to the outside world looking at us?' I continue slowly, bringing the canoe to a stop on the water.

'It's a true—'

'Auntie, the mapping project . . . *Shey* it was young *girls* they chose to do it! To give us opportunity and skills. Not just because we're young but because we're women. We're in a fishermen's community but the future, the future of *Makoko,* is female,' I declare passionately like a politician drunk on the sound of their own voice.

Auntie Bisi straightens up in the boat and watches me with what looks like admiration on her face.

'You want me to talk to him?' she proposes as a nearby boat moves towards us. We wave to the passersby in a boat that has been badly battered by the elements. As the man inside steers, a woman is scooping out water pooling at the bottom of the boat with an enamel cup. I imagine, without her action, they would be submerged in a matter of minutes.

'Well?' Auntie asks again once we're alone on the water.

'I do, but will that be enough?' I say diplomatically before reaching for the thing I really wanted from her. 'I know if

it comes from the community leader, he will listen to him,'
I propose innocently while Auntie Bisi scratches away
furiously at something caught between the folds of her
wrapper.

She loses herself in her thoughts for so long that I feel my
hopes ebb as they prepare for imminent disappointment.
Reaching for the oars, I ease them into the black water and
bring us back into motion.

'Auntie?' I call, rousing her from her reverie.

'Maybe, maybe not, he might listen,' Auntie Bisi replies at
last. 'But who *does* every leader listen to?' she adds enigmatic-
ally as a playful look washes over her face.

Mrs Elsie Akinbami, our community leader's wife, is an
elegant beauty. Despite being on the leaner side, a youthful
plumpness to her face and upper body indicate living well. I
imagine that, standing next to her husband, they'd look like
the number ten in human form.

It was through Mama Jumbo's grapevine that we'd confirmed
her regular church of worship. Then, assured of Mrs Akinbami's
attendance, Auntie Bisi and I got decked out in our nice regalia
and headed out to the Friday evening service at Christ the
Redeemer to try and catch her.

As the priest commands us to rid ourselves of every burden
and sin, I crane my neck to better admire Mrs Akinbami's
bronze lipstick from where we're sitting. It doesn't look like
gloss, but as though the sun setting behind her is gently kissing
her lips as it fades into the background. She'd been wearing

sunglasses when she arrived, ones with tortoiseshell frames so pronounced it seemed as though an animal was holding onto her nose before she removed them.

Auntie Bisi surrenders to the service, but I fidget beside her, wondering how we will make it to Mrs Akinbami when church has ended. What if she isn't a lingerer? Will I be stuck on a canoe in the real Venice with Samson as my escort? The thought is enough to make me catch the Holy Ghost like the woman on the end of our bench, twitching like a handkerchief in front of a fan.

'What we can be assured of, however, is whatever awaits all mortals upon death is the love of Christ,' the priest says to a hearty chorus of amens.

Latching onto his voice, I try to follow his words, but they pull me through a maze that closes in on me and before I know it, Auntie Bisi's shaking me awake to stand for God's blessing at the end of the service. Everyone's on the move then, but Auntie's hand in mine is like a vice as she cuts through the throng in front of me and pulls us towards Mrs Akinbami as she finishes off a conversation with the priest.

'Good evening, Ma,' Auntie Bisi traps her with her voice and a slight curtsey, and I do the same behind her. 'Can we please have a word? This is Yemoja, the Pearl of Makoko—'

'Oh *yes!* Yemoja,' Mrs Akinbami says warmly in an astonishingly deep voice as she turns towards me. 'Your family was at our place a few days ago, correct?'

'Yes, Ma,' Auntie Bisi replies quickly. 'It was that we wanted to talk with you about,' she adds as we veer to one side of the church, away from the noise of our neighbours, so that we can chat in peace.

'As you are aware, your husband has already chosen two people to represent Makoko overseas. Yemoja is to go along with a companion. Her father would like her to attend with another boy, but we feel like Makoko would be better served by a *woman* appearing alongside her,' Auntie Bisi preaches before pushing me forward to stand between her and the community leader's wife.

'Yes, Ma,' I butt in urgently. 'The world should know we are fishermen and fisher*women* here. After all, it is women cooking and selling the fish! And I am just one face among many! There are plenty other girls like me here,' I complete the phrase I've committed to memory for this moment, hoping that she takes the bait. The air around us throbs with electricity as we await her response.

'I couldn't agree with you more! Is there someone else you have in mind to accompany you to Europe?' she asks.

'My friend, Idunnu,' I say immediately. She's the only person I can think of after Mama Jumbo who I'm wanting. Efe is too young, and Maureen is married and would be too much headache. With all Idunnu's lifelong plotting about leaving Makoko, she's the only person I know who has the right documentation and the personality for the road ahead.

'In your wisdom as our leaders, if you feel that greater representation of Makoko's youth and females might be beneficial . . .' Auntie Bisi says before Mrs Akinbami interrupts her gently.

'Leave it with me,' she says with an exaggerated tip of her head. 'I will send word after I've spoken with my husband.'

We've done all we can. The rest is in God's hands. After thanking her profusely, I watch Mrs Akinbami depart before she's swallowed up by other worshippers and we quickly make our escape on the *Charlie-Boy*, like giddy children after the school day has finished.

'Do you think she will talk to him?' I ask Auntie Bisi hopefully while observing evening shadows dancing across the surface of the canal.

'Never underestimate the power of prayer,' Auntie Bisi replies with a knowing wink.

17

'Lagos Babe.' That's what my friends have started calling me due to all the time I've been spending on the mainland. That's how separate our community feels from the city. Curiously, the nickname is just for me, although Idunnu has been here too for the meetings in preparation for our trip in January, along with Jonathan Omotaya Akinbami, the son of our community leader, and Dr Hariri from the general clinic.

H2All have been treating us like dignitaries. A cool car service comes to pick us up and take us to Lekki for their meetings at the Sheraton Hotel conference centre since their main office is in Abuja. These sessions, plus the time I'm stealing to spend with Prince before my travel, have made me less of a mermaid, but I've been telling myself it's practice for the trip to Switzerland. Though from what we've been told, if you squint at the mountains at night, they resemble water rising.

Prince and I are officially boyfriend and girlfriend despite what Maureen and Efe think, that I should be keeping an open mind now that my star has risen. But I know it's a nonsense.

Telling my heart not to *be-doum be-doum* is like telling the sun not to appear again. Try as you might, it's there the moment you open your eyes.

The moment had caught me by surprise that morning in Ebute-Ero. Having successfully negotiated two beautiful guinea fowl from a trader in the market, he'd held them up for my approval as though he'd killed them himself.

'They were the last,' he'd announced triumphantly before stuffing them in his bag for easier transport. 'They're off the market, and so are you,' he declared softly while inspecting my face.

It had taken a moment for his meaning to land. As he'd studied me, I'd glimpsed the vulnerability behind his bravado, the question lurking behind the bold statement. I'd reached out and taken his hand, sealing our pact with our palms, and we'd continued shopping, my head high up in the clouds.

My shiny, new passport is burning a hole in my pocket as I wait for Prince to arrive. I sit at the restaurant next to the Tejuosho Ultra-Modern Shopping centre in Yaba that has quickly become our meeting place. Not for the cheap food, which he complains uses far too much oil, but because it's just outside of Makoko, meaning I don't have to stress about being seen by anyone in my family and he doesn't have to come as far in the slivers of time he has available. I want to remove my passport again, to look at my picture, but I'm nervous as I know it's a precious thing. Who would ever think months ago that *I*, Baby, would have a passport and would be preparing for a trip in the abroad? You can lose your whole mind just thinking about it.

I'm taken aback when he arrives wearing a button-down shirt. Then I remember his interview at a new restaurant opening up on Victoria Island.

'*Oya*, let me see,' Prince asks noisily, drawing the attention of a man eating chin-chin loudly on the bench not too far from us. I laugh and extract the passport from my bag. It's so fresh, so crisp it looks counterfeit.

'My face was shining,' I confess dramatically before his fingers locate my passport photo to reveal the glare of the overzealous photographer that somehow managed to magnify my forehead for the humiliating duration of five years.

Prince chuckles at the picture before handing it back so I can tuck it away.

'I love it! I love you,' he announces suddenly, shocking me as I stand before him. My mouth is temporarily out of service, so I fling my arms around his neck and squeeze him tightly enough to communicate that the feeling is mutual.

'I still no believe you dey travel,' he says with a wistful expression that makes me instantly feel like crying. I've been trying to focus on the excitement of the upcoming trip, especially with Idunnu as my sidekick, but leaving Prince will be hard even though we don't see each other that frequently.

'How was your interview?' I ask, trying to distract us from our unhappiness. He doesn't seem disappointed that I didn't repeat his declaration moments ago. I suspect because he already knows. 'What was the place like?'

'I can't wait until you come back . . . Baby, if you see the inside? This Rendez-vous—'

'Rendez *who*?' I interrupt him as his hands are flying up like a conductor as he prepares to describe the new venue in detail, from its industrial glass and cement facade that somehow looks like an upside-down boat plonked on land to its sleek white interior and dining booths in camel-coloured padded leather. There's even a swimming pool next to the outside bar.

'*Yepa!*' I exclaim dramatically after his epic description of the fusion of African and French cuisine they offer, which finally culminates in him revealing that he got the position. 'Will you remember me when you dey hang out with VIPs on VI?' I tease him, but there is a nervous knot in my belly.

'Na *me* go remember *you*? Says the person leaving here to go and do celebrity tour for outside?' Prince quips loudly. 'Just better return, you hear me?' he warns, reaching out to tap my forehead gently with his forefinger.

'Will you come and collect me if I don't?' I ask him playfully, enjoying the sensation of his touch on my skin.

'You dis girl . . .' Prince lets out an exaggerated sigh before looping his arm territorially around my neck.

Papa has been resigned but respectful after Mr Akinbami's representative came to our house to deliver the news Auntie Bisi and I had prayed for. Not that he'd ever admit it, but I'm sure a part of him was secretly impressed by our coup. Maybe I'm not so much of a baby after all, which is the only way he sees me most of the time.

A spark had switched back on inside Idunnu when I informed her that she was coming with me. She hadn't even taken time to think about her job at the hotel or Moses. She'd just leapt out of her chair to grab and suffocate me with her chest until I begged her to let go.

'Are you *serious*? I can come with you? Na lie, Baby!' she'd repeated over and over until her laughter was replaced by panicked breaths as the realisation that she was, at last, leaving like she'd always wanted.

'Ten days, all expenses paid, *Swizza Land*,' I whooped, pretending to rain money over her like an Afrobeat singer in one of their music videos.

'Wait o!' Idunnu had put a pause on our celebration as a mischievous expression came over her face. 'Let's go and tell Efe,' she'd said before roaring with laughter.

At home, I'd replayed her elation at the prospect of leaving the community, so much more emphatic than my own. We'd fantasised for years, but my moment was coinciding with a new relationship. Was what was waiting on the other side any better than what I currently had? Then I'd thought about Prince's words at the hotel, about it being okay to be afraid. I let my worries bubble gently in the background like a slow-cooking soup and focused on other things.

Time had accelerated rapidly ever since Helen had made the formal invitation for us to come to Europe. I had no idea where those nine weeks had gone. One moment it felt as though January would never reach, but before I knew it, Christmas had come and gone, and Charlie Boy was counting down from ten to ring in the New Year.

'Baby, Baby! The year we fly!' Charlie Boy squealed before holding his arms out wide to mimic a plane's flight.

This trip was as much for him as it was for me. Not just the chance to go up in a plane – even more powerful than a drone – but to experience something beyond what we'd ever imagined. My brother wouldn't grow old, wouldn't catch a fish, or marry. His life had been cut short so senselessly. I felt the pressure of my obligation to him as well as the expectations of the larger community. The people counting on me had grown exponentially since my picture had appeared in the news. I didn't want to let anyone down.

'*Yes-o*,' I agreed, amused by the confusion of his Iron Man-like pose while wearing his Spider-Man T-shirt. 'The year we fly,' I'd repeated dutifully, hoping he didn't catch on to my reservations.

Mama used to say that it's only by knowing hunger that we can appreciate food. She was hoping to teach us patience, or perhaps she was distracting us from the ache we were feeling sometimes, when the fish weren't biting and the money had been small. Either way, she'd been right. There's a sweetness from getting something where before, there was nothing really on the horizon.

As I watched Efe and Maureen over the last few weeks while Idunnu and I prepared for Europe, my long-held views about the two of them started to change. Even though they were my closest friends, I was always dismissing Efe's childish behaviour and Maureen's inability to see beyond herself, but this was no longer true; they'd changed or were in the process of evolving as much as I'd done this year.

Maureen's transformation was inevitable after so many years of wanting to be married. But now that she'd achieved her goal, while she lorded it over us every now and then during our conversations, she also had more time for our own stories. Perhaps married life wasn't as interesting as she'd cracked it up to be. I'd expected Efe to bristle about my extended spotlight and the fact that I'd included Idunnu for the next chapter and not her, but she'd been unexpectedly graceful about the upcoming trip that truly only *she* was prepared for, having spent a lifetime filling her brain with lots of nonsense from magazines in the salon about people from the abroad. She was also the only one with a wardrobe fitting for the road ahead.

Since Tayo had chopped all my money, there was no real way for me to prepare in the way I might have. Even the small stipend H2All had provided for us hadn't gone solely towards preparations for my trip but pressing things for the household that was now running at a deficit, thanks to the person whose name can no longer be said out loud at home.

'What about these?' Idunnu asks, holding a pair of flip-flops in the air at us.

'Don't you know it's cold where you are going? You want to lose your toes?' Efe cackles and shakes her head over Idunnu's ignorance as we sit in her bedroom, watching her assemble the things she plans on taking in her new suitcase.

I'm equally clueless and happy to defer to Maureen and Efe, who guide us towards taking sneakers and covered shoes, even though the ones I have pinch my little toes one way so that when I wear them too long, I start to see Jesus.

They've both brought some of their good clothes to Idunnu's for us to pick from. If they can't go with us abroad, then they live vicariously through us and their borrowed garments for our days mingling with politicians, dignitaries and – if Efe's prayers are realised, TV stars and musicians – who have been known to make an appearance at the big meetings and parties. Not that there's any proof we will be anywhere close to that action.

Idunnu had let me take my pick first of their offerings, not that it mattered as we could share once we got to the other end, but I'd been secretly eyeing Efe's green dress with the low V in the back since she bought it last year and had reached for it, hoping to be transformed into a beauty by the material. Mama Jumbo had already gifted me a pair of black trousers and a wool skirt as well as two sweaters for the cold. And when Auntie Bisi's employer had learned of the trip, she'd given Auntie Bisi a coat for me, one so thick it took up almost half my suitcase, along with a blazer that makes me look like a working professional.

As we focus on fashion, I soak up this rare moment of closeness where we're all together in the way we used to be when we were younger. It's not something I could have considered; the way life has naturally moved us away from each other even though our deep feelings bind us. I'm grateful for their support and momentarily wish they could both come with us; what a trip to be with all my girls in the abroad! But I know it's a temporary feeling. Maureen telling us all how to behave for days on end; I'm not sure which of us would be the first to push her off a Swiss mountain.

'What will you say if they start asking you questions?' Maureen probes as Idunnu is looking at herself in one of Efe's tops that made her breasts look like two eggs inside a frying pan. I'm the only one shaking my head in a 'no' fashion; the other two approve of the slinky top and she throws it to one side on her mattress with the other garments destined for Switzerland.

'That is what the others are there for . . . to speak for the community as a whole—' Idunnu answers, well versed after our mainland meetings about what to expect at the other end.

'The focus na for climate! How the lagoon is changing. How we can get clean water,' I chip in and reach out to catch the headwrap that Idunnu throws towards me. The tropical flower print fabric is so soft, I'll be able to wear it as a scarf as well as on my hair.

'How we will deal with the water level rising on account of Samson's tears once this one has departed,' Efe jokes and I flick the end of the scarf in her direction.

'Any question, we can answer,' Idunnu continues decisively. 'All that matters is we dey go.'

I wake up from a nightmare bathed in sweat and sunlight streaming into the bedroom window. I'd opened the curtain at some point during the night to let more air in before falling back asleep into a series of disturbing dreams. In my final one, it had been Children's Day, the May public holiday, which meant a day off from school for the students in primary or secondary and a day of festivities all over the country, Makoko included. Face-painting, singing and dancing and even the spelling competition we held, the prize of which had been a scholarship a few years ago. I don't remember which NGO had been responsible for it, and apparently neither do they, as it had never made good on its promise.

I'd dreamt that Charlie Boy had been at the God of Salvation Ministry with its small bank of sand next to it that allowed people to occasionally have gatherings there. For whatever reason, this was where the spelling bee in my dream had been taking place. I was sitting between Mama and Papa, watching my brother standing in a line along with his classmates. His teacher was in front of him, prompting him to spell the word *ocean*, and I'd held my breath observing his little mouth pushing out the letters OSUN. I'd flinched inwardly at his mistake, but the crowd around us had exploded into applause, and his teacher had beamed proudly as he was crowned the winner of the competition. The time for awards had come, but when I'd turned to my right, Mama was no longer by my side. Up in front of me, Charlie Boy too had disappeared.

A search for them had ensued, but I'd instinctively known where to look and sprinted back home to check underneath the stilts of our hut. Mama was holding Charlie Boy in her arms atop a pile of sewage as if they were on a mattress at home. It's when I started to weep that Mama opened her eyes, except she was no longer Mama at all, but Osun herself with silvery blue pupils eyeing me cruelly.

'Who told you to leave?' she asked from her position despite the fact that I hadn't moved; I was still in the canoe, metres away from where they were. I felt the boat lifting under me as though something had pushed it from underneath the water, like in the story of my birth. All at once, the lagoon began to rise like someone pouring water into a glass. As the boat was submerged with everything around it, my lungs burned with liquid. It was only as I'd been on the point of choking that I'd sat upright in my sleep before my coughing fit woke me fully, banishing the dream's hold on me.

The nightmare was my brain's way of addressing the fear I'm feeling about leaving Makoko despite it being something I've always hoped for. That much Mama taught me about bad dreams. Now that the prospect is so close that I can touch it, a part of me wishes all of this was happening to someone else. Before Prince, before the drone project, it's what I yearned for, but perhaps it's *too* much. *Isn't Europe, on top of my current blessings, unnecessary?*, I ask myself, knowing how much Charlie Boy would laugh at me if he knew the extent of my fear fear.

I bathe and complete my household chores before focusing on my trip. I'm ironing the last garment destined for my new case when Papa exits his bedroom before fussing in the living room as though he's looking for something behind me. When I turn towards him, he backs away briefly and pretends to search through a loose pile of papers on one of the mounted shelves sloping towards the floor. I resume my activity, steering the heavy iron carefully around the collar of Maureen's star print ankara dress, but I can feel his attention on me and set the iron aside before I burn her cloth.

'Is everything okay?' I ask him, praying that he hasn't had another change of heart despite me being in two minds about travelling myself.

'Don't disgrace us over there, you hear me? You carry heavy stone for all of us; not just the family, but for *Makoko*,' Papa proclaims, his shoulders agitated by the weight of his message.

'I know, Papa,' I reply quietly.

'Just do what you can,' he continues while approaching me slowly. 'Remember where you're from . . . And don't let anyone take advantage.'

'No, sah,' I answer quickly.

He nods at me curtly before pulling me into an awkward bear hug. Before I can acknowledge it taking place, it's over, and I'm staring at the shiny spot at the back of his head where there's no longer any hair from a combination of ageing and lying in the same position on his mattress.

'You're truly your mother's daughter,' Papa mutters on his way down the corridor, as much to himself as to me, who only manages to catch his words before his bedroom door closes.

I have Mama's face, her vision and some of her gentleness, but I know I possess his obstinacy too. Retrieving the iron, a tear rolls down my cheek and sizzles as it touches the hot plate. I go back to pressing my fabric, tracing the elaborate fishtail hem of the dress while replaying Papa's words – as close to any blessing as he'll ever give.

I sail towards the Third Mainland Bridge, lured by the orange lights casting tiger stripes across the water. It's not too late, a part of me thinks traitorously. I can stay here and just go to the drone programme. I don't need to go abroad after all. But as the breeze blows through my hair, I take a mental snapshot of my view, bottling it along with other moments to take with me on the journey that I accept I can't back out of.

I recall my farewell with Auntie Bisi, so contrasting to the minimal exchange of words with Papa that occurred earlier in the day. Extracting some money out of her bosom, she'd pushed the notes into my hand. Not naira but US dollars.

'From Mrs Dozie,' she'd said gently with a nudge before I could refuse her gesture disguised under her employer's kindness, no doubt out of guilt over what Tayo had done. 'Na small but use it carefully, you hear me?'

'Yes, Auntie,' I'd said softly, suddenly saddened by her imminent departure.

'You have a chance here, Baby, with this moment God has granted you,' Auntie said, pointing up towards the ceiling. 'Lord willing, from it you can pay for your education. It can even take you far away from here, like that boy wey dey do art . . . Now he dey for *America*,' she continued approvingly, reminding me of the community's last major success story.

'But what if—' I'd started, but she'd fielded my question before I could ask it.

'Your father is your father. The time has come for you to think about only *yourself*, Baby.'

Across the water, I hear the sound of other canoes; the ebb and flow of conversation moving towards the community and away from where I bob by myself, nothing between me and the unobscured vista of the lagoon. One good thing to come was that the trip would at least put much-needed distance between Papa and any notion he has of Samson and me, I tell myself. It's not even a case of me being too picky; more that I'm not in a hurry. How did Mama Jumbo put it? There's more to life than this water.

There are other ways of doing things, no need to rush to the altar in these new times when women can be anything. It's one of the reasons I like Prince. There's no suffer-head with him; no one pressuring me, himself included, about his intentions.

I take my time and enjoy one of these final moments of solitude, where I'm able to clearly hear my own thoughts. When we're in Switzerland, there's no telling what each day will entail. After predictable days on the lagoon, moving from one chore to another, the world spreads wide open before me like the body of water supporting my boat. It's overwhelming.

'Four more days,' Charlie Boy announces his presence as he shifts on the wooden seat in front of me. His silhouette is highlighted in the glow from the bridge. His begging puppy eyes, the small scar on his left cheek from when he fell over trying to hang onto his kite, his front tooth that hadn't fully grown by the time he died, that made his perfectly imperfect smile.

'Four more days,' I repeat before Charlie Boy asks me again to tell him what I've learned about where we are going.

Once more, I inform him about the mountains, the pictures I've seen on the internet, of snow falling from the sky, even though I have a hard time believing we might encounter that ourselves. I tell him about pine trees so tall and tapered they look like swords and one kind of green we never see here where everything is black, brown or dirty.

'What of the plane?' he wants to know before letting out a huge yawn that makes me copy him. Checking the time on my phone, I pick up the oars and start to slowly make my way home.

I repeat our itinerary. Two different planes to board as we have a connecting stop in Amsterdam. When we arrive in Zurich, we'll go to Davos by train.

'Will they let me go with you?' Charlie Boy asks abruptly, his eyebrows furrowing with apprehension.

'Of course, they will,' I reply forcefully while he taps out a tune with my empty water bottle against the canoe.

'Are you sure? We won't get in trouble if I come too?' He presses on until I pull a silly face that makes him stop being serious and he starts to laugh.

'How can I enter plane without you? It's even because of you that I'm going sef!' I say incredulously, watching his shoulders slacken before he reaches down to scratch at his ankle forcefully.

'It's okay if you can't take me as well,' he declares after a moment of silent reflection. 'You'll be fin—' he continues before I sharply reject his notion in their tracks.

'Ah ah, am I not Robin?' I ask jokingly in anticipation of his swift reply.

'Robin na Batman's sidekick, not Spider-Man's!' Charlie Boy takes the bait and is appalled by my apparent ignorance.

'*Really?* Who is your own then?' I ask him, watching his moon-tinged features deep in concentration for a full thirty seconds.

'I'm more of a lone ranger,' Charlie Boy says cheekily, all other thoughts forgotten.

Since Mama Jumbo has given me the day off, I'm free to spend some time with Prince.

It's a great relief for me to be able to mention him, for him to be real in front of one adult in my life. Not that I'm keeping him a secret. If anything, I'm saving him from our family drama and the pressure of marriage so he can be free to focus on his cooking career.

It would have been a good day on the lagoon for customers, I surmise from the number of people waving their hands to try and flag down a canoe. Tunde and Aziz, two of my staunch competitors, pass me on the canal with their full load of passengers headed for the community as I'm travelling in the other direction with only me on board. We greet each other with a nod before an argument breaks out in one of the canoes about water being allowed to penetrate the vessel. The large pig reclining with his tapestry of black spots watches the commotion from behind the jetty while running its nose through mounds of garbage.

I take my time at the market, buying the things we need that won't spoil so that they can continue to eat without me while I'm gone. Kemi knows some basics, and if they get desperate, Iya Rose next door will offer her help. While haggling over yam, I catch a glimpse of someone I'm convinced might be Tayo and try to follow his profile inside the busy marketplace but quickly lose him in the crush. I haven't forgiven his conduct, or the fact that he stole from me twice since Papa's money was from my good fortune, but a tiny part of me feels pity for him now that he is lost to us and we cannot say his name at home.

I'm surprised that he hasn't returned asking for mercy or claiming to have been brainwashed into bad behaviour by his peers. It's hard to imagine him fending for himself, hidden in the community or on the mainland itself. But there was always a hardness within that boy. Even underneath Papa's hardened exterior lies a molten centre. The same can't be said for Tayo. What is it they always say? When you allow the wrong people inside your house, stuff will come up missing.

After picking up the dry goods, I kill some time at the shopping centre while Prince is running late. I'm looking at the giant television in the window of an electronics shop when he comes up behind me and puts his hands over my eyes. Only he would do such a nonsense, plus I can recognise his smell: the Palmolive coconut soap he bathes with, along with the scent of lemon juice he uses to remove cooking aromas from his skin.

'Na you,' I say jokingly, feeling my heart rate quicken as he turns me around to face him. Instinctively my gaze drops to take in his T-shirt, but there's no empowering message this time. Instead, his white T-shirt, so new it still has the fresh fold marks on it, bears my photograph from the newspaper more supersized.

'What is it?' Prince asks innocently as I beat my face on his chest before looking around to see if anyone else can see the two versions of me inside the mall.

'You dey craze!' I laugh in spite of my embarrassment as we walk. Luckily, while some people are observing his shirt, no one seems to connect the image on it with me by his side, perhaps because the cheap print job has blurred my features. Even my brown skin is verging on the side of purple or blue.

'Na you dey make me crazy,' he replies with a smirk. 'You wan chop? I hear there's a place close by that sells the best sausage rolls!'

We have a relaxed meal together and when I come back from the bathroom, a plastic bag is sitting on our table and Prince is zipping up his backpack.

'What is this again?' I ask him with faux exasperation, preparing myself for more practical jokes at my expense.

'Open it now,' he demands hurriedly before I gingerly peer inside the carrier bag.

I blink as I look between him and my gift, speechless, as I extract the Infinix phone in its sealed box. He helps me to tear away the wrapping to get to the device inside, which is good as my fingers are no longer cooperating.

'Was this the one you wanted?'

I stare at him. I can't even recall telling him about a smartphone, much less a specific brand, when I don't pay attention to such things. I'd abandoned the thought of it after Tayo's antics in any case.

'Prince! You can't . . . This is too much. Are you serious?' Words are forming a go-slow on my tongue as he pulls out the phone and carefully removes the protective cellophane from its screen.

'So you can be taking proper *fotos* of your trip,' he says. 'You can't be going abroad with your ye-ye phone,' he adds, sneering at my mobile with its cracked screen on the table next to my hand. 'Are you alright? What is it?' he asks, concerned as I fall silent. I can't help it. I know if I open my mouth in this moment, more than words might come out.

I picture myself exiting my chair and throwing myself into his arms before the owner of the restaurant chases us out of their establishment. I'm certain that if Prince holds me now, I won't let go. Switzerland be damned.

I watch him bring the phone to life and walk me through its basic functionalities, marvelling at the way he understands it intuitively while I try to keep up, so I don't forget everything

255

later. He slides the phone over to me and holds onto my hand affectionately over the handset.

'Baby,' he says, though it comes out in the form of a question.

Thank you, I'm fine. I'll miss you; I love you. I think them all at the same time, but none of them will budge from my lips. I conjure up my girlfriends and imagine how a fusion of the three of them would respond in this situation.

'You okay?' Prince adds, studying me intently.

'Chef . . .' I say quietly while nodding my head at him. 'You don butter my bread.'

After a sleepless night watching the ink fade from the sky only to remain in the water, the morning finally comes. Surprisingly, there are tears from Afo and Kemi, not due to my imminent departure, but from fatigue that has accumulated from mounting adrenaline as the day grew closer. I'd stopped telling them to be quiet as they'd whispered in the dark, fantasising about my *holiday*, as they referred to it. The sound of their voices comforted me and supplemented my own excitement when the nerves crept in.

In the afternoon, Uncle Jimi holds both of them under his arm while Papa and I hug briefly before we head out to the deck with my suitcase. We all watch the water silently until the boat appears.

When the house is no longer visible, I turn my attention towards the water, drinking in the six o'clock rush hour as we navigate the waterway while keeping a close eye on my suitcase, balanced carefully in the boat.

I meet Idunnu on land, clutching her own new case tightly and shining her teeth. Her headwrap makes it seem as though a protrusion is growing out of her forehead and I touch my freshly prepared braids instinctively, long wide cornrows that had required one fresh pack of Expressions; no reusing old hair this time.

We step gingerly through the muddy pathway – avoiding letting our travel bags touch the ground unless it's on a dry patch – until we're out on the road and waiting for the car to come ferry us to the airport.

Idunnu's chatter distracts my mind until we arrive in front of the market, where we meet the other two members of our group along with Ngozi, our escort this way and back. The airport is heaving with people as we follow behind Ngozi as though we're her baby chicks as she guides us through the lengthy process, checking our papers, weighing our suitcases and passing through machines to check inside our bodies. Everywhere, speakers are making announcements as we go from one cool spot to a warm enclosure to wait in an even hotter line before we finally make it inside the plane.

A pretty white woman in her bright blue uniform beams at me as she checks the boarding slip in my hand before guiding me down one alley of the plane with her hand. Idunnu is chattering away behind me and bumping me with the large handbag across her body as I fold my shoulders in to avoid knocking into people as they settle into their rows.

Copying others around us, we click ourselves into our seats and play with the buttons above our heads as the women and men in uniform parade the length of the plane as though they're doing fashion show. Finally, after counting us all and ordering some people to open their blinds, the pilot introduces himself over the speaker and then one of the women begins to tell us what to do if the plane has an accident. I listen to the instructions with one ear and to Idunnu with the other, who is panicking while making a sign of the cross. I pray inwardly, to God, to Mama, and when I look up, the plane people are taking their seats before the cabin lights are dimmed, only they have not taken power as the plane is still moving.

Closing my eyes to escape Idunnu, I pretend we're already in flight, soaring over the Third Mainland Bridge. I think I see Charlie Boy down in the water below, waving furiously at the plane's tail lights, but that can't be right; he can't be in the lagoon and here next to me, which is where I want him to be, holding my hand tightly as we fight over dominance of the window seat with the view over the aircraft's wing.

As the pressure squeezing my hand increases, I crack my eyelids to see Idunnu, her teeth flashing like pearls as she smiles back at me nervously. Peering through the window, I notice we haven't even moved. But to me, those few seconds in the past feel like hours ago. In the dark outside, Charlie Boy is gone, but he'll come when he wants to, I reassure myself while pushing deeper into the headrest. There are too many people around in the plane; we prefer our time when we're alone.

Suddenly, the jet starts to race over the tarmac with the speed of Usain Bolt for about the same amount of time as it would take for me to do the hundred metres sprint. I hold my breath, but when the plane's wheels begin to lift off the ground, and my heart behind my chest is pulled towards the ceiling, I exhale deeply.

'Stop your moping! Na *adventure*, not an ending . . . Are you ready?' Idunnu squeals excitedly, gripping my arm with the force of a vice.

'Let's go,' I say outwardly to Idunnu, and to Charlie Boy inwardly, as we inch up and up into the sky.

Air

18

Ngozi is a shining example of what an education can bestow on a person. Not much older than Idunnu and I, she exhibits the poise one only has from proper schooling and the good manners not to hold our lack against us. It was hard not to admire her as she steered us through not one but two airports and dealt with our complaints and hunger after arriving in Amsterdam so early in the morning that the only source of sustenance we could attain was via vending machines as we waited for our connecting flight into Zurich. Schiphol Airport had been one massive space centre, or so it seemed, but it had been too early to wander.

Our guards had gone up immediately upon meeting her, suspicious of her evident oyinbo mannerisms, despite her outer ethnicity. I wasn't convinced her core was Nigerian, that she hadn't been whitewashed in Europe or wherever she came from, but our need for her was greater than our reservations as we braved our unfamiliar surroundings. So, out of desperation, Idunnu and I had warmed to her quicker than we'd both anticipated. Ngozi handled officials with the same amount of grace and care as she did us, I noticed, but it was incredible to watch her accent, along with the pronunciation of her name, change as we left the African continent and landed in Europe. By the time we reached Davos, her Nigerian intonation had disappeared entirely and she began speaking as though she had multiple ice cubes in her mouth.

Upon our arrival at Zurich Airport, both Idunnu and I had been dry-eyed from a night of flying.

'Shey we really dey here?' Idunnu had asked, refusing to believe her own eyes as the realisation that we'd truly travelled started to sink in.

As we'd set off from Lagos, we'd watched the same films on our miniature screens inside the chairs in front of us in the plane and polished off all the food it would have been wiser to save for the gap in between our travels. The other occupant of our row was a man who acted as though he was in charge simply by being allocated the aisle seat. Either that or because he'd carried a briefcase. Idunnu claimed he'd opened it when I'd gone to use the bathroom; all she could glimpse inside it was a jumble of papers and a scrawny pen not even worthy of our supply-less schools in Makoko!

I was grateful I'd heeded Efe's advice as we'd exited the plane, having been greeted by air so cold it chooked my brain. I'm surprised we hadn't turned into statues in the corridors we walked down as we followed the signs towards passport control. I'd originally wanted to put my coat inside my luggage, daunted by the prospect of toting it around for the duration of the flight in the sweltering heat of Lagos, but Efe had warned against it. I shielded myself from the icy wind while Idunnu shivered in her double sweater combination beside me. She'd accepted the scarf I untied from around my handbag gratefully and wound it around her head dramatically.

'*Fada, which kind cold be this?*' Idunnu had cried out to the Lord for salvation as we waited in a line inching its way towards the booths manned by white officials waiting to check our paperwork to allow us into the country.

'Don't worry, you'll have a chance to go shopping properly,' Ngozi had remarked gently, masking her amusement.

Ngozi had gone first, explaining we were in a group before ushering us up one by one and guiding us past the immigration desk until we'd all made it through and could go and retrieve our luggage. All the Nigerians that had been on our flight seemed to have disappeared when I wasn't looking. The flight to Amsterdam had been more populated with our people than our connecting flight, where we'd been in a sizeable minority alongside other Africans and foreigners from other countries. We were promptly diluted again in the sea of travellers in the Arrivals Hall and by the time we collected our suitcases from the moving conveyor belt, we were mere beads of sand inside a full kilo of beans.

Zurich Airport was much more than its Nigerian counterpart had been. It easily had more shops and restaurants than the shopping centre in Yaba. People were coming to the airport, I'm convinced, as somewhere to spend time even without having any intention to fly. There was a large train station on the lower floor and small small kiosks everywhere, selling a variety of goods.

Inside all the activity, though, had been *order*. No person shouting about their lost luggage or some other committed injustice, or people hovering around to beg you for change, using their small babies to pluck on your heartstrings. Announcements filled the air in an impenetrable language and police officers walked the airport in formation, looking authoritative and not as though they were in search of someone whose pocket they could terrorise money out of.

Before we'd left the airport, Ngozi helped us at the currency exchange and then both Jonathan Akinbami and Dr Hariri had bought hats they'd pulled over their ears forcefully. Idunnu had wanted gloves but baulked at the eye-watering Swiss prices that threatened to chop her money and decided against it. We'd waited for our taxis to arrive to take us to the train station, mesmerised by the clean air and the sight of our breath exiting our bodies in front of us, like blowing bubblegum made of ice.

I'd been exhausted from too many nights of fitful sleeping prior to our flight, but as we sat in the back of the taxi, my face had been pressed against the glass, alert as I'd taken in the city, so different to what I'd seen of Lagos.

The traffic was organised; roads perfect with clear signs, while trains – that are called trams – ran alongside them and people got on and off without the usual chaos that ensues on our buses back home. It was clear Switzerland would tolerate no type of a nonsense. Everywhere we passed pristine erected buildings, in grey and white, or completely in glass. The sky was filled with cranes and the lines powering the trams. On the main roads as we stopped by traffic lights, we'd seen statues;

men, women and children cast holding strange positions in stone the colour of Badagry oysters. In front of the railway station, water poured out of the mouths of the severed heads on the base of a fountain. It had shocked me and arrested my gaze, but the locals had passed by like it was nothing, like it was somebody shitting inside the lagoon before turning around and going about their business.

Ngozi settled us inside a bright fish restaurant that was thankfully warm before going to purchase our train tickets while the four of us picked through our meals slowly. I'd devoured my selection: a fish burger despite the fish being barely recognisable as it had been a square encrusted in orange breadcrumbs, yet surprisingly moist and tender. The men had chosen more wisely, opting for a plate laden with salmon, potatoes, spinach and a sauce resembling the custard Mama Jumbo sold in packets that only required boiled water to be added. The thing that had saved me was copying the man that had ordered just ahead of me. I'd pointed to his burger with the two pieces of breaded fish inside, unlike Idunnu's miserly choice, which looked like the kind of thing you'd have served to a child. When Ngozi returned, she could tell we were still hungry and when she came over to the table brandishing her own tray of food, she'd bought us two large plates of shrimp covered in breadcrumbs along with potato fries.

While we waited for our train to arrive, Ngozi installed Dr Hariri in the railway station's prayer room while our community leader's son made loud calls on his mobile phone from a nearby large armchair that if you put money inside the box next to it, would vibrate to give you a massage. We'd secured our luggage in a storage locker so we could move freely around the station and Ngozi took the opportunity to lead Idunnu and me out of the station on foot to a gigantic clothing store nearby. In this H&M, Idunnu had bought a coat on sale and some gloves. Then we'd purchased matching marked-down sweaters; mine in yellow while Idunnu chose the black version.

On our way back to the station, we'd clutched our shopping bags proudly and I'd momentarily forgotten the cold as I passed other fountains on the streets. People stopped to drink this free water. Even with the yellowed leaves that had fallen from the few trees that still had some foliage this winter, the water inside the stone sinks on the pavement was crystal clear.

'Shey you've been here before?' Idunnu asked Ngozi, who nodded while typing into her phone.

It was obvious that Ngozi was familiar with Europe, as nothing seemed to surprise her. As Idunnu and I had slowed naturally to watch people bending over to drink briefly from the tap or to fill their aluminium water bottles before heading off, Ngozi beckoned us to the fountain so we could drink. She snapped a photo of Idunnu, wearing her new black coat in one light puff-puff material, her head bowed towards the arc of water. When I bent down after her to sample it myself, I understood the expression that had come over Idunnu's face. It was the coolest, freshest thing I'd ever tasted.

I'd passed the railway station in Yaba several times but had never seen the trains coming in. Either way, I could guarantee that the trains at home were nothing like the ones in Switzerland. We'd waited for our train to Davos on a long platform that had been crowded but good-mannered as people had stood in an orderly line along the platform, waiting at different points for the train to arrive. With our outer layers, the cold was easier to bear, but occasionally the wind penetrated my braids almost as though someone had been stroking my bare scalp with the tip of a knife.

Finally, the train showed up, a huge beast of a machine in sleek silver that filled the length of the platform. As we filed into a compartment, I pictured the buses back home on Lagos mainland, winding through the streets like an army of yellow battle-scarred ants with their mangled exteriors, broken windows and missing doors. With more passengers than seats sometimes, as people routinely clung to the sides of the vehicle, unafraid of traffic.

On the train, there'd been no fuss; people moved towards free seats until the train was almost full capacity. No one checked our tickets before we entered, but Ngozi advised us to keep them handy for the train's conductor.

'Please o! They go collect am . . . Keep it well.'

Idunnu and I chose a two-seater, facing the direction the train was moving in, while the others occupied a four-seater with a table in the middle on the opposite side. I was surprised by the graffiti on the railway tracks as we left the station, but soon the tapestry changed, giving us a brief glimpse of a large body of water, which Ngozi explained was a lake. It was so blue against an even paler blue sky with clouds like balls of cotton wool, so different to our own smoked-filled skies back at home. On the hills behind the lake, houses appeared to stand on each other's shoulders; a little bit like Makoko from a distance except with white facades instead of our tin huts. Idunnu slipped away with the motion of the train, but I tried to stay awake, watching the scenes rolling outside the window, large patches of countryside between stations whose names hurt my eyes as I struggled to make sense of them. Inside the train, a family caught my eye, two parents travelling with their daughter and son. The way the mother fussed over them sharing their snacks made me think of Mama, of the four of us in our old house. Dura had been married by then and living with Tokunbo. Mama had been trying to get me to share my biscuits with my brother when Papa arrived home unexpectedly that afternoon. On our deck, he'd excitedly removed the pouches of FanIce from his carrier bag, still partially frozen. He'd even bought some for himself and Mama, when normally he'd have complained about such frivolousness. I'd torn off the edge of mine hastily to suck the softening vanilla ice cream, savouring the spontaneous moment of pleasure before it melted away.

As the stretches of green land between small clusters of civilisation grew, I succumbed to the motion of the train like the others, allowing my body to ease into the soft back of my seat as I fell asleep. I dreamt I was on water being shunted by a canoe on the lagoon trying to overtake me and woke up just as the train was passing over a bridge. As it turned in a sweeping circle, I caught the deep arches over which we were passing, which caused my stomach to lurch. It struck me then, the difference in the terrain as the train moved seamlessly from one level of land to another, over water and earth. Either side of the train's carriage was framed by impressive hills and far-away mountains. In the distance, large clouds pooled like smoke and there were so many trees, the kind they were always showing on Christmas images, that I was certain we were heading towards a forest.

Houses appeared with white roofs and the ground became more covered with a white lining the closer we came to our destination. Another lake appeared, framed by yet more ghostly trees, and I shook Idunnu awake to catch the spectacular view, the jagged mountains around us crested with a blanket of white.

'We don reach?' Idunnu yawned, her eyes widening at the scene in front of us.

I nodded at her, feeling the train slow as it pulled into the Davos Platz station. I wondered which of the four of us from Makoko would be the first to step out and put our feet onto the snow that awaited us. I took a long time retrieving my suitcase to ensure that it wasn't me.

19

Switzerland is one kind of a torture. Outside, the cold feels like a slap in your face before it seeps inside your bones and freezes your skeleton so that you can't move. You can't even call for help as your mouth is shivering. When you're indoors, you sweat heavily as the temperature of their heating is so high you want to remove your clothes like the small children who run around Makoko naked. But you can't do it because your body's stinking, and if you go out again dressed foolishly, the cold will kill you.

The place we're staying is the colour of a sweet, as are many of the other hotels we drove by on the way: butterscotch, strawberry, or toffee. They aren't very big but are striking, given most of them resemble birthday cakes with thick elaborate icing. All of us are on the same third floor, with Idunnu and me in rooms next to each other that have the same view of a cable car in the distance.

My eyes lit up when I first saw the small vehicles trekking across that tiny metal line. I'd risk the cold to try it, even if the thought terrifies me, but Idunnu won't hear word, no matter how much I try to convince her it's the same as flying.

We'd all been able to fit in the large vehicle that had come to collect us from the train station, while a burly taxi driver smelling of cigarettes had piled our suitcases carefully in the boot, all without holding his hand for *dash* after ferrying us. Helen had been waiting at the hotel reception when we arrived after the brief drive, smiling proudly as though she hadn't entirely expected our group to make it from Lagos.

'*Welcome*,' she beamed at us warmly before she and Ngozi exchanged kisses on the cheek. She pointed to the gentleman by her side as she introduced him.

'This is Mr Novella. He'll be your coordinator while you're in Davos for many of the events this week,' she'd explained as the sharply dressed man fiddled with the orange tie that was the only thing not gelling with his dark grey suit.

'Please . . . Call me Thierry,' Mr Novella had said, beaming at us approvingly.

'*Good afternoon, Terry*!' we'd all chimed in harmonious unison like schoolchildren.

Dr Hariri and Jonathan, who were taking their roles as Makoko ambassadors very seriously, reached out for a handshake, pumping Thierry's fingers so vigorously that two spots of red appeared on both of his sunken cheeks.

Then, in the lounge room with its porridge oat wallpaper, we'd had a brief welcome drink and meeting before leaving to discover our individual rooms. Ngozi had knocked on our doors to deliver a welcome pack from her organisation. Inside had been Swiss biscuits and chocolate, a map of the area as well as a ticket to the Kirchner Museum. It had also included a small brass bell on a leather handle and most importantly, a Lebara SIM card, allowing us to call home without worry.

In a small way, my room reminded me of home; the ceiling was composed of wooden slats, albeit the colour of honeycomb, that mirrored the shade of the other wooden features in the room like the doors and side tables. My bed was two single mattresses pushed together and topped with crisp white linen. Like the hotel room in Ikeja, it had its own bathroom, but the room in Switzerland also came with a flat-screen television and a small balcony outside my room displaying the hill of Christmas trees and the cable car line.

Idunnu and I met in the hallway, having both had the same idea of coming to visit each other's suites. We started with mine first before exploring her own, an almost identical offering to the one belonging to me, apart from her wood being painted white and her room having red accents and no balcony.

She'd already scattered the contents of her welcome pack on her mattress as we'd sat down to discuss our impressions so far.

'Wetin happen to Jonathan's face? You know how long I've been waiting to *yap*,' Idunnu said before squeezing her laughter into her pillow. I laughed with her, conjuring up his new look for our trip overseas, the thin moustache over his top lip that was more like a line of dirt he forgot to clean off.

'Idunnu, you are *bad*,' I declared in mock shock, even though I'd wrestled with the urge to tell him to scrub it off myself.

'Remember on the plane how Dr Hariri tucked his blanket around his neck like—'

'*Superman!* Even when he got up to use the toilet,' I interrupted Idunnu loudly as wild cackles escaped our mouths once again. Tears sprang from our eyes as we relived some of the moments between our flight and our arrival in technicolour before lapsing into a wistful silence.

'The only thing I'm fearing is the food,' Idunnu confessed quietly. 'Do you think they will have rice?' she'd asked sheepishly.

'Yes o! They have everything in the international,' I claimed with more conviction than I possessed. I'd had the good sense to carry two packets of Mama Jumbo's Indomie in my luggage. Worst case scenario, I would use the kettle to boil water and prepare the dried noodles in the small cup in my bedroom.

I went back to my room to switch over my SIM card and call home. There'd been no answer from Papa, who rarely answered his phone in real-time, preferring to squint at his screen while trying to read text messages that came through long after messages were of any meaning or relevance. I sent a brief text telling him of our arrival before slipping into a long-awaited sleep on the soft cloud of my bedding.

I was awoken by the knocking on my door and wiped the sleep from my eyes, for one moment still thinking I was back home since my body was hot. My throat felt dry from the heat and my nostrils burned as I rose from the bed and acclimated to my surroundings before I hurried for the door. Ngozi had changed into a soft brown sweater that made me feel sorry for the animal she'd plucked for its wool. Her hairstyle rendered her outfit more elegant. She had cornrows like me, only micro ones braided towards the top of her head so that she would tie the ends into a bun. That, along with her black rimmed glasses, gave her a stylish, educated appearance.

'You're still sleeping? In thirty minutes, we're going to eat,' she'd announced authoritatively.

I raced to get ready, eager to try out my shower and the fresh-smelling products waiting for me on the bathroom countertop.

We hadn't dined at the hotel as I'd imagined, but instead walked a short distance in our new winter wardrobes to a nearby bistro filled with a mix of locals, judging from the sound of the language, and foreigners like ourselves. Thankfully, they'd offered us menus in English and after seemingly fifty potato dishes, we'd stumbled upon a selection of roasted meats that were accompanied by either another style of potatoes or rice. Ngozi had ordered shrimp cocktails for the table as well as garlic bread, which was surprisingly sweet and warm and had left us all with shiny lipstick. Only Jonathan had been feeling adventurous, opting for the same main dish as Ngozi, a potato cake filled with bacon, onions and egg, but when it had arrived, anybody looking at his face could tell he was missing the bite of hot pepper. Ngozi had spoken to a waiter on his behalf, who'd returned with one bottle of red liquid that had barely pinched and mostly tasted acidic. Still, Jonathan had poured it on generously.

Dr Hariri had gone for rice like us, but instead of meat, had chosen king prawns.

'*Kai*! Is that what they're calling *king* here? Then what is *prince*?' Idunnu had joked, her mouth falling open comically at the sight of his measly plate. As we laughed, I'd thought briefly of my Prince, at the mention of his name, while Dr Hariri had fought to control his laughter to stop the ye-ye Swiss shrimp from devastating his windpipe.

Helen and Thierry had joined us as we were finishing our main course and reading through a menu with all sorts of flavours of ice cream. All of us had refused, given the outside temperature, so Dr Hariri and Jonathan progressed to hot drinks while Helen, Thierry and Ngozi shared one bottle of white wine. Idunnu had tried a glass, but it was only fatigue that made me refuse. Thankfully, when we were back at the hotel, having run through our itinerary for the next few days, she'd revealed that I hadn't missed anything.

'Tastes like cow piss,' she scoffed while making a face at the remembered flavour.

'To go with the cowbell!' I replied speedily, having since understood the significance of the gift in our welcome packs, the ornament worn by their Alpine cattle as a way to keep track of them.

Ngozi knocked on Idunnu's door, where we were residing, and asked if we wanted to come to her room. We accepted and were shocked to discover hers was even bigger than our own, with a small living room before her bedroom. My body sank into Idunnu as our weight was accepted by couch cushions the texture of pounded yam. As we made small talk with Ngozi, who'd temporarily slipped back into a Nigeria-lite accent now

277

that it was just us, I began to wonder if a part of her was lonely since she was travelling alone. The divider between her and ourselves began to disintegrate the more we talked nonsense in her living room, about Afrobeats musicians and American celebrities. The sky behind her large window deepened and darkened until all that was visible were pinpricks of lights inside a sombre blue.

'You get plenty schooling?' I asked, envious of the gulf between us as she briefly recapped her years in education. Born in Nigeria, she'd gone to London at sixteen to finish her schooling before studying at university. The more she talked, the more daunted I was about the days ahead and our role in them.

'Don't be afraid,' Ngozi reassured us. 'It's mostly for *foto*! To put real faces on people dealing with these difficult issues,' she'd explained while cleaning her spectacles with the end of her sweater. Without them, she'd blinked repeatedly at us as if one of us had switched off the lights until she'd safely repositioned them on her nose again and her pupils reappeared.

'How long you don dey work for Helen?' I asked.

'This is my third year with H2All. Before that, I was at Care International,' she told us. 'My father was a board member of another UK NGO allocating grants all over the world, so giving back is in my blood,' she continued and I didn't dare ask her what she was meant to have taken.

'She is so *correct*,' I said, attempting to broach the nerves I felt around Helen before Ngozi interjected.

'I promise you, underneath her professional layer, Helen's actually very nice. No need to stress.'

'*Shey* we'll have chance to sightsee?' Idunnu asked before being overcome by a large yawn she didn't try to hide.

'*Eeehn.* You will see what there is to offer,' Ngozi confirmed.

'Including the lake?' I asked eagerly, having picked up one of the flyers about it in the hotel foyer.

An image of me and Charlie Boy languishing on its powder blue surface sparked in my mind as Idunnu's obvious fatigue triggered my own.

'Even the lake,' Ngozi nodded before echoing our yawns and bidding us goodnight.

20

It's easy to fall asleep in the cool tranquillity enveloping the town, but it's the quiet that wakes me up. The blanket of snow covering everything falls silently but heavily on top of my dreams.

Despite the temperature outside, I've been sleeping with the window open. The heat inside the room is too oppressive for me and unnatural in the way it radiates through the small confines, like food inside a cooking pot. As I drink my tea, looking out of the window, I notice the thick layer of snow that has reformed since last night and recall Idunnu out on my balcony, enjoying the stillness of our surroundings on our free day.

We'd been seduced by the snow falling outside the window, fat snowflakes drifting into view under the streetlights. Letting the cold air into my room, we'd headed to the balcony and raised our faces towards the sky as we'd tried and failed to catch snow on our tongues, but it had been harder than we imagined. Instead, we found ourselves quickly covered in the icy sprinkle as it landed in our hair and on our faces like peppery stars.

Checking the time, I confirm what my body already knows. It's early. There's no major time difference between here and back home, but I'm finding it hard to settle because it's hard to believe we've travelled at all. Of course, it's real; I'm away from Makoko, in a cold place where the language sounds like something grating my ear, and there's no Papa looking stony-faced, no smell of fish or foul. Still, as I floated through the hotel with Idunnu, trying to familiarise ourselves with our habitat, it felt as if we were in the midst of a shared hallucination. Any moment, I could wake up on the deck in Adogbo with Auntie Bisi staring over me and telling me I hit my head and fell into a coma.

With no one to communicate with at this hour, I turn my attention to the window and watch as the darkness slowly drains out of the receding night like dye from clothes in hot water. There are similarities between the light here and back home. The grey glaze the sky is washed with during the daytime *was* confusing at first, only theirs wore a blue petticoat whereas in Lagos it was reddish, and the crisp, fresh Swiss air – like mentholated ointment under the nostrils – quickly reminded you of your location while the force of the wind was reminiscent of being whipped with a cane until you were on the verge of tears.

Without Mama Jumbo to stop me, I've already killed fifteen minutes in the bathroom, flushing the toilet with abandon to witness the crystal-clear returning water no matter how many times I push the handle. Outside, activity begins to perk up, perhaps preparations for the forum that officially commences tomorrow or for the ski slopes itself.

'Which kind person go dress to climb to the top of a mountain then slide down on two rickety sticks?' Idunnu had voiced our collective thoughts out loud the day before. But it's something I'd like to see with my own eyes, even if my brain will refuse to believe it.

I ease the glass door open, bracing myself for the gush of freezing air that pours in through the doorway and clears away the internal heat. Sliding the door back further, I relish the chill blowing through the leggings and T-shirt of my nightwear as I crane my neck over the balcony to observe the noise down below. A lorry makes a series of beeps as it parks before men exit either side and start to remove things from the boot; what looks like a large screen and some kind of audio-visual equipment. The moment I take a step back, some snow shifts from the awning above my balcony and just misses my feet in my slippers from the hotel. The droplets of water that manage to catch my ankle remind me of the time I accidentally scalded myself when cooking. I'm mesmerised by the balcony railing, which is topped with a heavy fringe of new snow that's almost uniform all the way around.

Against all sense, I reach out to touch the snow with my fingertips before spontaneously scooping up a mound and spooning it into my mouth like it's fufu. The snow breaks down easily in the warmth of my cheeks, leaving the taste of metal on my tongue. *Charlie Boy wouldn't be able to control himself if he were here in real life*, I tell myself, as I imagine him in the face of all this temptation. His greedy mouth would have licked the entire railing clean as though it was a lollipop.

Prince's voice is deep and croaky when we speak. For a moment, I pretend he's here in the room with me, under the thick duvet enveloping me following my foolish flirtation with the outdoors.

'You no fit call person again?' His laughter gets clogged up in his half-asleep throat and I picture him sitting upright in his hotel room and looking at my photo in the paper.

'*I rang you!*' I proclaim indignantly as he chuckles a million miles away.

'I know. I'm sorry. They're trying to kill me since I've told them I'm leaving. Anyway, enough about me. How far? What's it like?' he asks.

As speedily as I can, I recap the past few days, the flight over and the cold and white of our location. When I tell him about the food, he's disappointed that we've yet to sample some of the local dishes.

'Baby! If you come back here without at least trying fondue, I will kill you myself,' he promises loudly.

'Which one is fondue?'

'Na cheese wey dey melt . . . with other things. You for dip bread or vegetables inside,' he explains patiently, with a hint of amusement in his voice.

'That is what you are calling food? What kind of ye-ye chef are you?' I make fun of him from a safe distance.

'When you return, I will show you what kind I am,' Prince replies, his voice deepening to a kind of predatory animal level. I feel my body begin to soften and wrap up the conversation as quickly as I can before it gets too saucy, or I quench my Lebara from one phone call.

Almost as soon as we hang up, Papa flashes my phone. One brief ring and the phone is dead. A signal for me to call him since there's no way he'll use his credit to call me in the abroad. I compose myself, shaking off the memory of Prince in my head as I dial him back quickly.

'*Baby* . . . Thank God for journey mercies! How far?' Papa asks as soon as the call connects.

I inform him of our arrival, assuring him we're in good hands, not just with the community leader's son and the doctor but also the NGO's representatives, while he makes sounds on the other end bordering on approval. Before I know it, the phone is hijacked by Kemi and Afo's voices, battling for domination of Papa's handset. I'm secretly grateful for their interruption, which disguises the fact that Papa and I would naturally have exhausted our conversation if not for their appearance.

'*Baby! Baby! How are you? What can you see?*'

I field their rapid-fire questions as queries of my own swirl around in my brain as I try to conjure them up back at home.

It's hard to imagine them accosting Papa in his bedroom that's decidedly off-limits, even without it ever being expressly communicated. It's early enough for breakfast, but I don't know who's preparing it in my absence. It's strange to contemplate them carrying on with life without me. Despite being relieved of my daily chores in this temporary exile I've been granted, I notice sadness gnawing at my centre and suddenly my eyes feel prickly. Papa manages to rescue his phone for long enough to say goodbye while shouting at them about international costs and I stare at the phone for a few minutes after they are gone before going to take a shower. As the water pools at my feet, I think of Charlie Boy. Maybe it's because I can only ever envisage him on the lagoon that he hasn't come yet. I can barely believe that I myself have travelled, crossed the sky to a whole new planet, it feels like. It's too much suffer-head; this new-found interest in me. I've done nothing to deserve it.

In the hotel restaurant, Idunnu and I are sporting our matching sweaters over breakfast before we venture outside. She's also wearing one tangerine-coloured lipstick that's popping against her complexion and I admire her ability to remain unfazed in the midst of even more attention. We already stand out here and I'm not entirely comfortable with the scrutiny. Some faces greet us with generous smiles, but others are stares of glass that try to look through us as if to remind us of what we should know: that we don't belong.

In our heavy coats with our layers underneath, Idunnu and I are shielded from the cold. It's only our faces that are freezing: my earlobes, eyelashes and my teeth if I talk for too long.

We walk down the promenade looking at the vibrant window displays of all the stores we can't afford. Davos is certainly a place for millionaires. Over breakfast, we'd overheard some people at a nearby table referring to it as the *Magic Mountain*. They were right; it would certainly take a magician to allow you to live here permanently. I'm sure what all those people bragging on Banana Island earned would be considered mere kobo compared to a Swiss salary.

We pause to admire the window display outside Benetton, the huge poster bearing a beautiful mixed-race child wearing a colourful headband covering each ear with a woolen puff-puff. It's exactly what I need as my ears are burning from the cold. I half expect that when I reach out to touch them, they'll break off in my hands like ice blocks.

On another windowpane, a striking ebony-skinned woman with a close crop and gap-tooth smiles at a redheaded man. *This could be me*, I think fleetingly, remembering my first photo-graph in the newspaper, only she's beaming while I feel as if my generator has suddenly quenched its fuel.

The hot pink sweater she wears is bold against her complex-ion. It's surprising to see our faces so large and included in the advertisements. And then, almost by witchcraft, a black man in running gear appears, nodding at us briefly as he passes by.

We'd already stopped in some of the food shops earlier but decided on this large Migros, welcomed by the warm-coloured M outside its front and the roomy aisles just beyond the door. Our intuitions were right as the prices are a fraction lower than at its competitors. Both Idunnu and I are trying to hang on to as much of our stipends as we can, quenching our hun-ger on the hotel breakfast buffet and the meals bought for us by Ngozi. Enticed by the cooked food display, we linger in front of the heated trays, warming ourselves in the low heat they emanate while we make our selection.

The supermarket is so clean and vast. Rows and rows of neatly stacked shelves with everything perfectly sealed and labelled. Workers in their black vests are checking produce and replenishing shelves without yelling at customers. It's a sight to behold.

Prince's voice pops into my head as I explore the food packed in aluminium tins, but I push it to one side as I reach for the piri-piri chicken. Idunnu chooses a noodle dish and a long sausage before we pick up drinks and some snacks; she has the bright idea to head to the spices. It's the best we can do. We buy two jars of chilli powder: one for us and the other for Jonathan.

I want to explore more but happily agree when Idunnu suggests returning to the hotel to eat our food instead. The cold is plenty and there's a minibus coming to take us to see the lake in the afternoon. On the walk back, we take turns holding our shopping bag, so that we can warm our fingers underneath the takeaway swiftly losing its heat.

'God forbid! How can you do that?' Idunnu glares at me with disgust when I absentmindedly scoop some snow off the back of a bench and put it to my lips.

'What's the matter?' I reply. '*Try* it—'

'How do you know a bird hasn't wee-weed on that?' she asks, flashing her eyebrows at my hand.

'Is it *yellow*?' I challenge defensively before surreptitiously allowing what remains in my hand to drop to the ground.

We turn on to Telestrasse, which also leads back to the hotel. After passing the small supermarket, a packed place catches my eye. It could be a coffee shop or a bar that's crowded

with men even before lunchtime. I turn and see Idunnu looking at it too, its LINGO signage in pink neon. As a waitress
comes out to deliver some drinks to the table by the window,
I study her scanty outfit as well as the man's attention on her
behind as she turns to give his companion a drink. It's then I
look properly inside the place and see it's equally full of women
in next to nothing, most of whom are languishing in little
groups looking idle. I even spot some black faces within them
as we pass by and the men in the window turn their intrusive
gazes over towards us.

'*Tufia-a*!' I exclaim after we're a few metres away, momentarily channelling Mama's indignation and language as Idunnu
shakes her head beside me.

It's not the fact that there's prostitution here that is shocking
me, but the casualness of it on display, between a florist and a
sandwich shop. For some women in Makoko, selling themselves is the only way to make a living, but it's not something
that's done out in the open. One would expect it to be less
brazen in a town full of rich people.

Mama Jumbo pops into my head suddenly and a flood of
homesickness washes over me. I recall her anger at the art show
we'd attended and the woman at our table that had brought it
about by her snooty attitude from being on the same table as
people from the ghetto. As we'd left the venue, Mama had
yapped the woman to Auntie Bisi as she'd passed us.

'Just because you get money, no be say you get class.'

Maybe the same could be said for the people of Davos.

★

I'm running to catch Charlie Boy. It makes no sense since we're in Makoko, so how we're running on the surface of the water, I don't know, yet there I am, sprinting after him. Splashes whip my legs, burning like the flecks of snow did earlier in the day as Charlie Boy weaves and zags in the direction of the bridge while I race behind him, trying to stop him from getting away. The next thing I know, he's being lifted up into the air. I never even noticed his kite, the end of the string in his hands, before his legs are pulled off the ground. Lunging at him with all the force I can muster, I grab hold of his ankle. It feels so small and fragile in my hands as I grip on to him. But the laughter, *his* laughter, which has been the soundtrack to the dream playing in my mind this whole time, stops as we begin to fall and fear invades my body as I look down at the black water below.

I don't know what to do. Some invisible force – maybe the kite – is tugging him upwards, yet my weight is pulling us down. I don't want to be the reason we're dragged and drowned in the water, but I'm paralysed as he twists his ankle, locked in my grip.

'*Baby!* You have to release me,' Charlie Boy says in a tone so ominous as he turns to face me that I immediately wake up and find myself bathed in sweat in in my hotel room bed.

I blink myself into consciousness and reach for the phone charging by my bedside. Barely two hours have passed since my head hit the pillow, but I feel as though I've been asleep for a full day. I peel the duvet off my damp body and go to open the window. The reason for my disturbed dreams, I tell myself,

289

is that the artificial heat in the room has accumulated with no source of freedom.

I gulp some fresh air while watching the eerie glow of moonlight coming through the hill of trees in the distance. I taste the sourness of my tongue, unaccustomed to the alcohol that we'd consumed over dinner at a hotel not far from the convention centre after our afternoon filled with activities. My rum and Coke had tasted like Coke with bitters; the alcohol had barely been discernible inside the drink, but after a short while, people in the restaurant and bar had begun to sway as I observed them, their voices swelling uncomfortably in my ears until it had been time to leave.

We visited Lake Davos in the afternoon. We all took turns reading the information on the signposts outside about the lake that was one and a half kilometres long with the deepest level of fifty-four metres. Making the short walk along the trail, we stood in front of the lake, fringed with forest and distant mountain peaks rimmed with snow. As we approached, the lake itself wasn't what I'd been expecting but resembled a sheet of frozen glass with a thin dusting of snowy icing on top. The sun's rays bounced off its surface like someone shining torchlight from heaven, a luminescence that came to a stop on a thick patch of snow beyond which the lake beamed in the liquid blue hue of a mouthwash.

It was hard to process the blanket of undisturbed water without stilts and houses on top of its surface. Around the lake was only a smattering of houses; if it hadn't been so cold, we could surely have counted them. The only thing floating in the lake were large white water ostriches that Ngozi told us were swans. Of course, there'd have been fish inside the lake, but it never occurred to me that anything without scales would be able to survive such freezing climates.

In almost a single file, we'd walked by the lake, all lost in our individual thoughts as we compared this vision to the life we knew back home. Then Ngozi had fielded questions in her best tour guide impression about fishing and boating here. I took my time at the back as we strolled, trying to lengthen the distance between me and the others while I waited for something to happen and stared intensely at the water, willing Charlie Boy to emerge from its depths. If he'd been anywhere, it would have been the lake, irrespective of the daytime it had been and the inky sky under which we normally met.

Closing my eyes, I pictured my canoe on the surface of the lake, the only one on the water with the clouds in the sky scrolling by at a rapid rate until darkness descended. As vivid as my image had been, I could feel in my marrow that he wasn't coming – he wasn't anywhere nearby.

My eyes stung with unshed tears as I scoured the horizon for hope of his appearance. He'd wanted so much to be here; I hadn't contemplated a scenario where he didn't show up. I felt the nerves mounting in my body, pulling at my fear and scratching away at the old wounds of my loss.

I'd sworn I'd never leave him again the day we'd found him. It hadn't made sense at the time, but then Charlie Boy had come back to me and we'd found a way to be together since then. I'd made good on that declaration to stay with him. But it had never crossed my mind that *he* could leave me.

'Are you there?' Idunnu's voice had tickled my ear before she waved her gloves in front of my vision to rouse me from my stupor.

I laughed, watching it exit my mouth in smoky puffs as we took in the view in front of us.

'It's so beautiful,' Idunnu said heavily before checking where the others were ahead, on the verge of approaching the water-front restaurant.

'Na so,' I replied softly, hoping I'd managed to mimic her sentiment.

Both Idunnu and Dr Hariri had vetoed riding in a ski lift, repulsed by the idea of being exposed to the elements as well as being only held in place by a steel bar and God's graces. So, we'd taken the Schatzalp funicular railway, a mini one-carriage train that pulled us up a three-hundred-metre incline high above the town. The leisurely pace of the train did nothing to quell our mounting nerves as we squeezed our palms while crammed in next to chatty skiers clad in bulbous outfits, anxious to get to the snow-stacked pistes.

The hotel at the top had been a presidential palace of gigantic proportions. The view from the balcony where we'd taken photos and had some drinks had been exquisite; the clouds hanging above the jagged mountain tops had reminded me of the smoke rising from the fish smokers back at home, varying shades of grey and salmon depending on how the light struck, while mist rose from the valley below out of which peeked the tips of freakishly tall trees. The hotel was situated in a beautiful botanical garden with thousands of alpine plants, not that we could tell one from another. As the waiter had backed away to capture us sitting around our table, I'd felt us all grinning like fools while he snapped our image.

'It's like we've travelled up to heaven,' Ngozi declared dreamily as her body nudged mine.

'*Or freedom,*' Idunnu had whispered, her icy breath tickling my ear as we'd posed.

We'd literally been on top of the world, but as I'd smiled at the phone in his hands, all I could think about was that day on the lagoon after I'd flown the drone. The camera in that other man's hands that had taken my photo; the reason that had brought us all here to the magic mountain.

'Why you dey so quiet?' Jonathan asked us, swirling his second drink around in his tumbler. The ice cube at the bottom of his glass was one centimetre smaller than its vessel, in one solid orb that looked super chic. It hadn't dissolved as the whisky around it disappeared down his throat.

'*I know,*' Ngozi chipped in, nursing her go-to glass of white wine. 'Me, I didn't behave so well at your age,' she continued, appraising the two of us as Idunnu and I sat by each other's side.

We both giggled in lieu of a response, aware of our slight constraints despite the absence of our parents. I wasn't quite sure what they'd expected of us. Maybe they imagined the carnage of uprooting two lionesses from the jungle and installing them inside a mall.

After the mountain, we'd ended up at a larger chain hotel near ours, packed with bodies. Unsure of the etiquette, it was clear we were foreigners from the way we remained clumped together, awkwardly, in the lounge chairs, unaccustomed to such social settings. A mixture of men and women in suits had converged with others more casually dressed in slinky outfits and expensive-looking denim. Everyone seemed to have pressed hair, makeup and fragrance as they tipped cocktails down their necks and the room buzzed with a hundred different conversations but few of them in our languages. The lagoon had always seemed so noisy and chaotic when I was trying to pilot my taxi, but how I longed for its music of voices, the floating refuse obscuring my path daily, the riot of colour of our people's mismatched and tattered clothing compared to this sea of navy suits and endless black trousers.

Ever since being in a new world, it was as if something had chopped my voice. I couldn't speak for Idunnu, but I felt more like a fish in the bottom of a boat, taking frantic gasps of oxygen while praying for someone to toss me back into the water where I came from. I could also hardly tell anyone I was missing my brother, but his prolonged absence had clearly deflated my balloon.

'Work begins tomorrow morning, so you better enjoy yourselves,' Ngozi teasingly ordered us while coaxing us towards the pizza pie that arrived on a silver platter. Against my better judgement, I'd accepted another drink, trying to keep up with Idunnu, who undoubtedly had more practice than me as a result of her employment.

Casting my glance around the hotel's bar, I began to notice more black and brown people and fixed my attention on some of the women at the bar with their long weaves and second-skin dresses, wondering what had brought them to this part of the world. Idunnu tapped my leg surreptitiously underneath the table when one of the women got up from her stool next to one old-looking man beside her. I'd assumed she was with the man next to him with whom he'd been conversing most of the time, however, when she stood – after arranging one big handbag on her shoulder – her fingers had reached out to take hold of the old man's hand possessively. In her high heels, she'd easily gapped the top of his silver hair, which was long at the edges with a wide hole in the middle. Perhaps he wasn't aware of it, or she hadn't told him for fear he'd stopped buying her presents. I almost broke Idunnu's finger as I gripped her tightly while watching the man squeeze the woman's backside for one second as if he was testing melons at the market before he nudged her towards the doors leading to the elevators. Idunnu had squealed but had the good grace to pretend it was drinking her icy cocktail through the straw that had been the cause of her momentarily pained expression.

Back home, Idunnu was always a joker, but this trip was the first time I'd seen all the teeth inside her mouth. She couldn't stop smiling in this new country as a result of her independence. The two of us left to use the toilet together, shaky on our legs as we escaped our table and pushed our way through the growing crowd in the hotel foyer. There was such a lively party atmosphere that it was hard to believe the world's leaders were here to talk about big business for real. I noticed Idunnu's walk change on our way back towards the bar, either through inebriation or because she was trying to blend in with all the *sophisticats* mingling inside the hotel, and reminded myself to tease her about it afterwards.

While passing the bar, we both slowed down to watch the television screen mounted above it that no one seemed to be paying attention to. It was on a music channel, and in the blink of an eye, the blonde-haired woman driving in an open-top car on the screen disappeared and was replaced by Tiwa Savage in her yellow bubble dress and cornrows down to her ankles. I was so excited to see a part of Africa, a part of home up there, inaudible on the television that I pondered fleetingly if that was how Idunnu had felt when my photo had been in the paper.

We didn't notice the man who approached Idunnu, but suddenly he appeared, tugging at her arm and asking if we were twins before offering to buy her a drink. It was a temporary moment of cold water, shocking the fuzzy edges caused by our earlier drinks as I felt myself recoil instantly from his attention. Behind the man in his suit was his friend, dressed identically, who lifted the glass he was drinking in our direction. As Idunnu began laughing, I pulled her away forcefully, hoping her good spirits didn't encourage him to follow.

'Baby, why you vex *so*—' Idunnu giggled theatrically, trying to disguise the fact that I'd just ruined her star moment in a way Mama Jumbo might have done, had she been present.

'Nothing is for free,' I hissed sourly, turning around quickly to see if the man was in pursuit. Thankfully, he hadn't been and was back in conversation with his friend.

We'd travelled to Switzerland for serious business. Idunnu didn't have the same obligations as I did, but I still didn't want her misbehaving in front of the other representatives. I wasn't here for someone to try and toast me or to massage my body parts in public.

My chest grew warm, as if the embarrassment I felt was an additional layer of clothing I suddenly wore that I was desperate to remove. Dragging a reluctant Idunnu back to our table, I felt on display in the crowded bar as laughter sprouted all around us like instantly blooming flowers whose aromas made me nauseous.

But if we were a spectacle, Idunnu sashaying behind me had no awareness of it at all.

21

It's not even light by the time we're assembled in the hotel reception, but we're all up and ready, adrenaline making it hard to sleep now that the forum has started and our holiday is over.

The conference is a short distance away – we could probably have travelled via foot – but the NGO is taking pity on us, not wanting to have four ice blocks from Nigeria representing them in Switzerland, I imagine, as our bones rattle inside our skimpy layers of clothing underneath our overcoats. Not only are there vehicles all over the place, reminding me of the grid-lock of Lagos, but these cars look so fresh; nothing battered, no vehicle missing a door, no driver yelling through his window and no one accosting you with goods for sale. All we see are large vehicles that Jonathan guesses have bulletproofing to protect the men inside. We even spot some limousines for the super high rollers.

There's security *everywhere*. It's not that noticeable at first; what I see is the large number of bright orange jackets, people directing cars and guests to different areas and through various lanes as the traffic moves slowly, all on the same route. Then men emerge from their camouflage; their uniforms echoing the dark sky around them, machine guns on display for all the world to see. Of course, there would be a heightened sense of security at an event like this – that Presidents and leaders of the world's largest companies will attend – but it's nice to see the officials staying in one place. Not making *guy* when they approach the cars to put the fear of God into you about their unchecked authority.

Once outside in the crisp morning air, we follow the flow of people moving towards the conference entrance via an inflatable white tunnel. It looks like something set up for children to play with.

'It's called an *igloo*,' Ngozi explains to us as we repeat the word for the shelter built from the snow itself and used in some of the coldest parts of the world. For a moment, I'm taken back to the plane, the sensation of enclosure and artificial light as we travel through the plastic contraption into the large building and get our bearings inside a sea of professionals.

Dr Hariri and Jonathan naturally form a pair while Idunnu and I inch our way behind them, drinking everything in so we can remember it all later and take it home as keepsakes, or presents, seeing as we won't be able to afford any real gifts for people given how expensive everything is in Davos. There are queues of people standing all over the place, flashing lights and bars set up every few metres as if discussing business is thirsty work. Ngozi and Thierry confer at the front of our group while guiding us towards a coffee bar at the same time and settle us at a table so we can have a quick breakfast.

I sip my tea, eyeing everyone around us in the beige hall-way. I thought we'd come early, but the people around us are so alert and engaged in activities. It's easy to see from the demeanour of people congregating at the circular bar a few feet away from us that business is already being done. No time for playing.

Idunnu's head drops towards her cup and I know she's fight-ing the sleep still wrecking her body. Her hair is flat on one side; I'm guessing she didn't have time to fix it before we departed, but she's still done her face well once again in make-up, and for a moment, I regret not doing more than my lip-gloss and the only gold earring I have. I try to chase away the inse-curity I'm feeling, but it won't go. It clings to me like a mess I'm convinced anyone near me will be able to smell. The reality that I – that we – have no business being in this setting.

Under the guise of needing the toilet, I take Idunnu on an exploration mission, moving through the central lounge into a plum-coloured area with standing vases taller than each of us, filled with flowers that would certainly cost a fortune. Idunnu squeals before pulling my arm as she watches someone pass by quickly, but I don't recognise the Indian man in his forties. He's not wearing a suit but a loose sweater on top as he hurries by without us having time to read his name badge, but Idunnu swears he's an Al Jazeera reporter she's seen on the television at work in her hotel back in VI that's constantly trained to that channel.

We accept the free backpacks that are being given out; another welcome pack, this time specifically for the conference, and I momentarily picture Prince and me moving around Lagos with matching appendages on our backs. I know Kemi would want it, but I'm keeping it for myself. Inside the bag is a notebook, a map of the congress centre and a device to go over our shoes, to stop us from slipping in the snow.

The venue is a veritable labyrinth. After walking up and down identical corridors, I stop trying to trace my steps. There are plenty of minders there; helpers pointing people to one side or another, so I know there's no way to get lost even though a large part of me is wanting this very thing rather than to be put on display.

One lounge blends into another, all populated with strangers in similar outfits. There are more women than I expected, although very few others that look like me. They stick out as our paths cross and we exchange knowing looks and wordless nods in a sea of whiteness.

A flurry of commotion occurs as an important-looking oyinbo man crosses the flow of traffic in the hallway, followed by six security members. Helen and Ngozi exchange excited looks before revealing that the man is in fact extremely well known in the UK, unbelievable as that is. After all, how does someone *even* become a chancellor of chess and checkers?

We begin our day of sessions in the Humanitarian Hub, where I feel Helen's gaze on me, so I turn my attention towards her. I take it for a maternal move as her expression softens, or recognition that she's the reason I'm here or vice versa. Either way, I don't want to disappoint her. Squaring my shoulders, I tell my brain to concentrate. Not three hours have passed, but I know for certain that I'm a different person.

So many things I'm learning. Some I've already forgotten; my mind wants to explode.

The world's billionaires have the same wealth as the poorest *sixty per cent* of humanity. It's a truth I can't even begin to imagine. Idunnu and I repeat it over and over again to ourselves like a nursery rhyme, so we won't forget it, and I keep scanning everyone we pass in case I'm in the midst of one of those people who are most certainly at the forum.

There are hundreds of thousands, even millions of us in Makoko, and that's only one spot in this world. One pin-prick on a map. Over half of the world's population is living in poverty and all their money combined is the same as two thousand people: some breathing the same air I'm ingesting? It's a knowledge that can drive you mad.

'Can you imagine such a thing in Makoko?' Jonathan's voice brings me back to the latest topic, the rapidly biodegradable bottle that was unveiled at the conference. A game-changer if it ever came into effect worldwide.

'The implications for the community would undeniably be phenomenal,' Dr Hariri chimes in using some very big English while Jonathan nods profusely beside him before adding his own thoughts.

'What got me was the discussions about the future, you know, having the bottles break down easily – unlike plastic – and then *feeding* the ecosystems? Talk about *amazing!*' Ngozi's eyes light up as she repeats the brief lecture that had accompanied an exciting demonstration.

To me, it's inconceivable; Makoko without its mountains of refuse: our community minus the ever-growing waste that is as much a part of the landscape as the houses and the dirty water. I'm trying to picture it – our settlement surrounded by the kind of water I've seen in my short while here – when Idunnu excuses herself to go in search of a refreshment for her dry throat. She's the only one seemingly bored by the conversation, but I accompany her, not wanting her to feel excluded from this situation we're in.

'Isn't it incredible, thinking of all these things coming home?' I say while declining the offer of juice when a waiter a few feet away points towards my tumbler. I try to visualise myself paddling in see-through, unencumbered waters; to envisage a time ahead that looks different from the way we have always known it.

'You people can stay there with your make-believe ... No be my future o,' Idunnu mumbles with a bitter twist of her lips that bursts my bubble before draining her glass loudly in a way that quenches all further conversation.

After lunch, we're free to attend any meeting sessions that take our fancy, so Idunnu and I copy Dr Hariri and Jonathan as they enter a room to listen to a discussion about sustainability. I understand about three out of every twenty words that are uttered quickly by the six people sitting in front of us on the panel. A few minutes into the event, I peek over at Idunnu; her head is tipped to one side and her mouth is open. In another session, it's my turn. I doze gently, listening to their murmur around me like nearby mosquitoes, and wake up when a woman's voice begins a passionate argument over something to do with culture.

We emerge from another breakout session, spilling out into the corridor like a slick of oil mushrooming over the lagoon's water, and are met by servers with trays of drinks and snacks. I'm relieved as my breath is surely stinking from keeping quiet for so long. Carefully, I use one thing they say is fish on a dry cracker to brush my mouth when no one's looking.

Large television screens are mounted all over the place, capturing some of the sessions going on in other venues and rooms behind closed doors. There are all other kinds of fancy technological equipment as well, goggles some people are trying on and miniaturised robots being powered by men with computers. My thoughts turn to Efe and how much she'd love this; two of her greatest passions in one area, although I have a hard time picturing any of these men in their business suits asking for her hand in marriage.

'Are you okay, Yemoja?' Helen asks, appearing out of nowhere and making my soul stand to attention. She has a way of sneaking up on people, I've noticed, a slow glide that makes her seem as though she's further across the room than she is until she strikes. 'You looked a little overwhelmed . . . How are you finding it?' she continues, sweeping her blonde hair behind her ear with a manicured fingertip.

'Yes, Ma, I'm fine,' I say, pasting a smile on my face before she thinks I'm ungrateful. There's also something about her that I find unsettling, despite her outward kindness. Maybe it's a sense that she's wanting something from me that she's not yet saying, or perhaps I'm my father's daughter after all, deeply suspicious of all outsiders.

'It's a lot to take in,' she proclaims sympathetically before waving at some people walking by. 'Tomorrow will be a bit more intense, but it's good you get a feel for it today,' she adds, picking a loose thread off my shoulder I wasn't aware was hanging down.

'Please, Ma—'

'*Helen* . . . You can call me—'

'Will I have to talk tomorrow?' I ask as the enormity of the feat presents itself in my mind now that I've seen some of the meeting rooms and heard some of the things coming out of people's mouths. Lagos was one thing; all I had to do was read a winner's name off an envelope. Surrounded by all these strangers here, I doubt I'll even be able to say my name.

'Not if you don't want to, Yemoja . . . But you guys have put in a lot of practice. You'll be absolutely *fine*.'

I try to return the smile that she gives me, but my lips stop working and something in my face causes her to bend down and whisper in my ear.

'Malala was the face of female education in spite of the Taliban . . . Greta's leading the charge for the environment! Right now, you're the Pearl of Makoko, our *water warrior,* who can help us have very necessary conversations about how we

end the clean water crisis devastating so much of the world . . .
It's marketing *gold*,' she continues, looking at my blank face
kindly. I don't know the people she's talking about; maybe I
will meet them tomorrow. 'Never mind. You just focus on
being the face and let me do the heavy lifting,' she whispers
conspiratorially before she disappears again.

By late afternoon, we've seen Richard Branson, whom the
Virgin planes are belonging to, the President of France, and a
woman Idunnu swore was Agbani Darego. All attempts to
convince her that our former Miss World would *never* sport
1B/27 colour combination braids were passionately rejected.

I slip away briefly to ease myself, leaving Idunnu stalking a
platter of melon wrapped in ham in between her schmoozing.
How she can create conversation with strangers out of thin
air, I'll never know. When I return, I see her enjoying her
five-star lifestyle and standing alongside the man that had
been eyeing us greedily the night before as though we were
chewing sticks. It's hard to tell for sure as I approach them;
many of the men appear so similar in their black, grey or blue
jackets. It's only their age, height and sometimes hair colour
that separates one from another.

For a second, I'm envious of her obvious ease, but my
irritation quickly pushes that aside. As long as I've known
Idunnu, she isn't one to go chasing after men. Maureen or
Efe, I could understand, but this kind of behaviour isn't some-
thing I expected from Idunnu, who is usually more forthright.
It's almost as if by borrowing Efe's clothing, some of her

mannerisms have rubbed off on Idunnu, who was usually as disinterested in appearance as I was. But as I watch her, winding her body like chewing gum as he says something to her that makes her laugh, I'm realising that Idunnu and I aren't as similar as I once thought. Maybe the cold is messing with her brain and causing a strange reaction, or being far from home is allowing her a freedom that's making her take chances to forget her past self, or Moses even. But I'm bothered by her unusual behaviour as it unsettles me. Either the trip is revealing a new side to my friend I never knew existed, or she's pretending to be someone else, which is another cause for concern. I can't even begin to imagine what she could be discussing with that man, but as I near them, they break apart and she comes up to me with an innocent expression on her face.

'What did he want?' I ask as Ngozi waves at us from a distance, beckoning us over to where a row of journalists is standing in wait.

'*Mcchheww* . . . What does any guy want?' Idunnu replies slowly before a smirk creeps over her lips.

I slept better yesterday evening, no doubt a result of the busyness of the day. We'd had a quick dinner at the hotel restaurant after the conference before disappearing to individual corners to unwind. I called Papa and reported on all the people we'd seen at the conference, then Idunnu had knocked on my door to tell me she'd just come from exploring the spa area downstairs in greater detail. In addition to the sauna and indoor

307

swimming pool we knew about, there was also a hot tub that some other guests had been discussing.

I reminded her that neither of us had swimming costumes, but she'd won me over with emotional blackmail.

'Is that what you go tell Efe when she asks what we did? That you no get costume?' she'd yapped, and after a few seconds of reflection, I'd given in.

We rode down to the spa centre located in the basement and waited for the lone swimmer in the pool to leave. Given the hour, the sunbed and the sauna were closed, but the pool and the hot tub were still open. Stripping down to our underwear, we wrapped ourselves inside the thick hotel towels and went to the hot tub, squealing as we put our fingers inside the bubbling liquid.

'It's *really* hot,' I'd declared incredulously, laughing as Idunnu flung off her towel before submerging her body into the water. I imagined Charlie Boy 'enjoying' the tub with us. He'd probably squirm like a live fish thrown into a pot on the fire.

'*Oya now!*' Idunnu shouted when I'd hovered next to the tub, glancing at her taut belly when she raised herself to flick some water in my direction.

'I dey come,' I said before stopping myself a moment later. 'Wait. Let me take foto first,' I remembered.

'See your long face,' she'd scolded me after a quarter of an hour of sighs and silence. The warm water pulsed against our skin in the quiet of the swimming pool area in front of us, soothing away all the knots trapping my shoulders during the day. 'Why you dey vex?'

'*Me*? I'm not angry,' I replied, rearranging my face to look correct.

'Are you missing home?' she asked wisely, turning her head carefully to avoid her hair making contact with the water level as she shifted to face me.

I nodded in response, casting my gaze over the pool illuminated by artificial lights in the water that gave it a pink hue before turning to a soft green. My brother's image pressed against the backs of my eyeballs. I replayed the recent memory of all of us dancing to the radio in my mind.

'And you?' I countered, turning the tables.

'*At all*,' Idunnu had declared emphatically before twisting her lips. 'No Idunnu this, Idunnu that . . . This here na *living*.'

'Na lie,' I said, not entirely believing her before she flicked some water in my face playfully.

'Na true! No be long time we talked about this? Getting away? Me, I'm counting every day and thanking God each second. But you, your face is frowning. I mean, isn't it what you imagined?' she'd asked at the very moment my phone buzzed and the awakening screen showed Prince's name.

'O-*ho* . . . Is it really Adogbo you're missing or your man for Lagos?' Idunnu queried shrewdly as she eyed my phone. I'd wanted to read his message but restrained myself due to our watery confines. 'You see? It's okay for you. You get Prince, even all these plenty people after you now, since you're famous. There's nothing waiting for me back home,' Idunnu said, her pupils glazing over until no warmth remained.

'You forget Moses?' I looked at her, shocked she could disavow her boyfriend so readily.

'If only,' Idunnu had sighed deeply before raising herself out of the water.

I leave my hotel room feeling eyes upon me. Turning around slowly, I smile at the couple also exiting their room as Idunnu's door opens. I can read the question in their faces as the four of us enter the elevator together and ride in electrified silence before arriving at the hotel lobby. Wondering how I'm staying in this room by myself when I could easily be the black maid pushing the cart down the corridor and waiting to clean the suites after the guests. Idunnu, too. The maid – clearly West African from her features – had looked at us with a mixture of incredulity and admiration when we'd first spotted her in her grey uniform. Idunnu had smiled widely while I'd felt like a fraud.

If it's possible, there are more people than the day before, crowding into the central lounge, swelling in the corridors as cameras rattle off photos at an alarming speed. My face is sticky from the glare of overhead lighting and the nerves I'm feeling even before we begin. I catch Dr Hariri reviewing the notes he carried in his attaché case while Jonathan is exhibiting the calm that came from his birth rite. I suspect that as soon as he opens his mouth, all the wisdom gained from his father and ancestors would issue forth without him having to break a sweat.

I squeeze my fingers tightly as I sit on the edge of my chair and keep my eyes fixed on the exit. If I have to bolt from here, there's little standing in my way unless they have security disguised in plain costume at each of the meetings.

From the first row of audience seating, I can feel Idunnu's torchlight glaring at me and willing me to make contact. She makes a victory sign when I do. Jonathan reaches over from his chair to slap my arm as people begin to fill the room; the shock of his forceful touch is a welcome reminder of home. Switzerland is too much air-kissing and softly softly. I'm grateful for the fleeting sting of my skin that forces me to pay attention.

People take their seats swiftly, and before I even know it, we're underway, with Helen making a rousing opening speech. Our session looks more mixed than some of the others we've attended, where we've been in the clear minority inside the audience. I notice a group of Indians in the last row, an East African woman not far from Idunnu's seat and two men with small caps on their heads. As I observe the engaged faces filling the chairs opposite us, I think that this must be their equivalent of church as they nod at intervals to what she's saying.

'If we're indeed to make the world a better place, then it must be for *all* of us and not just some who look a certain way. If recent times have taught us anything, from social injustice to our response to the world's greatest crisis since the 1800s, we have a responsibility to do *better* . . .'

Idunnu wiggles her eyebrows at me to attract my attention. I watch her fidgeting before I understand the meaning of her message and sit upright in my chair.

'It's imperative that we stay on course to meet our 2030 commitment to provide safe and affordable water to everyone on this planet. Achieving our sixth goal means not just providing adequate sanitation, but investing in *infrastructure*, reducing pollution and *eliminating* the dumping of hazardous chemicals and materials, protecting our precious resources . . .'

I let Helen's voice wash over me like the light from the presentation flashing up on the big screen behind us for the audience. We have our own smaller screen facing our direction, aimed at Helen that we can see too, painting a spinning globe with positive colours as figures relating to her speech appear and disappear. I lose concentration for a while as she discusses their latest project in the Democratic Republic of Congo. It's the word *Makoko* that pulls me back into her talk and I notice all the attention coming in our direction.

All at once, my heart no longer feels like a heart behind my ribcage but like a small, frightened bird that senses a predator outside its nest. Scared as I am, I console myself with the fact that we're only in a small room and not the main auditorium, where some others are speaking in front of hundreds. Still, I pray underneath my breath while Helen introduces us to the audience before more photographs and statistics appear on the screen.

'This settlement has largely been overlooked, like so many others, until one recent photo shed more light on the plight of this extraordinary community going about their daily lives amidst *very real* challenges,' Helen continues, pointing towards me. 'Yemoja, whom some of you might already recognise, was piloting a drone as part of a community-wide mapping pro-ject when her picture was taken. One moment captured on camera that allowed us a brief glimpse into her world and the issues faced by her community.'

I feel myself becoming lightheaded as I bribe my mouth to speak when the moment comes, but thankfully, Helen forges ahead, giving Jonathan and Dr Hariri equally memorable introductions before she continues on with more data.

Both Mama and Charlie Boy must be smiling down on me because I hear Helen call upon Jonathan, who begins to speak about the people of Makoko. I wasn't wrong; years of eavesdropping on community issues by his father's side before being passed the baton are in effect on the stage for all to see, myself included. I watch Adogbo come to life under blown-up images of people going about their day, hawkers on the water, women covered with sweat and smoke over trays of caramelis-ing fish, men labouring on the lagoon, their taut muscles powerful and glinting under the sunlight. Dozens of children with smiling faces dance across the screen, in doorways, on the water in plastic tubs, playing on mounds of sand in Apollo; all of those images are amidst a backdrop of black water and endless garbage.

Dr Hariri goes next, describing the issues faced by the poorly equipped general hospital that runs mainly on local donations. Malaria, typhoid and cholera that devastate our numbers as much as diarrhoea and starvation. It's all things we know. Still, it knocks my brain in a new way; this map that's forming with all the information being put to us. The link back to the lagoon, with its bad drainage, poor sanitation and lack of clean drinking water that's at the root of our problems.

Time moves quickly as I listen to the three of them speaking, turning my head from one to another as though I'm watching a football in the legs of children back at home. Before I know it, the audience are throwing their hands up for questions and the room falls silent as I hear my name.

'How are you finding Switzerland?'

I search the crowd until I find the source of the question. A woman who surprisingly looks so much like Helen that I double-check on her location on the stage in case she's done her shapeshifting again.

'*Cold*,' I reply and the room immediately breaks out into laughter before I can say anything else.

The woman who asked the question continues to look at me and I see Ngozi nodding her head encouragingly, urging me to continue.

'It's very different to what we're experiencing back home. Everything is clean and organised—'

'What are you enjoying the most?'

The microphone being carried around the room by a helper has landed in the hands of a white man reminding me of the Father Christmas that had been on the billboard in front of the fish market throughout the holiday season.

'I like . . .' I begin, wracking my brain for what I can communicate. My nerves have retreated after listening to Jonathan and Dr Hariri handle the audience. All I have to do is keep my eyes on Idunnu as I respond. 'Everywhere there is *clean* water since we arrived in Switzerland . . . There are drinking fountains in the streets with fresh water. And in my room, there's running water,' I continue, latching onto my theme once I've started. 'We visited the lake and there wasn't anything inside it. Just *clear*! Even how you are recycling here . . . Everywhere different, different coloured dustbin! That is how the lagoon could be.'

My voice drops with the end of my statement and the applause that greets me is overwhelming. Through the clapping still ringing in my ears, I hear Jonathan answering another question. The sound is far away, as though my head is underwater, so the words are muffled. As my ears pop, I peek in Ngozi's direction. She gives me two thumbs up and I exhale as I recline in my chair.

The worst part is over. I've held my own in front of all these people. When the news goes back home, I won't have let anybody down.

The morning meeting is followed by a workshop at a nearby hotel with a variety of NGOs also focused on clean water as well as climate change issues. Not much is required of us except to answer a host of similar questions when put to us. It takes me back to school days, not the pressure of story time and being forced to entertain classmates with a tale pulled from your imagination but being trotted out for visitors to bestow upon them an anticipated greeting. It makes me think of the kids back home on the lagoon, acting out for the foreigners that enter our waters. If they're lucky, they'll make a few naira out of it or have their picture taken. But after years of piloting my own canoe, I no get time for that show-business kind of attention.

We crisscross Davos, between event venues in different hotels before ending up back in the congress centre. Photographers snap our pictures in all locations and the journalists at the hall – who are only allowed little pockets of time – throw questions at all of us at once and wait to see who answers. Idunnu even chimes in, mentioning the much-needed solar panels that would put an end to the need for generators and the diesel required to power them. I'm shocked when her voice emerges, considering how little interest she's shown in pageantry before this.

As the day elapses, I begin to understand why I'm here. As a taxi driver, I have a unique overview of the lagoon. As a youth, I have an insightful perspective about our future. We're not the only ones here in Davos who aren't businesspeople. Ngozi points out a young man who's a refugee that still lives in a camp and has been pivotal to discussions for a few years. Throughout the day, my awareness grows of people as young as Idunnu and I, walking amidst officials and leaders with ease.

The day brings us a sighting of an apparent computer giant. He'd crossed the floor in an unhurried, casual manner while smiling at people that it was hard to believe his importance. A man of his worth in Lagos and security would have cleared the entire corridor.

In a slow moment in the central lounge, I'd watched the mounted television, capturing silent titbits from many of the sessions taking place. After a series of serious-looking men, a woman appeared on the screen in a sharp head-tie and navy blue ankara skirt and blouse. Her name flashes on screen and I see she's Ngozi's namesake, Igbo like my mother. Her cheeks even remind me of Mama Jumbo, who I miss so deeply as soon as she appears in my mind. I prod Idunnu, who watches the screen with me, admiring this woman holding her own among experts.

'Na de former finance minister,' Dr Hariri proudly declares, having recognised her, although the text from the discussion taking place is about immunisations.

I watch Ngozi Okonjo-Iweala's command of her knowledge in awe, imagining what she's saying in real life as she pauses on the screen before counting something off with her fingers. For two days, I've been feeling like a fraud in this strange place. Little did I know that my countrywoman was one of these world-leading power brokers invited to the conference, skillfully standing her ground.

Davos is equal parts business and party. After back-to-back meetings, there are drinks everywhere, with no end of locations to choose from. Jonathan's in his element, wetting his lips with a well-deserved brandy after a day of speaking valiantly on our behalf while Idunnu, Dr Hariri and I sip soft drinks and watch the world go by. We haven't seen much of Thierry today, but he soon comes over with Ngozi to toast the end of our sessions. It's Helen who takes her time, working the stuffy room as she's pulled into one group after another before she can tear herself away.

'Let me say again how *well* all of you did today,' Helen repeats once she's settled around our tabletop with a glass of bubbly wine in her hands. 'I've had so many people asking about Makoko and how they can help . . . We – no, *you've* – started a very important conversation,' she adds, raising her glass up in front of her, and we all clink each other's glasses excitedly.

More mini snacks appear on trays that we try and catch before they disappear down people's mouths. A woman approaches Helen for yet another conversation and Helen introduces me before coaxing us a little distance away from the table.

'I'm sorry, work doesn't end. But that's also a good thing,' Helen smiles at me as she taps my shoulder affectionately. 'Yemoja, I'm particularly impressed with your composure. I'm sure that wasn't easy for you,' she says gently, and I nod my head in agreement. 'As my husband would say: "*you try oh*",' she continues and I'm grateful that Idunni isn't here to catch my eye or I would be laughing in Helen's face over her clunky attempt at pidgin.

'Have you given any thought to what you want to do in the future?'

I stare at her blankly. Of course, I'm always thinking about the future, but without money or guidance, the future isn't something you choose but rather something that happens.

'I know about your interest in the drone project, which is very important for Makoko's present and future, and I think you're a *key* part of your community's future,' Helen says seriously. Behind her, a woman passes with something like meat pies, but I force myself to stay focused on Helen.

'You could be an asset in terms of changing Makoko for good. Bringing much-needed facilities to the area, raising awareness. If that's of any interest, then we'd be happy to contribute to your further education. I think you could have a really bright future in international development, back home or anywhere else you'd like to study if that's something you want?'

I smile in lieu of an answer. I'm so overwhelmed I don't know what to say.

I think of Auntie Bisi, who was wishing this very thing on me: some possibility to open up my world.

The woman with the pies holds the tray in front of me and Helen, but there's only one left sitting on its white lace doily. Helen nods swiftly and winks knowingly in my direction and I reach for it before it's gone.

By dusk, Charlie Boy still hasn't appeared, no matter how much I'm wanting it. It's the lack of water, I assure myself, before going to my balcony to search the inky blue horizon, hoping the effect will be the same and I can conjure up my brother. But it's fruitless, and after several minutes in the cold, I return inside, defeated.

The balls of my feet ache from the pressure of my good shoes that I've been wearing for two days straight, and my eyes feel so strained and gritty. Briefly, I picture myself running my eyeballs under a tap before popping them back inside my head.

Days in Davos are passing by speedily, but they're filled with so much activity, it feels like we've been here far longer than we have and my tiredness doesn't ease even with the comfort of a proper mattress. I chew on my tongue as I watch the moonlight creeping across the far wall. Idunnu is here enjoying her best life, but all I'm thinking of is home.

I thought my brother would come with me. He'd always wanted to fly after all.

I hadn't stopped to think what leaving Makoko would mean in terms of leaving Charlie Boy behind, not to mention other reminders of the community. What I wouldn't do for some *swallow* to pass my lips, or a tiny piece of panla straight out of the fire, smoky from the cardboard lid trapping the flavours inside the fish and deepening its burnt caramel colouring. I miss the taste of Maggi cubes and scotch bonnets, the sting of onions tickling my eyeballs and making them water. I'm even missing the smell of Kemi's armpit under my nose and the words Afo sometimes mutters as he's sleeping. My hands long to cook, to chop and peel and stir instead of simply receiving plates from people of interesting-looking food that's sadly lacking in seasoning.

Papa hadn't answered his phone when I tried him after returning to the hotel. My head was still swimming from Helen's words, the prospect of her offer that was the greatest one of the many that had fallen on me in the past few months. I'd called Auntie Bisi instead and her scream was so loud it was as if we'd been communicating via speakerphone.

★

I'd barely registered the rest of the day at the congress centre after Helen had spoken to me. I'd snuck away to write a message to Prince and to read the gibberish Efe had sent, the chainmail that demanded forwarding on to fifteen other people to beget God's blessings. The fact that she'd included me in the abroad and was willing to chop her credit demonstrated her level of desperation.

After the conference centre, we'd made a short walk to a nearby bar, stopping beforehand outside the Rolex shop so Jonathan could take a photo. I spotted the man Idunnu had spoken to the day before among the plenty people squashed inside the small wooden venue that smelled of beer and boiling vegetables. Idunnu saw him too, but she hadn't said anything to me about him while we were there.

I push the covers off me in bed and feel my temperature instantly plummet without the thick protection. But for just a few moments, I want to remember what it's like back home to sleep with nothing, perhaps just the whisper of a mosquito net before the holes in ours became so large that the only point in its continued use was to entertain the insects.

So much has happened, and while I'm still happy I have Idunnu here to share it with me, it doesn't feel the same without being able to talk to Charlie Boy, even though I've been keeping things hidden from him. Did he know that before I flew here?

I recall his doubts suddenly, his query about being allowed to come. I'd assured him that everything would be okay. I wrestle the guilt I have about leaving him behind and add it to the burden I carry about not watching him properly. I count regrets as they come to me until my eyelids start to grow heavy.

I hear Idunnu shifting next door, or so I imagine, as it's hard to know for sure which direction the sounds are coming from in the hotel.

She's been through a lot this year. Sometimes I forget due to her tough exterior. I wonder why she doesn't understand that she's having options too. As I contemplate her outward composure and confidence, the way her fear doesn't show, I realise how resentful I am of this ability she has, especially for this trip we're on. You would think she'd spent the whole of her life travelling. That nothing we've encountered is new. However, the feeling subsides and is replaced by my embarrassment.

I'd expected her to respond more cheerily when I'd told her about my chat with Helen, but she'd been dismissive when I brought up my concerns later on in her room.

'You know how many people would kill for thing dem dey offer you? You don't know how lucky you are to have all these options,' Idunnu had said as we'd sat, flicking through endless channels on the television to find one playing something in English we wanted to watch.

'What about London? Like Ngozi?' she'd suggested before rattling off another half dozen places across the world where I could continue my schooling with Helen's help. I kept silent as she'd polished off the packet of biscuits we'd bought together with our money. 'This is your moment. Why is it causing you stress?' she'd asked, conking my hand gently with the remote control.

If I could answer her question, my spirit wouldn't have been as disturbed. It was one thing to chart my own destiny, but the pressure of being obligated to others or even letting them down was paralysing. I couldn't put my fears into words. I'd bitten down on my irritation about her abruptness or perhaps her jealousy that all these things were happening to me. But her demonstrative lack of appreciation that we were here because of me was bothering my mind somehow. I'd experienced this fleeting impulse to pierce her happy bubble and reached for the first thing my mind thought of: the man from the bar.

'Wetin? You and your friend no dey talk today?' I'd asked, trying to provoke a reaction, but she'd only cackled in a way that irritated me further.

'There are plenty of men here looking for *business* on top of business,' I continued, stressing my words as I tried to get a rise out of her. 'Heaven forbid,' I said, shaking my head and grabbing for the pack of peanuts she'd been reaching for before she finished that too.

'Look at you,' Idunnu replied, flicking her fingers at me. 'You think it's that simple ... Don't you know we play the cards we're dealt? We're not the only ones with a hard life—'

'*Eeehn*, but is that the only option?' I said, sated now that I could see Idunnu sparking to life. 'Selling your body?' I argued, picturing some of the more shameless girls that sold themselves on the mainland before coming back to make yanga with all the things their men had bought them and making fun of those who had less.

'See you, who made you judge and jury?! Is the body any worse than selling your mind?' Idunnu raised the question in a tone that suggested she already knew the answer.

The moment Charlie Boy appears, I wake up from my dream. I don't even remember it; I've barely been asleep since leaving Idunnu's room. Squeezing my eyes shut, I try to retrieve scattered pieces from my reverie, hoping that will make him return and that this time I can hold onto him. It's not fair that having this experience abroad means losing him and there's no one I can talk to about it who'd understand.

I try and remember the last words we'd exchanged in the canoe, but my mind is watery; random images appear before floating out of my grasp. I feel robbed. Not in the way of Charlie Boy not being here, but if this was indeed *it*, then I hadn't even had the opportunity to say goodbye.

I always feared this day would come when he'd disappear forever. When Charlie Boy would go to Mama for good instead of staying here to keep me company. I just always believed that when the moment finally arrived, I'd be prepared. I'd be mature, like a snake shedding its skin for further growth. Instead, what I feel is like a lizard with its tail chopped off.

I know I can live without it, but it's not the same. *Things* aren't the same without him. While I understand objectively that my brother has passed, he's still a part of my present and I've never truly contemplated a future without him.

Is that the price to pay for being offered new things? That I have to let go of older ones?

If it is, I'm not sure I'm ready to pay.

22

Now I know what's in store at the forum, I'm less anxious to face the day. I shower, relishing the hot water pulsing from the massage jets above my head and watching the soapy swirls disappearing down the drain like magic.

I wait a few moments for Idunnu in the corridor, and when she doesn't appear, I knock on her door in case she's sleeping. It opens slowly, and when I see her, she's still in her bedclothes, her face stained with old make-up.

'Idunnu, how far?' I ask, listening to her nails assaulting her scalp as she scratches her hair in a way that leaves it looking more unkempt.

'My tummy dey pain me,' Idunnu says, dropping her gaze downwards. 'I can't spend all day running to the toilet,' she adds, and I picture the unfortunate scenario at the conference venue.

'Tell Ngozi. Maybe she has some medicine—' I offer, but she shakes her head before releasing a large yawn.

'It's okay, I'll just sleep. Maybe I'll feel better quickly then I can come . . . The woman on reception says it's not far to walk,' Idunnu replies softly.

I feel my morning cheer diminish as it dawns on me that she won't be with me today. Just seeing her face in the crowd, even as an occasionally unsatisfactory support, had been helpful. Maybe the universe is punishing me for my wickedness the day before, I think, recalling my snap judgements and feeling remorseful as she shivers in front of me as I delay her meeting with her bed.

'What about breakfast?' I query as I step into the corridor. I doubt she has any food left in her room at all.

The word perks her up and she licks her lips instinctively.

'Please, Baby . . . Bring something for me,' she pleads with a tilt of her head and I nod in return. I only manage a few steps from the corridor before she yells at me to wait and to come back. She's changing her mind, I hope, as I turn around to meet her at the doorway with a smile.

'Can I? Abeg, let me borrow Efe's dress?' she asks.

'Aren't you sick?' I respond, inspecting her closely for any signs of pretence. She'd been fine yesterday, so if she was holding a grudge, then this was a delayed reaction.

'*Eehn*, but must I *look* it?' Idunnu replies sharply, putting me in my place.

As the rest of us ride to the centre, the roads are clear. The ever-present snow here isn't falling from the sky, and the streets have been scraped at some point in the night, leaving dirty grey banks of melting snow that remind me briefly of the gutters on the way to the lagoon. *Idunnu's lying if she believes she's going to walk to this place*, I think to myself, while entertaining the vision that plays in my head of her trying to balance her ankles on the slippery slush.

I try to capture the day for Idunnu, who's missing it, and for people back home, taking photos whenever I see others rushing to pull their phones out to snap away at someone passing with a square of security around them. It's always surprising to see who the real superstars are here – they look just like everybody else.

Hovering outside the Ideas Lab, I attempt to read the lips of the cluster of people inside as they talk animatedly about topics beyond my understanding. Now that we're less in demand, the sessions are starting to make my head swell and ache. I've reached my maximum capacity for what I can take in. After a long meeting involving someone high up at the South Africa Reserve Bank, we file out in search of sustenance.

We stumble upon a new venue, or perhaps we've eaten there before, but they've redressed the room. Either way, the first thing I see is the fountain in the far corner of the room, oozing *chocolate* – not water – but pure melted chocolate gushing down easily seven tiers into a wide silver basin below. Jonathan, most times unfazed, is equally as shocked by it, and we quickly rush over there together, me to taste and him to get some photos for his children.

So many fruits on offer at the table before us, like the fish in the market. I'm not sure whether fruit and chocolate go together, but no one has put their hand into the fountain to scoop the chocolate, so I emulate what the others before

328

me have done, opting for banana, watermelon and strawberries on my three skewers before placing them under the jet of chocolate. I've barely placed the tip of my skewer in my mouth when Jonathan laughs beside me as he takes my photo with his telephone. I don't even care what I look like or whether I have milk chocolate on my teeth.

A woman wears Mama's laugh fleetingly in a way that makes my body shiver as I scan the room feverishly in search of the maker of the sound. Suddenly I'm back at our old home, watching her hang our clothes out on the washing line before the sound of a metal fork scraping a china plate brings me back to the present.

My sadness turns to irritation as Idunnu reenters my brain. She's only replied to one of my texts checking on her in the morning. Ever since then, she's been quiet. I try her again, hearing her phone ring and ring until the line drops off.

Tell me you're okay, I write, pressing my phone screen hard as though that's the same as shouting. I'd hoped she'd be better by this point, that I'd see her floating down the steps to find us in Efe's long dress and attracting some attention with her shakara and her makeup. I shake my head at Ngozi as I return from my corner and we prepare to leave.

I'm grateful that we don't have to sit through another afternoon of meetings. Yes, we're here to help them with our agenda, but it's a lot of pressure and Helen's people know that, which is why we've been granted the afternoon off. There's a trip to a chocolate factory planned and some sightseeing, though no one appears particularly optimistic now that it's started to rain, not even when I propose revisiting the lake. It's frustrating being outvoted. I can hardly tell them why I need to go back, to wait for my brother.

By the time we arrive outside Weltner's, we've got our second wind, captivated by the beauty of the store's shiny windows with the impressive gold leaf signage. The sweets on display look like jewels, stacked in deep brown trays in a way that must be designed to drive people inside to buy. If a store like this was in Makoko, they would need to clean the window every hour as children putting their hands on the glass to see inside would dirty it in no time, but Davos doesn't appear to have many young children visible. Perhaps it's too cold for husbands and wives to be making plenty children.

'Davos is known for beer, but Switzerland is renowned for its chocolate, much like Makoko is for fish,' Thierry explains on the pavement as we ogle the window display.

'Are we going to a beer factory too?' Jonathan asks excitedly, relishing the opportunity to kick back and sample some beers even though our own are the best in the world.

'Well, we thought with the group . . . Next time,' Thierry replies, looking a little dejected.

We walk through the warm restaurant where they're serving food as well as cakes and chocolate until we arrive at a working kitchen space at the back. We're given aprons and hairnets by staff before they take us on a quick tour of the chocolate store, telling us about its hundred-year history before we turn back to the kitchen to take our places along the long bench and try our hand at making our own chocolate. The environment is so sanitary, so different from the way we run things back home in our smokehouses, and their labour appears much less intensive for the delicious outcome.

My mind is full of Prince as I'm stirring a bowl full of melted chocolate and following the instructions of an overeager Swiss gentleman, teaching us how to add our own flavourings before pouring the chocolate into mounds and freezing it. We all get to take away the truffles we made, and in the car, Dr Hariri gives me his own for Idunnu. I thank him, even though I'm in two minds as to whether I'll give them to her or not.

I make one last push for the lake before we return to the hotel, but Dr Hariri is tired and even Jonathan has had his fill of touristy activities.

'Don't worry,' Ngozi commiserates gently. 'I know you're missing the water! You'll have plenty of it when we get to Venice, I promise you.'

I pretend to draw small comfort from her words, contemplating whether it's not the actual water itself but its state that's the issue. Then turning my face to the window, I quickly pray that the lagoon in Italy is as filthy as the one we left back home.

At the hotel, I head straight to Idunnu's door and tap gently but there's no reply. I strike the wood harder, placing my ear against the door as if that will allow me to hear inside, but there's just silence. As the elevator pings down the corridor, the person that appears isn't her but a gentleman watching me curiously as I hover in the hallway, so I pull out my keycard and enter my room.

Helen had been right in her appraisal of my feelings here. Overwhelmed was the word. We'd prepared for the conference, but there'd been no way to know what it would truly be like to be here. How was it possible to feel alone amidst almost as many people as there was on the water? I'd experienced so many things in such a small amount of time and learned some valuable things, the most being that wanting to go somewhere wasn't the same as wanting to *be* there.

There's no answer from Papa when I call him, so I remove my business outfit and climb into my jeans and my new sweater before looking at myself in the mirror. Perhaps it's the location or the setting that's so different to the backdrop in front of the mirror at home, but I notice the changes to my appearance, the crinkles at the edges of my eyes and the hollows in my cheeks. All the running around in a new country has made me lose weight and my jeans no longer grip my thighs. If Maureen was here, she'd call me a pauper. Efe would say that I resemble the capital letter I.

I watch the world outside my window; the figures tiny as ants as they scale the mountain in the cable lift and fade out of view. The streets fill with people and empty at sporadic intervals, and I scan bodies over the balcony for Idunnu's frame, part of me hoping to catch her in a lie. When my phone rings, I leap for it, putting it to my ears before I even know who it is.

'Idunnu—' I begin in an accusatory way before I hear Prince at the other end of the line.

'Pearl? How you dey?' Prince asks, his voice steeped in amusement. I feel a physical ache from the distance between us. I didn't know I would miss him so much.

He keeps me updated about stuff happening in Lagos, protests against the government's proposed fuel price hike and the local squabbles in his kitchen. It eases my mind, not having to think about myself for one second, not having to solve the riddle about my future. But he can tell that I'm distracted and asks whether there's been any news since Helen and I spoke that day.

'No,' I inform him. 'But I'm sure before I come back, I'll have to tell her something. Just so the offer doesn't go away.'

'How can?' Prince replies indignantly. 'Once she has promised you, I'm sure it'll come to pass,' he declares authoritatively and I make a sound that hopefully conveys agreement.

He asks what I can see out of my window and I describe the scene while conjuring him up at his location, in one of his many T-shirts, leaning over a woman's stall in search of the perfect onion.

'In the end, what are *you* wanting? No one else can decide for you,' he ruminates philosophically and I drag myself away from my thoughts. 'Close your eyes,' he says before repeating his demand more forcefully as though he can tell I'm cheating from the distance.

'Don't focus on ten years or five years from now, but say within the next two years . . . If I ask you what your life would be like, what do you see? Are you picturing me? Just joking! Now try to imagine,' Prince commands before lapsing into a charged silence.

I sigh deeply down the phone before obeying, but my mind is blank no matter how tightly I squeeze my eyes. I listen to his breath through the phone, the steady rhythm as he finishes his credit trying to hypnotise me from afar. It's foolish, but it's working, I realise, as the nothing in my mind begins to peel away.

I was viewing it incorrectly, the image in my head, I realise. It was never blank but grey. The lagoon is what I see. Black oily water. The *Charlie-Boy* bobbing gently on top and—

'You see am?' Prince asks, interrupting my imagination, but I don't mind. I have a clearer picture of what I'm wanting now.

'Yes,' I reply with a laugh. 'And I love you too,' I announce boldly, all my prior hesitation gone.

Before I go to the others downstairs to head off for dinner, I try Idunnu's door again. My mind is made up to tell Ngozi or the hotel manager if she doesn't answer, but this time when I pound on the door, I hear shuffling behind the wood before it opens.

'Idunnu! Wetin happen? All day I dey call you,' I say angrily, watching my expression drift off her calm countenance like rubbish floating down a waterway.

'Sorry now . . . I was sleeping,' Idunnu replies sheepishly. I'm in two minds about whether she's lying as she drops her face from my scrutiny.

'For the whole day?'

'My stomach was running *now* . . . Shey I told you,' she repeats indignantly. 'Was everything okay?'

I nod my head in the affirmative as she clutches the side of the door. Her face is clear, devoid of any mask of pain.

'You coming to chop with us?'

'*Eeehn*,' Idunnu nods enthusiastically. 'Let me get my bag,' she adds before moving towards the bed.

Her door inches back a fraction as she relinquishes it and I spy the mess on her floor, her shed night clothes as well as Efe's dress that's no longer pressed like when I'd brought it to her but wrinkled as if she's worn it and then removed it carelessly. I also spy empty wine glasses but close my expression as she returns, clutching her bag and coat.

My phone rings the moment we enter the elevator. I'm expecting Papa from the number on my screen, but it's Uncle Jimi's voice I hear. As soon as I greet him, the lift begins to move and the already shaky connection between here and there worsens. We play a short game of *hello hello* until the lift arrives on the ground floor.

'Hello?' I say.

'HELLO? Baby, can you hear me?' Uncle Jimi shouts for the umpteenth time and Idunnu laughs, which in turn causes me to join in.

'Yes, Uncle, I can hear now,' I reply, putting my finger across the phone speaker to muffle our giggles. 'How far, Uncle? Where is Papa—'

'Na why I dey call you now, Baby! It's your Papa . . . He get accident for mill.'

23

At first, when Mama died, Charlie Boy didn't quite understand. He'd only been four, but death was something we all recognised as we grew, always hovering near to us like our shadows, given the conditions of the community. So, when it came for Mama after her long bout of sickness, somehow, the slap had still been too hard for him at that time and had peppered his brain. Every morning he would ask Papa where Mama was, and every night before he fell asleep, he'd harass Dura, enquiring when she was coming back. It was my sister who'd started his night-time obsession with the lagoon. She'd take him out so Papa wouldn't hear him crying. The journey and his sorrow would tire him, and she'd carry him home, sleeping.

It took a while for him to process the meaning of what had happened. Then he stopped asking about Mama altogether. Six months later, I picked up where Dura left off, taking him out on the canoe to watch night descending, waiting for planes to appear in the sky.

Mama's loss had been all it took to scramble Charlie Boy's mind. I'd suffered then too, but his passing had taken the greatest toll on me. Now they wanted to take Papa as well.

My head had been full of mosquitoes since talking to Uncle Jimi briefly on the phone. He'd told me what he knew about Papa's accident at the mill, where he worked occasionally to bring in some money. Papa had never enjoyed the mill, particularly after spending so many years as a fisherman. The work was tough, especially for a man his age with his poor health. His role had changed from a general labourer to wood inspector these days, but it was still a gruelling task in a difficult environment.

The accident had been caused by a problem with the log stacking and the large beams of wood had come crashing down. Most of the workers had managed to escape unscathed, but Papa and another fellow had been struck.

After I reported to the group what I'd just discovered, we decided against the restaurant we'd been heading out to and went to one closer to the hotel, filing into the small venue with steamy glass windows that smelled strangely of cleaning products. They'd tried to lift my spirits, praying for Papa before we ate our meal, but all I could picture was wood falling on Papa's head.

We'd ordered fondue, spiced melted cheese that arrived on a platter that resembled our cooking pots back home, only shrunken. There was even a miniature cooking fire underneath it that kept the cheese warm at the table, and tiny forks for loading our accompaniments onto. It was the Swiss version of ogi in terms of taste; Dr Hariri had really enjoyed it, as had Ngozi.

Papa had been to the general hospital. Of course, his accident would have to happen while I was in another country with the main doctor of the clinic.

'It's okay, Yemoja. The people there will look after him,' Dr Hariri had tried to assure me throughout dinner, but I'd had no appetite for food or his empty words.

It was hard to imagine proper care from a place that existed mainly on donations. Some of the long-established hospitals on Lagos' mainland had less than nothing in the way of basic medical supplies, so patients died needlessly due to a lack of equipment or even hospital beds. Even Chibuogo, Auntie Uche's daughter, had been turned away without the simple injection that would have saved her after stepping on a nail. She'd effectively come out of the hospital dead, Mama Jumbo had declared at the time.

Loss was something all inhabitants of Makoko experienced; it surrounded us like the lagoon. No one would dare drink the black water directly, knowing how badly it would harm the body, but it always found its way into us just the same.

None of my family members were answering their phones when I called them, but I sent the same message to Papa, Uncle Jimi and Mama Jumbo, begging for any kind of news. I sent a message to Prince, who texted back immediately with commiserations and even offered to go to Makoko in the morning to get news if I wanted.

Idunnu was coming down the corridor in her coat as I'd left my room to knock on her door. I was startled by her outerwear, imagining that everyone had been in their hotel rooms like I had been, even though this wasn't necessarily the case.

'Where did you go?' I asked, regretting the question as soon as I said it on account of its accusatory tone.

'Food 24,' Idunnu answered instantly, coming to a stop by me.

She wasn't carrying a shopping bag, but I didn't have the energy to challenge her as she opened the door to her room and I followed her inside to collapse on the foot of her bed and tell her what I'd decided.

'*Are you serious?*' Idunnu had turned to eyeball me after violently shrugging off her coat.

'*Yes, now,*' I sighed, checking my phone again even though no notification had come in. 'I must go back. For Papa—'

'When?' she asked before reading the answer on my face. 'But what about Venice?' Her voice climbed two octaves as she lay down next to me, so we both stared up at the ceiling.

'I know, but how can I continue travelling when Papa dey hospital?' I replied, distressed, listening to the loud footsteps that scurried down the corridor before the faint ding of the elevator bell sounded.

'What can you do for him if you're there?' she asked, strangely calm. She'd made a fair point and I had no response.

'You go come back with me?' I asked quietly after a long moment of silence and Idunnu sat upright beside me sharply.

'Baby, what are you saying?'

'Wetin—'

'This na *once* in a lifetime opportunity! How can you even ask me that?' Idunnu hollered like a wounded animal. 'Or is it because you're not enjoying yourself? *Haba*, it's just four more days on top—'

'Idunnu, my papa dey *hospital*,' I'd implored, tugging at her compassion. Even though his heart had hardened over the years, he was still my father.

'And may the Lord God protect him,' Idunnu replied before pacing her room agitatedly. 'But this is our one moment . . . Maybe not for you, but for me—'

'*So*, because you dey jealous me—'

'Ah, I'm not jealous o, Baby, I just no fit go back yet.' Idunnu picked up a sweater from the floor and flung it onto the chair, expending some of her pent-up energy. 'Please *now*! It's not new, what I'm telling you. But, of course, *you* want to go back?' she asked slowly and I nodded.

'You're my chaperone—'

'*Eeehn* . . . But only for the conference, *abi*? Venice is just vacation,' Idunnu argued soundly and for a minute, I applauded her effort. She was fighting for what she wanted. I understood her desire to stay on this luxury trip as much as I couldn't explain my need to be back in Makoko even if I couldn't help Papa.

'I can't lose another person, Idunnu,' I said, shocked by my own admission once it left my lips.

'You already lost your papa a long time ago,' Idunnu replied before screaming and recoiling from me, stunned. It had happened so instinctively, so quickly, I hadn't even registered striking her until I was witnessing her reaction. It was only then the stinging in my palm appeared.

Idunnu glared at me, frozen by the unexpectedness of my action in defence of the man I'd spent years complaining to her and our friends about. I was equally taken aback. I'd wanted to reach out to her, but my blood had turned to iron and my body refused to move. The moment she'd taken her gaze off me, I'd fled from her room.

She's not scary as she rises out of the waves. She *is* the wave, the water, I realise as I stare at her, transfixed by how the liquid appears to be her vibrant skirt before my gaze moves up the silver fish scale bodice of her outfit to take in her metallic crown and head-tie combination. Her long braids move like sea serpents, undulating behind her with the current, which is what alerts me to the fact that I'm under the water with her and having no trouble breathing.

Yemoja, I think, only I hear my name out loud as she's calling me and so I answer her.

'Yes.'

'You've done well,' she says, looking at me with such fondness that I at once register her familiarity.

'*Mama*,' I whisper. I immediately start to cry, but the tears that fall aren't liquid but cowrie shells, hundreds and hundreds of them that pool underneath me and slowly become a canoe. Once it's formed, I feel it begin to rise from the water, but Mama remains where she is, reclining against a rock with numerous fishes at her feet.

'*No!* Make it stop. I don't want to leave,' I beg as I try to climb out of the canoe, but she halts my movement by commanding the waves around me so they impede my exit.

'You have to. You can't stay here,' her voice says gently as my boat carries me higher towards the surface.

'*Please,* Mama . . . What of Charlie Boy? Is he with you?' I think to ask as my throat fills with flames and I become aware that my ability to breathe underwater is fading. I watch her as the gap between us widens and I grow faint from the lack of oxygen.

'He's fine. I have him now, you can let go,' she replies.

'I'm not ready! Let me see him,' I cry, but my mouth fills with brown water and I know then that I'm in the lagoon and not the clear aquamarine waves I'd been in when my dream first began. Now that I know my brother is with her, I'm even more determined to stay, to hold on if I can, knowing I won't survive this loss. 'Please! Don't make me do it—' I begin as bits of refuse charge into my open mouth.

'You'll be okay, Baby. Now you must LET GO!'

I wake up immediately as if someone has given me an order and find myself staring at my hotel ceiling from the bedroom floor. I cough repeatedly to draw air into my burning lungs. My body is so drenched in sweat that I wonder if any part of my dream might have been real.

For the first time, I noticed placards in the crowds gathered. Perhaps the town's security had successfully managed to keep the people bearing signs away for most of the conference; had isolated the troublemakers until now in case they caused too much of a disruption. I read CLIMATE FOR CHANGE as well as CLIMATE JUSTICE NOW before a lone woman bellows about abolishing millionaires. She isn't holding a sign, so it's harder to spot her amidst the normality of people on the street, but when she opens her mouth again, she's caught. As she's led away quickly, most people ignore her outburst, seemingly unfazed by these isolated protesters threatening the harmony of the forum. *Maybe it's my own lack of peace that draws them to my eyeline*, I think to myself. I recognise my own people where before I was blinded by all the newness, by the shiny spectacle of Davos.

The morning is a blur that I push through as I retreat into my own head, consumed with my worries about Papa and ashamed about my behaviour with Idunnu, who isn't talking to me. After I'd left her room, I knocked on Ngozi's door. Once I'd been safely inside, that's when the tears had come.

'Please *now*, make I go home! Quick quick . . . I'm sorry for Italy,' I pleaded between painful swallows as Ngozi tapped my back gently.

There was no point in me carrying on with the trip to Venice. I wouldn't be able to see a thing in any case as all I could think about was Papa back home.

'What about the other side? What will you do from the airport?' she'd asked, raising a series of questions that were either destined to deter me or to help us see if there was any feasible way forward now that I was spoiling the trip for all of us.

'My friend will pick me,' I declared firmly, thinking of Prince, who I was certain would come to my rescue.

'Why don't you sleep on it and decide in the morning? If you—'

'I'm sure,' I'd said, but she'd made me wait while she got a hold of Helen.

After everything had been decided, Ngozi had pulled out her computer and I'd watched her navigate the internet and a series of websites until she'd procured me a ticket, departing the same day we were meant to leave for the Makoko of Europe, but in the morning.

Everyone could sense that something was going on between Idunnu and me, but no one had the courage to face it. Jonathan and Dr Hariri exchanged curious looks that I pretended not to notice and Idunnu flatly refused to make eye contact at all. Whenever I asked her a question directly, her response was polite but super icy in that way that cold drink hurts your teeth and is no longer refreshing. As I doubted an apology would resolve things, I'd kept quiet. Besides, while she might have felt a temporary pain when my hand made contact with the side of her face, I was the one who was truly hurting, and by all accounts, she didn't seem to care.

The workshop in one of the labs is the most relaxed one we've had so far and after the usual opening, there's a flurry of questions, but I'm no longer terrified. It's become almost second nature and I can't help the feeling I have of slowly becoming a performing monkey. I know exactly what to do to get the peanuts that are applause. I paste a smile on my face, but inwardly, I feel my resentment mounting for these people that are here to fix the big issues of the world. There's a thin line between them being curious about our circumstances and us becoming curiosities, though when I observe Idunnu and the others, they don't appear to mind that outward gaze. They're enjoying the attention in a way that I'm not. But it's only me that had Papa as a parent, I remind myself, as his feelings and mine merge momentarily. Apparently, it's only me that's feeling tired of being the entertainment.

At a mixer event, I'm grateful for the opportunity to lose myself inside the crush of bodies talking over one another in an attempt to be heard. I watch Dr Hariri in a rapt conversation with the refugee from the other day, while a group of women surround Jonathan as if they're waiting for him to bless them. Ngozi and Idunnu are bonding over something, which draws laughter from the two of them that chooks my eyes. I feel the impulse to cry even though I'm standing in the middle of a room full of merry people and fight to control the tears welling up in my eyes when I smell Helen's perfume next to me.

'How are you holding up, Yemoja? Any more news about your father?' she asks me with a concerned expression. I shake my head and shrug my shoulders as we stare off in the same direction in the absence of any other conversation.

'I understand why you're leaving, but still, I'm sorry you won't get to see Venice.'

'It's okay . . . This has been *plenty*,' I tell her truthfully and she smiles at my words.

'Let's keep talking, even when you're back home. You've got too much going on now, but when you're ready, we can continue that conversation about your education. Or how we can help, if you want it,' Helen says warmly before skipping off to chat to a group of people.

Back at the hotel, I skip the dinner downstairs in the restaurant with the others and opt for something in my room. The chicken that comes smothered in a yellow sauce is tasteless and surprisingly hard, but I eat it anyway, feeling it land in my stomach next to my anxiety about Papa and travelling home alone. When Prince flashes my number, I call him back so we can go through my flight details one more time. As I listen to his voice through the phone, I register the frisson of excitement about the prospect of seeing him sooner than anticipated.

I call Uncle Jimi to check if he's seen my message about me coming home and he tells me that Papa's awake, that they were waiting to rule out concussion from where he conked his head. They're giving him painkillers, but it's taking some time for him to respond. At the end of the call, I hang up the phone, satisfied with my decision to return early. I chase away the guilt that momentarily travels through me as I recognise my relief that Papa's still unwell. If they'd reported a speedy recovery, then I'd have jeopardised my trip for nothing.

More than I want Papa to be better, I don't want Idunnu to be right.

I inspect my suitcase before closing it. It's much fatter now with the things I've acquired from this trip and the gifts I'm taking back home, small as they may be. Idunnu and I managed to get two hats each from a company giving them away at the conference centre before they ran out. The blue bobble hats would be perfect for a fisherman during Harmattan when the wind can make it feel surprisingly cold, or even just to elevate Papa and Uncle Jimi's outfits. The hotel cleaner kindly gave me another pair of slippers that I packed for Papa. It's only Auntie Bisi and Prince that I got real presents for. For Auntie, it was a nice-smelling soap bar with real flowers inside. She'll never use it but will put it someplace for decoration.

Of course, for Prince, it could only be one thing. At last, I'd settled for a black T-shirt with the word DAVOS printed on it, along with a silhouette of the mountains.

Nestled in the corners of my luggage were also packets of sweets, biscuits and many small pots of jam I'd successfully smuggled from the buffet breakfasts, along with different flavoured herbal teas.

As I close the zipper around the case, I push away the sense of finality gnawing at me and think of canoes gliding through the water; children dancing to the music in their heads. My brother . . .

The others are downstairs when I head down and I force myself to eat as they chatter around me in the busy hotel restaurant. Idunnu had been the last one to appear and I imagined her debating whether to show up at all in her room before descending in the elevator to squeeze in at the end of the booth at the other side of Ngozi, so she didn't have to see me directly. When Dr Hariri inevitably began asking questions about Venice and their upcoming journey later in the day, I closed my ears, not wanting my jealousy to surface even though I'd made my choice.

Soon after Thierry arrives, my chaperone for the journey back to Zurich Airport, I go to perform one last sweep of my room before bringing my bag down to reception. Ngozi takes charge of checking me out while Dr Hariri and Jonathan coax me into a series of photos inside the hotel reception before I disappear. They drag Idunnu into the mix and she complies, stone-faced. Maybe they think we're fighting because I'm going back early – and mostly we are – but I know with my slap, I crossed a line and I don't know how to apologise. Moreover, after everything we've been through together, I shouldn't have to.

'Don't forget: when you get to Paris, you don't have to pick your bag. Just follow the connecting flight signs and keep checking the board for your gate.'

'Okay,' I say rather unconvincingly and Ngozi notices.

'You have a short connection, you hear me, so don't take time anywhere!'

'You ready?' Thierry asks, taking the handle of my suitcase from my hands. I nod and the goodbyes begin.

'Thank you for all your hard work,' Ngozi continues as she hugs me quickly. The trip had taken a toll and some effort, but it hadn't felt like *work*. I don't really understand what she's thanking me for, but I accept it anyhow, especially knowing I won't hear anything like that from Idunnu. As I bid farewell to the others, Idunnu takes an awkward step forward before

I leave, an involuntary jolt from deep inside her as if it's her soul that wants her to move, but she's trying to resist it.

'See you,' I say, staring above her shoulder at the emergency exit poster on the wall next to the reception desk.

'*O dabo,*' Idunnu whispers sheepishly.

'Goodbye for now,' I repeat back to her as I follow Thierry towards the waiting taxi.

As we make the journey in reverse, a part of it feels like a video being rewound; only I know I'm not going back to the same place, to the same starting point. I and everything have changed. I'd thought I was exactly the same, it was only people's interest in me as a result of my viral moment that had caused them to act differently towards me, but it begins to dawn on me as I catch pieces of my reflection in the train glass as Thierry and I sit opposite each other on the ride to Zurich, how I'm not the same Baby as the one that left Lagos a week ago. How could I be after this extraordinary outing to one of the most exclusive areas in the world? I was a fish out of water that had endured a long stretch on dry land and had lived to tell the tale.

Just as we reach Zurich train station, I get a text from Idunnu saying *sorry*. One simple word that has surely taken so much to transmit.

Me too! Shey you understand why I have to go?

I only have a minute to wait before her response comes back.

You did what you feel you have to do. If anybody understands that, it is me. Safe journey.

We take another connecting train from Zurich Main Station to the airport and Thierry stays with me through the check-in and even accosts a family standing a few people behind us in the queue. They have enough luggage for an entire village, mismatched cases spreading out over two trolleys in a way that is impressive and intimidating. But Thierry, using his management skills, asks if they can keep an eye out for me since we're travelling to the same destination and they agree, although who can say if they'll actually do it? He escorts me all the way to the departure gate and waits until the family appears so that I can fall into step after them.

Ngozi calls me once I've cleared security, almost as though she can see what I'm up to, to check that everything's okay and it is. I feel strangely at ease despite not really knowing where I'm going. In many ways, the airport is symbolic of my life. I'm surrounded by people, but the truth of it is I'm alone. There's no Mama, no Charlie Boy; *nobody* here to guide me on my way. I think briefly about the dream I had with Yemoja, that had made me feel loss initially, but as I'd woken up, I'd realised its deeper meaning. I simply have to have faith in myself and know that I have what it takes to arrive where I'm going safely.

In what little I'd seen of the airport in Paris, there'd been a poster welcoming travellers to *the City of Lights*. There'd been no way to witness this during the daytime, but as we descend into Murtala Muhammed International, it is Lagos that better bears that name. Like a million wicks flickering in the darkness sprawling out of the window, scattered and without meaning until a certain point where the yellow, orange and red dots converge to form rivers and rivulets that turn into main roads the lower we go.

Before we touch down, I close my eyes. I hear the gentle sound of the plane before my ears pop to reveal the rumble of the engine. A few rows ahead of me, a baby cries and cries in the dark plane that mirrors the outside world before its wheels graze the tarmac and we shift in our seats before the pilot resumes his smooth ride. I join in with the spontaneous applause that breaks out in my economy section as the cabin lights come back on and the baby falls quiet at last. The flight that was never silent, given who its passengers are, reaches its most tranquil moment as a stillness settles on the plane for just one moment before it disappears and conversations resume. Multiple phones are switched on and a flight attendant yells at two passengers for getting out their seats before they're allowed to. One man is unrepentant and keeps pulling his case from the overhead container until the woman rushes over to scold him.

My heart swells as the plane continues to slow but never quite stops moving. There's little to see now that we're on the ground, but the evening is lighter than it appeared from above and the black more translucent, like the lagoon's water revealing trees and the tops of nearby buildings. Somewhere out there, close by is Prince, waiting for me.

Reaching for my phone, I switch it on and wait for it to regain consciousness as the seatbelt sign above my head turns off and everyone gets up as though the small ping sound accompanying it is a starter pistol for the hundred metres.

351

I'm in a window seat again, so there's only so much I can hurry, but I gather my things quickly, hearing the notification sound on my phone as it connects back to the local signal. After the fourth ping, I check my phone, fearing something has happened to Papa while I was in the air. But there are no new messages from Makoko. I see texts from Prince as well as missed calls and multiple messages from Ngozi.

I start with the most recent one as the passengers begin to file out into the main aisle. I join the crush of people and come to a standstill after less than eight steps, all my attention swallowed up by my phone.

Can you PLS call as soon as you land? Idunnu still hasn't shown up and isn't answering – we've ALL tried to call her! If you know anything or have heard from her, we need to know.

'I say HELLO!' A passenger eyes me savagely; I'm causing a roadblock in the aisle by reading and rereading the message swimming in front of my eyes.

I turn to face the annoyed lady, my mouth hanging open as a result of what I've just read. She hisses at me as I hurry to catch the people ahead of me with Idunnu's trouble burning a hole in my brain.

Fire

24

For the first time, I'm truly aware of it. After the cool crisp freshness of the Swiss atmosphere, I notice our air, the distinct, familiar aromas of home.

From the moment I exited the plane to be greeted by the city's hot breath on my skin, I'd latched onto the scents of Lagos: fuel, sweat and rubbish. The memory of Davos peeled away almost as instantly as my coat had on the gangway outside of the plane.

When we came to Makoko the following morning, even before we'd arrived at the water, I could smell it.

Dirt, decay, shit . . . their heady bouquet striking deep chords on my heartstrings while around us, a tapestry of chaos, so contrasting to the sterile order of Davos, dazzled my senses. Maybe it was the same as Ngozi with her NGO work; the lagoon being an essential part of me in a way I hadn't appreciated before. I'd seen other water, clear and frigid as ice, yet in that form, it hadn't stirred me. But the unmistakable odour of fish and waste, the black waves: they *were* my blood.

I inhaled deeply, taking the pungent smoke of my birthplace deep into my lungs.

Reawakening the old fire-breathing dragon within me and reinvigorating the new one that has flown far away from here at the same time.

25

Sitting in the *Charlie-Boy* staring out across the lagoon, it's almost as if I'd imagined my trip in the abroad, as though it was just part of a feverish dream. Even now, as I wait for tail lights to appear in the dark sky, it's hard to believe that I was once up there looking down over this place, as I flew to mingle with giants.

I'd settled back into the routine of my former life seamlessly, preparing food for my cousins while replaying scenes of being waited on back in Switzerland. To think that we'd been speaking on the same podiums that major world leaders had used! It was hard to believe as I swept around the mattresses in our packed bedroom.

The trip hadn't been bad at all, only different. The unfamiliarity of it all had thrown me off-centre, but astonishingly, others like Idunnu had enjoyed the lifestyle that was strange in comparison to being on the lagoon.

My young cousins had been right. For me, it had been more of a holiday. Little did I know that for Idunnu, it was her escape.

Idunnu. Idunnu.

I listen to the sound of my paddle in the water as it strikes against the sides of the canoe, almost to the rhythm of her name. I try to remember the sensation of snow against my skin, the fleeting singe of my eyelashes and cheeks before the flakes melted away, leaving prickles of electricity on my exposed scalp. Is this what Idunnu was wanting all along, so much so that she would endure an eternity freezing? The chance to flee Makoko once and for all?

A part of me is desperate to be angry with her for leaving without telling me. But any sense of betrayal is masked by grief. I'd been so consumed with what was happening with my brother, I'd missed what had been going on right in front of me with my closest friend.

For so long, I'd imagined leaving was what *I* wanted. I'd attached Charlie Boy's dreams to my own when he could no longer dream them for himself. I'd gone abroad for *me*, but he'd had a big hand in it as well. Perhaps because he knew it was the only way for me to move on without him. But I'd never considered the full implications of what it would mean to live outside the community. However, when the opportunity had presented itself to go away, all I could really think about was home.

The night I'd returned to Lagos, after successfully navigating the airport by myself and gathering my bag, I'd gone through the exit to a wall of people; family members, security, drivers hustling for passengers, all of them shouting and screaming as travellers came outside into an added layer of heat. For close to a week in Switzerland, we'd been the indi-vidual faces in a sea of white. But once again, I was surrounded by mostly Nigerians of all tribes and complexions, twitching and pushing forward, threatening to break the invisible line beyond the arrival doors where loved ones waited for travel-weary passengers to emerge.

I'd scanned the crowd fearfully as I searched for Prince, ignoring men shouting as they offered taxi services and others waved fat bundles of cash, hoping someone wanted to exchange currency. I wasn't sure what I would have done if he hadn't come at all, but there he'd been, using his back-pack as a protective shield against the overzealous people in front of him, leaning against his body. When he'd seen me, he rushed forward with his hands out to protect me from strangers pushing past in their speed out of the airport and towards their cars for the gridlocked journeys back home on the road.

I'd hugged him tightly, reading the TOGETHER WE RISE on his T-shirt only when we'd pulled apart and he'd taken my suitcase off me.

'*Welcome home*,' he whispered before wiping the tears I hadn't even realised were running down my cheeks.

'Guess what happened?' I started to tell him about Idunnu, but his attention was focused elsewhere as he steered me towards the haphazard car park until he found what he was looking for in the long queue that was inching its way forward to where we stood. I saw the vehicle, the white car with the Viceroy's logo printed on its side.

'Let's get back first, Baby,' Prince said, pulling me into the car, where his colleague was behind the wheel. 'Then you can tell me everything.'

At his room in the hotel, I'd heard my anger as I recaptured what had happened in Davos, my incredulity at what Idunnu had done, as well as my embarrassment at having selected her as my companion. But after the first burst of my emotions subsided, I'd felt the guilt followed by the weight of our previous argument and questioned whether any of my actions had forced her into what she felt was her only move.

'You're not responsible for her behaviour,' Prince had remarked, trying to console me, but I wasn't sure if what he'd said was true.

Small dots of light appear in the sky above me and I recall looking over the lagoon from our seats on the plane. Idunnu squeezing the life out of my fingers before we'd set off.

You did what you feel you have to do.

Those had been some of her final words to me, I realise as I contemplate the fact that I might never hear from her again.

In her own way, Idunnu had told me her intention. Only I hadn't been listening.

All of my initial joy at being on home soil was swallowed up in the drama Idunnu's disappearance had brought.

My heart had been racing when I'd called Ngozi back the moment we got to Prince's hotel. She'd explained that Idunnu had chosen to remain at the hotel after checkout instead of going for a walk with the rest of them. Their plan was to meet for lunch at the pizzeria. When Dr Hariri, Jonathan and Ngozi had arrived at the pizza place at 12.30, Idunnu had texted to say that she'd gone to buy some last-minute things and they should continue without her. She'd be back in time for the car coming to drive them to Italy. But at the hotel, when they'd returned to retrieve their suitcases from the luggage room, Idunnu's had been missing, as was she. It was hard to imagine any scenario other than fleeing since she'd retrieved her belongings, according to the concierge.

Of all the people to kidnap in Davos, a lagoon dweller would not have been the one. Plus, Idunnu had rejected the first call that Ngozi had made and after that, her phone had been switched off.

When I'd been travelling back to Lagos, my thoughts had wandered to them continuing on with their European exploits. Cruising in a luxury vehicle through breathtaking country vistas for the four-and-a-half-hour journey. But I'd listened to Ngozi speaking as though she'd been recounting the plotline of a Nollywood film. Never could I have imagined them fretting at the hotel in search of Idunnu, who'd vanished into thin air. How on earth was she planning to sustain herself? I'd previously assumed that she'd blown what money she had on shopping.

I'd sworn passionately and repeatedly about not knowing what Idunnu had planned; Ngozi had heard the shock in my voice and hadn't accused me of being involved but had only begged me to keep trying to make contact with Idunnu from my location. I'd tried both her new and old number, calls and text messages, but wherever she was, she wasn't responding to me either.

The following morning, I'd called Ngozi again, but they still hadn't managed to track Idunnu down and Helen had been looped into the situation. They'd spent the night in the hotel, hoping that Idunnu would come back of her own accord and that the messy situation would be salvaged. Understandably, the trip to Venice had been cancelled and Helen had been forced to scrap her own flight back out of Zurich as they'd accepted the need to call in the authorities to inform them of the situation.

I'd been full of worry about Papa when I'd landed, but then the news had come about Idunnu, immediately doubling my capacity for concern. Where had she gone and how could she possibly survive in that place with what little she had? I'd slept fitfully in Prince's room, reviewing our last conversations in my half-asleep state as I attempted to find clues I might have overlooked in real-time when we'd been together.

Could she have run off with one of the men from the forum, or was she hiding somewhere in the basement of the hotel, waiting for the search for her to be called off in order to start a new life? She'd always wanted to leave Makoko, but not like this, surely?

When I'd arrived back at home, Idunnu was the second topic on people's lips after reassuring me about my father.

'Heeey! *DRAMA!*' Auntie Bisi had pummelled her breasts after hugging me tightly on our deck as dirty clouds hovered low in the sky around us as if they too were eavesdropping for gossip. Not a full day had passed, but the news had already been carried far and wide.

Dr Hariri, Jonathan and Ngozi returned to Lagos the day after, shell-shocked from the abrupt ending of their European experience. We attended a meeting at Jonathan's father's house to discuss what implications Idunnu's disappearance might have on the community once the news spread.

'The NGO's position is that they will keep things quiet, to not overshadow the real story, which was our presence at the forum,' Dr Hariri had informed the stunned gathering.

'It's true . . . You people did well and a global spotlight is shining on us like never before,' our baale began, looking proudly at us despite the awkward situation. 'Idunnu's behaviour hasn't changed that, no matter how shocking her action has been,' he'd concluded sagely as my lost friend captured all of our thoughts.

As everyone had debated H2All's statement, internally, my exasperation at Idunnu's actions battled my love for her. Part of me wanted them to drag her back here, yet I was equally impressed by her boldness *and* happy that she'd left us. Some members of Idunnu's family had been present, including her mother, whom her sister and cousin had needed to hold on tightly to keep her from slipping to the floor as her grief overtook her in dramatic waves.

'It's okay, it's okay, Mama. She'll return,' Bimpe had repeated unconvincingly to her mother, who was muttering to herself between various panicked outbursts, almost as if the news had been that Idunnu had died.

It struck me then – as my bones had turned to jelly, like boiled cowfoot – that in some way, my dear friend Idunnu had.

★

'Baby!'

'Yes, Papa,' I shout back, despite the short distance between our bedrooms.

I hurry to him, but the urgency in his voice is built in and not tied to any immediate drama. I wonder how long it will take until the stress no longer chooks my body about his health. Or perhaps I'll always have to live with the threat of losing him, until it's only me and Dura left.

'Please . . . bring my newspaper for me,' Papa asks, pointing at the chair on the other side of his bedroom.

I comply, handing him his paper and helping him shift upright with his new makeshift pillow that is a pile of his clothes underneath a wrapper. Although he grumbles as I pull back his curtain and open his window to dispel some of the stale air, he stops short of complaining outright.

I check the dressing on his leg. He has medicine from the general clinic to take but insists on using the ointment given to him by the traditional healer. Every evening, I rub the stinking ointment onto his limb that leaves a stain on it as well as on my fingers before I cover it with some bandage. Since he still drinks his tonic, I've taken to crushing his real medicine inside it. Not that he can tell; his mixed drink already has an unusual taste. But after all the trouble Mama Jumbo went to in taking care of his situation, the least he can do is use the medicine meant to make him well. She'd even arranged to pay for the balance of his fee at the clinic while I was still in Switzerland.

'You see this?' he asks, drawing my attention to the newspaper.

'Yes, sah,' I reply, reading the article headline upside down from my vantage point about the new composting toilet being built in our community.

'You young people . . . Your world is different. You've done well,' Papa says softly before clearing his throat. 'You hear me, Baby?' he adds, looking at me so intensely that I feel my eyeballs prickle. 'We thank God,' he concludes before shaking his newspaper vigorously.

It could have been so much worse. The accident at the mill had seen no casualties this time, only head wounds, broken ribs for Papa's colleague and a torn tendon for Papa, requiring a knee brace and many weeks of inaction to allow him to heal. But no walking means no working, so it's a good thing that we have money from H2All.

He'd been shocked when I'd arrived back from Switzerland early, though he'd hidden it well, or perhaps the painkillers he'd been on had helped him as he floated in and out of his delirium, talking to Mama, who must have come to watch over him until I could return. It struck me then, as I'd watched him communicating with her, that what Idunnu had said to me in her hotel room – the day I'd hit her – had been right. I'd spent almost a decade talking to Charlie Boy, who had passed, as though he was in the present. It had never occurred to me that a part of Papa had died that same day. I'd been scared of losing someone I'd lost many years earlier; only I hadn't made that connection.

It might even have been why my brother had appeared to me in the first place. Why he'd stayed so long until I'd gone away.

Only then had he decided it was safe for him to go away too.

I miss Charlie Boy so much there's a physical ache, like when I once banged against a canoe and had a bruise the size of a belt around one side of my waist. I only knew what *I* felt; I hadn't considered what Papa must have endured with losing Mama as well as his son.

'I'm sorry,' I begin before Papa moves forward so swiftly that his pillows drop to the floor.

'What are you sorry for? You this child—'

'For Charlie . . .'

'Baby, Baby, Baby,' my father's eyes grow wide as he chants my name while flapping his hands theatrically. 'Don't even finish your sentence!'

'I should have—'

'*You* are full of blame. *I* am full of blame, even now! Is any of that bringing him back? My daughter, I have been holding on to you too tightly. I'm sure that's why you left, why you wanted to go. And I thought I had lost you as well by trying to keep you close. But you returned and I'm so thankful,' Papa proclaims as slow tears run down the grooves of his wrinkles.

It's the most he's ever revealed to me about his feelings and I'm taken aback by Papa's openness. I'd never once read his control over me as a sign of his affection.

'Listen, you'll always be *my* Baby, but you're a strong young woman with your mama's head on your shoulders. Whatever you do, you will do well,' Papa declares proudly with a firm nod of his head.

As he reaches over to brush away my own tears with his dry palm, I at once see the parallels in our journeys, how neither of us had been ready to process our situations until now. I settle the pillows behind him and gather his scattered paper while we compose ourselves and face our truths silently.

He hadn't wanted to let me go in the same way I'd felt about my brother.

26

The following week, Ngozi had asked to come out to Adogbo to see me. I'd picked her up at the waterside for her virgin voyage, but the shock of confronting the lagoon for the first time scrambled her mind. Guiding her into my canoe, I'd taken her slowly across while she prayed loudly and begged me repeatedly not to tip over.

'Yemoja, don't drown me, *abeg*!' she hollered comically, gripping the sides with all her strength.

'As if I can . . . Shey it's only your shoulder it go reach,' I giggled, reminding her that the lagoon is only five feet deep.

For all the poise and intellect she'd displayed throughout our passage to Europe, she'd transformed into a child when presented with a little discomfort on home soil. Many Lagosians had never ventured to our side, much less the ones who had studied overseas, so I'd understood her evident shock and hid my amusement from her despite the awkwardness of the situation.

At home, we'd sat on the deck and she'd met Afo and Kemi before I'd taken her inside to briefly greet my father. Papa covered himself to receive this outside visitor, asking for his good shirt earlier in the day and pairing it with his new bobble hat from the abroad, bearing the Zurich logo so there was no question where it came from. As Ngozi bent sheepishly in front of him for a few minutes and enquired about his well-being, Papa had been more concerned with thanking her for all her help during our trip, heaping a thousand journey mercies and blessings on her, that had made her blush and steam up her glasses before we retreated to the deck to watch the world go by above the water.

I'd told her many times that I hadn't heard from Idunnu, but clearly, Ngozi had needed to see me up close for my truth to penetrate. I felt sorry for her, for the position that Idunnu's absconding had put her in. She seemed shaken by the event, no doubt for the responsibility that had fallen on her shoulders as we'd technically been under her watch. Idunnu had cost Ngozi her reputation. She might also have cost me my future with H2All's sponsorship though she had assured me that wasn't to be the case.

'Helen wants you to know that even though this situation is unfortunate, we stand by you,' Ngozi had said before waving at a canoe of chattering children that passed by.

'Thank you,' I responded sheepishly. 'I'm grateful.'

'We'd like you to carry on being an ambassador for our water programme. And as Helen said, the organisation is behind your educational aspirations. Just let us know what it is you'd like to do. Are you still participating in the drone project?' she asked.

'Yes, I am,' I'd confirmed as we watched a family navigate the lagoon. I'd been relieved that Helen hadn't blamed me for

Idunnu disappearing in Switzerland, but it hadn't lessened my internal guilt.

Back in Davos, Idunnu had referenced those very opportunities given to me but I'd taken them for granted due to my homesickness. I was glad that they were still open to me even though I was still undecided about asking for help. As fortuitous as H2All's kindness was, there would always be a stain based on how things had ended. I feared too that I'd always bear the weight of obligation I'd felt with Helen, who wanted me to be the face of a cause.

I just wanted to be me.

One of Mama Jumbo's workers had followed next, waving to me as we exchanged a brief flurry of words before I resumed my sitting position beside Ngozi. So many expressions had fought for dominance over her face as we sat together people-watching and observing life in the community. What little she'd seen had moved something within her. I think we'd been a fiction for her before then, but suddenly via some exposure, we were no longer figures on paper and in charts but *real* people.

'What will happen to Idunnu when they find her?' I'd asked, fearful for my friend and the possible repercussions she might face in her unknown path. She would be welcomed back by the community, but were there other ramifications I wasn't even aware of?

'The chances of that are slim . . . *We thank God*,' Ngozi whispered, staring glassy-eyed over the waterway.

I'd let her enjoy the scenery in quasi-silence. I hadn't filled the air with forced conversation as her ears and eyes absorbed everything around us.

'Now that you've come, what do you think of Makoko?'

'It isn't . . . I expected . . . I can't believe that I haven't . . .
Wow,' Ngozi declared before releasing a sigh so heavy we'd
both laughed. 'It's really something,' she said, shaking her
head at the black, oily water.

'Na so,' I'd agreed, brimming with pride.

I see Wunmi in a canoe and wave furiously before continuing
my fast rowing to meet Efe. She's leading some girls who all
look my way. They stare at me with a mix of wonder and
pride. The poster-child Dream Girl, despite me officially yet
to start with the team.

I'd arranged to see Maureen and Efe at the canteen a few
days after my return, having spent most of my time with Papa.
Efe had been speechless when I told her what had happened
after I'd left Davos. She kept staring at her phone in disbelief,
rechecking the last messages she'd exchanged with Idunnu
before she'd gone silent.

'She didn't say anything when you dey for Switzerland?'
she'd inquired for the tenth time; her eyes were large as
oranges in her head. 'Poor Moses!'

'I swear,' I'd replied, crossing myself in front of her. 'It's a
mystery . . .'

Maureen, who'd listened without interrupting, had been
ambivalent about the situation and shrugged her shoulders
dismissively after taking in the full story.

'What was it I've been saying about her?' she proclaimed, rolling her eyes at me knowingly, even though

she'd never uttered anything profound about Idunnu in her life.

'Her mouth is too sharp . . . Mama says never take your eyes off a sharp knife,' she'd declared before sitting back in her chair sanctimoniously.

Briefly, I'd imagined the type of snappy comeback that would have fallen from Idunnu's lips, had she been there with us, and bit down on my feeling of regret. I held back the words working their way out of me on her behalf, for fear of being christened with the same expression. I knew better than ever how dissimilar Idunnu and I really were.

'Baby, you said Idunnu took her case?' Efe posed the question slowly as though her mind was still working on a calculation after we'd finished speculating about our friend's whereabouts.

'*Eeehn*,' I'd replied quietly, facing her across the sticky table.

'Okay then . . . I hope you were the one carrying all my clothes?' she asked, unamused.

After Maureen departed, our talk circled back to our missing friend and Efe and I exchanged memories of Idunnu wistfully, missing her side cracks.

'I couldn't do it, but I'm happy she did,' Efe had announced proudly, shocking me with her maturity when I'd perpetually dismissed her as the youngest of the crew.

'Me too,' I'd admitted quietly as my mind imagined Idunnu in half a dozen scenarios from our trip. As a new hotel maid, dancing in a seedy bar, or maybe she'd landed a blue-suited whale in Swiss waters?

I was only concerned with her welfare and not how she would need to make her living out there in the world. Idunnu would forever be my friend, doing the best she could under every circumstance. We could only hope to do the same.

Remembering her disapproval of my rush to judgement of some of the women in Davos that evening in the hotel, I'd polished off my drink beside Efe, regretting that I wouldn't get the chance to debate once more with Idunnu, or even to apologise.

Efe had been too annoyed about her dress to show me what she'd been working on. But she'd called after she'd calmed down and asked me to meet her the next Friday at the entertainment centre at the end of her salon shift.

I'd taken my time to get there, relishing familiarising myself with the feeling of being over water after so long on land. Once there, I'd squeezed my way through the loud teens waiting for their turn on an even noisier computer game that involved one kind of ghoulish monster on the old television screen. In the corner, some boys played pool without the black ball and shared the one cue between each turn.

Efe was at the back of the room, typing away furiously on one of the two computers, when I called out to her.

'Wait,' she'd said, pointing me away from her monitor so I couldn't see the screen while she finished her secret work.

'Oya . . . Look,' she'd instructed, beckoning me over finally.

I'd squinted at the screen to better understand what I was looking at, but Efe had become impatient.

'I've been running it since you were away . . . Na Fundunited page I created,' Efe announced excitedly, scrolling down the page like a computer expert. I had watched behind her as she talked me through the intricacies of her *Makoko Pearls* project.

'Your newspaper foto don dey inspire me,' Efe had laughed cheekily as she awaited my reaction. 'Here, you get information about the community and we can keep adding updates like *this*,' she explained, dragging the mouse over to another tab. 'People can make a general contribution or donate for the specific things,' she'd pressed on as I studied the individual projects she outlined: street lamps on Apollo, the creation of composting toilets, as well as the procurement of solar panels.

'Efe, na you really do all this?' I'd remarked incredulously, moving to squeeze her tightly while she giggled beside me.

'I also created a Facebook page,' she'd replied, clicking on another tab on the computer, 'and next we can do Insta—'

'Wait-o . . . Go back first! So that figure is our *money*?' I'd asked as the realisation sunk in that she'd already been close to hitting half of the target goals she'd set.

'You know I don't play, Baby,' Efe made a face while shrugging her shoulders. 'Now, next time, *young* or not, you know who to take with you when they ask you to fly somewhere!' she'd yapped dryly.

Idunnu has been on my mind so much it's no wonder she visits me in my dream. I'm chasing her through the Swiss airport, although every time I almost catch up with her, more passengers block my path. My throat is raw from screaming her name. I shout over the departure announcements, but she refuses to turn around. Suddenly the airport scene vanishes and we're at the top of the mountain peak the cable car had ferried us to, riding in a ski lift. I feel the icy wind in my ears and see the blanket of snow beneath our dangling feet. Gripping the iron bar across our laps so tightly I feel as if my arm might break, I look over at Idunnu, shining all of her teeth.

'This is what you were wanting?' I say, knowing the answer even before I ask.

'*Yes*,' Idunnu replies enthusiastically.

I cannot stop her. She opens the iron bar and slips off her seat, whooping with delight. Surprisingly, I don't fall with her but watch her terrifying plummet towards the treetops, dreading her impact. But Idunnu disappears into the snow drift before coming into contact with anything.

When I wake, I find Kemi sitting over me as if she's been observing me the entire night.

'What is it?' I ask her, rubbing away the dried spittle from the edges of my mouth.

'You're a very noisy sleeper,' she declares accusingly and then moves off to disturb her brother on his nearby mattress.

Before heading to my shift at Mama Jumbo's, I stop over at the shipping yard in Uncle Jimi's boat. Samson's hard at work, bent over a boat motor while two men argue in the background behind him over Lord only knows what. But he's unaffected by the squabble as he knocks the end of a screwdriver with a hammer before removing the fan blade.

He can still sense when I'm coming and looks up at me before I reach him. The accident at the mill had thankfully distracted Papa from my romantic life, but the moment I'd reappeared on the lagoon, Samson had made the excuse to cross my path, in case I needed his help tending to my father.

The situation with Idunnu had taught me that life is short. She'd spotted a chance and had taken it. No hesitation. No fear. She was choosing to live on her own terms, and in my own way, I was learning to do that too.

I wasn't as brave or stupid as her yet, and so I hadn't told Papa about Prince, but in a valiant *being-more-like-water* move, I'd invited Prince to Adogbo for a day on the lagoon and had made sure to run into Samson. From our demeanour, it was obvious to anyone that had seen us that I was taken. Koku had pointed at us before opening his mouth wide, but nothing had come out, and behind him, Samson's lips had struggled with a smile before he dropped his head. As much as I'd wanted to feel sorry for Samson's dashed hopes, I'd only felt relief.

Asking him to help me procure some canoes was the next best thing I could offer him. It made sense for the bottom line of my business and underneath his shy shy, he was a good person.

'Baby,' Samson laughs as he greets me. 'Something told me you dey come today,' he says, wiping his hand with a cloth pulled from the back pocket of his jeans. 'How far?'

'Na me supposed to dey ask you,' I begin, looking around the yard where he's working for any evidence of the progress with my project.

My eyes drift to a canoe covered with a dirty sheet about ten feet away from where we're standing.

'Is *that* it?' I ask impatiently as his lips split into a smile.

Samson clears the sheet away and I take a look at the canoe underneath, the original *Charlie-Boy* rendered new in its fresh coat of paint: red and blue like Spider-Man with bright white lettering. I exhale gleefully as I drink in the shiny upgrade, in stark contrast to the nude, battered wooden boats that drift by endlessly on the crowded waterways.

'There's one thing remaining I go fix—' Samson begins, but I cut him off before he can go into his explanations.

'One down, two to go,' I say and he nods in agreement before wiping a bead of sweat off his forehead.

'When are you starting the drone thing?' Samson asks and I pull my thoughts away from my taxi empire to my more imminent role ahead.

'Next week . . . It's *official*,' I declare excitedly. The adrenaline rush I felt in my inaugural piloting experience washes over me briefly before my nerves announce themselves.

'Another Dream Girl is born?' He laughs quietly.

'That's only *one* dream o,' I reply cheekily. 'Me, I get plenty!'

It was Mama Jumbo that had given me the idea that buried the seed inside me many months earlier when we'd talked about her vision of the future.

When Prince had asked me to close my eyes during our phone call while I was in Davos, all I could picture was the lagoon, the weight of the canoe over the water, the security of the paddle in my hand.

I'd envisaged myself staring at the Lagos skyline in a brand-new boat with a motor like Uncle Jimi's had been gifted with thanks to Samson, not just in one place but in many locations on the water, the way Mama Jumbo sells her wares using multiple workers. Taxi drivers have one of the most reliable sources of income on the water. If I had more boats, then that would be a steady income stream.

With the money I had remaining, Uncle Jimi's connections to spare and scrap materials and Samson's time, I could start with three canoes on the water. One to be manned by Afo, who was shaping up to be more of a man than Tayo, wherever he was, and Wunmi had already expressed an interest in driving the other for the free access to a boat. Their bright colouring would be free advertising on the lagoon, a way of standing out and attracting customers.

The taxi business is my vision for now and that's okay. The drone project will give me more skills and there is still Helen's offer of help on the table. Who knows what can come of that?

'Hmmm . . . see my competition!' Mama Jumbo had complained half-heartedly when I'd revealed my idea to her after coming back to work.

There'd been a mixture of surprise and pride on her face. I'd clearly learned more from her than she'd ever anticipated. I had *fire*, in fact, me and all my friends did, when you think about it.

'Sure you don't want to sell small small for me in your canoes? Make we do *collabo*?' she'd asked in all seriousness before chuckling deeply and I'd had the feeling that conversation was only just beginning between us.

Letting a boatload of people pass ahead of me on the canal, I spy a small child in its mother's arms. I realise how swiftly time has passed since I was their size and age to where I am now. You grow up quickly in these waters, but I'd matured so much over this last year and months that I barely recognised myself.

The women had seen it first; Mama Jumbo and Auntie Bisi. Like it or not, Papa had been forced into a slow acceptance as circumstances had worked against him. The entire community had helped soften his rock so that he no longer only viewed me as a child.

My time overseas made him afraid. Losing me to the abroad and losing me to the drone project right here are two entirely different things. Or perhaps *me* going away and representing the community showed him that I'm an adult who can determine *when* and *if* she needs another fish!

'Meanwhile, I hear you are to marry a prince!' Papa's words over dinner replay themselves embarrassingly for the hundredth time as I sail away further into the distance in my nightly ritual.

His statement had taken me completely by surprise, causing a few ofada rice grains to go down the wrong pipe as I coughed up my dismay at the table.

'Papa, *I*—' I began desperately.

'It's fine, Baby,' he'd assured me with a wave of his hand. My eyes darted to my cousins, who had thankfully cleared out onto the deck so that I at least bore this awkward exchange without an audience. 'Mama Jumbo confided in me after my accident . . . I understand that there are some things that are easier to say to another woman.'

379

'I was going to tell . . .'

'Shey you know what you're doing . . . But he should come and see me—' he'd continued sternly while waiting for me to clear his bowl away.

'Yes, Papa,' I'd replied hurriedly, eager to end the talk.

'That's the way we do things. It's just *protocol*. Then we can discuss your marriage . . . In *time*! If that's what you're want-ing,' he'd added to my great relief.

To distract from the conversation, I'd surprised him with my taxi business idea, and he understood that my canoe hadn't gone to Samson for repairs. He seemed pleased, especially with the idea of Charlie Boy's name living on so proudly on the lagoon that took him. It made me see that if even the most inflexible of us are capable of change, then one can never stop hoping for a brighter future.

I'd always considered Makoko to be small – and too small-minded – for me, but now I know it was just my thinking. It's the change within me that transforms everything else.

I'm the Pearl of Makoko, and the world is my oyster.

Who knows if the government will succeed in robbing us of our land? With the world's eyes upon us, that will be harder to do. But with the help from overseas, with the donations com-ing in directly to us so that no official can chop them and the awareness growing about our part of the world, we can change the way we exist little by little.

My phone screen illuminating cuts through the darkness as I drift aimlessly on the water listening to the deep hum of a much larger trawler in the distance. I know it's Prince even before I reach for it and read his message. Still determined to find a Swiss recipe that I like, I magnify the photo he's sent of one clear brown-looking soup topped with grated cheese and feel my stomach rumble enviously after hours of inactivity.

Next week? I text him with confidence, knowing he'll make time in his schedule even as he adjusts to his new job at the restaurant.

Okay o. If you no go for abroad first, now that you be international businesswoman!

I laugh as I read his response, my voice bouncing off the shallow waves around me and stirring up the life underneath. I still can't quite believe that Papa knows about our relationship and that I'm not sleeping peacefully in the arms of Jesus in the afterlife!

You know a fish cannot live on land, I remind Prince before tucking my phone away.

A tiny golden pin-prick brightens the sky before another one appears. I follow the almost invisible tail lights of a faraway plane as I row, and whisper a silent prayer for Charlie Boy, who's missing out on the scene.

These days I no longer wait for him as I clear my head on the water.

He's not coming back the way he used to, but I know he's looking down just the same.

Author's Note

Yemoja's is but one imagined life on the water. There are thousands more – in reality – doing the best they can in incredibly difficult conditions.

I was inspired by a YouTube video featuring some of the food from within the Makoko community, but what blew me away more while watching was the ingenuity with which everyday living is carried out on the lagoon. Things we have learned to take for granted in our daily existence, such as clean water running freely from a tap, or flicking on a light switch in the evenings, all painstakingly considered in order to make life work . . .

All those key aspects of how to function – tackled with alacrity and dignity.

The more I discovered about the community, the more enamoured I became with Makoko and the many people who call it their home.

As worldwide conversations about the environment and climate change escalate, and some global leaders take steps back which mean that *many* of the goals of the 2030 Agenda for

Sustainable Development are unlikely to be met, it's never been more important to add our voices to the chorus before it's too late to sing.

So, while we focus on the planet at large, it's my hope that we spare *more* than thoughts for those presently living in less fortunate circumstances, within communities most greatly impacted by these devastating – and preventable – changes, and help out financially, where possible.

With that in mind, I've set up a fundraising page for anyone who would like to provide monetary assistance to the people of Makoko. More information can be found at www.makokopearls.org.

For those donating elsewhere, I encourage you to research thoroughly to ensure that your money truly reaches the community directly.

Acknowledgments

Ajebowale Roberts, your passion for this novel has been extraordinary from the outset. A fiercer advocate I have honestly yet to meet! Thank you for your guidance and for taking such great care with your editing, for your improvements and for singing Baby's praises so loudly! Thank you for making me feel like I'd created something worth getting excited about. The little girl who adored the school library within me thanks you for welcoming her so warmly into the world she always wanted to join, and the woman that she is now (speaking awkwardly in the third person) continues to be appreciative of your unceasing kindness.

Thanks to my agent Niamh O'Grady, and to Emma Capron and the wider Quercus family for all your work. Thanks to Tosin for their cover, and Adeola Opeyemi — I'm grateful for your Pidgin polishing!

I would also like to thank the fantastic travel journalist, Pelu Awofeso, for guiding me through Makoko, and Agunto Oluwatobi Ambrose, a teacher from the Morning Dew Nursery & Primary School. Thank you for taking the time to share your experience of life on the water and for welcoming us so warmly to your incredible school. Thanks to Farida Ladipo-Ajayi, founder of the Bookworm Cafe for curating the books I donated to the school's library. It was heartwarming to see so many young ones eager to learn and I'll forever remember their lovely reception. Tolu Onile-Ere – I'm delighted that you were my companion inside those waterways. Thank you also to Priscilla Nzimiro Nwanah for sharing your amazing images and footage from your own Makoko research with me, and to Tassa Chabouni for your immediate and generous contribution.

Thank you muchly to my 'sensitivity reader', Sesede Simeon, for your insights into the community. To my family and friends, thank you for your continued faith and for urging me forward. Mariama Abudulai, Donna Muwonge, Meron Abraham, Rebecca Allen-Cavanagh: thank you for your support, your help, for taking the time to read rough passages and for your early feedback, and – more importantly – for making me laugh in those moments where I was between words.

The late Biyi Bandele was a phenomenal artist, creator, visionary, historian, griot and friend. I was continually inspired by his photography. His images weren't voyeuristic or exploitative, they were mirrors capturing people in their daily motion in all their full glory. I will miss his vision even though his incredible work across all forms remains for us to cherish. I'm so grateful to be able to include one of his images here, taken on the lagoon in 2022, entitled *Water Babies*. I believe artists drink from a communal well, so I was deeply moved by our moment of synchronicity when I came across his photo, and I'm honoured to be able to feature it in the book's end pages.

Simon Toyne, your unearned support has been incredible; I remain indebted to you for taking time out of your schedule to offer me advice time and again, and for the agency intro.

In an industry that largely involves silence and rejection, I cannot overstate how grateful I am to the following people for their timely words and encouragement throughout this oftentimes lonely writing process and especially with this book – Irenosen Okojie, Silé Edwards, Kemi Ogunsanwo, Cari Rosen, Elise Dillsworth, Andy Hine, Sharmaine Lovegrove and Edwidge Danticat.

To Martin, otherwise known as *l'homme qui porte sa femme* . . . Thank you for refusing to view me as anything else but a writer until I had no choice but to believe it myself. Thank you for making every version of this book better with your *sous-cheffing*, your wisdom, and your Spartan support. Most importantly, thank you for wearing me down about getting our eternally shedding cats that have made our lives infinitely better, and peaceful sleep a thing of the past. They are undoubtedly worth its sacrifice.

And to *you*, dear reader. If you've made it this far, then thank you for journeying along with me. There are millions of choices on physical and virtual shelves, so I'm elated that you picked this to spend some time with. Books are *truly* magical but a magician requires an audience. So, thank you for coming to – and sticking around – for the show!

Water Babies, Biyi Bandele

Author Bio

Born in Nigeria, Chioma Okereke grew up in London and studied law at UCL. She started her writing career as a performance poet before turning her hand to prose. Her debut novel, *Bitter Leaf* (Virago), was shortlisted for the Commonwealth Writers' Prize and her short story, *Trompette De La Mort*, received First Runner Up of the inaugural Costa Short Story Award. *Water Baby* is her second novel.